MW00639128

ANNIE LeBLANC IS NOT DEAD YET

ANNIE LeBLANC IS NOT DEAD YET

MOLLY MORRIS

WEDNESDAY BOOKS

NEW YORK

First published in the United States by Wednesday Books, an imprint of St. Martin's Publishing Group

ANNIE LEBLANC IS NOT DEAD YET. Copyright © 2024 by Molly Morris. All rights reserved. Printed in the United States of America. For information, address St. Martin's Publishing Group, 120 Broadway, New York, NY 10271.

www.wednesdaybooks.com

Designed by Jen Edwards

All emojis designed by OpenMoji, the open-source emoji and icon project. License: CC BY-SA 4.0

The Library of Congress Cataloging-in-Publication Data is available upon request.

ISBN 978-1-250-29006-9 (hardcover)
ISBN 978-1-250-28971-1 (ebook)

Our books may be purchased in bulk for promotional, educational, or business use. Please contact your local bookseller or the Macmillan Corporate and Premium Sales Department at 1-800-221-7945, extension 5442, or by email at MacmillanSpecialMarkets@macmillan.com.

First Edition: 2024

10   9   8   7   6   5   4   3   2   1

For Margot, always

ANNIE LEBLANC IS NOT DEAD YET

PROLOGUE

The plastic tub lands on the counter with a thunk. Ryan Morton towers behind it, hands shoved into the pockets of her jean jacket and eyes fixed over my shoulder as though she can't be bothered to look at my face.

Surprise bubbles up in my throat. For a second, I don't know what to say.

"Where did you get these?" I manage eventually as I pick up the tub and hold it to the fluorescent lighting that beams down from above us.

Inside are what appear to be at least thirty individually wrapped candies, perfect little balls in a bright, glossy red. Atomic Fireballs.

Ryan hops over the counter and sheds her jacket and backpack in one fluid motion before tossing them toward the back office.

"Me and my mom were in Orange County yesterday and we

found those at this dinky little candy shop." She says it with such nonchalance, as though it's nothing. Ryan punches her code into the cash register, whose drawer opens with a ping. "They had like eight thousand tubs because you're still the only person who likes those disgusting things."

I twist the tub around in my hands so that each red ball inside has the chance to catch the light. She's right: I'm the only one out of the three of us—me, Ryan, and our best friend, Annie—who could stomach an Atomic Fireball, a candy so radioactively spicy, my mouth would still be tingling an hour after eating it. Dudley's Bakery used to stock them and I'd grab at least four tubs whenever Annie, Ryan, and I would stop in on our way to San Diego, but they haven't had them for a long time. Plus, I haven't gone to Dudley's in a million years, not since Annie died. Not that the three of us hung out a lot around then anyway.

When I look at her again, Ryan is bent over the cash register, her lips moving silently as she counts the bills. Even though she's ignoring me now, she's still aware of me, watching her. I can tell by the way her back stiffens, unmoving beneath her red T-shirt. I bite the inside of my cheek, trying not to smile. This gift, this conversation—it's small, but it's the first time Ryan has spoken to me in a week, since the night her mom threw the Country Kitchen staff a graduation party. It feels like a peace offering. An apology.

Before tucking the tub underneath the counter, I pluck out a candy and unwrap it, pocketing the little plastic wrapper in my khaki shorts. The Atomic Fireball gets to work sizzling my mouth almost instantly, the sweet cinnamon flavor giving way to heat.

"Thank you," I say quickly to Ryan. The Atomic Fireball is a glorified marble in my mouth, garbling up my words. "For this." I tap the tub's lid. "Thank you for this."

She doesn't respond, just drops quarters into their slot one by one.

Around us, the air is thick with the smell of apples and butter. The bakers in the kitchen behind us have been baking apple pies since midnight, ready for the crowds of tourists that pour into the Country Kitchen pretty much from the second we unlock the doors. I straighten my visor and glance at the clock above the serving hatch. Three more minutes until opening time.

Ryan slams the register drawer shut.

"The lady there said she's gonna stop carrying Atomic Fireballs because nobody buys them anymore," she says. "So if you want to prove there actually are weirdos out there that like them, you should probably go soon."

The candy knocks against my teeth as I bend my mouth into a half smile. "Yet another argument for my mother to buy me a car," I say.

Ryan turns around, her eyes not quite reaching me. Instead they land on the counter, where my fingers drum against the glass surface.

"I have one," she says, before glancing away.

I open my mouth to respond, but nothing comes out. Is Ryan trying to shove in my face the fact that *she* could get there if she wanted to, or is she offering to drive me? Coming from Ryan, one option feels cruel, but likely. The other feels . . . impossible.

The front door to the Country Kitchen swings open, unleashing a sound so earsplittingly loud, I shrink into my shoulders and clamp my hands over my ears. A woman in a lemon-yellow suit with shoulder pads at least half an inch thick appears in the doorway holding up a bullhorn, which, at the sight of me cowering, she brings down to her chest and then smiles apologetically.

"Sorry!" she calls. "Got a little carried away there."

In her other hand is at least ten balloons, all of which are pink except the shiny one in the middle, "Congratulations!" written across it in rainbow bubble letters. The woman, I would recognize anywhere. It's Ruth Fish, president of the Lennon Historical Society and organizer of pretty much anything that goes on in this town. Beside her is a small bald man with a practically ancient camera hanging from a strap around his neck. I've seen him at festivals before, the Mr. and Mrs. Apple Pie pageant and the Fourth of July parade. He's a reporter for the *Lennon News*.

"We're not open yet," Ryan says to them, frowning. "That door was locked."

"Sometimes good news just can't wait," Ruth says as she approaches the counter. "Because you, Wilson Moss, have won this year's Welcome Back!"

She presses down on the bullhorn again, slightly quieter this time, and thrusts the bouquet of balloons at me.

I stare at them with wide eyes, my mouth dropping open. As it does, the Atomic Fireball falls onto the floor and skitters across the tiles. A camera flashes.

The voice that comes out of me is quiet and incredulous. "Me?" I say. "I won?"

I'm not even sure I'm speaking at all until Ruth nods enthusiastically.

"You did it, sweetheart!"

I won. Me, who got last place in the fifth-grade spelling bee after getting "brain" wrong. Who could never even win the cake walk at the Halloween carnival, which consisted only of walking around in a circle and sitting in a chair with a picture of a cupcake taped to the back when the music stopped. But if I won Welcome Back, that means—

"Who?" Ryan is suddenly at my side, angling her body so that she blocks Ruth and the reporter from my vision. It's jarring, going from having almost none of her attention to suddenly having all of it. "Who did you pick?"

"I—I—" I stammer, eyes darting helplessly between Ryan and Ruth, as though the latter can somehow help me.

Everything about Ryan is electric. "Wilson," she says slowly, carefully. "Who are you bringing back from the dead?"

I brave a glance at her. Her brown eyes are alight with something I'm almost afraid to identify.

"I'm sorry," I whisper back.

She takes a tiny step away from me, her gaze leaving mine and dropping to the floor. "No," she says, almost breathless.

"I'm really sorry." I can't stop looking at Ruth, whose brow is furrowed in confusion. "I—" I start to say. "I picked—"

"No." Ryan jabs her finger in my direction. "Don't say it. Don't you dare say—"

But she knows what I'm going to say. Because of course it's her. It could only be her.

I swallow hard, the taste of cinnamon sour in my mouth.

"I'm sorry," I say again. "I picked Annie."

ONE

There are a few things nobody tells you about bringing your best friend back from the dead:

1. The dead don't always arrive on time because, apparently, they need bathroom breaks or something on the way back from the afterlife.

2. Not everybody is going to be happy you've chosen said person to come back. They're not like POWs, where their return is universally celebrated. It's more like the Rolling Stones going back on tour, or the arrival of another *Twilight* movie.

3. The ceremony isn't necessarily cult-y or weird. There aren't any black robes or virgin sacrifices, which is probably a good thing. As the Resident Virgin Dork of Lennon, California, I would definitely be at the center of that pentagram.

These are the things that are running through my head as I sweat my face off on the small stage rigged up at the head of the football field, the last remnants of an Atomic Fireball disintegrating in my mouth. Not the fact that my best friend, who I hadn't talked to for over a year before she died, is on her way back to the land of the living. That, in most cases, this is not the hallmark of a best friend, and that by even calling Annie this, I'm basically confirming that I'm the loser everyone already suspects I am. No, I'm preoccupied with the fact that nobody ever seems to want to touch me in a way that is neither accidental nor platonic.

"What is wrong with me?" I mutter under my breath.

"What's that, sweetheart?"

Ruth Fish smiles down at me. Her baby-pink lipstick matches her pale pantsuit.

I blink up at her and feel a blush spreading across my neck. "Nothing."

She reaches out a hand and squeezes my shoulder. "It's okay to be nervous," she says.

"I'm not nervous," I say quickly.

This is a lie. I am very nervous. In fact, I don't think I've ever been this nervous in my entire life. Over the sounds of Bruce Springsteen playing from the stadium speakers, I can feel the eyes of everyone in the audience on me, their gazes somehow burning even stronger than the sun. I sink lower into my plastic chair and bring my comic book up so it covers my face, like that'll make any difference. Besides a squat podium and Ruth Fish, I am literally the only thing on this outrageously small stage, baking like roadkill on the artificial turf of Lennon Union High School's football field. They could've at least held this event somewhere with shade, but because I'm the youngest Welcome Back winner in Lennon's history, hosting the ceremony at my school was the most obvious choice. Forget the fact that I graduated over a week ago and therefore am no longer an attendee of Lennon Union, that I'm nearly eighteen and technically almost an adult.

"It won't be long now, honey," Ruth says as she grabs her phone from underneath the stage's central podium.

Ruth Fish is the kind of person who adds "honey" or "doll" or "dear" to the end of every sentence. She has the sugary sweetness of a little old grandma from Minnesota, even though Lennon is so far south, I can practically see Mexico from my house. Even though that by being the president of the Lennon Historical Society, she's got to be into some seriously dark shit.

I swallow hard and focus on the football field, on the balloon arch sagging down from the goalpost fifty or so yards away. THIS IS EAGLE COUNTRY is spray-painted on the grass in burgundy and white, leading up to a banner with the words WELCOME BACK, ANNIE scrawled across it in uneven writing. One of the *N*s in Annie is smaller than the other, as though it were crammed in at the last second after the sign-maker spelled Annie's name wrong. Other than this and the streamers draped across the bleachers, the football field basically looks exactly as it did during the entire last season, when our team lost so many games, even the players' parents stopped showing up.

"Hi, Wilson," a voice says from a few feet away. The reporter from the *Lennon News,* who put the picture of a bewildered-looking me on the next day's front page, my mouth dropped open so wide you could practically see my tonsils. He's somehow wearing a khaki jacket in spite of the heat. "I'm Tom Bradford from the *Lennon News*. Could I get an interview with this year's exciting winner?"

He makes it sound like I beat the Russians in a chess tournament, not that my stupid name was drawn out of a stupid bowl. I didn't even plan to put myself in the running for Welcome Back; one second, I was cramming my visor into my backpack after a shift at work, and the next I was scribbling my and Annie's names on the back of a receipt for a bag of Doritos. It was like my subconscious and fine motor skills were actively plotting against me, conspiring to bring about what could either be the best or worst thing to ever happen in my life. But once our names were in the bowl, I couldn't take them back.

Before I can answer, Tom runs a hand across his bald head and peels a tiny notebook out of his pocket. "Why'd you pick Annie"—his eyes search the notebook pages—"LeBlanc?"

"I, uh . . ." I start to say, but look down at my shoes instead.

It's a fair question, but one not even I'm sure how to answer. How does one say without sounding pathetic: *Annie was the best friend I've ever had and even though she didn't talk to me for a year before she died, I still think about her all the time and I'm pretty/sort of/mostly sure that if she were to come back right now, things would be different because she won't be around that school or those people, although I'm not totally sure, so now that I think about it, maybe—*

"Wilson?" Tom prompts.

I blink. "She is—uh, she *was* my best friend," I stammer eventually. "I mean, with Ryan. That's—she's our other best friend. Was. We were best friends. We were the three best friends." I swallow. "There were three of us."

"Ryan Morton?" Tom says. "She was with you when you found out you won."

Standing next to me in the newspaper picture, a scowl so deeply cut into her face, it looked almost painful. Of course Tom the reporter knows Ryan Morton, daughter of Terri Morton, owner of the most famous restaurant in Lennon.

And then, without warning, Tom turns and waves to someone in the crowd. "Ryan!" he shouts. "Come on up here."

A figure rises from the crowd from somewhere within the first few rows. Ryan Morton walks slowly up the center aisle, looking annoyed at having been acknowledged.

As she climbs onto the stage, Tom points his pen at her. "Ryan, Wilson says you were best friends with Annie too."

Ryan's face morphs from a look of vague disinterest to one only someone who knows her favorite nail polish color as a kid was called Macaroni Sunshine could recognize as sarcastic glee.

"Oh yeah, totally," she says.

The only thing more surprising than Ryan Morton admitting she was ever friends with Annie LeBlanc—sarcastic or not—is the fact that she's even at this thing. Ever since finding out I won Welcome Back, she's been ignoring me again, the Atomic Fireball peace offering firmly off the table.

"So, how do you feel about Annie coming back?" Tom says.

Nobody waits for me to answer.

"Oh my god," Ryan says, "like, unbelievably psyched. Ever since she died, life has been basically unbearable. Like, who cares that she transferred to some elite private school for rich kids with con artist parents the year before and never talked to us again? We *are* disgusting."

Tom is dutifully taking notes while I curl my fingers around my comic book and pray for death. My nails dig into the front cover of *Buffy the Vampire Slayer: Wolves at the Gate,* the one where

Dracula comes back. It's my favorite issue in the series, mostly because Dracula is the best character ever. It's one that used to make me feel calm when I was a kid, but now all I feel like doing is shredding the pages and disappearing into the rubble.

"Do you have any plans for the summer?" Tom asks.

I open my mouth, but all that comes out is air. Since finding out I won Welcome Back a couple of days ago, I've been agonizing over what Annie and I would do for her one month on Earth. The notebook in my nightstand is crammed with lists of activities I scratched out one by one, none of them feeling right. Because even though I technically put Annie's and my names in the bowl, I never, for a single second, thought I'd actually win.

"Of course we do." Ryan flicks her long brown ponytail over her shoulder. "First, we're gonna go to the beach, then we're gonna go shopping, and then we're gonna have a sleepover and a slo-mo hot-girl pillow fight!"

Ruth Fish, her phone call finished, apparently having heard all this, clears her throat and nudges me and Ryan backward.

"That's enough questions for now," she says. "Pictures? Anyone? Tom, do you want another picture of the girls?"

Ryan and I stand about a foot apart while Tom snaps pictures with his camera. In my green-and-blue flannel shirt and thrift store denim shorts, I can't help but feel a little underdressed standing next to Ryan, who's wearing a long off-white bohemian-style top with lacy sleeves that hang past her wrists. Peeking out of her shirt is a gold necklace with a tiny *R* charm on it, one she's been wearing every day since we were kids, when Friday night sleepovers at her house were as reliable as the sun.

"Tom, let's get pictures with Annie's parents, too," Ruth says when he's finished.

She leads Tom back to the crowd, where a couple in clothes even I can tell from this far away are expensive sits in the front row. Mr. LeBlanc is in a white summer suit like something out of a movie about the South, while Mrs. LeBlanc wears a long army-green dress and a straw hat whose brim is as wide as a Hula-Hoop. Mrs. LeBlanc's smile opens wide as Tom introduces himself, Mr. LeBlanc shuffling forward in his chair to shake his hand. They start to talk, Mrs. LeBlanc tipping her head back to laugh in a way that rich women do on TV, as though they expect everyone in their immediate vicinity to join in.

And then, without warning, the crowd falls silent as a pickup truck appears between the far goalposts on the field. Ruth Fish quickly pulls Annie's parents onstage so they're standing right next to me. She begins talking into the microphone, but all I can hear is the blood rushing in my ears. My comic falls to the floor, sliding somewhere underneath my chair.

This is the first time I realize I don't actually know how this is supposed to go; does Annie skateboard down the aisle? Fly out of the back of the pickup truck with makeshift angel wings? I file through memories of the other Welcome Back ceremony I went to, but they happen only every ten years, so it's fuzzy. All I remember is seven-year-old me sitting at the back of the crowd, drawing on my hands with permanent marker.

For a second, as I stand here, my heart thudding and skin overheating, I think I might be sick. I think I might actually projectile vomit onto Mrs. LeBlanc's dress, which probably costs as much as I make in an entire month. Somewhere in the commotion, Ryan has left the stage, disappearing back into the crowd.

Part of me wants to run away, just dip the fuck out of here, but then I remember that I'm the one who did this. I picked

Annie. Even if I did put our names in the bowl on a whim, even though I never thought in a million years that I'd actually be standing here, there was still a part of me that wanted this. That still wants this, more than anything.

A man in a San Diego Padres jersey emerges from the truck and jogs around to the passenger side. He swings the door open, revealing a figure sitting motionless in their seat. I have to blink into the sunlight to make sure I'm not hallucinating, but there she is. Annie LeBlanc lowers herself onto the artificial grass, wearing a short dress covered in bright, sparkly pink sequins, her long blond hair draped over her shoulders. Everyone in the crowd turns toward her, phones up, waiting.

Two

DAYS UNTIL ANNIE LEBLANC DIES: 30

As Annie stands there, someone in the crowd breaks into applause. It's gentle at first, then picks up momentum, thundering by the time Annie starts walking down the center aisle. She's barefoot, a pair of gold high heels looped around her wrist. Everything transitions into slow motion as I watch her do this: Annie's movements, the tiny squeaking noises Mrs. LeBlanc is making from beside me, the clapping. I know this is a once-in-a-lifetime opportunity, giving Annie a second—albeit brief—chance. Her death was so sudden, and now she can be with her family again, sleep in her own bed, do all the things in Lennon that she used to love. That *we* used to love. But my brain is still humming with worried questions, the same ones that have been swirling around my head ever since Ruth Fish told me I'd won.

What if Annie didn't want to come back?
What if Annie doesn't want to see me?
What if this was all a big mistake?

I twist my hands in front of my stomach, cursing myself. What was I thinking? There's no way Annie will ever want to hang out with me again, not when I'm the same nothing she left last time. And while last time the only person who knew the full scale of my humiliation was Ryan, now all of Lennon are guaranteed to see I have approximately zero friends and always will.

It's only seconds before Annie reaches the stage, but it feels like hours. For a moment I think I must black out, that I'll come to in my bed and realize it was all just a dream, a plot from one of my comic books. But then Annie's here, collapsing into her parents as her mother lets out a choked sob.

I just sort of watch this part with the awkwardness it deserves, like a kid waiting their turn to see Santa Claus. I squirm and clench my hands, trying to look like I'm not actively searching for the nearest exit, trying not to look desperate, until finally Annie turns to me.

"Wilson?" she says.

Annie stares up at me, her eyes wide in disbelief. And then every part of me is sure, sure this is the moment where Annie cringes quietly at the sight of me, says a polite hello, and then doesn't talk to me again for the rest of the summer. Maybe she doesn't even say hello, maybe she just runs. But as I'm imagining everyone in the crowd pointing and laughing at me like something out of a 1950s fever dream, Annie leans in to hug me, her arms looping around my neck.

She buries her face in my shoulder. "It's really you," she says softly, her arms tightening.

At first, I'm stiff, waiting for her to pull away, but when she doesn't, I tentatively let my hands reach up around her back and pull her close. Then, just like that, I settle into her, my worries melting away like ice cream. It's so easy. She even smells like Annie, all vanilla perfume edged with rose. The smell of my childhood. Her nose is the same shape, slightly crooked at the end, and she's wearing the gold hoop earrings she bought with the money she saved up from the lemonade stand we ran that summer when we were ten.

I don't know how long we stay like this, the crowd around us fading into nothing. Annie's mom and her expensive dress don't matter, I can't feel Ryan Morton's anger simmering quietly from the crowd. Ruth Fish announces something into the microphone again, and Annie pulls away. Everyone in the audience stands and begins to disperse, making plans to get somewhere with air-conditioning. A few people stop to stare at Annie, one family even sending up their youngest kid to ask for her autograph. Annie blinks at him for a second before realizing it's her he's talking to. She shakes her head quickly, as if to clear fog from her brain, and when she stops, her confusion is replaced with a smile. She bends down and graciously signs the kid's notebook. Pretty soon there's a small line of people extending from the stage, waiting for Annie, and it's only now that I realize just what I'm up against this summer. It's not even just me and Annie's parents, but the entire town that's vying for her attention. She's a local celebrity.

"Okay, okay, give her room to breathe," Ruth Fish says, breaking the line with a wave of her perfectly manicured hands. There's a small groan from the crowd. "She's here all month, people. Lennon's a small town; you'll see her around."

Annie waves politely as the people turn to go. "So," she says to me as we watch the last of them leave, "do I have you to thank for the fact that I'm back on the Lennon Union football field, a place I swore I'd never return to after—"

"Robbie Bennett streaked during that game freshman year," I say, finishing her sentence and momentarily forgetting my nerves. But the ease is gone in a blink, replaced again with anxiety. "Yeah, yes, you do," I stammer. Now that I can see Annie's face better, she doesn't look as much like the old Annie as I first thought. Dark circles hollow out the skin under her eyes where her mascara has smudged, and her hair looks flat and lifeless, devoid of the bright silkiness that practically glowed in the pictures on her socials. "I mean, you don't need to thank me. I just mean, if you were asking, was it me who brought you back, then the answer is yes. I did."

"Well, thanks anyway," Annie says. Her eyes scan the football field, the concrete bleachers and the mustard-yellow goalposts, the steep slopes bordering the stadium that are pockmarked with dried brush and scrubby bushes. "It's weird being back here."

Mrs. LeBlanc turns around and says to Annie, "Sweetheart, we've got reservations at the Rainforest Café in a few hours."

The Rainforest Café is Annie's favorite restaurant of all time. It's a giant space whose insides are decked out to look like a rainforest, complete with vines and leaves hanging from the ceiling, life-size elephant statues, and a massive tank crammed with tropical fish. Their food is mediocre at best, but Annie always had dreams of being a conservationist, so every year on her birthday, from ages seven to twelve, we'd pile into her dad's car and drive two hours to the Rainforest Café in Ontario Mills for lunch.

Mrs. LeBlanc's eyes land on me and she smiles, revealing bright white teeth. For a second she looks startled at my presence, as though I haven't been standing next to her for the last five minutes.

"Wilson, honey, look at you!" she says, recovering quickly. "No more purple hair. Is this your natural color?"

My hands go up to my shoulder-length hair, mousy brown and split at the ends. "Yeah," I say, trying to smile back.

Annie dyed my hair with purple Kool-Aid once when we were eight, and it stayed in for about three days.

"Wil, you coming to lunch?" Annie says.

I catch the look Mr. and Mrs. LeBlanc exchange, even though it lasts only a half second. Annie misses it, too busy watching me and waiting for my answer. If I don't go with them, I know that by leaving Annie alone with her parents, there's a chance this whole thing, Annie actually wanting to spend time with me, could disappear. But I also know that look, the one that says I'm not wanted. The last time I saw Annie, she'd given me the same one. Seeing it again sends a chill of shame down my back.

"No, you guys go," I say, doing my best attempt at appearing nonchalant. "I've got a bunch of stuff to plan for this month."

This isn't a complete lie. I do, in fact, have a lot of planning to do, mostly because I haven't been able to bring myself to do any of it at all.

Without warning, Annie gives me another hug. As though she can sense the nerves radiating off me like lightning bolts, she squeezes her arms tight around my shoulders.

"I can't wait," she says.

I nod like I believe her.

Annie and her parents leave in the same direction from which she came, Annie tucked under their arms. I know I should be happy for them, and I am. But part of me can't help but wonder how long it'll take for Annie to not want me at lunches with her parents again, if this was the one and only time it would happen while she's alive.

As soon as the thought enters my head, though, I shake it away. Now that Annie's here, I have to believe this time will be different.

"I told you not to bring her back," a voice says from behind me.

Ryan Morton is watching me with her arms folded, the WELCOME BACK, ANNIE banner pressed against her chest. Suddenly it all clicks: that's why she's here. Not because she wanted to be, but because she was Lennon Union's ASB president last year. They must've asked her to carry out her presidential duties for an extra week after Joey Franklin, the incoming president, was busted for smoking weed on the tennis courts behind school.

"No, you didn't," I say. "All you did was roll your eyes."

After she stormed into the back office and wouldn't come out for forty-five minutes.

At this, Ryan rolls her eyes again. "I think even you can read between those lines," she says, scowling.

Sometimes I forget there was a time when she wouldn't look at me like this, when she actually smiled at the thought of a sleepover at my house. Seeing her scowl at me, nerves prickling my scalp, I can feel my renewed sense of determination starting to crumble. I'm used to Ryan acting exasperated with me, mostly for stuff at work, like when I pretend a microwavable bag of egg-fried rice counts as lunch. But here, the look on her face isn't as mad as it is disappointed.

I glance back toward the direction of the parking lot, where Annie and her parents have disappeared. "It won't be like last time," I say, swallowing hard.

Ryan snorts. "People like Annie don't change."

"Says the girl who was a vegan for approximately four days before going absolutely apeshit on a pepperoni pizza." Ryan's brother, Mark, appears behind her, dragging a string of balloons.

Ryan squints at him. "I am nothing like Annie," she says. "Also, I couldn't help but notice the way in which she just, um, I don't know, dicked off?" She throws an arm toward the slowly emptying parking lot. "I did not decorate this stadium so she could go back to her house and eat caviar off Marie Antoinette's best china."

Mark picks up the tail end of Ryan's banner. "You literally made a banner on the flip side of Christmas wrapping paper," he says. He twists the paper around, revealing thousands of Scottie dogs in bright green scarves. "And you spelled her name wrong."

As he speaks, Mark's shaggy hair falls into his eyes. He's the only person I know who can get away with talking to Ryan like this, but that's what you get for being a twin, I guess.

Ryan tugs the banner away. "It was an easy mistake." By the way she says it I can tell it wasn't a mistake at all. "And reusing old wrapping paper is called being *economical.*"

"Annie just got back from the dead," Mark says. "Sorry she's not desperately trying to be insulted by you."

"She doesn't know I'm going to insult her," Ryan says.

"Believe me," Mark says, "she knows."

The fact that either of them are talking in my general direction is astonishing. While the three of us have worked together for the last year or so at the Country Kitchen, they both usually do an incredible job of pretending I'm not even there. Sometimes I like to tell myself it's because Ryan is preparing me for when she goes to UC San Diego in August and leaves Lennon behind, but even I know that's mostly the self-delusion talking.

"She's probably in shock," I say. "I'll see her later, when she's settled in."

That is, if her parents haven't already dragged her halfway around the world on a private yacht. When I told them I was bringing Annie back, they didn't even invite me inside. Mrs. LeBlanc just burst into tears and practically slammed the front door in my face.

"See, Ryan?" Mark says, gesturing to me. "Some people aren't as annoying as you."

"Don't act like you don't care she's back," Ryan says. Her high ponytail swings behind her like a pendulum. "We all know you had a picture of Annie as your phone background for like three years."

I turn to Mark, my mouth slightly open. He splutters a laugh that's half incredulous, half pissed.

"You little fuck," he says to his sister.

"So are you going to draft up a custody agreement with Annie's rich friends?" Ryan asks me, ignoring him. Mark busies himself with the wrapping paper, his cheeks an unexpected shade of pink. "You know, dividing her time?"

I suck in a deep breath. Even though the last few days have been a roller coaster of emotional highs and lows, I've prepared for this. It's what I've been telling myself over and over again every night as I lay in bed and stared up at my ceiling, panic squeezing my lungs.

"She can't hang out with them," I say. "Even if her friends see her, they won't *know* it's her unless they're from Lennon, which they're not. That's, like, rule number one of Welcome Back."

Saying nothing, Ryan rolls her eyes yet again. She knows I'm right.

"Is that really why you want her to hang out with you?" she says. "Because she can't hang out with anyone else?"

I fold my arms across my chest. "That's not—I didn't mean it like that," I say. "You're twisting my words around."

Ryan pushes her lips together and gives me a pitying smile. "Am I?" she says, then turns away.

I watch as she catches up with Mark, who's now untying balloons from the chairs along the aisle. They shove each other back and forth until Mark wrestles Ryan into a headlock and they're both laughing, Ryan magically able to forget my existence when conversations like this have the power to keep me awake for weeks. Her voice, reciting words she's never even said, at least not out loud, circles my head.

As soon as she can, Annie will ditch you again.

You're giving her free passes she doesn't deserve.

You're going to let her walk all over you. Again.

And that might be true. But here's something else that's true: Even though Annie and I hadn't talked for a year, even though thinking about the last time we saw each other makes me physically sick, there hasn't been a single day since she died when I haven't thought about what would've happened if we'd just stayed friends. Would she still have died? Would things between me and Ryan still be weird? And would my life—if I could even call it that—still feel like a never-ending series of implosions?

By bringing her back, Annie has another chance at life, however brief. We have another chance. *I* have another chance. And this time I won't waste it.

THREE

DAYS UNTIL ANNIE LEBLANC DIES: 29

My time with Annie was always going to be limited, even from the beginning.

It's been known, even when we met back in first grade, that Ryan and I would go to Lennon Union High School and Annie would go to Del Monte, a private high school in Rosita, which is a town about a half hour away. Del Monte is the kind of school that looks like it's part spaceship, half-chrome, half-eye-wateringly-white stucco, like a villa on a Greek island in the year 4000. Ryan wasn't totally wrong when she said it was for people whose parents are con artists; a lot of local politicians send their kids there, including the guy who got arrested for selling ferrets on the dark web. But Del Monte is also where Annie's mom went to high school, where all the framed field hockey jerseys and pictures of the team celebrating their win at the California high school girls' field hockey championship hanging in her mom's office are from. Annie's mom is from

Rosita, and moved to Lennon only once she married Annie's dad, but she was still on the Del Monte alumni association, planning expensive proms and charity drives for kids only marginally less fortunate than the ones at Del Monte. So it wasn't a surprise when Annie went there for high school; what *was* a surprise, though, was that it didn't happen until our junior year. Because when Del Monte was having a new theater built for their drama department, a major gas leak was uncovered— turns out money can't guarantee you air quality—which forced the school to close for two years while they fixed it and battled a lot of pissed-off parents with expensive lawyers. The school opened again the summer before our junior year, just in time for Annie to officially transfer.

After that, I expected her to leave my life in some way. We were going from seeing each other every day at school, walking home together with Ryan, and religiously watching afternoon reruns of *The Price Is Right* to not carpooling anymore, not having lunch together, or not even having the chance of matching classes. But we would make it work. We still had the weekends and the evenings when Annie didn't have field hockey practice. She still lived in Lennon. What I didn't expect was for her to completely disappear, to stop returning my calls and texts and even the occasional handwritten note I'd stuff into her mailbox. That, and for Ryan to leave me at the same time.

Holding the laptop at this angle is making my neck sore, but I don't want my little sister, Bernie, who's snuggled next to me on our mother's bed, to see the screen. Ever since I saw Annie yesterday, I can't stop thinking about her, even more than normal. The fact that I haven't heard from her makes it worse. I scroll through the digital print of the *Lennon News* I paid $1.25

for last year for what must be the thousandth time, Atomic Fire-ball clicking against my back teeth, until I find the right article.

LOCAL TEEN DROWNS ON 18TH BIRTHDAY

BY TOM BRADFORD | DECEMBER 18

Last week in the early hours of December 15, Annie Le-Blanc (18) died at her home in Lennon at what was sup-posed to be her 18th birthday party. A spokesperson for the Lennon County Sheriff's Office confirmed Miss Le-Blanc died as a result of an accidental drowning in the fam-ily pool. No foul play is believed to have occurred. There will be a closed ceremony for Annie later in the week. Her parents, Rick and Mary LeBlanc, have asked for privacy.

And that was it. An underwhelming punctuation mark to the life of my best friend. Nothing about the sound of her laugh, or the way she made increasingly detailed photo collages for each one of my birthdays. She'd died in the pool I'd been swimming in a thousand times, the one whose dark deep end went down eight feet. Annie once confessed to me that she had to wear water wings until she was seven; combine that with the likely chaos of her birthday party, and I didn't have much trouble imagining how things could get deadly. I wasn't even invited to her funeral. Mr. and Mrs. LeBlanc held it at their house for just family, probably too afraid the rest of us commoners would leave marks on the walls with our sticky, malnourished hands. If Len-non was to live up to small-town stereotypes, rumors would be flying like Frisbees, but Lennon was not like other small towns, and for once, everyone seemed to mind their own business.

"*I'm* the one who's supposed to be helping *you,*" Bernie says.

A small paper bag materializes under my nose, its contents rattling around at the bottom. Before Bernie can see the computer screen, I close the PDF of the *Lennon News* and snatch the bag from her so I can cinch its top with a thin red ribbon from my pile. But when I pull the ribbon tight, the bag rips in half and a handful of candied almonds spills across my shorts. My mother, Jody, looks over at me from the end of her bed and raises an eyebrow.

"Easy there, Incredible Hulk," she says. "We want the guests to get the wedding favors *before* they get ripped open."

"We have like three hundred extra bags," I say as I chew the last fragments of the Atomic Fireball. My mouth burns with a sour tang. "Apparently eBay only sells them in quantities of millions."

Even though Jody can't read my mind—no matter how much she swears our once-connected bodies make us inherently telepathic on some level—I can feel my cheeks burn as I try to push thoughts of Annie and the news article out of my head.

I grab another bag and tie it closed with a ribbon, carefully this time. Splayed out at the end of the bed is the binder I made for Jody's wedding, filled with vendor information, receipts, color schemes, and table plans, all organized into carefully labeled folders, while scattered around me and my sister are the remains of our mother's wedding favors. They consist of seventy-five little brown bags, a sack full of sugared almonds coated in a shiny kiss-me red, matching red ribbon, and a hundred mini wooden hearts with the words WITH LOVE FROM DR. AND MRS. DAVID KRAMER carved into them.

"Remind me why you agreed to this insult to feminism?" I say, holding up one of the hearts.

Jody sighs. "You know how traditional David's family is. It was this or wear his great-grandma's wedding garter."

Bernie and I shudder.

Dr. David is the kind of guy who irons his underwear and has had his own health insurance since he came out of the womb. He's never even slept over at our house; he always makes this big show of saying good night and then leaves, even though he's usually back at seven the next morning to drive Jody and him to work, which is the dentist's office he's owned since he graduated from college at Professionals "R" Us. I'd hate him if he wasn't so fucking nice.

From the other end of the bed, Jody pulls an orange jumpsuit with glitter on the collar over her shoulders.

"I thought you and Dr. David were going to trivia night at the Nickel and Dime," I say. Lennon's worst bar. "You didn't tell me it was parole night, too."

My mother zips up the suit and stands in front of the mirror, her shoulders rolled back. "I've never worn this before," she says. "Every time I put it on, I keep hoping I'll like it." She turns to us and sweeps her hands down the front of the jumpsuit. "Is it really that bad?"

I grimace. "Not if you're a member of TLC."

Bernie shakes her head at me. "Your references are extremely outdated."

I sigh through my nose. Even my ten-year-old sister knows I'm a loser.

Jody unzips the jumpsuit and shrugs it off, revealing a hot-pink bra. Every minute I get through without thinking about Annie and her parents is a win, even if I am just watching my mother struggle into black-and-white-striped pants that make her look like Beetlejuice.

Having finished her half of the wedding favor assembly line, my sister has moved on to watching muted YouTube recaps of a UN meeting on our laptop while the Foo Fighters play over it from Spotify. The subtitles streak across the bottom of the screen at lightning speed as Bernie looks over the lip of the laptop and says to our mother, "What's the capital of Nigeria?"

Jody chews her tongue as if in thought. "Luxor?" she says after a few seconds.

A laugh explodes out of me. "That's a hotel in Vegas," I say.

"Luxor is a city in Egypt, too," Bernie says. She's already smarter than me and Jody combined. "The capital of Nigeria is Abuja."

"Abuja," Jody says, rolling the word around in her mouth. "Abuja."

"I'm pretty sure they're not going to ask about African capital cities at the Nickel and Dime trivia night," I say.

"It's general knowledge," Bernie says. Then, to Jody: "What was the name of the first dog in space?"

But Jody's distracted. She gives up on the pants and lets them fall back to the floor. A few outfits later, she decides on a short-sleeved velvet shirt tucked into high-waisted black jeans. It's better than the skintight purple shorts she'd wear to my soccer games, or the lace crop tops she usually reserved for grocery shopping. But most of that stuff went to Goodwill after Dr. David showed up, swapped instead for things that look more like clothes than costumes.

Even though I keep my eyes trained on the ribbon I'm failing to tie into a neat little bow, I can feel my mother glancing at me in the mirror between flicks of her mascara wand. She's desperate to talk about Annie, but she knows better than to ask.

When Bernie's video finishes, Jody ushers my sister into our bedroom to finish packing for her dad's house tonight.

"There's twenty bucks in the tin, so order pizza from Lucello's or something for dinner," she says to me from the doorway. "I'm working tomorrow from ten to seven, so if I don't see you in the morning, remember I need you to pick Bernie up from Cass's after dinner. Bernie says his new wife has eight meals a day, but they should be done with their first round of dinner at about six."

"Amanda's pregnant," I say to my mother.

Jody rolls her eyes. "Don't remind me."

The next few minutes consist of Jody trying to convince my sister she doesn't need to bring her goggles, to which Bernie responds with a torrent of facts about Lennon's extensive wildfire history and did my mother not know how much smoke in your eyes stings? Jody finally manages to get her through the door ten minutes later, Bernie quizzing her on the first five American presidents, by which point my playlist has finished and Spotify automatically starts cycling through random nineties pop music. I click back to the playlist titled "Michael Stipe's Army," named for the lead singer of R.E.M. Jody and I made it a few years ago and have been slowly adding and subtracting songs as they fall in and out of our fashion, but they're always from the nineties and almost always alt-rock. No matter how hard I try, I can't ever seem to listen to anything other than grungy, moody nineties music, but that's because when I was growing up, it's all Jody ever listened to.

I finally manage to cinch the knot on my ribbon bow, a wooden heart dangling from what's mostly the center. I toss it into the pile of finished favors on the floor next to me. Grabbing another bag, I begin dropping in exactly ten almonds, but even with Michael Stipe's voice in the background, I can still feel the silence around me now that I'm alone. Aside from comics, my playlists are normally one of the few things that can help erase from my mind the fact that I ate lunch by myself in the library again, or the way people laughed when Mrs. Edwards accidentally called me "Bill" in AP European History.

I slap the laptop shut, the stillness settling around me like a shovelful of dirt. Shaking out my shoulders, I wedge the wedding favor stuff back into its cardboard box and try to distract myself with thoughts of what I'm going to order from Lucello's. But as I make my way to Jody's bedroom door, I pause in front of the pictures lining her wall.

Jody has always had a million friends, a number that has only doubled since she met Dr. David. She's the type of person who gets invited to somebody's wedding after talking to them at a bar for five minutes. She has this way of connecting with other people that I've never been able to understand, always asking the right questions, never put off by the fact that somebody *looks* like they wouldn't be her type. She had me when she was seventeen, so to say my upbringing was unaverage would be an understatement. I spent the first two years of my life strapped to her chest while she traveled up and down the California coast. As a toddler, instead of using building blocks, I was constructing houses out of Radiohead tapes. Jody's mom died before I was born and she never knew her dad, like me, so we were pretty much on our own from the beginning, my mother getting out only at night, when our neighbor Mrs. Milton came over to watch me and chain-smoke in our recliner.

In the pictures on her wall, Jody is always at the center of the crowd. No matter what, she's smiling, and in most of the photos, at least one person is staring at her. There's even a picture of Jody standing behind a birthday cake and next to the birthday girl as she's blowing out the candles, and yet all eyes are on my mother, who's staring straight at the camera, her mouth open wide in a laugh.

I pad through to my bedroom and toss the laptop and wedding box on my bed, sitting down hard on my comforter. I know I shouldn't be surprised, but I can't help but think about how lame it is that even my mother and her fiancé have plans tonight. No matter how many times I look at those pictures, I'm always reminded of how much more of life Jody had lived by the time she was my age. She had a tattoo and a newborn before she was even legal. For Jody's fifteenth birthday she snuck into the Whisky a Go Go in Hollywood to see Weezer play. For my fifteenth birthday, I watched *Spice World* three times in a row with my mother and sister, then threw up at the end of the night—not from drinking too much, but because I'd eaten too many Sour Patch Kids.

Next to my bed is a small nightstand that used to belong to Jody when she was my age. It's still covered in Green Day stickers, its sides painted neon yellow with purple stripes. I slide open its tiny drawer and pull out the spiral-bound notebook I once used to take notes in calculus, but that now is filled with ideas of what Annie and I can do over the next month. I spent hours googling the best things to do in San Diego, which, at just an hour's drive away, is the nearest major city to Lennon. Whale watching, going to the San Diego Zoo, seeing a baseball game at Petco Park. But they all feel wrong. Hollow and forced.

As I'm flipping through the notebook, a single picture drops from the back pages. The picture is crumpled, its once glossy surface spider-webbed with stiff white creases. The three faces in its center are smiling, arms looped around each other's shoulders. Me, Ryan, and Annie on our last day of tenth grade. Nothing in it suggests this was the last day we would all be friends, that in just a few hours everything we'd spent however many years building would be gone. And along with it, just about everything in my life.

FOUR

DAYS UNTIL ANNIE LEBLANC DIES: 29

Somewhere in between me ordering pizza and making two more wedding favors, I fall asleep on top of my comforter, notebook facedown on my chest. The sound of someone settling into Bernie's bed across from me wakes me up.

"Holy freaking god," I exclaim at the figure propped up on the edge of the bed, their legs dangling over the side. I sit up straight, my heartbeat pulsing in my throat. Somehow a few sugared almonds drop down my shirt at the sudden movement. "How'd you get in here?" I say, shaking them out.

Annie nods toward the open window above my nightstand. "Front door was locked, so I tried the next best option. You should really lock your windows. And get curtains." She pinches one of the sugared almonds from my lap and pops it into her mouth. "What's all this?" she says, crunching down hard with her back teeth. But before she can swallow, she spits the gooey red remnants into her hand. "Holy shit, that's disgusting."

"They're sugared almonds, the official candy for boring weddings," I say. Now that we're on my turf, my words seem to be coming easier. "Jody's getting married. I wanted to give everyone gift cards that said *See you at the next one,* but apparently Starbucks doesn't make them yet."

The picture of me, Annie, and Ryan is still lying next to me on my bed. Before Annie can see, I cram it into the gap between my bed and the wall, my heart pounding. Somehow, she doesn't seem to notice.

"Oh my god, your mom's getting married?" Annie's eyes light up as she clasps her hands together at her heart. "When? To who? I have all of the questions."

As my heartbeat returns to normal, I can't help but feel a little caught off guard by how nice Annie's still being since the ceremony, even in just a few words. But then, what did I really expect? It wasn't like she ever bullied me on the internet or dropped a bucket of pig's blood on my head at prom. The explosion that ended it all wasn't even directed at me.

Holding up one finger, I say, "First, to Dr. David, the owner of Toothy Smiles, on Main Street. You'd think only a predator would call his business Toothy Smiles, but he's surprisingly normal, at least for Jody." The second finger goes up. "They're getting married in a couple of weeks, no thanks to Jody. In the last three months, I've planned every single aspect of this wedding, down to the color of the stamps on her invitations."

In true Jody fashion, everything between her and Dr. David has moved lightning fast. They'd dated officially for only two months before they got engaged, though, to Jody's credit, they *had* worked together and been friends for a year before that. As if starting a relationship and pledging your forever to the person wasn't enough for one year, Jody then insisted they get married this summer. And yet, I'm not allowed to call it a shotgun wedding.

I point to the binder now lying on the desk at the end of my bed. Annie lifts an eyebrow before shuffling over to it.

"Wow, this is kind of impressive," she says as she flips through the pages. She pauses on the one where I made a collage of different colored hydrangeas. "When did you get so organized?"

"I've had to be organized when it comes to Jody," I say. At least, if I don't want the water to get shut off. "And now there's the wedding, which obviously has twelve million moving parts I have to put in the right order."

It was never a question who would plan Jody's wedding. It was always going to be me. That's just how my mother and I have done things since her first marriage blew up; she's the hormonal teenager and I'm her frumpy governess, at least until Dr. David showed up.

Annie cocks an eyebrow. "Are you bitter about any of this? I can't really tell."

I smile sheepishly. "It doesn't help that it all kind of came at the worst time," I say. "The wedding is happening while you're here, which we obviously didn't plan. I didn't win Welcome Back until after the save-the-dates went out."

"Oh god, I don't care about that," Annie says, waving the thought away. "I can help make the playlist if you want. I'm well-known across the California coast for creating chill vibes. Or at least, chiller vibes than any of the weird dad music you listen to."

"I do not listen to weird dad music," I say. She and Ryan loved to tease me about the fact that the vast majority of the songs on my phone were released before 1999. "But your help would be good. Jody said she wants songs by Olivia Rodrigo and I have no idea who that is."

"You don't—" Annie says, then stops and rubs her forehead. "Never mind. Just leave it to me."

In skintight black workout shorts and a matching halter top, her hair pulled back in a slick ponytail, Annie looks like an Instagram girl, the ones who pose half naked next to a bowl of yogurt. I do a quick sweep of my bedroom for anything embarrassing: the My Little Pony collection that Cass bought for my seventh birthday is under my bed, along with Jody's pile of *Tiger Beat* magazines from the nineties, so all that's left is Bernie's and my beds, the dresser and nightstand we share, my desk, and a small bookcase by our bedroom door.

It feels weird, though, seeing Annie in my bedroom, with my things in the background. It's like seeing your teacher or a celebrity at the doctor's office. I have to blink a few times to convince myself she's even here. The last time Annie came to my house, it wasn't actually my house but Cass's, Bernie's dad. I lived there from ages five to fifteen, before he and Jody split up and we moved here. Even this won't be my room for much longer, not when Jody moves us all to Dr. David's house after the wedding. His place is small, but there's enough room for me and Bernie to share there, too, not that I even should. Now that I'm almost eighteen, I'm supposed to be on my own, figuring something out, but that would only work if I actually had somewhere else to go.

It occurs to me for a second that maybe the bareness of my room is just as embarrassing as my shoebox full of My Little Pony dolls. There aren't any framed pictures of me with people my age. All that's on the walls are posters for the Smashing Pumpkins album *Siamese Dream* and Liz Phair's *Exile in Guyville,* with sparkly flower stickers covering her exposed nipples. Looking at it all now, I realize it's almost *more* of an advertisement for the friendless pariah I've become since Annie and I stopped being friends.

As Annie makes it to the section of the binder devoted to the wedding cake, the doorbell rings.

"Pizza," I say to her as I scramble off the bed, relieved at the excuse to get out of my room, if only for a second.

I return in a few minutes with a large pizza box. A cloud of steam floats upward the second I open it, reaching the ceiling and blossoming across the popcorn surface. I reassemble myself on my bed and grab a slice before pointing at the box.

"You want some?" I say to Annie.

"If it means I'll get the taste of turds out of my mouth." She lunges for the pizza box. As she shovels a slice into her mouth, her eyes roll into the back of her head. "Oh my god, this is amazing. You'd think they'd have pizzerias in the afterlife, but no, it's all detox smoothies and granola."

The slice of pizza lowers slowly from my mouth as I stare at Annie in disbelief.

"I'm obviously joking," she says, plucking a pepperoni off her pizza and popping it onto her tongue. "And no, I don't know whether Heaven or Hell exists, so let's not even go there." She slaps her thigh with her free hand and gapes at me open-mouthed. "God, it feels so weird being back. My parents just keep looking at me and crying. They've hugged me so many times today, I'm surprised their bodies haven't just, like, absorbed me." Annie throws a hand toward my window. "I had to sneak out of my house and walk here. My mom actually asked if she could brush my hair today, which, like, yeah, okay, that's super sweet, but it's also very, very weird."

A pepperoni gets trapped at the back of my throat as I choke in surprise. "You walked here?" I say in between hacks. "There are mountain lions and coyotes out there."

"Relax, I'm already dead," Annie says. "I'm pretty sure it can't get much worse."

"Oh," I say. There's not much I can say back to that. We chew our pizza in silence until a thought occurs to me. "If you don't know whether Heaven or Hell exists, does that mean you don't remember it?" When Annie looks at me, I elaborate, "The afterlife."

Annie shrugs. "Not really. I remember having a sort of left-over warm feeling when I got here, but, like, a happy warm, not a fire-and-eternal-damnation warm." She bites into her pizza again. "I bet there's something in place that makes sure I don't actually remember. There was probably some sketchy dude a million years ago who tried to make a bunch of money by telling people about the afterlife."

I nod. That sort of makes sense.

"What about my funeral?" Annie says. "Please tell me you sang at it."

"I—no," I say as I glance down at my lap. "I didn't go. No-body did." When I look up at her, she's staring at me, frowning. "Your parents didn't invite anyone except your family."

Annie raises her eyebrows. "Well, that's depressing as hell," she says.

"Someone made you a Facebook page, though," I say, scrambling to open my laptop.

I click through to Facebook and the RIP ANNIE LEBLANC

page. I swivel the computer around so Annie can see. "They made it after you died," I say as Annie begins to scroll. "I don't know who. It's mostly people from Del Monte; I kinda found it on accident."

What actually happened was, I stumbled across the page as part of an hours-long mission in which I searched the internet for any other information about Annie's death and found mostly nothing.

Annie clicks through to the pictures people have posted, which are primarily group shots with her beaming at the back. There's one of her at a cast party from her high school's musical, a team shot after a field hockey game. And she fits right in, her hair glossy and smooth, perfectly applied lip gloss looking as though it's got some expensive name like Apricot Fantasy.

When we were growing up, Annie lived only a couple of houses down from Cass; that's how we became friends. One day Annie's dad brought her over to Cass's house with a plate of brownies and a tiny seven-year-old Annie cowering behind his legs. Her mom was a freelance architectural consultant who mostly gave design advice to cookie-cutter housing estates in northern San Diego and her dad owned an antiques shop on Main Street that he had inherited from his dad. It wasn't until we were in middle school that Mr. LeBlanc started making real cash by loaning out some of his antiques to big production companies in Los Angeles. And while Mr. LeBlanc's headquarters moved to LA, the family never followed. Very few people ever leave Lennon, because you may not know when you need its perks. The town has a way of picking and choosing who gets to stay, mostly people who have married locals or are notorious do-gooders. Because Mrs. LeBlanc is technically from a half hour away in Rosita, she's one of the lucky few. So instead of moving outside of Lennon, they brought the outside of Lennon to their home in the form of a new kitchen, a professional landscaping company, a heated lap pool, and a detached guest house/home gym in their backyard.

Sometimes it was almost worse that Annie never moved away. Even though she still lived on my old street, it felt like she lived on Pluto. The last time I actually talked to her face-to-face was on the last day of tenth grade, when me, her, and Ryan had lunch together at the Fish Grotto in San Diego, just like we always did whenever another school year had ended. But after that, it was as though someone had flipped a switch. One second, I existed in Annie's world and the next, I didn't. After Annie started at Del Monte, I barely saw her or her parents in town, and when I did, it was only really from afar. If they saw me, they'd mostly pretend I wasn't there, except the one time when Annie's mom fled the deli because I'd walked in. She actually dropped her basket full of groceries on the front counter, as though by existing, I was reminding her how much she didn't want to be there. I started to fear going into town, walking down the streets that used to feel like home. Every time I did, it was just another memory, another reminder of what I'd lost.

In the photos on my computer screen, Annie's hair goes from dark brown to platinum white and then a medium blond, her face getting thinner and thinner as the day of her death draws nearer. Right after she died, I flicked through each picture so many times, I'd practically memorized every face, embarrassing, pathetic thoughts circling my head. What made those people with her more interesting than me? What made Annie return their calls and not mine?

"Who's Ashley Turner?" I say from over Annie's shoulder.

While there are close to three hundred people on the RIP ANNIE LEBLANC page, at least a quarter of the posts are by someone named Ashley Turner, a girl with purple hair she probably dyed to piss off her important parents, and whose Instagram and Facebook are locked down so tight, I can see only her profile picture. But even with that, I can tell she probably smells like diamonds and teenage boys' dreams.

"We did field hockey together," Annie says, the constant scrolling onscreen reflected in her eyes.

They were clearly best friends, but I appreciate Annie sparing my feelings and not mentioning it. It's Ashley who posts every so often to keep the RIP page going, asking for pictures and organizing a memorial event on the six-month anniversary of Annie's death. If I had to guess, I'd say she made the page. When Annie died, part of me wanted to drive out to Rosita and meet Ashley myself, get some sort of information about Annie's last days, but the other part of me remembered that the only time I did something like that, it did not go well.

Watching Annie scroll through these pictures, I can't help but wonder if she's got the same pit of longing in her stomach that I used to get as I looked through them, except she's wishing she could be with her other friends, the ones who now wouldn't know her name. Without her smudged mascara from yesterday, she looks brighter somehow, and younger. Like the Annie I used to know. She wraps her ponytail around her hand, letting the hair slide through her fingers before repeating the movement all over again.

"Okay, enough about me," Annie says suddenly as she shuts my laptop and hands it back. "It's your turn. Tell me everything I've missed." She points at my head. "Are you between shaved heads, or is this actually a wig?"

I frown. "What are you—" I start to say, but then I remember.

Every year, Lennon Elementary's fifth-grade class puts on a D.A.R.E. pageant that's meant to discourage kids from taking drugs. For our turn, Cass, who had been sheriff for a couple of years by then, volunteered to be our emcee, and asked all of us what we wanted to be when we were law-abiding, drug-free adults. My response was that I wanted to be Sinéad O'Connor in the "Nothing Compares 2 U" music video because I liked her shaved head. While Jody had never been prouder of me, Annie and Ryan (and Cass) never let me live it down. It became a running joke in our friendship, a bargaining chip for them. *I'll give you my last cookie if you shave your head. Shave your head and you can pick what movie we watch.*

"It's a wig made from real human hair," I say. "From my feet."

Annie pets the ends of my hair. "It's so soft," she says. "But seriously, give me the *Access Hollywood* version of your life in Lennon but, like, from the last year."

I swallow. This is the part when I'm supposed to tell her that the most exciting thing to happen to me in the last two years is that the Travel Channel filmed an episode of *Haunted Hotels* at the Gold Rush Inn and I managed to get my elbow into a frame just before the third commercial break. But admitting this to Annie would inevitably unearth the whole fact that her transferring to Del Monte was the catalyst for my spiral into friendless loserdom, and I didn't bring her back to make her uncomfortable, which is inevitably what would happen if I brought up the black hole otherwise known as my social life during the second half of high school. Because what if, by telling her, I make her feel bad, or remind her of my social pariah status, thus making her not want to hang out with me again? What if I ruin this whole thing before it even really has a chance to get started? It's already going to end in twenty-nine days anyway. I can pretend nothing happened for twenty-nine days.

"Nothing's really changed," I say. Aside from the fact that my family as I once knew it exploded and I have no friends. "Luke Perry from the original *Beverly Hills 90210* died." At Annie's arched eyebrow, I shrug. "I don't know, Jody was really sad about it."

"I can't believe you still call your mom Jody," she says. "The only people who call their parents by their first names are therapists and serial killers."

I smirk. "It's kind of hard to call someone with such an extensive collection of pleather bandeaus 'Mom.' I mean, it's all kind of toned down since Dr. David appeared, but Jody will always be a Courtney Love fangirl at heart."

Annie laughs. "I guess that's fair. And speaking of dysfunctional, are you still friends with She Who Shall Not Be Named?"

She means Ryan. I swallow and briefly wonder how to answer this question. But it's actually pretty simple.

"Not really," I say. "We haven't been friends since you transferred schools."

Aka, when you ditched me.

"Wait," Annie says, frowning. "You guys haven't been friends since then?"

I shake my head. "I mean, we work at the Country Kitchen together, but it's not like we actually talk. Plus, she's leaving at the end of summer for college, so I'm pretty sure I'll never see her again."

"Damn," Annie says. "Does this mean we can't spend the summer there in our old booth, eating our weight in apple pie and hot chocolate bombs? Because if so, I will catch the next bus back to Hell, mark my words."

This thought hits me like a brick to the face, but Annie doesn't seem to notice. Apple pie and hot chocolate bombs at the Country Kitchen used to be our thing when we were little, almost every day after school, when calories and sugar consumption meant nothing. Annie wanting pie with me would mean she's somewhat prepared to hang out at least occasionally for the next month. Her offering to help me make the playlist for Jody's wedding would also point to this, but she could've just been trying to be nice. That, or make fun of my taste in music. But the fact that she's even here right now, in my bedroom, suggests she isn't planning on exclusively ignoring me this summer. That maybe this whole thing might actually be okay.

"What about your parents?" I say slowly.

Annie frowns again. "What about them?"

"Aren't they gonna want to spend the next month with you?"

"I mean, yeah, but not *every second* of *every day*. Can you even imagine? We're going to LA to see my cousins in a few weeks, which, by the way—*waste of time*. Only my aunt is from Lennon, so nobody else will know it's me. My mom says they think I'm some foreign exchange student from Canada who my parents are hosting."

At this, I feel a twinge of guilt. Everybody talks about what a gift Welcome Back is, but I hadn't really considered how hard this might be for Annie, her having a chance at life again, but only a glimmer. A window into what she had, knowing that in a lot of cases she could look but not touch.

"Otherwise, my parents know you brought me back," she continues, "so I'm gonna hang out with you. You might just need to work something out with them, but *Rick and Mary* can be reasonable." She stares at me for a second, letting her words hang in the air. Then she sticks out her tongue in disgust. "God, calling them by their names feels so unnatural."

I laugh, feeling a warmth spread slowly across my chest. This is why Annie and I were so close; while Ryan brought a sometimes baffling level of intensity to our friendship, things with Annie were always easy. I always worried about what Ryan thought of me in a way I never had to with Annie, at least not until the end.

The pizza box is still open between us. I peel up another slice as Annie does the same.

"Well," I say mid-bite, "wait until your mother wears a mesh bikini top to a rave and then get back to me."

FIVE

DAYS UNTIL ANNIE LEBLANC DIES: 28

Lennon, California, was once a mining town that's now a living, breathing homage to its gold rush heyday. Most of the buildings on Main Street and their saloon-style architecture are designed to look exactly like they would in the 1800s, with dusty brown wood and old-timey signs. Back in the seventies, the town council even made a law that says any new building on Main Street can't have an exterior that looks any newer than if it were built in 1913, resulting in the town looking like it's been permanently trapped in a cowboy time warp. We had a Dairy Queen and a Subway once, before I was born, but everyone was so offended by their invasion that they refused to eat there, and both eventually closed.

I wind my way down Main Street, past the thrift stores, tiny cafés, and the saltwater taffy shop. Everything feels so deliberate, from the discarded wagon wheels instead of planters and barrels for trash cans, designed specifically to attract tourists up from San Diego in their giant SUVs. But by the end of their visits, there's something about Lennon that stops them from wanting to be here anymore; they suddenly long for Frappuccinos and Target, their expensive waterfront hotels. Lennon's quaintness suddenly looks less charming and more boring, more isolating. It's Lennon's way of crowd control, making sure the population stays down, that there aren't too many people competing for Welcome Back, but that we still have a steady stream of tourists with a distinct taste for apple pie.

Unless you're born here, Lennon has to choose you specifically to stay, like it did with Annie's mom. As a kid, I thought I'd stay forever, lucky to have been born here. I liked the nostalgia, the way Main Street looked like something out of a Halloween movie from the nineties, before kids start getting picked off one by one. But after Annie and Ryan left my life, all I could see in the streets and the storefronts, the parks and the festivals, was what we used to have. What I no longer had. Suddenly the piles of autumn leaves tastefully gathered on street corners and the way Main Street always smells like apple pie, even on trash day, started to feel weird. Contrived. Creepy.

The Lennon Historical Society sits all the way at the top of Main next to the old post office. It's just a small wooden building with an American flag draped over the porch. At the end of the ceremony two days ago Ruth Fish asked me to come by her office to pick up the pamphlet on Welcome Back she forgot to bring.

Last night Annie and I finished the entire pizza and researched music for Jody's wedding playlist until midnight. As we huddled on my bed debating which line dance to put on the list—Annie was steadfast in her argument for the "Cha-Cha Slide," but I would hear of nothing other than "Macarena"—I could almost imagine things were like they used to be, with Annie sleeping over at my house, Jody and Cass watching *Cops* in the living room. For the first time in nearly two years, somebody other than my mother and little sister was in my room listening to music with me and wondering aloud how much nineties Britney was too much nineties Britney on a playlist, and not because they had a chemistry project to work on, but because they wanted to. For the first time in two years, all those nights I spent reading comics in my empty bedroom felt like fifty thousand miles away. The fact that I had only twenty-nine days left of it didn't even cross my mind until I turned the lights out to go to sleep.

The Lennon Historical Society's tiny building is half office, half museum. The far half of the room has two desks stacked to the ceiling with papers poking out of manila folders, while the front consists of two scraggly red couches with a rack of pamphlets behind, its shelves crammed with brochures for activities in Lennon and San Diego. I grab the pamphlet with a rainbow parakeet on the cover thinking it'll be for the San Diego Zoo, but it's actually for the Bailey Higgins Science Center, a place in downtown San Diego we used to visit on field trips, where we'd watch movies about killer whales and outer space in its giant golf-ball dome theater.

When I slide the pamphlet back into its place, I catch the wall behind the rack; it's completely covered in pictures. The ones directly beside the front door are grainy and brown, with cowboy-looking dudes standing in a line in front of the old bank on Main Street. When Welcome Back started in the 1800s, only men could win, and most of them just brought back old rivals so they could have the satisfaction of killing them again. As the pictures extend around the corner of the room, they slowly sharpen into color. Men and women standing in front of elaborate floats for the Fourth of July parade, posing in the apple orchards at the old Apple Pie Festival. In 1960, the first woman—Ryan's grandma Wendy Young—won Welcome Back, and in 1990, they lowered the minimum age for people who could win from twenty-one to sixteen.

As I near the end of the photo wall, I pause on the picture whose inscription reads WELCOME BACK 2000. It's nothing that extraordinary, just some woman with bushy brown hair and dark round-framed glasses who's dressed in baggy jeans and a matching denim jacket. There's something about her that looks weirdly familiar. Maybe it's the fact that her jacket is dotted with splotches of pink paint, and that this fashion monstrosity vaguely reminds me of something Jody would wear.

I circle back to the start of the photo wall and the very first picture, dated 1840. Even though the dates stamped underneath each photo on tiny gold plaques slowly increase to the present and the images look more and more contemporary, they each still have that weird, undeniably old-timey outdatedness that surrounds everything in Lennon. It's this and Ruth Fish that are the only constants; because at the back of every group photo, there she is, even in the very first one. But instead of it being Ruth Fish as I know her, the plaque underneath labels her as LUTHER FISH. In spite of the cartoony handlebar mustache and the dark hat that looks like a deflated basketball on her head, I can tell it's her: same heart-shaped face, blond hair, and sharp, knowing eyes. Only in 1960 does she appear in the photos as

I know her now, her trademark pantsuit going from white to turquoise to tangerine orange.

"I will never stop regretting that mustache."

Ruth Fish appears over my shoulder, the sound of her voice tickling the inside of my ear. My hands instinctively fly up to cover my head as I let out a yelp.

"Jesus Christ!" I exclaim. "Where did you come from?" I didn't even hear the door.

Ruth chuckles and steps around to my side. Today she's in head-to-toe magenta, the edge of her suit jacket collar studded with silver rhinestones.

"Sorry, sweetheart," she says. "You'd think I'd have learned by now how to approach people without scaring them to death." She holds out a hand to touch my arm. "I forgot I asked you to come by today. Come sit, come sit." She waves me over to one of the desks, then leans in and drops her voice to an excited whisper. "So, how's everything been so far with Annie?"

"Um, good, I guess," I say. "She's staying with her parents, so I haven't seen her that much yet."

Today, she and her parents went to San Diego, where they're probably eating diamond-encrusted escargot on a recently landed spaceship.

Ruth nods. "That can happen sometimes, when the Returned have multiple loved ones still alive. It's like a tug-of-war, you know, trying to fit in time with everyone." She mimes pulling me back and forth, then waves it away. "You'll figure it out, everybody does. So, the literature." A pamphlet with a group of people linking arms on the cover materializes on the desk. Ruth flips it open to the front page and brushes her fingers down the glossy paper. "We like to give these to the Welcome Back winners, along with their Returned. It goes over the fine print, what you can and can't do, that sort of thing."

"Fine print?" I say.

I probably should've assumed there would be catches that came with Welcome Back, but I guess when it's something that's happened in your town every decade since basically the dawn of time, the details don't really cross your mind.

"Just about what would happen should Annie get in an accident while she's back or write a hit single. You know, that sort of thing."

"Oh," I say, like those two things are even mildly on the same level. "Sure. And what would happen, exactly, if she, you know, got in an accident?"

Ruth's face doesn't show a hint of self-consciousness. In her deep pink power suit, she's all smiles, her blond hair so sprayed into place, it looks almost like concrete.

"Well, it depends," Ruth says. "But in most cases, she wouldn't die again, she'd just be severely injured."

"What if her head gets chopped off?"

Ruth blinks at me. "Okay, in that scenario she'd die early," she says. "But as I said, in *most* cases, she'd just get hurt. It's all in the pamphlet, see . . ." Her eyes scan the list of rules outlined on the second page. "'Though the Returned cannot *usually* die again,'" she says, reading the words aloud, "'they can be severely injured. This includes, but is not limited to being: impaled, shot, run over, suffocated, asphyxiated, drowned, or dropped from great heights.'" She thumps her finger against the page, as though she's just proven that water does, in fact, exist. "So, there you have it."

"Keep Annie away from sharp objects," I say, nodding. "Got it."

"I'll be here if you've got any questions, but otherwise I'll see you and Annie at the Fourth of July parade. Just make sure you wear sunscreen, because it can get pretty darn hot on top of that float, and—"

My brain stutters. "Excuse me?" I say, cutting her off. "I have to ride on the float?"

"Of course you do. You won Welcome Back, silly girl." Ruth swats my arm playfully. "Winners always ride on the float with their Returned. This year's theme is America the Beautiful, so I'm thinking you girls could dress up in American glamour, you know, like Marilyn Monroe or Jayne Mansfield. We've set the float up so it's got flowers from all over the country representing all the different ecosystems. It came to me in a dream one night, I'm just—"

As Ruth rambles on, I make sounds as though I'm listening, but really, she lost me the second she said I'd have to stand on top of what is essentially plywood on wheels, dressed like Marilyn Monroe, sweating under the summer sun in front of the entire town. Just the thought of it makes my head swim.

Ruth is still talking as I slide the pamphlet off the desk and into my clammy palms. I mumble something about needing to pick my sister up and move toward the door as quickly as I can.

"If Annie has any questions, just send her my way," Ruth shouts after me. "And let me know if you need any help with your float costumes. Don't be strangers!"

Outside of the weirdly detailed list of ways Annie can be killed or heinously maimed while alive again, the pamphlet Ruth Fish gave me is pretty useless. Most of the information in it, I already know:

1. One winner is chosen every ten years. That winner must be sixteen years or older; from Lennon, California, or have been settled here permanently for a minimum of twenty years; and not convicted of any felonies in the United States of America, Mexico, Canada, or Puerto Rico.

2. The Returned must be from Lennon, California, or have settled here permanently for a minimum of twenty years prior to their death.

3. The Returned is allowed back for exactly thirty days, after which they must return to the afterlife at noon on their final day.

4. Though the Returned can be seen and interacted with by members of the public who are not from Lennon or who have not been settled here permanently for a minimum of twenty years, it is not physically possible for said members of the public to know about Welcome Back or recognize the Returned as they were in their previous lifetime. Anyone caught attempting to circumvent these restrictions will have their Returned sent back to the afterlife, and they, along with their Returned, will be ineligible for winning any future Welcome Back contests.

The rest of it is just boring stuff about tax codes and intellectual property, should the Returned want to take up a part-time job or invent something half-interesting while alive again. It says nothing about what to do if the bona fide sovereign of your town tries to strong-arm you onto a float while dressed as a beauty queen and parade you in front of everyone you've ever met.

I shove the pamphlet deep into my pocket and swipe my forehead with the back of my hand. Cass lives on the other side of town, but because Lennon is basically the size of a Post-it note, that means he's only about twelve blocks away from my house. Even still, the change from shitty, run-down one-stories to the nicer, woodsy brick houses is palpable.

Cass's front door is propped open by a white rocking chair, a fresh vase of pink roses poking up from a nearby table. I jog up the steps and knock loudly on the doorframe. This doorway is one I've crashed through so many times, I've lost count, but now that it's not mine anymore, I know I'm not allowed in any farther. As I wait, I glance down the street at Annie's house, a few yards over. A Range Rover is parked neatly in the driveway, tall lanterns I'm sure they've never lit staggered up the porch so that the front of their house looks like something out of a magazine.

"Hey there, Wilson P," a voice says from inside. Cass appears at the end of the hallway. "How'd the ceremony go? It must've been the quietest shift I've ever had."

Cass is wearing his sheriff's uniform, his pants and shirt one giant block of khaki. He pulls up the waistband of his pants around his stomach, which swells over the lip of his belt.

"Oh, you know," I say, shrugging, "eventful."

He rubs the dark stubbly beard growing along his chin and the top of his neck. "Yeah, I heard about Mary LeBlanc's hat," he says.

I smirk. For some reason the woman from the picture in the historical society comes back to me, her denim jacket with the pink paint that I know I've seen somewhere before. Like Mary

LeBlanc's hat, it's so unnecessarily loud, designed to be noticed. It reminds me vaguely of a jacket that Cass's mom made for me for Christmas one year, except instead of paint, it was covered in little embroidered butterflies she'd stitched in vibrant purple and pink thread.

Cass leans back into the house and grabs something off the table by the door. He hands me a thin book with a squashed gold bow stuck to the front. On its cover is a picture of an actress I recognize but whose name I can't remember, her smiling face looking up from a birthday cake. It's a comic book: *Chilling Adventures of Sabrina*.

I suck in an excited breath. "Oh my god, I really wanted to read this," I say, flipping through the pages and scanning the comic, the panels filled with jagged drawings in sharp reds, yellows, and muddy watercolored browns.

Cass is watching from over my shoulder. "It's pretty good. I might even go so far as to say it's better than *Afterlife with Archie*." *Archie* is by the same writer as *Sabrina* and is basically perfect. I lift an eyebrow. "I said *might*," Cass insists.

"Thanks," I say, gesturing to the comic. "This is really cool."

"Can't give up on the tradition, not when it's your last one."

Ever since Cass and Jody got married when I was in kindergarten, he's been buying me comic books as a present on the last day of school. It used to just be *Buffy the Vampire Slayer* issues, but we've since graduated to edgier, mostly weirder things.

Glancing up at the house that used to be mine, I say, "So, are you gonna get the new baby into comics too? Because if you are, I feel like you shouldn't start with *Buffy*. Not unless you want them to peak by age three."

Cass widens his eyes. "Bernie told you about the new baby?" he says.

What she actually said was that Amanda, Cass's new wife, had thrown up egg salad sandwich all over the dashboard of his cruiser, and Jody read between the lines.

"I heard it's a girl."

Cass pulls out a pack of cigarettes from his back pocket and wedges one between his lips. He nods slowly. "It's a girl," he repeats, fishing out a lighter. The cigarette's edge comes to life with a little circle of orange. "Amanda's got all our weekends booked until the baby is here. I forgot how much stuff there is to do to get ready for a baby." He lifts his cigarette and smiles at it sheepishly. "Starting with stopping smoking. But then I've gotta paint Amanda's studio, figure out how the hell to strap the new car seat into my cruiser . . ."

Amanda's studio sits at the back of the house, but it's perfect for a baby. While it's pretty small, it gets amazing light in the afternoon. I know this because it used to be my room.

"Please tell me you aren't gonna name the baby something cliché like Katie or Sarah," I say. "Or, like, Mary Elizabeth."

Cass frowns. "My grandma's name is Sarah."

I give him a sympathetic smile. "Is that why you're so cliché?"

He rolls his eyes and nudges me with his elbow. "I wanted to name the baby after the worst band of the nineties, but turns out somebody in Lennon already did that."

My look of smug sarcasm deepens into a scowl. I'm not cool enough for Wil to be short for something exotic like Wilhelmina or Willow. I'm named after my mother's lame, most unbelievably boring favorite band ever, Wilson Phillips.

"So, how's your mom?" Cass says quietly. "Everything okay?"

Somehow our conversations always steer back to Jody, Cass checking up on her, cringing at the word of every new boyfriend.

But that's what happens when your now ex-wife walks out on you, I guess.

So I say what I always say: "She's good."

Cass nods. "Wedding must be coming up soon."

It's my turn to nod. He wasn't invited for obvious reasons. "Three weeks."

The air around us is heavy with summer, so thick you can practically chew it. Cass's house is surrounded by dense oak trees, his dried lawn stretching out to meet a line of woods. There's a tree not far back with a crooked branch about three feet up; it was my favorite place to read comic books when I was younger, especially in the fall, when the ground was sheltered under a blanket of orange leaves.

"Cass, have you gone—" Amanda appears in the hallway beyond the front door but stops when she sees me. This gives Cass the opportunity to toss his cigarette away before she can see it. "Oh," she says, her smile tight-lipped. "Hi, Wilson."

Amanda's long red hair descends to the middle of her back, a light pink dress floating around her calves. Of course she looks perfect as a pregnant person, all watermelon boobs and a bump that's 100 percent baby and 0 percent pizza. We spent the last days of Jody's pregnancy with Bernie at Moo's in town, my mother knee-deep in a vat of cinnamon ice cream.

"I'm just heading out now," Cass says to Amanda. When she turns away, he murmurs to me, "Amanda's parents are on their way up from Encinitas for the week. She's ordered a fifteen-pound turkey I've gotta roast tomorrow. Forget that I'm doing a twelve-hour shift tonight. We'll be lucky if I don't burn the whole house down. Instead of *The Walking Dead,* I'll be something like"—he pauses, thinking—"the walking *dad.*"

"That'd make a good comic," I say as I stare down at the one in my hands.

But my words drift off as I zero in on the birthday cake, at the warm glow lighting up the lower half of the girl's face. As I do, a tiny light bulb flickers to life over my head.

"Oh my god," I say quietly. "I know where I know her."

Cass frowns. "Who, Kiernan Shipka?" he says, pointing at the girl on the comic cover.

"No," I say, then squint at him. "When we met, you barely knew who Christina Aguilera was. How do you— Never mind." I tap the cover. "The woman from the picture, the one in the paint-covered jacket from the—" But as Cass's frown deepens, I realize there's no point in explaining it to him. "Forget it. Is Bernie ready to go?" I lean as far as I can toward the front doorway without actually going in. "Bernie!" I shout, unable to contain the nervous panic creeping into my voice. "Let's go!"

Cass sets a hand on my shoulder. "Wilson, what's wrong?" he says.

"N-nothing," I stammer, my brain flickering between memories of the picture in the historical society and the pictures on another wall, ones I've looked at almost every day of my life. "Can you drive Bernie home? There's something I gotta do."

Cass's look of concern only heightens, but I don't give him the chance to ask more questions before I tear back down the porch and break into a sprint.

"Thanks again for this!" I shout behind me, lifting the comic over my head.

Most of the time I curse the fact that Lennon is so freaking small, but today it works in my favor. I'm home in less than five minutes.

I barrel into Jody's empty bedroom and turn on the light, illuminating the hundreds of faces staring back at me from the pictures on my mother's wall. My heart hammers in my throat as I scan the frames, searching for the right one. Up near the top right corner is the picture of Jody and a group of girls gathered around a birthday cake covered in neon-green icing and the words *Happy Birthday, Stacey*. Standing in the middle, Jody has one arm on her pregnant stomach and the other around her friend Stacey, a small girl with a mouth full of braces and bleached-blond hair. But just behind them is a woman in a denim jacket with patches of pink who's adjusting something on a table filled with presents.

"Gotcha," I whisper, plucking the frame off the wall.

It's the same woman. It has to be. Not only would it be weird and mostly impossible for someone to make an identical version of the same ugly homemade jacket, but the woman in the picture has the same frizzy brown hair and oversize glasses.

I shut my eyes as I do the math. If Jody was pregnant with me when this picture was taken, that would mean she was seventeen. Jody was born in 1985, which means this picture was taken in 2002. And if this picture was taken in 2002, that would mean it was two years *after* the woman in the denim jacket was brought back from the dead.

"Holy shit," I say, the picture slipping from my hands.

The frame drops onto the carpet, facedown, so all I can see now is a sheet of black cardboard and the little metal hook that keeps it attached to the wall.

For some reason, this woman was allowed to stay.

Which means maybe Annie can too.

Six

DAYS UNTIL ANNIE LEBLANC DIES: 28

As I make my way back to the historical society—fast-walking this time, because I'm not a machine—my confidence from just a few minutes before is already starting to wane. Is it really that impossible for two people to have made the same ugly jacket? Maybe it's not even homemade, maybe they actually paid for it. Or maybe it *is* the same jacket, and the women were twins. The dead lady could have left it to her twin sister in her will, and the second lady felt so bad about the way she'd treated her sister in life that she punished herself by wearing the tacky jacket. It all seems unlikely, but not beyond the realm of possibility.

Ruth Fish is exactly where I left her, except this time there's a salad in a small blue Tupperware sitting on her desk. At the sight of me she pauses, fork midair and spinach dangling.

"Wilson," she says, her eyes flicking to the neon open sign in the window, which is now off. "Did you forget something?"

Without stopping to answer her, I beeline for the picture on the other side of the room and grab it off the wall. I hold it up next to the picture I've brought from home and here it is, right in front of me. Proof that this is the same person. Or twins.

Ruth drops her fork back into her salad and watches me curiously. "Wilson, what are you—"

"Her," I say, setting both frames down on Ruth's desk. I jab my finger into the woman's face. "Is this the same person?"

Ruth slides a pair of reading glasses out from one of her desk drawers and slips them onto her nose. She squints down at the pictures.

"That's Andrea Smithson," she says.

"So it's the same person?" I say. "They're not twins?"

Ruth gives me a look. "Honey, do you think two women would wear that jacket?"

I sit down hard into the chair across from Ruth's desk. "I knew it," I say, suddenly feeling light-headed. "Why didn't you tell me there was a way Annie could stay back?"

"Because there's not," Ruth says.

"But Andrea Smithson came back in 2000, and the birthday party picture was taken in 2002. She got to stay longer than thirty days."

Ruth sighs heavily and folds her hands in her lap. "There have been certain cases in which the Returned have been allowed to stay back permanently, but those were *very* unique circumstances." She leans forward and drops her voice, as if to convey the seriousness of what she's about to say. "It doesn't happen for just anyone and it's not something we even fully understand. That's why I don't like to advertise it."

"But it *has* happened," I say. "It *can* happen."

"Well, yes," Ruth says, glancing down at the pictures of Andrea. "But if you're looking for a way to keep Annie back, I don't know what to tell you. It's different for everybody."

"What happened with Andrea Smithson?"

With another sigh, Ruth snaps the lid back onto her salad, giving up on it. "Her situation was a little bit of a strange one," she says. "Andrea died in a car accident. Her husband, Joseph, went to jail because the police found drugs in his system and he was driving. But when Andrea's sister brought her back, Andrea found out that Joseph had been drugged in the restaurant they were dining at; turns out his ex-girlfriend was the chef. Joseph got out and the ex went to prison. She's up in Chowchilla now, over at Central California Women's Facility."

I squint at Ruth, trying to make sense of her story. "And that helped Andrea stay alive . . . how?" I ask.

"Oh," Ruth says. "Right. Well, we *think* it's because she righted a great big wrong, and Lennon rewarded her with a second chance. You see, the way it works is, all the Returned get dropped off just at the edge of Lennon, over by the power plant, in a bus. And when their month is up, the bus comes and takes them back at noon. But with Andrea, the bus just never came."

Somehow this feels like the most absurd part of this whole thing.

"I'm sorry, you expect the Returned to get back on a bus and wait to die again?" I say. "What's stopping them from just, I don't know, *running away*?"

"The rules," Ruth says simply. "If they don't return to the bus stop on time, they still go back. The bus always finds you."

"But how do you know the bus wasn't just late?"

Ruth shakes her head as though I've just asked her the most obvious question in the world. "The bus is never late," she says, smiling.

"So what happened to Andrea Smithson? Did her getting to stay back mean everyone outside Lennon who knew her from before got to find out she was alive again?"

Ruth lets out a loud cackle. "Oh god, no," she says. "Can you imagine? That'd be our secret out." She shakes her head again. "No, no, outsiders could still see Andrea, of course, but they could never know she'd died. Lennon makes sure of that. Haven't you wondered why nobody else brought it up to you that there's a chance Annie could stay back after it worked for Andrea? Lennon has a way of protecting its secrets." She scans me up and down. "You must be very special."

My eyes drop into my lap, unable to take the weight of Ruth's warm smile.

"But I've never seen Andrea Smithson around Lennon," I say. It's a small town. That jacket would stand out. "Where is she now?"

If I can just talk to her, maybe I can figure out how she managed to cheat the system, to make Lennon think she was worthy of a second chance.

"She's dead," Ruth says. "House fire."

My jaw drops involuntarily. "You're saying she died, came back from the dead, and got to stay alive, only to die horrifically *again*?"

Ruth pats my hand. "Just because she got to stay back doesn't mean she gets to live forever. It just means she gets to be the same as the rest of you." Ruth chuckles.

"Is that the kind of thing that happened for everybody who was allowed to stay back?" I say. "They righted some wrong?"

"Well, like I said, it's only happened a handful of times, but that's what it looks like. The first one was Adam Franklin, back in 1850, who found out his death had been a murder-for-hire."

"So it always has to do with crime?"

"Not necessarily," Ruth says. "The only other time it happened was in 1930, with John-David Peters. He and his twin brother were separated at a very young age, when his father took John-David's brother to live in France and John-David stayed behind in Lennon with his mother. After John-David died of cancer, his wife brought him back and he managed to track down his brother, who was running a little tailor's shop in Nice."

"And then what happened?" I say.

"What do you mean?" Ruth says.

"What was the wrong they righted?" I say. "Did they find out their dad was secretly smuggling drugs and they turned him in? Or that their mom was, like, Princess Anastasia?"

"No," Ruth says. "That was it. They were reunited."

"*That* was the wrong?" I say with disbelief. "That two brothers became un-estranged?"

"I told you, I don't make the rules. I just sign the paperwork."

As Ruth begins pulling out hand-bound booklets on Lennon's history that she made herself, I nod and make sounds of agreement while my thoughts race. My hands feel electric, my fingers fidgeting nervously in my lap. I've got plans to make, bullet points to list out in my notebook, and actions to execute with laser precision. Because I finally know what I'm going to do for the next month.

I'm going to bring Annie back for good.

SEVEN

DAYS UNTIL ANNIE LEBLANC DIES: 26

For the next couple of nights, I barely sleep. My brain is too hyped up, as though permanently fixed to an espresso IV. All I've done is pace the floor in my living room as midnight turned to one o'clock in the morning, then two, then three, then pretty soon I find myself eating my fourth bowl of Cinnamon Toast Crunch and watching as the sun comes up in a tie-dye haze of pink and orange.

Last night I ripped out all the ditched activities I'd written down for me and Annie in my notebook and started fresh with a list of ideas on how I can keep her back, most of which are completely absurd. So far my best theory is that Annie's dad is actually part of some prop mafia in Hollywood that's spent the last few years stealing antiques from small-town museums across America, and now Annie has to track them all down and return them to their rightful places in history. Annie's dad never gave me criminal vibes—he actually looks a little like Ed Sheeran but somehow even less threatening—but I figured, desperate times.

Because as I watched the sun come up this morning, my eyes stinging from the lack of sleep, that's all I felt buzzing up and down my arms. Desperation. Desperation to get this right, to keep Annie back. The opportunity makes Welcome Back look like amateur hour, because who cares about thirty days when I could have my best friend back for good?

My biggest problem now, though, as I walk beside Annie down Main Street to the Country Kitchen, is that I can't actually tell her about any of this; Ruth Fish made it very clear to me as I gathered Jody's picture frame and made my way to the door for the second time in only a few hours.

"But see, this is why I don't like talking about Andrea Smithson and everyone else," Ruth said. She'd already grabbed her salad again and was peeling back the lid, her not-so-subtle attempt at telling me to get out. "Not only is it completely different for every person, but it's also not something you can force. We've had a few people over the years try to keep their Returned around, but you can't just bend Lennon to your will."

In essence, I could steer Annie in the right direction, but I couldn't actually tell her what to do or why she should do it. This also meant that I couldn't ask her a lot of questions, at least not without arousing suspicion.

"So," I say slowly, drawing out the word as the Country Kitchen edges up on our right, "do you know where your dad actually gets his antiques from?"

For the entire walk down Main Street, Annie has been mostly quiet, taking in the historic building fronts and endless rows of American flags. Today is the perfect day, all clear blue skies and trees so green, they look Photoshopped. No matter how weird I think this town is, Lennon always looks beautiful in the summer. It goes out of its way to make sure of it.

There are some people on the street that, when they see Annie, literally stop to stare at her open-mouthed, but each time, Annie just smiles politely and tightens her arm in mine.

Since she got back, she's spent most of her time with her parents tucked away in their house, or down in San Diego, but Annie's parents and I did, somewhat, come up with a kind of agreement. This morning Annie had reported to me that after much discussion, her parents had agreed to a schedule: we'd alternate our days with Annie, except for the weekend they were going to Los Angeles to see Annie's cousins. She'd spend her nights with them and have the occasional sleepover at my house. And they still reserved the right to, at any point and for whatever reason, ask her to stay with them.

I had no choice but to agree. Because even though Annie is technically spending more time with them, I was surprised they even agreed to let me have any regular time with her at all. Plus, she's their kid. I get it.

Annie shrugs. "I don't know, garage sales, mostly," she says to my question. "People also just give him stuff because they don't know what else to do with it."

"But he doesn't, like, go out looking for certain things?"

"Not really, not unless it's something he doesn't have and he knows people need it. But he's got warehouses out in the desert filled with stuff. There's not a lot he doesn't have anymore."

I peel a piece of paper out of my back pocket and try to glance at it without Annie noticing. "Do you know if he has a"—I squint down at the picture of the weird-looking bronze horn that was stolen from a museum in New York back in the nineties—"Chinese gu? You know, like a metal cup thing?"

Annie pauses on the sidewalk and squints at me, her blue eyes glinting. "What the hell are you talking about?"

I shove the paper back into my pocket and sigh. "I have no idea."

The Country Kitchen is an exercise in beigeness. Aside from the forest-green plastic padding in the booths and the cherry-red T-shirts and matching visors Terri Morton, the owner and Ryan's mom, makes us wear, the restaurant is all shiny pine: wooden walls, stout wooden tables, and secondhand chairs, plus a long, glossy counter topped with glass and pictures of the Country Kitchen back when it opened in 1957 stuck underneath.

As we make our way inside, Annie and I sidestep the line of people that extends from the cash register at the front counter all the way out the door and onto the sidewalk. As the best apple pie place in Lennon, the unofficial apple pie capital of California, the Country Kitchen is a mecca for tourists looking for a healthy dose of butter and nostalgia.

Annie grabs a booth at the back of the restaurant, near the office. It's where we always used to sit, Ryan ping-ponging back and forth to the kitchen with trays of apple pie and hot chocolate for us. The floral wallpaper is slightly more faded and Annie is obviously older, but otherwise, with her here, the scene looks exactly the same as it did when we were kids. Minus the crowd of middle schoolers who swarm her, firing questions and asking for selfies.

"Are you a ghost?"

"Are you even real?"

"Have you ever met Kobe Bryant?"

"Um . . ." Annie says.

She shoots me a panicked look as one of the kids throws up a peace sign and snaps a picture with her, the flash temporarily blinding them both.

After ordering Annie a hot chocolate bomb, I slip into the back office. Sitting at his mom's computer with his back to the door, his red Country Kitchen visor flipped upside down and twisted backward, is Mark Morton. At the sound of me stepping into the office, he turns.

"Oh shit," he exclaims.

He yanks the visor off his head, unleashing an unholy amount of dusty brown hair that falls around his face. With one quick swoop, he brushes it backward.

"Sorry," I say, starting to back away.

"No, no, it's fine," Mark says. "You just startled me. What're you doing here? I thought Mom gave you the month off."

"She did," I say. There's a narrow line of cubbyholes hanging beside the office door. I point to it and the stack of white envelopes poking out. "I just came to get my paycheck. And eat pie."

The only way I could convince Annie to come here was by promising pie and reassuring her that Ryan never works Mondays. I forgot about Mark, though.

"Oh, right," Mark says.

As I flick through the envelopes, I can feel Mark watching me. Embarrassment creeps up my neck when I remember how awkward I was in front of him and Ryan on the day Annie came back. I can imagine the way the two of them must've made fun of me when they got home, calling me a social leper.

But when I glance up, Mark isn't looking at me. He's staring at his visor, which is twisted in his hands.

I pocket my paycheck and nod at his hat. "You can keep wearing it backward," I say. "I won't judge you."

Mark jolts at the sound of my voice, his face pulling into a tight smile. "I just really feel like I could be the one to bring the look back," he says.

"I didn't realize it went away," I say.

He sighs. "It didn't in my heart."

Along the back wall of the office is a row of faded green lockers. I swing open my locker door, revealing a pair of jeans, two empty water bottles, a pencil bag I forgot about, and three oranges that are definitely too old for human consumption. Mark rolls himself over the linoleum in the office chair toward me and holds out a small round trash can.

"Thanks," I say, scooping the water bottles out of my locker and tossing them into the trash.

"It's more for me than it is for you," he says. "My mom makes me go through everyone's lockers every week to look for drugs, and I'm pretty sure those oranges are starting to go radioactive."

My eyebrows shoot up. "Are you serious?"

"About the radioactivity or the drugs?"

"The drugs."

It's his turn to lift his eyebrows. "Why, are you holding?"

His fingers grip the edges of the trash can, going milk white as they strain against its plastic lip. Even in his official Country Kitchen uniform—kitschy T-shirt and khaki shorts—he still looks impossibly cool, his hair swooshed back in a way that would take me hours but on him just comes naturally. It's not immediately clear when looking at Mark that he and Ryan are twins, as their twin-ness is mostly in subtler things like the slight curve in their upper lips, the shape of their eyes, and the way they look when they frown.

"I'm really sorry about my sister the other day," Mark says suddenly. "She can be kind of a lot when she's mad. I usually try diffusing the situation with sarcasm, but sometimes that only pisses her off more."

I press my lips together and chuck the oranges into the trash can one by one. "It's not your fault," I say above the hollow *thunk, thunk, thunk.* "The whole thing is weird, so I just try not to react."

Mark shrugs. "Sometimes you gotta, though. It's how you earn Ryan's respect. She doesn't like it if you don't punch back."

I chew my tongue with my back teeth, the image of Ryan's face as she reminded me I shouldn't have brought Annie back drifting into my head. That mixture of disappointment and anger.

"Why does she get so mad like that?" I say eventually.

"Who knows," Mark says. "She was so mad when she found out Sandra Bullock had won an Oscar for *The Blind Side,* she cried."

"That was a really subpar movie," I say. "It's one of my mom's favorites. That's how I know it's subpar."

"I agree," Mark says. He brushes his hair back with his hand. "But Ryan feels things really hard. Like, *really* hard. She's always been weird about Annie, even when we were little."

I nod like I know what he's talking about, but was Ryan weird about Annie when we were kids? All I can remember is the three of us as best friends, dressing in matching denim overalls for twin day at school, being here, crying together when Annie first learned how to use Google and we found out Santa Claus and the Tooth Fairy weren't real. As far as I knew, things didn't crash and burn until the very end, over a plate of shrimp cocktail.

"Did you really have a picture of Annie as your phone background?" I say.

It's Mark's turn to look embarrassed. "Oh god," he groans as he slings an arm across his eyes. "Ryan was supposed to take that to her grave."

"What was it even a picture of?" I say.

Mark drops his arm and squints at me with gold-brown eyes. "If I tell you, you have to promise not to tell anybody," he says. "And if I find out you did, I'm gonna send a SWAT team out to wreck your house."

"I'm not sure that's in their job description," I say.

"Completely irrelevant," Mark says. "But seriously, I'm trusting you not to talk. Unlike my evil traitor of a sister."

I nod and wave for him to go on.

"Okay." He draws in a deep breath. "Do you remember when we all went to Six Flags for Ryan's and my birthday and my mom bought us the picture of all of us riding Riddler's Revenge?"

Riddler's Revenge was an outrageously tall bright green roller coaster that Annie insisted we ride. I couldn't even make it halfway up the first incline without sobbing.

"It was that picture."

I frown. "But that was a picture of all of us, not just Annie."

"That's the really pathetic part," Mark says. "I, like, zoomed in super hard on Annie's face and took a screenshot."

I bring my hands up to my mouth and cackle. I'd be embarrassed by the sound of it if I hadn't just learned Mark was basically the saddest stalker ever.

"I know, I know," Mark says. He's laughing too. "It wasn't even a hot photo. It was all pixelated, and everybody was screaming. I was a very uncool thirteen-year-old." Mark pushes himself to his feet, the chair rolling backward. "Well, this has been a super-fun humiliation sesh, but I have to go to the bank before my break is over." He sets the trash can down at my feet before moving toward the door that leads back into the restaurant. As he opens it, he says, "I think this might be the most I've heard you talk since elementary school."

My eyes shoot down to the floor. He's right. Even I'm surprised at how much I've said to him and Ryan over the last couple of days, as usually all they get from me is an ambiguous shrug when they ask if I have any rolls of nickels in my cash register. But with Annie back, things already feel different.

"Yeah, well, I'll probably go back to not talking any second now," I say, looking up.

Mark's fingernails click against the doorframe as he drums his hands on the wood. Instead of leaving, he pauses in the doorway and stares at me.

"Nah, you should keep talking, Moss," he says. "I like the sound of your voice."

At this, the sensation in my throat can only be described as a cross between the Sahara Desert and Jody's face after she puts toothpaste on a zit. It's so dry, I can barely swallow.

"Okay," I say, because that makes sense.

But Mark is already gone.

It takes an entire six minutes for the color of my face to go back to normal. I know this because I check it constantly in my phone camera, pressing the backs of my hands to my cheeks, my skin so hot it's practically sizzling. All I can hear is Mark, his words bouncing around my skull. *I like the sound of your voice*. What does that even mean? Does it mean he likes the sound of my voice *specifically,* or that he likes it because it means that by hearing it, he won't have to exclusively hear Ryan complaining?

Once my face has finally cooled to a level that won't make it immediately obvious how flustered I am, I grab one of the imperfect pies that Taylor, our head baker, keeps on the kitchen's side counter for employees to take home at the end of the day for free. The crowd has mostly died down, diminished now to just a couple of people huddled around the front counter. Annie is still at the back booth, her hands wrapped around a plain white mug whose wisps of steam gently waft against her chin. Her eyes are closed as she inhales.

"It's as good as I remember," she says when I approach the table. A sludgy brown lump bobs on the surface of her mug, the remnants of a slowly disintegrating hot chocolate bomb. "I've burned my tongue four times trying to drink it, but I don't even care."

"Well, make it five, because you've gotta down it," I say, shooting a nervous glance toward the door. It's ten minutes round trip to the bank from here, give or take five minutes if Mark runs into anyone he knows, which he definitely will. Even still, I don't want to take any chances. "We need to go."

Annie frowns. "What's wrong?"

"Nothing," I lie, tapping my fingers against the table's surface. I can't risk telling her about Mark, not here, where his cousin is currently in the kitchen skinning apples into a sink. "It's just, I don't know"—my eyes scan the restaurant—"everybody's looking at us."

This part isn't a lie. As soon as I turn toward the other tables, at least seven people glance down, suddenly super interested in their cheap paper plates.

Annie nods at the empty booth across from her. "Relax, they're looking at me, not you," she says. "I'll be done in five minutes. Just let me have this."

I push my tongue against the inside of my cheek and slide into the booth, my bare legs squeaking against the plastic padding. In the back of my head, a voice whispers, *Because why would anyone be looking at me?* This thought makes my cheeks reheat. I know it's pathetic and not what Annie meant, but I can't help it. But when I eventually meet her eyes again, Annie isn't looking at me. She's watching the front door as she leans down and lowers her voice.

"I thought you said Ryan doesn't work on Mondays."

"She doesn't," I say, twisting around in my seat.

But sure enough, Ryan is crossing the floor with strides so long, she's almost floating. I snap my head forward and slide down into my seat, as though that'll make any difference; we're right by the back door, where she'll have to go if she wants to get behind the main counter. Annie actually puts a hand over the side of her face Ryan will pass, but it doesn't matter; once Ryan reaches us, she charges past without so much as a middle finger.

I don't know whether to be relieved or disappointed; relieved because we've potentially just avoided a fistfight, or disappointed that rather than finally move on so the three of us can make the most of Annie's time back, Ryan is pretending we don't exist.

"What's she even doing here?" Annie says.

I shrug. "She's not supposed to be," I say, my eyes trained on the back door, which is still swinging in its frame. "On Mondays it's just me and Mark—" I pause. That's why Ryan's here, because I'm not. "Oh shit," I say, frowning. "She's covering for me."

Without even having to look, I know Ryan's behind the cash register. Its drawer slams so hard that the tip jar rattles on the counter beside it. Working with her for the last two years, I've grown to know every one of Ryan's sounds. The way her shoes squeak on a newly washed floor, the swish of her ponytail when she tilts her head to count change.

An older lady with pink-white hair and a lavender cardigan is stooped over the counter. Ryan leans in to hear her and nods slowly. I try to remember the last time she and Annie saw each other before the Welcome Back ceremony, when they actually talked like normal people. But all I can remember is that afternoon at the Fish Grotto, the one where everything between us exploded. That can't be the last time they were together, can it?

The words fall out of my mouth before I can stop them: "Are we really going to ignore each other all summer?" I say.

Even though Ryan and I barely talk anymore, it still feels impossible, the fact that the three of us have this incredible chance and we're just going to waste it.

Annie lets out a breathy laugh. "If we're lucky. I did not come back from the dead so I could watch Ryan and her rage suck all the joy out of everything like a happiness vampire."

I bite the side of my tongue. "She's not always like that," I say.

The day I found out Annie was coming back, things with Ryan felt different, at least before Ruth came charging into the Country Kitchen threatening to deafen everyone with her bull-horn. Ryan had given me a gift, maybe even offered to hang out with me again. Things felt, somehow, momentarily—easy. It was like that night at the graduation party had never happened; or maybe it had, but like it'd at least ended differently.

"Who's she even friends with anymore?" Annie says.

"Lots of people," I say, but this answer doesn't feel right. "And also, nobody."

Annie frowns. "What does that mean?"

Ryan is the type of person who can inject a room with energy without even trying. It's like all she has to do is exist. And while Ryan puts absolutely no effort into impressing anyone, that doesn't stop people from chasing her. That's the thing about the Morton twins—everybody loves them.

"I mean, I'm pretty sure she dated someone new every single week of senior year," I say. "Even Emma Corey-Smith for like three days."

Annie covers her mouth with her hand as she erupts into coughs. "Emma Corey-Smith," she finally chokes out. "Who 'married' her unicorn eraser in second grade?" She uses air quotes around "married" for obvious reasons. "Wow." Annie laughs. "Imagine getting dumped by a girl who was once married to an eraser."

"Ryan dumped her," I say. "Ryan dumps all of them. That's what I mean when I say she has lots of friends but also not. They all want to be with her, but she's done with them after a few days. It's like a social experiment for her or something."

She usually cuts each one off after a week, long before anything can even be considered close to a relationship. From what I hear, these dumpings mostly consist of Ryan saying she's "not into it" anymore. The longest one was with a senior when we were still juniors, which lasted a month. Even though he was going off to college at the end of the summer and was cool with long-distance, Ryan wasn't interested.

Her flings always end the same way, leaving behind a trail of teenagers who are sore from whiplash and confusion. Because

Ryan has this amazing ability to use her wit to bite, but in a way that leaves you wanting more, almost welcoming her jabs. It's masterful. Even I've left some of our extremely limited interactions wondering if Ryan had been insulting me or flirting with me, and if not the latter, why did I suddenly feel so flustered and warm?

"Yeah," Annie says, "a social experiment on how to be awful." With her pinkie finger, Annie scoops out the dregs of chocolate coating the bottom of her mug. "If I had to choose between spending five minutes with Ryan or having a sleepover with the clown from *It*, Voldemort, and Darth Vader, I would grab my sleeping bag." She sets the now empty mug back down and slides it into the middle of the table. "Let's roll," she says, and pushes herself to her feet.

"You can't actually hate her that much," I insist as I scramble to follow her. I drop my voice as we pass the counter, carefully skirting Ryan as she offers to help Cardigan Lady to her car. "We were so close. Remember how the three of us used to dress up for twin day in those purple overalls Cass's mom made us?"

Annie opens the front door with a ring. "That didn't even make sense," she says. "Three people can't be twins."

"Or when Mrs. Paulson caught me sending you a note in class and she threatened to show it to our parents? Ryan broke into the classroom at lunch and stole it."

Holding the door open for me, Annie says over her shoulder, "You're saying that like it somehow makes her less ridiculous. She *broke into a classroom* and *stole something*."

"Yeah, to protect *us*."

I know Ryan's sarcasm and coldness can make her difficult to be around sometimes, but Mark is right: Ryan feels things hard. Anger and disappointment, yes, but also protectiveness and loyalty. All the sleepovers, all the vacations we took with Ryan's parents to Palm Springs. Even though our birthdays are three months apart, me, Annie, and Ryan insisted on having joint celebrations every year. Our moms had to sync up our Christmas lists so none of us got something the other ones didn't. When Cass's mom died, Ryan and Annie stayed at my house for the entire weekend. When Annie's dog disappeared, we all snuck out at three in the morning to search the canyons behind her house. Everything we went through, we went through together. And now I'm supposed to believe it's all just gone? Again?

As we leave the Country Kitchen, I glance back over my shoulder only to see Ryan peering at me through the glass door. Annie is already halfway down the block, her eyes on a tie-dye shirt that says EAT TOFU, SAVE THE RAINFOREST in the Thrifty Coyote's front window. I wait for Ryan to look away, to pretend our eye contact was just an accident, but when she doesn't, I part my lips to say something. What, I have no idea. And for a second it looks like Ryan might too, but then she turns her focus back to the lady in front of her, speaking brightly in the fake voice she reserves for customers. I let out a long breath as the moment escapes. This, somehow, after everything, is when it sinks in that this is really how we're going to play this summer. Ignoring each other, as though we were never friends. As though all those years meant nothing. Everything about it feels wrong.

It's this thought that makes me bolt up straight, my shoulders pressed into my ears. Because it's so obvious, what I have to do. It's been in front of me the entire time, ever since Annie returned to Lennon and Ryan made that first ominous warning about the mistake I'd made.

"Fact," Annie is saying as I reach the Thrifty Coyote. Her face is pushed against the glass as though the front window is a portal overlooking outer space. "I was brought back to this earth for one reason, and one reason only—to wear this shirt."

But I'm not really listening. I know what I need to do to keep Annie back. The wrong I need to right.

I need to make Annie and Ryan friends again.

EIGHT

DAYS UNTIL ANNIE LEBLANC DIES: 24

The Walking Dad's origin story is almost totally mapped out. After the weird way me, Annie, and Ryan mutually ghosted each other at the Country Kitchen, I've spent most of my time trying to work out how I can get them back to a place where they can not only be in the same room without wanting to stab each other in the eye, but be in the same room and actually enjoy it. But the thought of achieving the miracle that is making them friends again after Annie expanded her list of who she'd rather hang out with than Ryan to Regina George and Lisa Rinna from *The Real Housewives of Beverly Hills* was starting to give me a headache, so today I wedged what I'm now calling the Annie notebook in the gap between my bed and the wall and pulled out my sketchbook instead.

Ever since Cass mentioned being the walking dad a few days ago, the idea for the comic has been hiding quietly at the back of my head, increasing in itchiness the more I try to ignore it.

Even today, as Annie and I watched reruns of *The Price Is Right* in my living room and I desperately tried to look and act like everything was normal, I could feel *The Walking Dad* trying to zombie-crawl his way into my sketchbook. And now, as I sit at my desk and Bernie lies on her own bed reading a copy of *National Geographic,* the cover of which has a picture of a monkey with glacier-blue eyes, it feels like the perfect distraction. I can't watch TV while drawing, so instead I've eaten so many Atomic Fireballs I can't feel my tongue anymore and have been listening to R.E.M.'s *Out of Time* playing from a tiny speaker in the corner of our room.

I can't decide whether I should make the panels of *The Walking Dad* mostly monochromatic, like *Ghost World* or *Chilling Adventures of Sabrina,* or if I should go Technicolor. Right now all I have are basic outlines of the different panels, Jerry the zombie and his kids just a bunch of jagged shapes moving through a world of half-sketched shadows.

All my favorite comics start with a seemingly random opening that leads to the title page. It's just story, story, story, then *blam,* TITLE. It has all the drama and punch power of a good movie. *The Walking Dad* starts with Jerry's tragic death by car accident. His daughters, fifteen-year-old Greta and five-year-old Ava, are now orphans. At Jerry's funeral, little Ava cries over her dad's closed casket and wishes he could come back to take care of them as their new guardian/overbearing great-aunt watches from the shadows. Somehow the universe hears Ava's wish, and that night, after the girls get home, there's a knock at the door. When they open it, they find Jerry standing in the pouring rain, his face half melted and his decaying limbs broken and twisted. He is . . . *dun, dun, dun!* The Walking Dad!

After that, I have no idea what happens. But it's a start.

Throwing all my brain power into *The Walking Dad* also means I don't have to think about Mark. I haven't let myself dwell on him and what he said, much less tell Annie. The only other person who might actually be able to decipher what Mark meant is Jody, but she's on a date in Rosita. Not that I ever *would* ask her. The last time I talked to Jody about anything even remotely relationship-oriented, she went behind my back and invited the girl's entire family over for dinner, and we'd only made out like three times over the course of a marine biology project. Plus, now that I'm further away from the Mark thing, the less meaningful it all feels. Mark probably just meant he liked hearing the sound of my voice because it confirmed to him that, after years of mostly silence, I could, in fact, speak at all. Besides, I wasn't the one whose barely recognizable picture was his phone background.

My thoughts shift back to *The Walking Dad,* to the hardships this tiny, complicated family will crash into; maybe the great-aunt can embark on a custody battle with Jerry, arguing that the unsanitary nature of his rotting flesh makes him an unfit father. Or maybe the only job Jerry can get is something like folding clothes in a department store warehouse, where he won't be seen by and terrify the customers, which means he won't have enough money for Christmas presents.

I've always liked drawing comics, ever since I was a little kid and Cass and I swapped issues of *Buffy*. Maybe it's having the ability to create a new world, or being able to do so without needing a lot of words that might screw it up, but it's always been something I could lose myself to and not feel bad about. When I was younger, I used to let myself think I could do this for real—draw comics—but I'm not that naïve anymore. I know comics have made sort of a comeback recently, but I can't shake the feeling that it won't last long. Even the *Lennon News* dropped their daily comic strip a few months back because they thought comics were pointless, and this is coming from a media outlet that reports on the rabbit showmanship category of our annual farmyard pageant.

For this reason, every time I sit down to draw something new, a mixture of excitement and sadness weighs in my stomach. Excitement, because that urge to *make* is so strong and consuming that giving in to it feels like a rush, but sadness, because I know drawing will probably only ever be for me. Because the only time I ever showed somebody outside my family my comics, it basically ruined my life.

It was a day of lasts. The last day of tenth grade, but most important, the last day when Ryan, Annie, and I would go to the same school. It wasn't something any of us said out loud, not on the drive into San Diego, not as we waited in the Fish Grotto lobby, but we could feel it hanging between us, thick as a cloud of smoke. It was obvious in the long silences that hung between us, the way we'd catch one another's eyes and quickly look away. But I was working my butt off to make everything feel normal, my voice fourteen octaves too high, my overenthusiasm for the new shrimp salad the Fish Grotto had added to their menu sugary and pained.

The Fish Grotto was a bougie restaurant on the San Diego harbor. It sat on a dock that hovered over the bay, so that when you looked through the floor-to-ceiling windows, all you saw was an endless stretch of blue above and below. The food wasn't anything amazing, but the tablecloths were white linen, we each had four forks—the purposes for which, we had absolutely zero clue—and Ryan's mom dropped us off at the door so we could feel fancy together. It was everything. The three of us had been going there since we were thirteen and Annie got a phone, our parents reassured by the fact that we could at least call someone if any of us were kidnapped.

But this time there was no giddiness at being in San Diego on our own, no matter how hard I tried to force it. After my initial attempt to spark some kind of excitement, the three of us sat at our table by the window staring at our menus wordlessly, even though we each already knew what we were going to get. For once, the view of the ocean through the glass and the gently lulling waves weren't exciting; there was almost something aggressive about the way the water sloshed underneath us, digging a pit in my stomach I couldn't shake.

I waited until after we ordered to give Ryan and Annie their gifts. We always gave each other something on the last day of school, usually matching jewelry or hard rock candy from Dudley's that would get stuck in our back teeth for days. This year I'd spent nearly two months making their presents, speeding through my homework so I could meticulously pore over them every night. It was an entire comic book I titled *The Lennon Chronicles*. It starred me, Annie, and Ryan as monster hunters that fought the demons who wound their way up the CA-78 into Lennon. Annie was the designated nerd—every monster-hunting gang needs one—and Ryan was our badass wild card who usually reduced the villains to nothing with a swift kick to the face. I fell somewhere in between, the quiet protagonist the monsters somehow always found first.

Their faces gave nothing away as Ryan and Annie silently flipped through the pages, me reaching across the table and nervously pointing to different panels in the comic. There was Ryan's *Toy Story* sleeping bag she brought to every sleepover, there was the Country Kitchen and our favorite booth. On the opening page were five panels, the first of which depicted Ryan sleeping in her bed. A shadow flickered across her bedroom wall, but when it knocked over a picture, Ryan woke up. It was a vampire who claimed he'd seen Ryan's future as the leader of Southern California, when the vampires won a makeshift civil war and took over. Would she join them? Would she be their queen?

Then, the title screen: EVER AFTER.

The next few pages followed me and Annie as we fought to get Ryan back, to show her that the vampire's vision was rigged. He claimed to have seen it in a fortune-telling well, but his plan was to actually just use her as bait for me and Annie and then kill all three of us. When Annie and I went to rescue her, I looked into the well myself and saw my, Ryan's, and Annie's real future; in it, we'd moved to a lake house in the middle of nowhere. Eighty years old, frail, and yet still totally badass, we lived out there just the three of us, best friends always. We killed the vampires, celebrated with apple pie and hot chocolate bombs. Blah, blah, blah.

"Wil, this is amazing," Annie said under her breath as she flicked to the last page.

She slid the comic book under her chair, her face breaking into a smile that didn't reach her eyes. Ryan, meanwhile, was flipping through her copy with such force, I was surprised the pages didn't rip. Her jaw worked quietly over her tongue, her eyes fixed on the characters as the staked vampires turned to dust. When she finally reached the end, she snapped the comic book shut and stared straight ahead without a word.

The tension at the table was so thick, I could almost see it, crackling over our glasses of sparkling lemonade like a thundercloud. Annie and Ryan made no move to grab the gifts they'd brought, and then it dawned on me that they must be embarrassed for me, because I clearly didn't remember some conversation we must've had about not getting each other presents this year. It wasn't like I'd spent a million dollars on the comic; the only real money I'd spent was on photocopying it at the library, a measly $2.45. But from the way Ryan's fists curled so tightly into themselves that her knuckles turned yellow white, I could tell suddenly that it wasn't that I'd gotten them a gift. It was the comic itself. Something between us, already strained that day, had snapped.

"So, do you have to wear a uniform now that you're a private school princess?" Ryan said suddenly.

Annie laughed as though it was just a harmless joke, but even I could feel the icy edge to Ryan's voice. "Accordion skirts and blazers all the way, baby," Annie said. "Nothing says private school like a bunch of teenagers dressed as tiny businessmen. But a few years ago some of the girls staged a protest where they all wore pants, and they got sent home every day."

"Mmm," Ryan said, nodding. "Groundbreaking."

Annie lifted her eyebrows. "I thought it was kinda cool."

"That is cool," I said quickly. "Do the girls get to wear pants now?"

"Well, no," Annie said. She adjusted her hands in her lap and avoided Ryan's eyes. "But the teachers all had a meeting about it."

"Siiiiiiiiiick," Ryan said in a faux surfer-bro voice.

I shot Ryan a look, but Annie spoke before I could even try to diffuse the situation.

"What's your problem?" she said.

"I don't have a problem," Ryan said. "I just think it's really cool you're going to a school that cares so deeply about whether or not the girls are allowed to wear the same ugly pants as the boys."

"It's not about getting to wear ugly pants; it's about having the right to choose," Annie said.

Ryan gave a smile that was all sarcasm. "I'm pretty sure if you're going to a school that costs twenty grand a year, you've got plenty of rights."

"You looked up how much my school costs?" Annie said.

Ryan hooked a thumb toward me. "Wilson did."

My mouth dropped open. "I—I just wanted to know," I stammered.

"Wow, that's really cool of you guys to get together and shit-talk my school," Annie said.

"I wasn't shit-talking anything," I said, panicked.

"You weren't?" Ryan said. She tilted her head when she looked at me. "I was."

"Ryan," I hissed. "What are you doing?"

"What?" she said, having the nerve to sound genuinely confused as to why anyone would be mad. "Honestly, I'm happy Annie finally gets to live out her dream."

Annie's eyes narrowed. "And what dream is that?"

Ryan smiled again. "Being a bougie-ass bitch."

Time just sort of stopped then, the tables around us melding into a blur of white. I knew that this was the part where I was supposed to say something, to pop the tension bubble with a joke and make things go back to normal, but my mouth was so dry I could barely swallow. It was at this point that our waitress brought out our food, throwing down our orders and scrambling away as though if she stayed too long, she might somehow get roped into the argument we were obviously having.

Annie ignored the lobster ravioli in front of her. "Well, if it's between that or scraping apple pie filling off the floor for the rest of my life, I think that choice is pretty obvious," she said. "It's no wonder you're always so angry, Ryan. I'd be pissed too if I knew all I'd ever be is Lennon trash."

At this, my stomach caved. I glanced quickly at Annie, waiting for her to take it back. But she had this glint in her eye like she'd finally gotten Ryan, pinning her against a wall and refusing mercy. I wanted her to look at me, to give me some indication that she didn't mean it. Because whether she realized it or not, that jab didn't just hit Ryan. It hit me, too.

"You know what?" Ryan said. Her head bobbed rhythmically as she stood and tossed her napkin onto her chair. "You're right: I am Lennon trash. And no matter how much money your daddy throws around, it's all you'll ever be too."

She reached down into her ice cream glass of shrimp cocktail and grabbed a fistful. Then, without warning, she hurtled the shrimp at Annie's face. Ryan has small hands, but she must've thrown at least fifteen shrimp, sending them bouncing off Annie's cheeks and into her eyes. One even landed on her head, catching in her hair. It felt like hours that I sat there, watching as the shrimp fell onto the table, but it only could've been a half second. Within moments, Annie shot into the air and fumbled for her glass of lemonade. She promptly tossed it in Ryan's direction, but her aim was off and so the lemonade landed mostly on a woman at the table next to us.

The staff was frantic, waiters and waitresses ushering Annie and Ryan to different corners of the restaurant, trying to pat down the woman whose white dress was stained yellow. There was so much yelling, threats to call the police, and the entire time all I could do was sit there and stare open-mouthed at the table. It looked like someone had set off a shrimp firework, peppering the carpeted floor with their little pink bodies.

That was how our friendship ended. It's also why I'm not allowed in the Fish Grotto anymore.

I've had a lot of time to think about why *The Lennon Chronicles* sucked so much that it obliterated my friendships. Firstly, it's completely ridiculous. A vampire gang takeover *and* fortune-telling well? It's all over the place. Second, there are about a billion plot holes. How am I so sure my vision of our future is any more valid than the vampire's? Couldn't mine be a lie too?

But most important, IT IS FUCKING CREEPY.

The ending basically consists of me human-hoarding my best friends in a remote, undisclosed location where the only people we need for literally the rest of our lives are each other. It screams, *I will murder you and stuff your body like a teddy bear*. After reading it, Ryan and Annie clearly thought I stole their underwear and kept it in a shrine in my closet. This realization must've put them both so on edge that a fight was inevitable.

After the Fish Grotto saga, I went a whole year without drawing, convinced that if it could ruin friendships, who's to say it couldn't also rob banks or kill people in some roundabout way?

Eventually I picked it up again, slowly at first, but more regularly as ideas for new comics crept into my brain against my will. But even still, no matter what I make, no matter how much it excites me or how good I think it might be, I can't ever bring myself to show it to anyone. Never again. Whereas before everything happened, it sometimes felt like drawing was the only thing I was good at. The only thing I wanted to work toward, that critical thing I could point to and say, *There, that's me. That's what I want to do. That's what I want to be great at.*

But that's all gone now. And sometimes I can't help but think that without it, what else do I have?

Nine

DAYS UNTIL ANNIE LEBLANC DIES: 22

The next morning, Jody is at the dinner table cutting out strips of antique newspapers I bought on eBay for the wedding table centerpieces as I pour myself a cup of coffee and go out to the porch to think. Later today Annie, Bernie, and I are going with Jody to Rosita for my mother's final wedding dress fitting. I've seen the pictures that Pam, my mother's maid of honor, took when Jody first tried on and ordered the dress, but there's something about seeing it in person that makes me weirdly nervous.

Coffee in hand, I curl up on one of the porch's plastic chairs and rest my chin on the mug's warm rim. Even though Annie's list of people she'd rather hang out with than Ryan is now longer than the Lennon phone book Ruth Fish insists on printing every year, I know I can reason with her. She's not like Ryan, who got into a screaming match with our sixth-grade computer science teacher when she thought he was laughing at me when really, he was watching a video of a dog sleeping in a flowerpot on his phone. At this point, the only way to get Ryan in a room with Annie is by ambushing her. From there, I can do the convincing. Because ultimately Ryan *can* come around; it'll just take a little effort. Like Mark said, sometimes the only way to earn her respect is by punching back.

But first, I have to actually get ahold of Ryan, a task made complicated by the fact that I don't even have her phone number anymore and can't message her. After her big showdown with Annie at the Fish Grotto, Ryan blocked me on basically everything. But failure isn't an option here; if I have to handcuff Ryan to me and drag her into Annie's general vicinity, I'll do it, even though doing so will likely result in me losing one or both of my eyes. Because if I'm successful, though I might be partially blind, I'll potentially have not just Annie in my life again, but Ryan, too.

I set my coffee on the floor and click the number I've got saved in my phone for the Country Kitchen. The street around me is quiet except for the sound of wind rushing over the dry grass slopes bordering the road and squirrels skittering up and down tree trunks. I'm wondering whether or not Ryan would come to my house if she thought I was dying and then wondering on a scale of one to ten how unethical it would be of me to lie about that, when somebody answers. But it's not Ryan. It's Mark.

I sit up straight in the chair, words trapped in my throat. "Oh, uh, hi," I stammer eventually. "Is Ryan there?"

"Not right now. Who's this?" Mark says.

I can tell by the way his voice only halfway reaches the phone that he's distracted.

"It's . . . Wilson?" I say.

I don't know where the question mark comes from. I know who I am.

"Oh, hey!" Mark says. A door shuts on his side of the phone and the line gets instantly quieter. "Ryan's driving to San Diego to pick up drinks for the party at Grant's house tomorrow night. Our cousin buys the beer for us, and while that probably means its consistency will be closer to sewer water, it will, at the very least, be alcoholic. Are you coming?"

Grant Lovelace is Mark's best friend. He also dated Ryan for about two weeks, during which he spent most of his time at the Country Kitchen drinking all our coffee. But outside of this and the fact that he went to Lennon Union, I barely know him.

It takes a second for this sentence to translate. That Mark has just asked if I'm going to a party tomorrow. At Grant's house.

I swallow. "I wasn't invited," I say.

Nerves and awkwardness are projecting off me like a bad smell. Mark and I have known each other for basically forever, and I've never had a problem talking to him before, during the four times he actually talked to me. But now that he's said something even vaguely flirty in my general direction—even if he didn't mean to—everything I can think to say to him turns to mush in my mouth.

Apparently, Mark doesn't notice. "Me and Ryan have been talking about it for the last three weeks," he says.

"That doesn't mean I'm invited."

"Do you think I'd talk about a party in front of you if you weren't invited?"

"Ryan would."

Mark pauses. "Yeah, okay, that's fair. Well, consider this your formal invitation: Wilson Moss, will you please come to

Grant's party tomorrow night? I promise Ryan won't be weird about it."

At this, my eyes bug wide in my head. "Ryan's gonna be there?" I say.

The second I ask this question, it sinks in how redundant it is. Because of course Ryan is going to be there, at the party for which she's picking up the alcohol.

"Are you kidding?" he says. "She lives for this shit. Ryan likes to pretend we'd all get caught if it weren't for her obsessing over every time someone forgets to take their shoes off in the house. But believe it or not, I can throw a cup into a trash can. You saw me."

For whatever weird reason, the idea of Ryan charging around Grant's party like a dictator in a tiny leather skirt makes me smirk.

"Technically you were only holding the trash can," I point out. "I did all the throwing."

"Semantics, Moss," Mark says. "So, are you gonna come? Annie's invited too, obviously."

"Annie?" I repeat quietly, but not because I didn't hear him. Something is only just now clicking in my head.

Annie.

At the party.

With Ryan.

This thought is enough to get my blood moving again, my heart picking up as I tap the fingers on my free hand against my thigh. It's the perfect solution, the perfect way to get Annie and Ryan into the same location without having to lie about why we're there. We're just two girls going to a party with our peers. No big deal. I might not have ever been to a real house party before, but I've seen *Mean Girls*. There will be drunk people, there will probably be puke. But if it means there's a chance Ryan and Annie can end the night in a group hug and therapeutic cry, I can handle it.

"Yeah, okay, I'll come," I say. "Do I need to bring anything?"

"Just your dancing shoes," Mark says. There's a long pause. "Please forget I just said that. Do you know where Grant's house is?"

Yes. "No."

Mark says he'll text me the address, and I have to stop myself from asking how he has my number, lest I look like I'm accusing him of being a predator. When a sudden wave of voices comes through from the Country Kitchen, he shouts over them before telling me he has to go. I hang up and stare down at my phone, wondering how I managed to earn this favor from the universe. Because the universe never does me any favors. I am usually the universe's bitch, destined to spend my weekends working and proofreading my mother's Bumble profile.

But even though I've just had this opportunity handed to me on a silver platter, I know the real hard work is only just about to begin. Now I have to convince Annie to go.

Everything inside the Blushing Brides Bridal Boutique is pink and cream, and that's not even an exaggeration. In the middle of the plush cream carpet is a giant padded pink pouf that's speckled with rhinestones, while the walls are swirled with a sparkly wallpaper the shade of cotton candy. The staff are dressed in matching pink pencil skirts with ruffly tops, their pink name tags featuring not just their names written in curly white writing, but their favorite wedding-themed movie. Even the chandelier, dripping with crystal pendants and twined with silk daisies— also pink, because *obviously*—is painted cherry-blossom pink, sending shards of rose-colored light across the room.

Annie stops in the doorway of the boutique, looking dazed. "I feel like I'm inside a cake," she says.

Bernie immediately collapses onto the pouf, her iPad held close to her face and little white earbuds poking out from the folds of her dark hair. On the drive down, she'd been watching a TED Talk about the potential for life on another planet, alternating between lecturing us on the ethics of colonizing Mars and asking Jody to turn down her Bikini Kill CD. Pam was the one who came with Jody to try on dresses at Blushing Brides, so I've never been here before and didn't know it was basically two mini malls away from Del Monte High School. When we passed it, I could feel myself sinking into my seat, cheeks flushing at the memory of the only time I'd ever been there. If Annie noticed, she didn't say anything; she just sat quietly in the back with my sister, nodding every time Bernie said something about the power of mathematics to re-create ancient life.

At the sight of the puffy pink garment bag hanging near the dressing room at the back of the boutique, Jody squeals. Kate, the woman with the pink butterfly hair clips and whose favorite wedding movie is *My Big Fat Greek Wedding,* makes a big show of unhooking the bag and sweeping it into the dressing room for Jody to try on.

"Girls, some apple cider?"

A woman whose name tag identifies her as Lorrie—favorite wedding movie: *27 Dresses*—appears with a silver tray of skinny glasses whose yellow insides sparkle lightly. Annie and I grab our glasses and wander over to a rack of wedding dresses hanging along the right side of the store. I take a tiny sip of my drink and watch over the lip of my glass as Annie peels apart the dresses, running her fingers along the intricate lace patterns and beaded swirls. Since I talked to Mark this morning, my brain has mostly been occupied with thoughts of how to get Annie to Grant's party. I know from her socials that going to the party itself won't be a problem—at least not how it is for me—just the fact that Ryan will be there. And I can't exactly lie about it, because the second we get there Annie will see Ryan and know that I lied, and then leave and never trust me again. This means I have to get Annie there *in spite* of the fact that Ryan will be there too.

Annie sets her cider on a glass countertop, underneath which are rows and rows of tiaras. "Do you think you'll ever get married?" she says to me before pulling out a giant princess-style dress with a heart-shaped neck.

I take another sip of my drink, shivering as the bubbles burst down my throat. "Somebody would have to want to go out with me first," I say. Mark Morton instantly pops into my head, closely followed by the feeling of complete horror at the fact that I'm essentially wondering if Mark Morton, who said he liked the sound of my voice *one time,* will marry me. "What about you?"

Annie moves in front of the floor-length mirror and holds the dress up against her body. "Yeah, I probably would've one day," she says as she twists from side to side. Her eyes lock with mine in the mirror. "But now, you know," she says, pointing to herself, "dead."

The cider surges back up my throat, sending me into a coughing fit that makes my whole body shake. Annie hooks the dress back onto the rack and whacks me between my shoulder blades as I bend over, coughing so hard my eyes water. When I finally stop, I use the back of my hand to wipe the cider that's dribbling down my chin.

"I can't believe I just said that," I gasp. "I'm so sorry. I forgot—"

Even though Annie's smiling, her eyes are sad. "It's cool," she says. "It's kind of nice that you forgot. It means we can actually have fun without being weird and emotional about it all the time."

"Yeah, but I shouldn't have even brought you here," I say, glancing around the room helplessly. "That was super insensitive of me."

This entire thing is beyond weird, how normal Annie is being and, in turn, how normally I'm treating her. Shouldn't we be skydiving over a volcano? Deep-sea fishing in enemy waters? What would I want to do if I had only thirty days to live? Probably not watch my friend's mother try on her wedding dress.

Annie laughs. "Wilson, seriously, it's fine. If I didn't want to be here, I wouldn't have come. Plus, it's nice to get out of Lennon. At least everybody out here isn't staring at me all the time."

I nod. Throwing my arms out, I glance around the room, eyes landing on the rack of wedding dresses. "Well," I say, "we could always just stay here and—"

Annie shakes her head. "Please don't suggest we start trying on dresses to help me live out the fantasy of getting married before I die," she says. "Because I will literally punch you in the throat."

A smirk inadvertently creeps across my face. If I can make sure Annie doesn't die at the end of her month back on Earth, we wouldn't have to play at her getting married. Maybe one day, she might actually for real.

"On that note," I say, dragging out my words, "I may or may not have plans for us tomorrow night."

At the end of the rack is a flowy wedding dress with long, lacy sleeves. Annie takes it down and smooths her hands over the drapey fabric.

"Are we breaking into somebody's house?" she says, frowning at a stray thread. "Because that's what it sounds like."

"Not exactly," I say. Does it count as breaking in when the people who own the house don't actually know we're there? "We may or may not have been invited to a party."

At this, Annie's frown lightens. "Whose party?"

I swallow. "Grant Lovelace."

"Grant Lovelace?" Annie squints at me. "Who's that?"

"Mark's best friend."

"Does that mean Ryan's gonna be there?"

And here we go.

I shuffle around to the back of the rack, where there's a dress whose train is so long and puffy, it looks like the head of a dandelion. "I mean, I don't know," I say, pretending to look closely at the ribbons lacing up the back of the dress. "Probably. I mean, there's, like, a good chance she will be. I guess. I mean, she'll likely be there, as in yeah, she'll probably be there. I mean, she will be there. Yes."

By the end of this useless ramble, I'm leaned so far into the dress that I can actually make out each individual honeycomb shape on the white crinoline skirt. When I brave a glance around it, it's clear by the way Annie's shoulders are spiked into her ears that she's not into the idea of going to a party with Ryan. Not even on the same block as Ryan.

I straighten up, panic swelling in my lungs. I know I need to say the next part if I want this to work, but it still makes me feel nauseated with embarrassment.

"Okay," I say, taking a deep breath, "I wasn't going to tell you this because I find the whole thing mildly mortifying, but Mark Morton is the one who invited me to the party, and I think that as he was doing it he was trying to flirt with me."

I blurt it out quickly in the hopes that maybe Annie will be too distracted with trying to understand what I'm saying to notice how hard I'm blushing. She turns, her eyes searching my face for some indication that this is just a trap.

Evidently finding none, she says, "Go on."

"He said this thing to me a few days ago about liking the sound of my voice, and I didn't tell you because I didn't think it meant anything."

"He said he liked the sound of your *voice*?"

"It made sense when he said it, but now that I'm saying it out loud, it sounds kind of creepy."

I pull my phone out of my pocket and unlock the screen before thumbing through to my most recent text. It's from an unknown number, just a few words, but enough so that I can't look at it without feeling dizzy.

Unknown
14695 Wildwood Drive. Better not flake
out, Moss. I know where you work 😉

At the sight of the tiny smiley face, my stomach does this thing that can only be described as a sneeze.

"What is it?" Annie says.

"It's from Mark, I think," I say, handing her my phone.

Technically this text could be from a serial killer setting out a trap to murder me. This seems unlikely, though. "When I talked to him on the phone, he said he'd text me Grant's address."

She peers down at the screen. "Holy shit, Mark Morton likes you," Annie says. Then, fast: "Not that that's surprising. I'm just shocked that anyone who shared a womb with Ryan could be capable of feelings beyond rage."

This thought makes my face go redder, if that's even possible. "Just because he was flirting with me doesn't mean he likes me," I say.

Mark Morton does not like me. Mark Morton could never like me, not when the vast majority of Lennon Union would do unspeakable things just for the chance to touch his hair.

"Oh, you're right, because he just likes to compete in the Flirting Olympics for fun," Annie says. She bats her eyelashes at me. "I personally have a gold medal in making eye contact and looking away."

"Okay, I'm not saying he's not flirting with me, but going from him inviting me to a party in a somewhat flirty way to saying he *likes* me feels like kind of a big jump."

"Why can you not just accept the obvious?" Annie leans in. "Are you acting weird right now because you've never . . . you know," she whispers.

"Never what?" I say.

"Kissed anyone."

Even though everyone else is at least fifteen feet away from us, I duck behind a dress and give Annie my most horrified look. Every hair on my body stands up straight.

"*No,* that's not it," I hiss. "I *have.*"

With three people, actually. A couple of times with Lena

Hendricks from my marine biology class, which promptly ended when Jody cornered Lena's mom at the deli and tried to invite her over for fajita night at our house; then there was that time at the party for the cast and crew of Lennon Union's production of *Hello, Dolly!*—which I'd helped cater on behalf of the Country Kitchen—when Scott Redwell kissed me in the boys' dressing room because he said I had "a face destined for the stage." Both times were unremarkable. It was the third one that was the worst of all, the one I'm still trying to forget.

"Okay, okay," Annie says, holding out her hands. "You're just acting like you haven't."

"Because it's *Mark Morton*," I say. "This is totally different. He and Ryan could have anyone they want. Why would he pick *me*?" At this, Annie rolls her eyes. "But," I say, "you know how we could find this out?"

"If you say go to the party, I'll scream," Annie says.

"I just—"

Annie lets out a shriek that's so loud, the noise of it reverberates in my bones. I shut my mouth quickly and stare at her, startled.

"I told you I'd scream," she says. At the panicked looks from Kate and Lorrie across the room, Annie waves. "I saw a spider," she shouts to them.

"We don't even have to talk to Ryan," I insist, my voice lowered. "We'll stay on the complete opposite side of the house to her. She won't come near us. We can make a game out of it where, like, for every step she takes, we take one in the other direction. It'll be like we're line dancing, but out of fear."

As Annie lets this thought sink in, she bites the side of her cheek. "I just—I don't really want to spend my time back here at some party," she says. "I was promised infinite hot chocolate bombs."

"We literally have three weeks for more hot chocolate bombs," I say. "I will get you one every day you're here if you come to this party with me. I know tomorrow is technically your parents' time with you, but I'll swap them. Besides, you love parties." From all those pictures on the RIP ANNIE LEBLANC Facebook page, you'd think she was Del Monte's personal party planner. "And, like, yeah, it'll probably be lame, but we can just go there and make fun of it ceaselessly like the callous *b*-words that we are."

Two years ago, I never thought I would be the one to have to convince *Annie* to go to a house party. Me, who considers live tapings of Nirvana concerts and a bowl of popcorn a party. Me, who can't even talk *about* Mark Morton, much less talk *to* him, without my entire face turning the color of Lorrie's and Kate's blouses. The thought of going to this party, with people I've spent the last two years watching but never speaking to like a giant freaking weirdo, makes me sick with nerves. But if I'm going to make Annie and Ryan friends again, I have to start somewhere.

There's a rustling from the back of the store as Kate holds open the dressing room curtain.

Lorrie claps and says, "Here we go!"

Jody appears in the open doorway in a long white dress that fits close to her body except for her legs, where it flows out and just barely skims the floor. Woven across the sleek fabric are thousands and thousands of tiny beads sewn on in thin swirling patterns. The dress has finger-width straps that loop around my mother's shoulders, the neckline plunging to about two inches above her waist, which is ringed with a thin white ribbon.

Bernie, seeing me and Annie staring, pulls her headphones out and sits up.

"Ta-da." Jody holds out her arms.

Annie's mouth hangs open theatrically. "That. Looks. Amazing," she says.

Even Bernie nods in appreciation.

Kate helps Jody up onto a small wooden box stationed in front of a floor-length mirror. Lorrie crouches down at Jody's feet, fanning out the bottom of the dress so that it sits perfectly over her heels.

"Wilson, what do you think?" Jody says.

I open my mouth to answer, but my throat is too pinched for words. One of my clearest memories as a kid is of Jody and Cass's wedding at the courthouse in San Diego. It was just the three of us, Cass in a too-small blazer, me in a puffy red dress with matching shoes, and Jody in a white sundress. After the ceremony, we walked around the shops at Seaport Village and ate soft pretzels. Right now Jody looks beautiful. She obviously looks beautiful, in a dress that appears as though it was sewn specifically for her body, but that day, that first wedding—that was perfect. This one suddenly feels like a kick in the stomach.

Everyone is staring at me, waiting for my response.

"It looks good," I finally manage. "Yeah, I like it."

Jody, completely oblivious to my unease, turns back to the mirror. "I want to wear my hair down, but it'd be a shame to cover up all this skin." She lifts her hair and piles it on top of her head, wrenching her right shoulder forward so she can see her back.

"You're going to look gorgeous whatever you decide," Kate says. She has her hands clasped at her chest. "Your fiancé had better deserve you."

Jody lets her hair spill down around her shoulders as she wrinkles her nose at herself in the mirror. "He does," she says. "He makes me feel like a whole person again."

Lorrie and Kate coo. My head goes light all of a sudden, my eyes filling with tears. Annie steps closer to look at the dress and pretty soon she, Kate, and my mother are talking about what makeup is best for covering moles as I back toward the door, mumbling something about the too-sweet air freshener making my head spin. I duck out of the boutique and blink into the sun, spotting a bench just outside the store that circles a huge planter filled with expensive-looking cacti. I sit down on the shady side and stick my legs out so that my feet are in the sun.

Jody has always been mostly chaos with a side of whimsy, but when she married Cass, things calmed down. He was five years older than her and already training for the sheriff's department, had his own house, had gone to college. There was no more backpacking from youth hostel to youth hostel through the Pacific Northwest, no more Lunchables for dinner, Bernie arrived. Everything evened out, maybe too much for Jody, because then it all fell apart. The fighting started. They tried therapy, but after a few sessions, Jody wouldn't go back. And then one day I came home and all our stuff was packed. Too occupied with Ryan and Annie disappearing, I was able to ignore the fact that Jody had obliterated the only real family I'd ever known. At least until I woke up one morning in a bedroom that wasn't mine and had no friends.

Things were weird for a while without the normalcy of Cass.

It was like Jody and I were missing our mother, the one who got us out of bed every day and made sure we brushed our teeth. That's when I stepped up with my spreadsheets and notebooks and binders. I had one for everything: grocery lists, monthly bills, Bernie's activities, school breaks. Everything in our house ran like clockwork, and that's not because I'm a poster child for teenage overachievement; in school, I was a straight-B student. But if Jody wasn't capable of looking after us, somebody had to. If I couldn't be good enough for Annie or Ryan, maybe I could be for Jody.

So for her to say that she's now a whole person again means she wasn't before. That everything we had together, that year and a half on our own when I literally signed her name on the electricity bills, wasn't enough. And I know Jody's the type of person who likes having a boyfriend around to change light bulbs and pick up pizza, but I thought we were doing okay. I thought *I* was doing okay.

"Fine." Annie appears beside me and sits on the bench with a sigh. "I'll go to this lame party with you, but if Ryan throws anything at me, I'm leaving. Immediately."

My head snaps toward her. "Seriously?"

"Yes. But I mean it: if so much as dust comes from her general direction into my general direction, I'm going to rip Ryan's face off and feed it to her. Do you understand me?"

I crack a smile and say, "Weird."

Blushing Brides sits on one edge of a mini mall, its middle filled with a parking lot whose blacktop is oven-hot in the sun. Directly across from us is a giant fountain that shoots streams of blue-green water into the air from a series of oversize fish mouths. There are a few people our age sitting along the fountain's edge laughing and drinking smoothies from the Jamba behind them. One of the girls there has purple hair and a long face, her yellow high-waisted shorts like something out of a hipster construction magazine. She's at least a hundred feet away, but still, I can tell there's something familiar about her. That purple hair.

"Oh my god, is that Ashley Turner?" I say.

It's Annie's turn to snap her head up. "What?"

"Over there," I say, pointing.

It hits me suddenly that by doing this, I've re-created my worst nightmare; I've basically given Annie the opportunity to ditch me for her old friends. Because Annie is charming. Her old friends might not recognize her, but she could probably integrate herself back into Ashley's life as someone else. But instead of skipping across the parking lot with both middle fingers pointed at me, Annie follows my eyes and then ducks her head down into her chest, slapping my hand away.

"Shit," she says under her breath. "I forgot they might be here. This is where all the kids from Del Monte hang out. God, how are they still here in the summer? Do they not have jobs?"

I squint at her, confused, and then I'm annoyed by my confusion. Is it really that bad that Annie isn't immediately abandoning me? Bernie emerges through the doors of Blushing Brides with her iPad held against her chest.

"Mom's getting her dress packed up," she says once she reaches us. "What're you guys doing?" She follows our gazes to the group across the parking lot, where one of the guys is splashing Ashley with fountain water as she squeals and pretends to run away. "Do you know them?" Bernie asks.

"Annie does," I say.

"Oh my god, could you make it any more obvious that we're talking about them?" Annie whispers loudly.

"They won't know it's you," Bernie says. "They're not from Lennon."

Annie's shoulders sink back to a somewhat normal level. "Shit, that's right." She throws her head back and sighs. "Thank *god*." At the look I give her, Annie adds, "What? Can you imagine if I just popped up? *Oh, hey, Ashley, remember the RIP page you made me and how sad you were when I died? Well, I'm back, baby, but get ready to feel it all over again in thirty days.*" Annie laughs darkly. "No, that fun tradition is reserved for Lennon residents only."

I nod, even though there's something about this reasoning that doesn't feel right. What if Annie doesn't want to see Ashley not because she's afraid of devastating her, but because she doesn't want to be seen with me? Not by her rich friends, no matter how ugly their shorts are.

Across the plaza, Ashley is now sitting on one of the guys' laps, alternating between drinking his smoothie and drinking her own through their respective orange plastic straws. I steal a quick look at Annie to see if she's thinking about the same thing as me, but now that she knows she won't be recognized, she's dropped her hand and is watching Ashley in the open. She's clearly not thinking about how or why I know what Ashley Turner looks like, because it's not just from the internet. I know Ashley because she was there the last time I saw Annie alive. The day I finally had to admit to myself that we weren't friends anymore.

It had been over a month since I last heard from Annie. She wasn't answering my calls or messages, she never came into town anymore. The only person I ever saw was her mother, who had no problem acting like I had the plague. There were a couple of times when I dropped by Annie's house, but I never made it past the front door because her mom would always tell me Annie was at field hockey practice or rehearsal or something. That's when I became convinced that Annie's parents were somehow involved in this.

It was always obvious that Mary LeBlanc never wanted to live in Lennon. Annie was only going to Del Monte because her mom wanted her to. Annie was always trying to make her mom happy, joining a community field hockey league in San Diego because none of the Lennon schools had a team, and then playing for Del Monte after her mom had been captain there her junior and senior years. That would be the key to me finally getting ahold of Annie; I had to do it when her mom wasn't around. Mrs. LeBlanc was obviously intercepting my messages to Annie, or acting as a brick wall anytime I came around. So instead of going to eighth-period PE, I took Jody's car and drove to Rosita. Del Monte was just getting out when I parked alongside the rows and rows of BMWs. The parking lot alone was bigger than Lennon Union, sprawling out in front of a series of giant white buildings that were lined with chrome. It was a Thursday, which meant Annie had field hockey practice right after school. After asking around about which field the field hockey teams practiced on—there were a weird number of fields—I waited on a bench outside the football stadium.

I know now what the whole thing looked like. I was basically no better than a common stalker, convinced there was some crack in the universe with my name written on it that everything I ever did or said to Annie fell through. It took only about fifteen minutes before the field hockey teams made their way up the paved ramp from the parking lot and into the football stadium, first the boys and then the girls.

At the front of the girls' team was a cluster of people I kind of recognized from Annie's pictures, all dressed in matching black Spandex shorts. Field hockey sticks were slung over their backs as they chattered happily to each other and passed me without a second glance. At one point as they walked by, one of the girls shouted Ashley's name and a girl with purple hair turned and answered. That night, when I would pore over Annie's pictures, I'd see her face again and again. Ashley Turner, Ashley Turner, Ashley Turner.

Bringing up the rear of the team was Annie, her head down as she typed on her phone. When Ashley said something to the group about a recent Del Monte party in which some guy had thrown a pumpkin out of a second-story window and it had landed on a car, Annie laughed. As she did, she looked up and saw me, standing there just a few feet away. For a second she looked too stunned to speak. I smiled, though I didn't wave or say anything. I must've known, deep down, that doing so would only call attention to me, force the rest of the field hockey team to form a link between me and Annie, something I had to know would embarrass her.

Only as Annie got closer, the team filtering into the football stadium one by one through the chain-link fence, did it dawn on me how pathetic I was being, how fucking weird it was that I was there, that I'd actually convinced myself this would be a fun surprise. So it wasn't totally unexpected when, instead of stopping to talk to me, Annie just ducked her head and kept walking as though I wasn't even there.

I quietly walked back to Jody's car, shame and embarrassment and rejection hot under my skin.

I left Annie alone after that and we never talked again.

TEN

DAYS UNTIL ANNIE LEBLANC DIES: 21

Jody is practically peeing her pants at the thought of me going to a party. She stands in front of her open closet flipping through hangers and pulling out different outfits for me to try on.

"What about this?" she says. She holds up a baby-pink slip dress that would barely cover my knees.

I wrinkle my nose. "Maybe if I wanted to look like Gwyneth Paltrow at the 1998 Oscars." I blink. "I hate that I just said that. That literally happened before I was born."

"It means I taught you right," Jody says, hooking the dress back onto the rail.

Annie is in my bedroom putting on her makeup. Her parents agreed to swap me one night with her for one of my weekdays so she could go to the party tonight and sleep over at my house. I poke my head into my room every few minutes to make sure she hasn't fled through the window.

Eventually Jody and I settle on a surprisingly tame black

T-shirt dress for me that I cinch around my waist with a braided leather belt. Despite Jody's protestations, I insist on wearing a long-sleeved blue-and-white-checkered flannel shirt over it.

"Nobody else's parents help them get ready for parties," I say, shrugging the shirt on. The comfortable feeling of the fabric calms my nerves from a 10 to a 9.5.

"I'm just happy you're going out," Jody says. "Taking a break from living the life of a widowed sixty-year-old accountant."

An unexpected pang of hurt beats in my chest. Does she think I enjoy being like this? All the notes and binders hoarded under my bed? But before Jody can catch on, I narrow my eyes at her.

"You're supposed to be warning me about orgies and stuff," I say.

Jody frowns as she sits on the edge of her bed. "Will there be an orgy?"

I shrug, ignoring the hurt so that it starts to dissolve. "How am I supposed to know? The last meaningful party I went to had One Direction–themed goodie bags."

When I return to my bedroom, I find Annie dressed in a tiny long-sleeved burgundy dress that belongs to Jody, her hair braided and wrapped around her head. Her eyes are flicked with perfect cat eyeliner, her lips a deep brown red. I still can't help but feel a little shaky around her after seeing Ashley at the plaza, wondering if I was embarrassing Annie, but I try to push the thought out of my head.

Seeing me, Annie tugs down on the hem of her dress and frowns, her hands on her hips. "When were you going to tell me you've made basically the most hilarious comic ever?"

At first, I squint at her, not understanding, but then I see my desk. Amid the tubes of mascara and liquid eyeliner pouring out of Annie's makeup bag is my sketchbook, open to a page of *The Walking Dad*. It's on the part where Jerry is trying to pick Ava up from school, but all the PTA moms complain that he smells too bad to be let on campus.

"That's—" I say, scrambling to grab the notebook. "It's nothing. Just something I was playing around with."

"It's amazing," Annie says. "I actually LOLed at the part where the mom sprays zombie man with Febreze."

"Jerry," I say without meaning to. When it's Annie's turn to look confused, I elaborate. "The zombie man. Zombie dad, actually."

Annie gestures to the notebook, now tucked under my arm. I'm so not used to people besides my sister and my mom being in my room, I forgot to hide the comic under my mattress.

"What're you gonna do with it?" she asks.

"What do you mean?"

"Like, where are you gonna send it?"

"Send it . . . ?" I say, still not understanding.

"Wilson, it's so good," Annie says.

I search her face for some indication that she's joking, that she's making fun of me, but she just looks surprised.

"You could at least try to get it in the *Lennon News*," she says.

I shake my head and open my underwear drawer. "Yeah, no," I say, burying the notebook beneath old pairs of underwear and tights I never wear, the nerves I felt from before edging their way back into my chest. "Even the *Lennon News* doesn't print comics anymore."

"Yeah, but this could give them a reason to bring them back. You're really talented, and they might—"

"Annie, no," I say. My voice comes out sharp and breathy. "Just stop."

It's enough to cut Annie off mid-sentence as she looks at me with concern. Does she not remember *The Lennon Chronicles*? Or has her life really been that freaking magical and carefree that she doesn't have to obsess over the epicenter of our friendship earthquake, the moment everything hit its boiling point and exploded?

"Va-va-voom," a voice says from my doorway. My mother is standing there with her arms folded across her chest. I've never been more relieved to see Jody in my life. Her eyes are on Annie, to whom she gives an approving nod. "Maybe I *should* be more worried about you girls."

I smooth a sarcastic smile over my face. "It's not like she can get pregnant," I say, then turn to Annie. "Can you get pregnant?"

Jody's eyes widen. "I definitely did not need that thought in my head," she says with a laugh.

"Thanks for letting me borrow your dress," Annie says.

"No problem," Jody says. "Go ahead and keep it. I don't even know why I have it anymore. I thought I got rid of all that stuff."

A head of dark wavy hair pokes its way around the corner of my bedroom. Dr. David. "Bernie and I are ordering pizza," he says, his eyes sweeping the room. "What do you girls want?"

He's still wearing his green dentist scrubs, the ones covered in tiny cartoon white molars that are wearing bow ties and giving a thumbs-up. I'd almost have forgotten he was here if not for the sounds of a *Judge Judy* rerun drifting in from the living room.

"It's just you, me, and the Bern tonight," Jody says as she

forks a thumb in our direction. "These floozies are going to a party."

"Excuse you," I say. "I'm not the one who threw her underwear at Billy Corgan."

Dr. David's pastel-blue eyes light up. "The bald guy from the Smashing Pumpkins?" he says. "I'm going to pretend I didn't just hear that." Then he blinks. "I feel like I say that a lot in this house."

"That's because if you didn't have spontaneous amnesia with Jody, you'd spend your entire life being pissed off," I say.

Jody finds a dirty sock on the floor near my bed and hurtles it at me. She misses by a mile, then turns her attention to Dr. David and smiles. "Get anything other than Hawaiian."

His face contorts with disbelief, as though Jody has just casually admitted she murdered his grandma. "What?" Dr. David exclaims. "But pineapple pizza is the best."

"Oh god, please tell me you're joking," I say.

"Pineapple on pizza is sacrilege and we will have none of it in this house," Jody adds.

He steps back around the door and into the hallway, mumbling under his breath, "How can I be part of this family if nobody lets me express myself?"

Jody smiles and calls after him, "You get used to it!"

Grant's house is on a quiet wooded road up the hill from Main Street. After the *Walking Dad* incident, Annie and I are careful around each other, our conversation disjointed and cautious. But the farther we get into Lennon, the more natural things become and the further away my sketchbook feels.

"Jesus Christ, I didn't know we'd actually have to hike to get there. I would never have worn long sleeves," Annie says. Her hair is starting to frizz around her face, a bead of sweat trickling down her forehead.

"You look great," I say. Standing next to her, I'm practically wearing a trash bag. I glance down at my outfit and realize with horror that this is actually true. "Shit, do I look like I'm wearing a trash bag?" I say, stopping in the street. I can already imagine the look on Ryan's face when she sees me; she's probably wearing something that makes her look like a *Teen Vogue* model, all perfectly tousled hair, her skin dewy and soft. "Do you think Ryan's gonna make fun of me?"

Annie frowns. "Of course you don't. And why do you care what Ryan thinks?" As she says this, she hocks up the sleeves on her dress. "I'm roasting. No wonder your mom wants to get rid of this dress. Has she ever actually worn it?"

"I think she bought it for Bernie's kindergarten graduation," I say.

Annie snorts. "I can't believe your mom was so cool about us going to a party," she says. "My mom never would've let me go without a full description of who would be there and what we'd be doing. But not for, like, all the normal reasons. She'd want to know because she's desperate to be there. If she knew we were doing this, she would literally be driving us to Grant's house and demanding text updates on what everyone's wearing all night."

"Is that what she did with all the Del Monte parties?" I say.

"What?" As she says this, Annie twists her ankle on a crack running along the edge of the road. "Shit," she mumbles under her breath. We stop as she rolls her ankle back and forth, one arm holding on to me for balance. "I mean, yeah," she says eventually. "Sometimes it was like she was trying to relive her own high school days with me. She did PTA with Ashley's mom, who Ashley always told about everything the field hockey girls did."

I nod like I have any sort of understanding as to what that would be like. Telling my mom everything. *Wanting* to tell my mom anything, much less everything.

After a few more seconds, Annie says, "One time we played make-out bingo with the boys' team at Ash's house and the next morning my mom already knew everything about it. But instead of, like, being horrified like a normal parent, she just wanted to talk about who I'd made out with. It was really weird."

"At least your mom's an actual adult," I say. "You're literally wearing my mom's dress right now, and it looks normal on you. Because it's from Urban Outfitters."

"I don't see how my mom wanting to know about my sexual history makes her more of an adult than yours, but okay."

Grant's house is a toffee-brown building with overgrown hedges. At first, we knock on the front door, but when nobody answers, we let ourselves in. There's a low hum of music coming from the backyard, so we move cautiously through the living room before making our way into the kitchen. When we emerge through the open set of sliding double doors that lead out to the backyard, everybody's conversations either stop completely or drop into whispers. I half expect to hear a record scratch from somewhere far off. Annie and I exchange glances, and I'm instantly reminded of what she said in Blushing Brides about everyone in Lennon staring at her. It's like we're onstage, one *wah-wah* sound away from realizing we're naked.

When Annie speaks to me, it's through gritted teeth. "Are we having fun yet?" she says, her eyes fixed on the crowd, as though by looking away she's leaving room for them to ambush her.

I open my mouth to answer, but before I can, Mark appears from around the corner of Grant's house.

"Holy shit, you guys are here," he says.

With Mark's attention on us, the conversations from before pick up again, with only a few people continuing to steal surreptitious glances at Annie. It's like Mark's presence has corralled everyone else into behaving in a way that's somewhat socially acceptable.

"Didn't you want us here?" Annie says, her eyes back on me.

"Yeah, of course," Mark says. "I just wasn't sure you'd show. You missed Grant overshooting a keg stand and landing in a bush, but I'm pretty sure it's already on the internet, so no worries."

There are about twenty or thirty people here, all of whom I recognize from Lennon Union. Grant's backyard consists of a big lima-bean-shaped patch of concrete that's fringed with neatly cut grass. A Ping-Pong table has been set up for beer pong while the rest of the people sit in lawn chairs scattered across the backyard or next to the keg by the side door. At the back of the yard is a line of trees, their tall trunks wrapped in Christmas lights. Ryan is nowhere to be found, a fact I can tell Annie realizes too as her shoulders sink in relief.

Mark takes a step back. "You guys want a drink?"

This thought makes me freeze. Do I want a drink? What would Jody do? But then I almost laugh out loud. Is that even a question?

"Yeah, okay," I say. Annie nods.

Once Mark turns away, Annie leans in and whispers to me, "How much do you wanna bet Ryan is hiding in those trees waiting to shoot blow darts at us?" She nods toward the trees at the back of the yard.

"She's not gonna do anything in front of all these people," I say.

"She threw a handful of shrimp at my head in front of an entire restaurant."

"Yeah, but those were people she didn't know. She'd have to live this down in front of our whole town."

Annie quietly works her jaw back and forth. "Yeah, a town she's leaving." She turns away, muttering behind her, "I'm going to the bathroom."

"Wait," I say, panic suddenly thick in my voice. Mark is making his way back to us, a red plastic cup in each hand. "You're supposed to be my wingwoman!"

But Annie is already inside the house. "Fly away, little dove," she says from the other side of the glass doors, her thumbs locked together and her hands flapping like bird wings.

When he returns, Mark passes a cup to me, its top heavy with froth. "So, how come you've never been to one of our parties before?" he asks.

I lift the cup and take a tentative sip. The beer is cold but sour and stings the back of my throat. I hold in the urge to spit it out and swallow instead.

"You've never invited me," I say, grimacing as the beer rushes down my throat.

"I still dispute that," Mark says. "But whatever. Anyway, welcome." He sweeps his arms out and gestures to the crowd. Nobody seems visibly drunk, but it is only eight o'clock. Mostly people are just standing around in loose circles and talking. It's actually pretty tame. "Have you grabbed a brownie yet?"

I raise my eyebrows. "Are those like a weed thing?"

"A weed th— What? No, they're not a weed thing," Mark says. He points to the kitchen. "Here, come on."

The kitchen is filled with more people from Lennon Union, mostly seniors who graduated with us but also a few rising ones too. As Mark and I cut in, there's a group of guys from the track team who give him high fives while a couple of girls gathered around the fridge eye me from head to toe, probably wondering how much I had to pay Mark Morton to act like he knows me. He doesn't seem to notice, though, as he places a gentle hand on the small of my back and guides me farther into the kitchen, the girls whispering to one another when they catch it.

Eventually the crowd dissipates, leaving just me, Mark, and an Ariana Grande song that wafts in from outside. Scattered across the countertops are a few bowls of chips, a stack of plastic cups, and a plate of brownies. Mark places one on top of a red paper napkin and passes it to me.

"I bake them for all our parties," he says. "And yes, I'm going to be incredibly needy and ask you to rate it on a scale of one to ten."

The brownie is sliced into a perfect square, its top marbled with what looks like peanut butter. No crumbs poke out from the sides; it's all just an endless, chunky fudge.

"You don't strike me as someone who likes to bake," I say.

"Do I detect a hint of sexism?" Mark says with a smirk.

"What— No," I say quickly.

Mark elbows me. "Relax, Moss, I'm joking. My mom owns an apple pie place; baking is kind of in my blood."

He takes a sip of his beer and leans back against the counter. The smell of chocolate and peanut butter is overwhelming as I lift the brownie to eye level.

"It looks perfect," I say. Over the surface of the brownie, Mark's eyes are fixed on my mouth. "You're watching me."

"Sorry, sorry." He puts a hand in front of his eyes. "Proceed."

My teeth cut through the brownie slowly, the fudgy middle like a thick quicksand. It's the perfect blend of chocolate and peanut butter: not so sweet that my eyes water, but subtle and delicious.

"Oh my god, this is amazing," I say, my throat heavy with chocolate.

Mark's hand lowers as he says, "Are you just saying that?"

"No way," I say as I shove the other half of the brownie into my mouth. "It's perfect."

But it's also really, really thick, the bite I've taken far too big. My chewing slows as I try to work my way through the peanut butter, but I probably just look like a cow chewing grass. Mark watches me with an eyebrow raised. I cover my mouth with my hand and try to smile, but as I do, a loose crumb lodges itself in my throat, leaving me hacking.

When I finally stop coughing and swallow, Mark is magically waiting with a glass of milk.

"It's okay, Moss. That can happen when you're an amateur," he says when I grab the glass from him and chug. "But don't worry. Now that I know you like weed brownies, I can bring you more interesting stuff at work."

The glass lands hard on the counter.

"What?" I say.

Mark bursts out laughing. "Oh my god, I'm joking," he says. "Do I look like the kind of guy who would drug girls at parties? Actually, don't answer that."

A long window sits over the kitchen sink and faces out to the backyard. Through it, I can see Annie talking to the guys from the track team, all of them laughing loudly at something she's said. Nobody seems to be staring at her anymore, the shine of her undeadness having momentarily worn off. Seeing her like this, in the middle of an adoring crowd, I can't help but imagine her at Del Monte parties. She never would have shoved an entire brownie in her mouth like an absolute dork. She probably would've poured chocolate syrup on it and then all over herself and made it look really hot.

Sitting on a bench just a few feet away are Ryan and Maddie Samuels, former head of the Lennon Union yearbook. Ryan, who must've snuck past me out to the backyard while I was trying to suffocate myself with baked goods, is wearing a short black skater dress, her legs draped over Maddie's lap and her long hair tied up in a bun. Mark is saying something to me about the cinnamon-sugar doughnuts he baked for their last party as I watch Ryan laugh so hard that she shuts her eyes and tips back her head. I wonder what Maddie could've said to make her so happy; Maddie, who used to claim she could see Bloody Mary's eyes in the drainage pipes behind our elementary school. To Ryan, who I've barely seen crack a smile in the last two years. When Ryan comes back up, she leans in to Maddie, says something in her ear. Maddie pulls away and smiles, and then before I know it, they're kissing. It's slow at first as they ease into it, but within seconds Maddie lifts her hands to the back of Ryan's neck, pulling them closer together like the rest of the party isn't there.

At first, I don't know what's weirder: the fact that Maddie is acting like nothing and nobody else exists even though at least half the party is now watching in a kind of stunned fascination as she and Ryan makeshift wrestle on the bench, or that Ryan lets her. But at least with Maddie, I get it, kind of. Knowing Ryan and the way her rage powers her like anger caffeine, the idea of getting anything else from her seems impossible. So, when you do, it's intoxicating. Feeling that for just those brief seconds, you're channeling Ryan Morton's sharp edges into something else. Something softer, but still crackling. Her attention becomes a kind of fire, burning in your blood or, in Maddie's case, a deep urge to claw Ryan's neck as though she's trying to peel back her skin like she's a human orange.

Sometimes if I shut my eyes and everything around me is still and silent, I can feel it again. That fire. Other times it hits me out of nowhere, when I'm watching *Buffy* reruns, or counting up the cash register at the end of the day as Ryan half-heartedly mops the back office floor. But then it's followed by embarrassment, remembering the look on Ryan's face when she pulled away. The horror and the regret.

A few weeks ago, at the graduation party. The night Ryan Morton kissed me.

With the exception of the bakers, most of the staff at the Country Kitchen are Lennon Union students, so every year when school gets out, Terri Morton throws a party. It's at the Country Kitchen, nothing fancy, just apple pie, cider, and homemade pizzas to celebrate the summer. But Ryan and Mark graduating this year meant Terri popped for a fondue bar and a fire pit in the back courtyard, over which everyone could toast marshmallows on bent coat hangers. I spent most of the night dipping spicy peppers into a curtain of melted cheddar while everyone

around me talked about college and their summer plans. It was
the same as the previous end-of-year parties, but this time I was
the one who was supposed to be joining in, excitedly relaying
all the big things I was going to do with my life. But all I could
manage was a tight-lipped smile as I shoved bite-size food skew-
ered with tiny toothpicks into my face.

The Country Kitchen's courtyard sits behind the restaurant,
usually just a patch of concrete with a few wrought-iron chairs
and a small table. But that night it was lit up by the fire burning
from a cylindrical pit ringed with mosaic tiles in bright yellows
and reds that caught the light of the flames. I slipped out just as
Terri was making a toast about everyone going off to bigger and
better things but always having the Country Kitchen as a home
base, and found Ryan sitting beside the fire, an open bag of jumbo
marshmallows on her lap.

At the sight of her, I took a step back. "Oh," I said, startled.
I knew from years of experience that being in a room alone
with me made Ryan uncomfortable. I could tell by the way her
shoulders would tense every time she walked past me, or the
strain in her voice when she had no choice but to acknowledge
my presence. "Sorry, I can just—"

But Ryan cut me off with a surprise shrug. "It's whatever,"
she said. She lifted the bag of marshmallows. "You might as well
stay while there're still some left."

Maybe it was shock, but I took the seat beside Ryan. In the
last few weeks, there'd been a shift between us. On the outside,
it was small—her asking if I wanted coffee before she went to fill
her mug, asking if I was going to Lennon Union's grad night—
but considering how limited our interactions had become, it felt
massive to me.

Ryan leaned down to untangle a coat hanger from the pile at her feet and then passed me one without a word.

"You're missing your mom's speech," I said as I grabbed a marshmallow.

The fire sparkled in Ryan's eyes as she said, "Exactly."

Outside was quiet except for the faint rumble of laughter from the Country Kitchen and the occasional crackle of the fire. Ryan and I stared into the flames, not speaking. At the end of the summer, she'd be off to UC San Diego, which, in reality, was only an hour away, but from the way her mom teared up every time she talked about it, you'd think it was on the other side of the world. At our graduation the day before, Ryan had gone uncharacteristically cliché, decorating the top of her hat with the UCSD triton in gold glitter. When we were little, we'd had a whole plan of what our high school graduation celebration would look like: Annie would be at Del Monte, but Ryan and I would sit next to each other during the ceremony—our last names meant we were pretty much always next to each other when organized alphabetically—and then we'd go to dinner the three of us at the Fish Grotto, spend the night at Ryan's house, and dig up the time capsule we'd buried in her backyard after that time we watched Jody's old VHS tape of *Crossroads* with Britney Spears. True to the movie, we'd each put in something related to the future we wanted for ourselves: Ryan, a snow globe with downtown San Diego; Annie, a stuffed poison dart frog toy for when she'd live in a tree house high above the rainforest floor; and me, the first *Buffy* comic from season eight.

"Do you remember our time capsule?" I said to Ryan suddenly.

She blinked at the fire and exploded with laughter. The

unexpected sound of it made me jump. I couldn't remember the last time I'd heard her genuinely laugh.

"You mean the shoebox we wrapped in a trash bag?" she said.

I laughed too. "Are you saying you didn't bother digging it up?" I said.

"Oh, I didn't have to. My dad did," she said. When I looked at her, she barked another laugh. "We only buried it like six inches down, so he kept running over it with his lawn mower. When he finally pulled it out, the whole top of the shoebox was shredded."

Something about this sent us both into hysterics, initially laughing at the thought of the shoebox representing our childhood dreams so carelessly demolished, and then even harder because the other person was laughing so hard. By the end of it, I could barely breathe.

I wiped my eyes with the heels of my hands. "What'd you do with all our stuff?" I asked.

Ryan's laughter slowly faded. She cleared her throat. "I threw it away," she said quietly.

I blinked. I knew Ryan wouldn't necessarily be sentimental over our time capsule, but I didn't expect her to get rid of it.

"Oh," I said, trying to downplay any sort of surprise, but I could tell my voice sounded strangled.

At that, Ryan looked at me for the first time. "I mean, I didn't think you'd even want it all back—"

"No, no, I didn't," I rushed. "I don't." I shrugged and laughed weakly. "It's probably for the best anyway, not having to dig all that stuff up now and be reminded of how disappointed even my eight-year-old self would've been with me."

Ryan's eyebrows met, her face bending into a frown. "What're you talking about?" she said.

"Oh, nothing, just that I, like, actually thought that by the time we graduated high school I'd be some big cartoonist, or whatever," I said. The end of my coat hanger was crusty with burnt marshmallow I tried to scrape off with my fingernails. "Which obviously wouldn't have even been really possible anyway, so I was basically setting myself up for failure. Not that I'm making excuses. I would've failed anyway—"

Ryan whipped her head around so fast, I could practically hear her hair whistling through the air. "Why do you always do that?" she cut in.

The sudden anger in her voice unbalanced me.

"Do what?"

"Talk so much shit about yourself." She threw her arms out on either side, knocking the bag of marshmallows to the ground. "Sometimes I can't tell who hates you more: you or the imaginary people in your head."

Ordinarily this kind of thing would've slapped me into silence, Ryan's bite just another reminder of how everything between us had fallen apart. But after her mom's speech and the way I'd stood next to the fondue fountain alone all night, it only made me mad. Who was she to tell me I was making up my loneliness? Imagining that I wasn't good enough? Ryan Morton, who had a new person falling over her every week, who had a neat little road map for her future and the same people at home every day of her perfect fucking life?

I turned my body in my chair so that its legs scraped loudly against the concrete. "Oh yes, please tell me more about these imaginary people," I said. "Says *you,* who acts like everything

I do is specifically designed to infuriate you. It's like you can't even be in the same room as me without rolling your eyes or trying to make me feel bad." As the words poured out of me, Ryan listened in silence, her eyes glimmering with what I could only guess was fury. "Where do you think it all started, Ryan?" I said. "*You* are the one who makes me feel like everyone hates me, when you—"

In one quick movement Ryan sprung up from her chair and lunged toward me. At first, I thought it was because she was going to hit me, her hands reaching for my face, and while they stung a little when they touched my cheeks, they were quickly followed by her mouth, landing hard on mine. Though my first thought was to panic, my eyes closed instinctively, almost like a deliberate attempt *against* self-preservation. Surprise burst up from the bottom of my spine like a firework, leaving my skin covered in a thin layer of goose bumps. What was happening? Was Ryan Morton actually kissing me, or had she slammed my face into the edge of the fire pit and knocked me out, resulting in some kind of pseudo love-hate sex dream?

Almost as if I had to make sure Ryan was real, my hands landed on her thighs, fingertips pressed into her bare skin. Once they were there, it was like they couldn't sit still, dancing up her waist and landing on the edge of her T-shirt. Ryan's hands slipped to the back of my head, where she gripped my hair between her fists, pulling me closer so that I almost stumbled up and out of my chair. Something about it felt hungry, almost desperate, and as her tongue found mine, I realized not only that I did not mind, but that I didn't want it to stop.

But when my hands accidentally slipped underneath her shirt and slid against the small of her back, Ryan pulled away and let out a little gasp, as though she couldn't believe what was happening either.

"I'm sorry," I said quickly. My heart was beating so fast, I wasn't sure how I hadn't passed out.

Ryan lifted a hand to her mouth, fingers landing lightly on her lips. I could see in the firelight that they were somehow already swollen from impact. Her chest convulsed like she was trying to say something or trying to suppress it, I couldn't tell which, until it became horrifically clear that it wasn't words she was battling—it was puke. Because half a second later she leaned over the side of her chair and threw up loudly onto the concrete, most of it landing on the discarded bag of marshmallows and the front of her shirt. She rushed to her feet, one hand clamped over her mouth, but she wasn't fast enough to beat barf round two, which was already spilling through her fingers.

"Ryan—" I started to say, but she didn't look back.

I stood just as Mark pushed open the back door, eyes wide as Ryan shoved past him. Once she was inside, he turned to me, standing motionless beside the fire.

"Jesus, Moss," he said, laughing. "What'd you do?"

That was when I burst into tears.

Eleven

DAYS UNTIL ANNIE LEBLANC DIES: 21

Mark leans in and clears his throat.

"So, I feel like we should address the elephant in the room," he says under his breath.

Reality snaps back into focus, Mark's face just inches from mine. His eyes are soft and he's biting his lip, waiting for me to say something back, but my body is on fire with shame.

"Elephant?" I say, breathless.

Is it that obvious that I'm remembering the time I kissed his twin sister and caused her so much mortification and regret that she threw up toasted marshmallows all over herself?

"As in, the actual elephant."

Mark points to a wall beyond the kitchen, in the living room behind a huge flat-screen TV. Somehow in between my nerves, I didn't notice it when I walked in. Crammed onto four shelves spanning the entire length of the wall are what look like a million stuffed animals, basically every animal ever: a toucan, an elephant, lions, llamas, and a really elaborate giraffe. There's even an aardvark, its long gray nose poking the face of a fat hippo.

I'm so relieved that he hasn't somehow read my thoughts, I could cry. What kind of degenerate eats a beautiful boy's home-made brownies and then reminisces about the way it felt to have his sister's *tongue* in their *mouth*?

"Oh. My. God," I say slowly as Mark and I move toward the animal wall.

Mark shoves his hands into his pockets. "Magical, right? Grant's mom knits one for him and his brothers every year for their birthdays and basically every holiday. She's been doing it since they were born," he says.

I stroke the paw of a panda. "She made all these?" I say.

He nods. "Yep. Grant and his brothers aren't allowed to touch them, though. She made me one for my ninth birthday, but don't remind Grant. He hates that I actually get to play with Timothy the hyena." Mark lets out a long sigh. "I wish someone would look at me the way Grant's mom looks at these stuffed animals."

Turning toward him slowly, I say, "I'm sorry, did you say *Timothy* the hy—"

But I'm cut off by an earsplitting noise from outside, some-one screaming as though they've just been stabbed. In the back-yard, Ryan is standing beside the bench with her arms thrown out, her face wet and shiny. Behind her, Grant is scrambling for a roll of paper towels on the beer pong table, his now empty cup on the ground. Maddie is still sitting on the bench, looking like she's trying not to laugh.

The entire party has gone silent, all eyes on Ryan. Mark pushes through to her and I stay back in the house, hovering in the doorway to the backyard.

"Are you fucking kidding me?" Ryan shouts as Grant haphazardly swipes the front of her dress with a handful of paper towels.

"What happened?" Mark asks.

"He dumped an entire beer on me," Ryan says.

Mark runs a hand through his hair. "Dude, come on," he says to Grant.

"She put my phone on Spanish again," Grant says, waving his phone.

"You literally took four years of Spanish," Ryan says. "Stop being so fucking bad at Spanish." When she twists the hem of her dress, beer waterfalls onto the ground. "I'm totally soaked." She points her finger in his face. "I'm changing into your clothes and I'm not giving them back, you dick."

With that, Ryan storms into the house, ignoring me as she passes. I don't know what makes me do it—a deep-rooted hatred for myself or the overpowering desire to seek the approval of people who clearly wish I didn't exist—but I follow her. The hallway leading to what I'm guessing are bedrooms is lined with family photos, each with Grant and his brothers as kids, all of them with the same dark curly hair. The only door that's shut is the one at the very back.

"Ryan," I say, knocking softly. "Are you okay?"

She mumbles something that faintly sounds like "fine," so I edge the door open. Ryan is standing on the other side of a bed wearing nothing but a black bra and underwear, her dress balled up in a little wet heap at her feet. At the sight of her naked stomach, tanned a deep, warm shade of bronze, that same firework of surprise I felt when she kissed me surges up my back as I clap my hand over my eyes.

"Oh my god, *get out*," she shrieks.

"Shit, I'm so sorry," I say as I scramble for the door again and slam it behind me. My chest is heaving as I stand in the hallway, forehead resting against the door. "I'm really sorry," I shout into the wood as I squeeze my eyes shut.

My first real party was always going to be an embarrassing shit show, but this feels ridiculous, even to me. Less than a minute later, the bedroom door swings open again, revealing Ryan in an LA Rams jersey that's so big it goes all the way to the middle of her thighs. She combs through her wet hair with her fingers, the tangles breaking with a snap.

"What do you want?" she says.

At the sight of her, I blink with disbelief. "Are you okay?" I say again.

She turns away and sits on the edge of the bed. "Yeah, I'm great. I love getting showered with skunked beer." She props her elbows up on her thighs and digs her hands into her eyes as she groans, "God, I hate these parties."

The walls of Grant's bedroom are covered in basketball posters, a framed Shaquille O'Neal jersey, and shelves lined with basketball trophies whose figurines all strike various sporty poses. His bed is basically the size of my room, his comforter a bright yellow and purple for the Lakers. Next to it is a small bedside table, which is stacked with books by John Steinbeck, Franz Kafka, and some dude named Nabokov.

I frown at the books. "I didn't know Grant could read," I say.

Ryan laughs softly through her nose. "Yeah, he surprised everyone with that."

I lower myself onto the bed beside her, careful to leave at

least a foot of space between us. I bite the inside of my cheek, the music from outside creating a low, constant thrum in the room.

"If you hate these parties so much, why are you here?" I say.

"Because what else am I supposed to do in this town?" she says before clenching her hands into fists and sighing. "Sorry," she says under her breath. "I don't—I just smell really gross right now and it's making me very mad."

"You don't actually smell that bad," I say. "Just kind of"— I lean over, pretending to sniff—"sour."

"Amazing," Ryan says as she slaps a hand over her forehead. "That's—that's my night, in a nutshell."

When she drops her hand into her lap again, her eyes tilt up to meet mine. Sparkling behind them is the same anger from the night of the graduation party, the night she found me so repulsive, her body actually had to expel any trace of me as though I was toxic. But why, then, would she kiss me in the first place? Was it because she wanted to shut me up? Or was what I was saying making her feel bad, and by kissing me she was trying to . . . what? Make up for it, but then she underestimated how gross she actually found me and realized it too late? And how pathetic did that then make me, that I'd actually liked it?

Ryan's eyes hold mine, her fingers flexing and unflexing in her lap. "Why do you like her so much?" she says, almost whispering.

I frown, trying to piece her question together. "Who?" I say. "Annie?"

The door cracks open and Annie pokes her head into the room. Ryan and I glance over at the same time.

"Wil, are you okay?" she says, her eyes not reaching Ryan.

Ryan twists her hair around one hand and stands. "I need to—" she starts to say to me, then looks at Annie and cuts herself short. "Whatever."

Now that the three of us are finally in a room together, the entire reason I'm at this party comes boomeranging back to me. Mark and Ryan had distracted me for a little while, but now I need to focus. Annie has only three weeks left and I'm no closer to making her and Ryan friends again than when she first came back.

"Wait," I say as Ryan reaches the door. "Can't we all just"—I throw my arms out weakly—"hang?"

Ryan and Annie laugh. "No," they say in unison, then look at each other and scowl.

"*You* don't want to hang out with *me*?" Annie says. "You're the one who threw shrimp at my head."

"You called me trash," Ryan says back.

At the sound of them arguing, panic wells up in my chest. This cannot go bad.

"Guys, come on, can we please not fight?" I say, trying to snuff out the desperation in my voice. "That was a long time ago and I really feel like—"

"You were acting like a dick," Annie says.

Ryan turns toward her, arms folded across her chest. "*I* was acting like a dick?" she says. "You'd been acting like a dick for years. You're the one who cried when you got a Benz and not a Beamer for your sixteenth birthday."

"Please stop, you guys," I say. "Please."

Annie narrows her eyes. "It was my grandma's old Benz and I cried because it had a CD player." She turns to me, looking for help. "Who the fuck listens to CDs?"

"You still got a car," Ryan says. "Everybody knows you couldn't wait to transfer to your shitty private school so you could ditch the rest of us. Just admit it."

"This isn't helping," I say, but neither of them is listening to me. It's like I'm not even here. "Please, just stop."

Annie takes a step forward. "I stopped hanging out with you because you threw *shrimp* at my *head*."

"Fine, that explains me," Ryan says before throwing an arm in my direction. "But why'd you ditch Wilson?"

Silence follows, the question leaving me breathless. So Ryan does know I'm here, but only as a prop she can use to make her point. I raise my eyebrows at Annie, waiting for her outrage on my behalf, but all she does is give me a quick glance before crossing her arms, matching Ryan's pose so that they're mirror images of each other.

Annie squints. "Why'd *you* ditch Wilson?" she says.

At this, I bark a laugh. I don't even realize it's coming until it's already out, just this loud explosion that's all at once confused and frustrated and just really pissed off. Annie and Ryan finally stop speaking as they look over at me with the same startled expression.

"I'm sorry," I say, slowly lurching to my feet. I suddenly feel exhausted. "You guys are hilarious. You both act like you're better than each other, but you're exactly the same. You want to act like she's some anger-management poster child"—I shove my finger in Annie's face—"but you clearly have no problem screaming back at her. And you"—I turn on Ryan—"you like to pretend her trying to leave Lennon was so horrible, but news flash, you're doing the same thing."

I cut through them toward the door and open it. I'm so sick

of listening to them go around and around and around trying to prove who did what, which one is worse, when they're identical. I'm so tired of hearing them bitch about each other that in this moment, I don't care anymore whether they're friends or not. I just want to get away from them.

But before leaving, I swivel around. "And yes, you're right. You both ditched me," I say, then stick up my middle fingers. The smile on my face is so brittle, it could crack in half. "So congratulations, ladies. You both suck exactly the same amount."

When I slam the door behind me, all I can hear from the hallway is their stunned silence. I know that by leaving them alone together, there's a very good chance they'll rip out each other's hair, but if I stay, they'll both see me cry and that's almost worse.

It takes me approximately three minutes of counting the amount of people at the party who have tattoos—eleven, though technically twelve if you count Carla Williams, but I don't because she only has the word "love" tattooed on the inside of her bottom lip and that's just gross—before I start to regret screaming at Annie and Ryan. Because while pointing out that they both simultaneously deemed me not worthy of their friendship, I also left them on the brink of what was almost definitely an all-out smackdown, thus ruining any chance I had of making them friends again. When Annie emerged from Grant's bedroom shortly after me, she didn't have any obvious bruises or chunks of her scalp missing, but the lighting out here is bad. Plus, she's made sure to keep at least ten feet between us, her eyes darting nervously over the party as she joins a very drunk Grant at the beer pong table. Ryan hasn't shown her face yet, which is probably for the best. In those few seconds between me walking in on her half naked and accusing her and Annie of being bad friends, things between me and Ryan were actually easy, like they were that day at the Country Kitchen before Annie came back. But now it's ruined. Again.

I know I should go home, but it's this or sitting between Jody and Dr. David in front of some reality plastic surgery show, and somehow watching Grant fire Ping-Pong balls across the table with his mouth seems like the less pathetic option. Plus, I can't help but picture the disappointed look on Jody's face at seeing me walk through the front door at ten. Just when she thought I was finally capable of doing something as normal as going to a party, I'd prove to her just how lame I am.

Mark Morton plops into the chair next to me, breaking my thoughts. He flicks his chin toward the Ping-Pong table.

"You and me are up next," he says.

"Next for what?" I say.

"Beer pong. Grant is currently tonight's undefeated champion and I don't have the energy to listen to him brag about it all week." Mark's arms are propped on top of his knees. Through the shag of his hair, he gives me a lopsided smile. "I volunteered us. I thought you'd be a good teammate because your head kind of looks like a Ping-Pong ball."

In spite of the last twenty minutes, I bite back a smile. "Is that all it takes?" I say.

He pushes himself to his feet and holds out a hand to me. "Pretty much."

At some point as I make my way over to the Ping-Pong table, it's agreed that Annie will join Grant's team against me and

Mark. And as it turns out, your head being generally Ping-Pong-ball-shaped is not all it takes to be good at this game; because within only a few minutes of playing, it becomes clear that I am, in fact, very bad at it. I keep throwing the ball either so lightly that it dribbles toward the cups or so hard that I pelt someone nearby in the legs. And I don't even have the excuse of being drunk. Mark drinks all my beer for me because every time I so much as smell it, I want to gag, so even he's looking a little wobbly, his eyes glazing over around the edges.

"You know you're supposed to get the balls into the cups, right?" Annie asks after I land a Ping-Pong ball somewhere in a rosebush.

Mark points his finger at her. "No smack-talking, LeBlanc. We discussed this." He leans in and whispers to me, "She's right, though. We're aiming for the cups, not the shrubbery."

I can tell Annie feels bad about what happened with us and Ryan by the way she keeps smiling at me and apologizing with her eyes, but every time she does I pretend I don't notice and look away. This has the effect of making her swallow big gulps of beer from the cups I'm not hitting with the Ping-Pong ball. Somehow, though, she's not even the drunkest person on her team. Grant is so hammered, he crammed an entire plate of pizza rolls into his mouth and keeps chest-bumping Annie every time they score another point, which is very, very often.

Annie whoops as she sinks another ball into one of the cups on my side of the table so there's only one left. Sighing, Mark drinks the beer as Annie lifts her own cup in triumph.

"Wil, if I win, you're finally shaving your head," she says before sipping her drink.

Mark hands me the ball, its surface slick and wet. I clench

my jaw tight and rub the ball on the side of my dress, feeling its smooth shell with my fingers. Ryan's breathy laughter sounds from somewhere over my shoulder and I glance toward her just in time to see her watching me. Her jaw is set and her gaze is so intense, I want to shrink away, but that would give her far too much satisfaction. Instead I close my eyes and let out a long breath. I lift my arm up and flick my wrist just slightly. My eyes open in time to see the ball gently arc over the table and land in the cup right in the middle of the triangle with a light plop.

I jump into the air and shriek, "I did it!"

But when I look back over at Ryan, she doesn't look impressed or even annoyed. She looks panicked. Everyone's attention has turned to the woods lining Grant's backyard, where bright blue lights have suddenly appeared, flashing across the trees so that it looks like the surface of the ocean.

Somebody shouts, "Cops!"

And then it's pandemonium, everybody running in different directions, hopping fences and ducking behind trees. Grant chugs beer from the last few cups on his side of the table before stuffing a bag of tortilla chips up the bottom of his shirt and disappearing into the dark.

"Shit," Mark says under his breath. He grabs my hand. "We gotta go."

I follow him to the back fence, my head swiveling wildly, looking for Annie and Ryan. Annie's side of the table is now empty and Ryan is gone too, her spot on the patio replaced with frantic teenagers shoving one another toward the back gate. Mark pushes a loose board in the fence so that it opens just enough to escape through.

"What is this, a cartoon?" I say, staring at it. "I can't leave Annie."

She might think I'm friendless trash, but I can't just abandon her. I'm not *her*.

"She probably went into the neighbors' backyard with Grant. We have contingency plans for this kind of stuff," Mark says. He waves me through the gap in the fence. "We don't have time to look for her, come on."

Slipping through the fence, I can hear shouting behind me as the cops make their way through Grant's house and into the backyard. Once Mark is through, he grabs my hand and pulls me into the woods, not slowing down until we emerge on a block I recognize as one not far from Main Street. Everything about it is quiet and dark, the windows on the houses mostly black except for the occasional blue haze from a TV. Mark and I stand in the middle of the street, panting, the sudden silence almost more unsettling than the sound of cops.

"I think we're good now," Mark says, giving one last glance over his shoulder. "Do you want me to walk you home?"

Nerves heat my cheeks. "You don't have to do that," I say quickly.

"It's cool," Mark says with a shrug. "I want to."

The two of us walk slowly down the hill toward Main Street, the faint glow of the streetlights coloring Mark's face orange. He's still holding my hand, and I don't know if it's because he's forgotten it's there or if he actually wants to. I shut my eyes against the night and try to focus on the way the scar underneath his thumb from where he cut his hand on a paring knife at work snakes along his palm, but all I can think about is whether or not I should tell him about Ryan. What happened at the graduation party. Would it be better coming from me so he could run away horrified *now*? I can already imagine the look on his face when he finds out I'm apparently the type of person who thinks about making out with *all* the inhabitants of Terri Morton's womb.

But it has been a few weeks since the graduation party, and I wasn't the one who started the kiss. In fact, I technically ended it. Plus, if I'm going to try to get Ryan to hang out with me and Annie, I'm going to have to act like Vomit Gate never happened. And judging by the way Ryan has been treating me since she kissed me, she's clearly trying to forget about it too.

"Okay, top five first party highlights, go," Mark says, breaking my thoughts.

When I open my eyes again, he's looking at me, smiling. His teeth are incredible, pure white and needle-straight. He used to wear headgear to bed every night when we were kids, and Ryan would put it on and pretend to talk with a lisp, but Mark and his perfect teeth clearly got the last laugh.

I pull in a sharp breath and count on my free hand. "Peanut butter brownies, knitted zoo," I say, thinking back. Four seconds of things between me and Ryan not being weird before I started yelling at her. "Not getting so drunk I puked, outsmarting the cops, and . . . oh! Getting the Ping-Pong ball in exactly one cup."

Mark frowns. "I didn't see that happen," he says.

"That's because the cops came basically the second I did it. The lack of recognition was actually really upsetting."

"Huh." Mark sweeps a hand through his hair and I swear if I were standing behind him I'd feel a breeze. He looks over and smiles at me again. "Well, I was involved in three out of five of those highlights—actually, since I drank all your beer for you, let's say four out of five." He squeezes my hand. "Jeez, Moss, you're not even trying to pretend you don't have a thing for me."

My feet stutter on the pavement, our hands breaking apart. My head is numb with the sound of alarm bells.

"I—I didn't mean—" I stammer, the words rushing around my mind too fast to make sense. "That wasn't what—"

"Moss, relax," he says, walking back to me. He puts his hands on either side of my face. My body freezes and every cell in me is aware of his, every tiny millimeter of his skin touching mine. Mark's eyes search my own until finally we're looking straight at each other. "I was just joking. I didn't mean to make this weird."

"You didn't," I say quietly. "I did." Suddenly the thought that's been in my head for the last few days is right at the front of my mouth, escaping before I can stop it. "Why are you being so nice to me?"

Mark's hands fall, leaving my cheeks feeling cold and stung. "What're you talking about?" he says. "I'm always nice to you."

My eyes drop to the ground, landing on my feet as they scrape against the asphalt. "No, I mean, you're talking to me. You never did before Annie got back, and now you . . . do."

Amazing. Absolutely A-plus talking.

"Okay, yeah, maybe that's true, but it's mostly because you're actually talking back to me now."

It's my turn to be confused. "What?" I say, scrunching my forehead. "In the four times you've talked to me in the last million years, I've always answered you."

Mark snorts. "I mean, sort of, but not in a way that makes it easy to keep talking." At my arched eyebrow, he elaborates. "Remember that time I asked if you were going to the New

Year's Eve fireworks and you told me you thought fireworks were a waste of time?"

"They *are* a waste of time," I grumble. "They're like Snapchat for the sky."

"Yeah, but that's kind of a conversation killer to someone who obviously thinks they're cool." He shrugs and steps toward me. "I don't know, you actually seem semi-open to talking to me now, so I thought I'd take advantage of it while I could."

He is standing so close to me. Like, so close. Even in the dark I can see the flecks of gold in his eyes, the way his teeth creep up over his bottom lip when he smiles. I'm too busy tracing the shape of his nose—slightly curved at first, but a perfect slope at the end—to hear the sound of a car approaching until Mark and I are drowned in blue lights.

We turn at the same time toward the headlights, squinting into their brightness. A door slams, followed by footsteps and another glowing bulb, a flashlight this time.

"What do we have here?" the voice behind the flashlight says.

Suddenly the light drops, revealing a darkened figure. His face is all business with a hint of surprise.

Cass.

Mark and I break apart as Cass walks toward us, embarrassment heating my entire body. Cass might not be my stepdad anymore, but it's still horrifying to think that the person who was my tooth fairy has seen me with a boy. Maybe on the verge of kissing a boy.

Cass drops his flashlight to his side. "Wilson P, you might be the last person I expected to find out here," he says.

An incredulous smile crosses Mark's face as he mouths to me, *Wilson P?*

I look away quickly.

"I've just heard about a party at the Lovelace house," Cass says. "You two didn't happen to stop by, did you?"

"No, sir," Mark says. He throws a hand toward me. "She never gets invited to parties."

My head snaps toward him. "Hey," I say at the same time Cass says, "Don't be a smart-ass, Morton."

Mark dips his head down to his chest so his hair falls in his eyes. Even in the darkness, I can see him smirking.

"We were just hanging out," I say.

Cass is silent for a minute as he glances between me and Mark. All I can hear is the sound of him breathing deeply through his nose, which I know means he's thinking. Maybe he can smell the beer on me and is wondering how I'll afford bail. He's a cop; he probably has a sixth sense for underage drinking.

I glance down at my feet, willing myself not to look guilty.

Finally Cass sighs. "Look, if you say you weren't there . . ." He flicks his flashlight on and shines it at my feet, motioning for me to look up. "Hey, Wilson. If you say you weren't at the Lovelace house, then I've got no choice but to believe you. But you two shouldn't be out this late, not with coyotes and other creepy crap skulking around."

"We were on our way home," Mark says.

"I happen to know you live on the other side of town," Cass says. He turns back to me. "I'll drive you home, Wilson. I'm heading that way anyways."

"What?" Mark says. "You're driving her home and I've gotta walk by myself and fight off werewolves or whatever?"

Cass rolls his eyes and opens the car door for me. "Good night, Morton."

Before ducking into Cass's cruiser, I give Mark an apologetic smile. He salutes me with two fingers against his forehead before turning away and disappearing into the night, along with whatever might've happened between us.

As Cass and I drive back to my house, the car is warm and quiet. On the dashboard, his radio crackles with voices saying something about a possible drunk and disorderly outside the Nickel and Dime. A few minutes later Cass pulls up to the curb in front of my house and drums his hands against the steering wheel.

"This is not how I thought my night would go," he says. "Here I figured I'd just drive around, break up a few house parties, ruin some kid's college career."

"There's still time for that," I point out.

Cass shrugs. "Yeah, maybe. But I'm hungry."

Silence fills the car again as Cass and I stare up at my house. The windows are completely dark, no sign of life beyond the cheap curtains.

"Really, though? Mark Morton?" Cass says suddenly. "That kid had more metal in his mouth than Apollo 13."

My eyes go wide as I press my forehead against the glass of my window. "I told you, we were just hanging out," I say.

"That's not what it looked like to me."

"Perv."

Cass laughs as I swing my door open and step out onto the sidewalk. "Hey, Wilson," he says, leaning over the emergency brake so he can see me. He swallows hard and looks down at his hands. "I'm all for you getting out, but just be careful, okay?"

I straighten up, unable to look at him. He and I both know what he's really trying to say: *Don't be like Jody.*

"Okay" is all I can say back.

He says good night and I slam the door, taking the porch steps two at a time. His words envelop me like a thick jelly. As if I would ever just be like Jody, as though one party would suddenly make me want to get weird with a bartender in his half drug den, half studio apartment, which is just what I assume happened when my mother ruined the only family I've ever known. But Cass is like me, someone who lives in their head, eating worries and anxiety for breakfast and then pooping out sarcasm. So I get it. Kind of.

Inside, my house is still and noiseless. My sister is asleep on the couch, her bare feet dangling over the side and an arm flung over her head. Bags from the deli are stacked up on the counter beside a mountain of six-pack cans of the girly alcohol Jody requested for her bachelorette party. I tiptoe down the hall to my bedroom and ease open the door. By the moonlight seeping in through my window, I can just about make out Annie's unmoving shape in Bernie's bed, on top of her comforter and fully clothed, including her shoes. As I carefully tuck a blanket I find in my closet around her body, Annie lifts her head from the pillow.

"Wilson?" she mumbles, eyes still closed.

"It's me," I say quietly. "Go back to sleep."

Her head lands back down with a thump. I change into rumpled pajama shorts and a T-shirt before settling into my own bed. I toss back and forth, trying to get comfortable enough for sleep, but my skin is still itchy from the night. I went to a party with my peers and nobody dunked my head in a toilet. Mark

Morton held my hand. But as I stare up at the darkened ceiling, one memory pushes through the rest—Ryan as we sat on Grant's bed, her supercharged whisper. What would've happened if Annie hadn't barged in? I know I need to move on and forget that Ryan ever kissed me, but would I have gotten the courage to at least ask her why she did it in the first place? And would she have done it again?

Annie's voice cuts through the dark, low and still sleep-drunk. "Wilson?" she says again.

A warmth in my stomach I didn't know had appeared evaporates. "Yeah?"

"I—I didn't know Ryan left at the same time as me," she says. "If I'd have known, I never—I never would've—"

"Annie," I say quickly. My chest is suddenly tight. "Let's not— We don't have to talk about this now." Here, in my bedroom, at whatever o'clock. Not when my body is still humming from the thought of tonight.

"Okay," she murmurs.

The silence returns except for the constant buzz from my neighbor's air-conditioning unit outside. But now my brain is occupied by different thoughts, stuck in a nervous, never-ending loop. If Annie had known Ryan left at the same time as her, she never would've what? Left? Died? Bought that pair of Birkenstocks? Maybe this is the moment I've been waiting for, the big explanation, the big apology. Because even though the thought of admitting it out loud makes me want to scrape my skin off with a spoon, part of me did, in some pathetic way, expect some kind of sorry from her. Something at the beginning, when she first got back, where she could just clear away the fog of the last two years that still lingered over our heads, and we could move on. I didn't necessarily need an explanation, just some sort of acknowledgment. That she *did* ditch me, and that it was wrong. That I'm not just someone she could throw away and pick up again like a mediocre Netflix show.

"Annie?" I whisper. She doesn't answer. I roll onto my side and squint through the inky blackness. "Annie?" I say again, louder.

But she's already asleep.

TWELVE

DAYS UNTIL ANNIE LEBLANC DIES: 19

The Cider Valley Apple Orchard sits on the outskirts of Lennon as you cross in from the tiny town of Santa Ysabel. At thirty acres, Cider Valley is the biggest of Lennon's seven apple orchards and easily the prettiest. In the fall, the rows and rows of apple trees hang heavy with red and green apples, the ground so covered in them, your shoes smell sweet for days. It's the perfect spot for a wedding, especially in the summer when the sun snakes between the branches and leaves the ground looking speckled and gold. Jody's lucky she got the date that she did; or actually, I'm lucky, because I'm the one who got Terri Morton to bribe Cider Valley's owner with the promise of them being the Country Kitchen's exclusive supplier during October—our busiest month—in exchange for them adding another day on which the venue is available for weddings. But today, as I follow Jody, Dr. David, and Claire, Cider Valley's events manager, from the clubhouse into the orchard's central courtyard, it is a less than perfect venue. Because apparently today is the one day of the year in Lennon that it rains.

Or almost rains. The sky is doing that weird thing where it looks dark and heavy all at once, as though the clouds are filled with marbles waiting to drop. There's no doubt that it'll storm; it's just a question of when.

"So, here's where we'll set up all the tables," Claire says as she waves her hand around half of the courtyard. "I've got written down that you'll have ten tables. Is that still right?"

"Yep," Jody says.

"Eleven," I interject. Jody looks at me. "Dr. David's cousins pushed their trip to Disney World back, so they're coming now."

Dr. David sighs and mumbles, "Joy."

Claire scribbles this new information onto the clipboard in her hand. In my arms is the box of centerpieces Jody and I have spent way too many hours making. They're mason jars we'd been saving under the kitchen sink for the last two months slathered in sticky Mod Podge and antique newspapers. There'll be six at each table; in them will sit tiny tea lights that, when lit up, will illuminate the newsprint and create a hazy glow around the orchard.

In the center of the courtyard is a rustic-looking gazebo, its weathered wooden posts wrapped in dense ivy. I set the box of centerpieces down just beside the gazebo's steps and pull Jody's wedding binder out of my backpack. After the final walk-through is over, I'll send Claire a recap of our meeting in an email.

"What about the lanterns?" I say to Claire. "You guys got our payment for that, right?"

This is a trick question. I know they did because I already asked in an email, and they confirmed it. But I need to triple-check.

Claire nods. I write this down.

Beside the central courtyard is the barn-looking building that is Cider Valley's clubhouse. It's where tourists who come to the orchard for apple-picking grab their old-timey baskets during apple season. Its kitchen facilities also mean it's where they stop for coffees, subpar apple pie, and, in our wedding guests' case, almond-encrusted salmon fillets or teriyaki chicken. Next to that is a line of incredibly tall apple trees that wrap all the way around the courtyard. On Jody's wedding day, market lights interspersed with paper lanterns will be strung between the apple trees and the gazebo, transforming the courtyard into a star-shaped landing pad that will be, if we play our cards right, visible from outer space.

Claire and I go back and forth about the rest of the wedding details as Jody stands beside me and pretends like she's had anything to do with planning this. The wedding cake will be delivered the morning of the wedding, as will the tables and dinnerware, which will be set up by the caterers. This will be followed by the florist, who has been instructed to fill approximately one large vase per table with white hydrangeas and five smaller vases per table with a handful of baby's breath.

A loud crack rings out from above us, and within seconds rain is unleashed from the sky. Grabbing the box of centerpieces, I scramble up the stairs to the gazebo, my clothes already mostly soaked through. I press the hem of my shirt into the most recent page in the binder, trying to blot out the raindrops that've already streaked my handwriting. Claire walks to the other side of the gazebo with Dr. David as she points to the stretch of grass where they'll hold the ceremony.

"At least it's raining today, which means we're not due for another downpour until four years from now," Jody says, sidling up to me.

"Yeah, maybe before global warming," I say, a little more irritably than I mean to.

The fact that it's raining right now has only reminded me that Lennon does, in fact, get rain, which means it could rain on Jody's wedding day, which means all of this could be ruined.

Jody frowns. "I thought global warming means everything is getting hotter," she says.

"Global warming can mean literally anything," I say back.

"Wilson, I'm joking." Jody sets a hand on my shoulder, which, to my surprise, actually makes me relax. "You've done an awesome job. The fact that we're even having the wedding here is a miracle. Everything's basically done."

I take in a deep breath, trying to keep my heartbeat steady. "I still have to finish the playlist," I say. "Plus, I need to send a game plan to Pam and everybody else about the rehearsal dinner and the morning of the wedding, because someone will have to let the cake people in, otherwise—"

"Wilson," Jody says, cutting me off. "It will get done. And if it doesn't get done, life will go on."

I know she's just trying to be helpful, but this statement still annoys me. Of course she thinks things will get done, or that life will go on. That's because I'm the one doing them. I'm the one making sure life goes on. And if everything falls apart, it'll be my fault.

From my back pocket, my phone buzzes. I retrieve it and

tap on my texts, where, underneath the same unknown number that'd sent me Grant's address, there now sits a picture of some scraggly coyotes and two new messages.

Unknown
HAVE YOU SEEN THESE COYOTES?
Unknown
WANTED: Evil coyotes suspected of stealing innocent teenage boy's clothes Wednesday night in Lennon. Armed and very, very dangerous. $10,000 reward.

Mark's number is still unknown in my phone because even after he'd texted me Grant's address, I couldn't bring myself to save it. The whole idea of him wanting to talk to me still felt preposterous, like some freak accident doomed to never repeat itself. But at the sight of his texts now, I can feel myself blushing like an idiot.

"What're you looking at?" Jody says. She cranes her neck so she can see my phone screen. "Who's messaging you?"

"Wow, invasive much?" I say, hugging my phone to my chest.

"Is it someone from the party?"

Jody says this in a way that makes it perfectly clear she's been desperate to talk about the party, but I've been holing myself up inside my room avoiding her. Now I'm out in the open, a deer with no shelter as the hunters close in. Instead of looking at my mother, I focus on the way the raindrops gather along the bottom rim of the gazebo roof before dripping onto the railing below.

"I don't know what you're talking about," I say.

"Oh, come on," Jody says. She's dangerously close to whining. "What did you do? Did you talk to anyone?"

At this, I give her my worst glare. "No, I went there as a social experiment," I say. "I just sat in a corner and observed my specimens until somebody called the cops and had me arrested for creeping everyone out."

"I'm just asking," Jody says. "You said so yourself, it was your first real party. I didn't know if you talked to anyone, you know . . . special."

"*Special?*" I say. "Who are you, my grandma? And even if I did, I wouldn't tell you. The last time I talked to you about that kind of stuff, you invited her entire family over."

"How many times do I have to apologize for that?" she says. "It was a year ago. I think it's time to move on."

The rain has reduced from a downpour to a drizzle. Dr. David braves it and follows Claire out onto the grass, where she's gesturing animatedly at an oversize gopher hole.

"Was Ryan there?" Jody asks.

"Yeah," I say slowly. "Why?"

She shrugs. "Well, I know things between her and Annie didn't end so well."

I open my mouth to protest, to accuse her of reading my notebook or gossiping about me with Pam, who works a few doors down from the Country Kitchen at the Thrifty Coyote, but then I remember that Jody knows about the fight at the Fish Grotto, but not because I told her; the restaurant called her, Mrs. LeBlanc, and Terri after they finally pried the last shrimp out of Ryan's clenched hands.

Instead I swallow. "Things with them are still . . . off," I say.

For a second, it occurs to me that I could tell Jody about the possibility of Annie staying back for good. Shove this impossible task onto someone else if only for a few minutes, feel the weightlessness of just having to exist without worrying about saving my best friend's sort-of life. But I know somehow, Jody would accidentally mention it in front of Annie or hint about it too openly. Something super unsubtle like elbow Annie in the ribs and say, *It wouldn't be the* end *of you to give Ryan a second chance. Eh? Eh?!*

"They're bound to be," Jody says. "Didn't Ryan throw french fries at Annie's head?"

"Shrimp," I say.

Jody nods somberly. "Sounds like Ryan."

"I just want us to all be friends again, for things to go back to how they were," I say. Telling Jody even this, being so open, feels weird, like something squishy and unfamiliar in my hand. My mother is annoying, maybe the most annoying person in the world; but at the same time, I can't pretend that confiding in her, confiding in *someone,* doesn't feel good. That the tables are finally turned in the direction they should be. "But every time they get within three feet of each other, they both get so weird."

"Maybe they just need to be reminded of the good stuff," Jody says. "You know, before Ryan hurtled shellfish across the table."

I scuff my foot against the wooden floor of the gazebo, where moss is creeping in around the edges of the planks. I'll need to bring this up to Claire. Does she have a power washer that could clean it up? Where could I get a power washer?

"What do you mean?" I say.

"Well, they were obviously friends for a reason. Maybe they just need to be shown why, and then they'll forget about all the bad stuff." Jody folds her arms across her chest and rocks back on her heels. "Like, okay, my best friend when I was twelve was

Britney Rogers, and when I say we were best friends, I mean we were *best friends*. We did everything together. Our families even spent Thanksgiving together a few times. But when I got my first job, she still wasn't working and she started expecting me to pay for everything. I drove everywhere, I bought her movie tickets and food whenever we went out with our friends. And she had money; her dad owned Ma's Diner. When she went to college in Santa Barbara, I was honestly glad she was gone. It meant I could actually afford new clothes and didn't have to listen to her emotionally blackmail me when I didn't have enough money for the both of us to do things. But then a few years went by and we didn't really hang out, and I started to wonder why we stopped being friends. So when she came back from college one summer and asked if I wanted to hang out like old times, I was kind of excited. I'd never been closer to a best friend since Britney."

Jody stares up at the domed ceiling of the gazebo, a dreamy smile on her face.

"So what happened?" I say, edging toward her. "Did you guys become friends again?"

"We had the best time," she says. "Honestly, it was like those years we spent apart never happened. She made us popcorn with M&M's, we watched *Titanic* and painted our nails until four in the morning. I felt so silly for ever thinking we shouldn't be friends."

I know most of what Jody says is actual trash, but for once she makes a good point. Of course Ryan and Annie don't know how to act around each other anymore; everything is new. It's like dropping two aliens onto Earth and expecting them to know about student loans and health insurance. If I could just remind Ryan and Annie about how things used to be between us, how they *could be* now, maybe it would trigger some sort of humanity in them. Something that suddenly made them not want to punch each other in the face.

"But what if by taking them back to that time, it reminds them of why they stopped being friends?" I say. Reminds them of why they ditched me.

Jody shrugs and gives me a sad smile. "I think that's a risk you're just gonna have to take."

I nod as this thought sinks in. I tried doing something completely out of character by going to the party, and look where that got me. Maybe nostalgia is all I've got left.

"Where's Britney now?" I say. "Did she move to Santa Barbara? How come I've never met her?"

Jody grimaces. "A week later she stole all my Red Hot Chili Peppers CDs and I remembered why I hated her." She sighs. "She still lives in Lennon. She waits tables at Heroes, which is why I refuse to eat there."

My stomach sinks, the vision of me, Ryan, and Annie wearing matching sets of denim overalls again getting fainter and fainter.

"I thought you hated Heroes because they always serve your food lukewarm."

Jody tilts her head from shoulder to shoulder. "That," she says, "and the fact that their head waitress is an asshole. Either way, no thank you." She must see my face drop, because she adds quickly, "The point is though, we reconnected and remembered what made us such great friends. Do the same thing with Ryan and Annie, and they'll see what they've been missing. Trust me."

Somehow, I'm not as sure.

THIRTEEN

DAYS UNTIL ANNIE LEBLANC DIES: 14

As Annie and I pull into the tiny parking lot outside the bike shop, my nerves are so strong I feel dizzy. At every stoplight for the last ten minutes, I laid my head on the hot leather of the steering wheel in Jody's car and took deep breaths, reminding myself I had to keep my cool or else Annie would know something was up.

Now that we're near the coast, the air is whip-thin and crisp. I try to even myself out with another deep breath, feeling as it fills every crevice in my lungs. On a map, Coronado Island is no bigger than a speck of dust. Half of it is a naval base and the other half is tiny and yet has outrageously expensive houses. It's been Jody's favorite place on Earth for as long as I can remember. Every Christmas Eve after dinner in downtown San Diego, Cass would drive us around Coronado to look at the houses lit up with lights while Jody debated which one we'd buy when she won the lottery.

The rectangular parking lot is for a small strip of buildings that consist mostly of cafés and restaurants with the bike shop all the way at the end. Hundreds of bikes crowd the window, hanging from racks bolted into the ceiling and lining the side-walk outside. Annie follows me as I sit on the wooden bench in front of the shop, hugging my backpack to my chest.

"Is this the part where you tell me why we came to Coronado?" Annie says. She's wearing the tie-dye shirt she got from the Thrifty Coyote, the one that says EAT TOFU, SAVE THE RAIN-FOREST on the front.

I shake my head. "Not yet. Almost."

I glance down at the time on my phone. Just a couple more minutes. In my shorts pocket is my last Atomic Fireball, its plastic wrapper crinkling underneath my fingers. I roll it around in my hand as I search for something else to talk about. Anything.

Apparently, Annie can read my mind, because she says, "Can you at least tell me what happened with you and Mark?"

My whole face practically goes up in flames. This is not the distraction I wanted. She and I still haven't talked about the night of Grant's party, her argument with Ryan. The next morn-ing, her parents came to pick her up just after nine, giving Annie enough time to change and shove in her mouth an old burger bun she found at the back of my fridge.

"What are you talking about?" I say, tilting my face away so she won't see me blush. "Nothing happened."

"Yeah, right," Annie says. "He was flirting his face off with you."

"He was drunk."

"So? Even I could see he was waiting for you to take him into the woods and make him into an honest man."

I groan and slap a hand over my eyes. "When you say stuff like that, I genuinely feel sick."

Palm trees line the parking lot, cloaking Jody's little blue car in shadows. My arms prickle with goose bumps as a breeze rushes by, despite the fact that it's at least eighty degrees outside.

"Seriously, though, nothing happened," I say as I smooth the bumps down on my arm. "We, like, held hands a little bit and then maybe he would've kissed me, but Cass showed up and did his whole macho cop routine and scared Mark off."

The sound that comes out of Annie's throat can only be described as earsplitting. "I knew it, I knew it, I knew it," she sings. "Is he texting you?"

My hand instinctively skims the rectangular shape of my phone in my pocket. "A little bit," I say. "He's working today, so we probably won't talk that much."

Since Mark sent me those texts about the coyotes, we've talked a little bit about the party and how Grant was grounded until infinity after his parents got a call from the cops and had to drive home in the middle of the night from their hotel in Arizona, where they were visiting Grant's older brother. Nothing about the fact that he may or may not have wanted to kiss me.

"Speaking of, can I borrow your phone?" Annie holds her hand out. "I left my phone in my dad's car and I need to text my mom."

I hand Annie my phone as a man with his daughter strapped into a plastic seat on the back of his bike wheels his way out of the bike shop. After Annie's finished texting and pockets my phone, she swivels around on the bench to watch them.

"Is this the same bike shop Jody used to take us to? I thought the building was red."

"It was, but that guy sold it to somebody new."

I read about it on the shop's website last night, when I checked that the place still existed.

Annie turns back around, her hands pulling at the hem of her shorts. "God, your mom used to take us here every summer," she says. "Can we still get ice cream from the hotel on the beach?"

I pat my backpack and say, "Jody specifically contributed to the ice cream fund."

When I told my mother that morning about my plan, she squealed with excitement and gave me twenty bucks for ice cream. Her especially generous mood could've had something to do with the fact that Pam was only five minutes away from driving her and the rest of their friends to Las Vegas for Jody's bachelorette party, but I tucked the money into my wallet without saying anything.

Right on cue, a black SUV pulls into the parking lot, dwarfing Jody's car as it turns into the adjacent space. Annie is staring at the curb, but I can't look away from the driver, my fingertips tingling with nerves and fear and a little bit of excitement.

When the door slams, Annie follows my gaze toward the girl in the parking lot, whose hands are now balled into fists at her sides.

"Are you kidding me?" she and Annie say at the same time.

It's Ryan.

Before I even get a chance to speak, Ryan is already back in her car. When I chase after her and yank on the driver's-side door, it's locked. She clutches her hands around the steering wheel, her expression hard.

"Just hear me out," I say through the glass. "I know it was wrong to trick you, but I knew you wouldn't come here if I didn't lie."

Ryan won't even look at me. Her eyes are fixed on some unspecified point over the dashboard as she locks her arms over her chest. "Yeah, and maybe that should've been a red flag," she says. "You literally lured me out here." She shakes her head. "I knew it was weird that you wanted to meet in Coronado instead of Lennon. I just drove an hour for absolutely nothing."

Technically it should have taken her longer than an hour to get here, but the way Ryan drives, I probably shouldn't be surprised. Last night on the phone I made it sound like I wanted to talk to her about the argument at Grant's house, but I couldn't do it in Lennon. Too many bad memories. It was a long shot that she'd even agree, but when she grunted her reluctant response, I knew I had them both.

"You made me feel like a dick just so I'd come out here," she says.

"No, you feel like a dick because you acted like a dick," I say. I practiced this part on the drive here, imagining this exact scenario. I was going to be strong. Determined. Honest. "I'm sorry for lying, but if you feel guilty, that's not my fault. All I said was I wanted to talk to you about the party; I didn't say anything about what. If you brought your own feelings to the table, that's on you."

Annie approaches us but stays far enough back so that if Ryan has a secret stash of shrimp in her car, she won't be able to reach her. "I thought we were supposed to be riding bikes around Coronado," Annie says quietly from behind me.

I turn so that I'm speaking to them both equally. "We are," I say. "That's why we're here." Annie's face shares the same skepticism as Ryan's, except hers isn't as twinged with anger. "Look, we used to love coming here. And I've never pulled a card like this before and I won't do it again, but you both owe me after Grant's house. You were like two hyenas fighting over a dead deer, except I was the dead deer and you weren't fighting over who was gonna eat me; you were fighting about who killed me in the first place."

"Hyenas don't eat deer," Ryan says. "How would that even make sense?"

"Yeah, where do you think hyenas live?" Annie says.

"Okay, fine," I say. "Then it's like—it's like when . . ." I can't think of anything smart to say with them both staring at me. "Okay, so it's like . . ."

Ryan rolls her eyes up to the ceiling of her car. "This is so painful," she grumbles.

"Well, look," I exclaim. "You can bond over the fact that I make bad comparisons." I glance between them both, desperate, but neither of them laughs. I can feel this opportunity slipping through my fingers, pulling me toward my last resort. The last resort I swore I wouldn't have to do. "Bike riding around here used to mean so much to us. Remember when we got that weird four-person bike-cart thing and it took us three hours to get to the other side of the island because Annie kept checking Twitter instead of pedaling?"

"Harry Styles had just released his first solo album," Annie interjects. "I'm sorry—was I supposed to ignore that?"

"Oh my god, you're so vapid," Ryan says. She twists her keys in the ignition and the SUV's engine comes to life.

"Wait!" I shriek, panic thick in my throat. I splay my hands on the glass of her window. "At least give it a chance. We'll get ice cream at the Hotel Del and eat it at the beach. It'll be just like it used to."

"Except it won't," Ryan fires back. "Wilson, we're not the same people anymore. I don't want to spend the day fighting and wheeling her ass around."

"You won't fight," I say. "There'll be no fighting."

Annie laughs quietly. "Pretty sure that's impossible for her."

As Ryan clicks her seat belt across her chest and adjusts her rearview mirror, it sinks in that I've got only one option left before she speeds out of the parking lot. My last resort.

"Look, I have an idea. Something that's going to guarantee you guys don't fight."

At this, Ryan glances over.

"But first, you have to turn off the car. Trust me, you'll want to hear this."

Indecision flickers over Ryan's face as she looks between me and Annie. Finally, after a few seconds, she twists the car keys again, plunging the parking lot back into silence minus the sounds of seagulls squawking and smooth jazz playing from one of the restaurants.

I rifle around my backpack and close my fingers on the small rectangular shape at the bottom of my bag. My hands are shaking when they finally lock around the hard plastic and pull it into the light, revealing a small battery-powered razor.

"I know you guys can do this," I say, my eyes trained on the razor's long plastic teeth. According to the internet, it's top-of-the-line, definitely high-powered enough to scrape my hair off in a few strokes. Dr. David accidentally left it under the bathroom sink after he and Jody went to a wedding together a couple of weeks ago. "We were best friends for like ten years before everything exploded, so I know you can ride a bike in the same general vicinity for forty-five minutes without screaming at each other."

"She can't even—" Annie starts to say, but I hold up a hand to stop her.

"I'm so sure you can do this that I'm going to make you a deal." I glance over at Ryan. "If you guys can go the entire way without fighting, I'll shave my head."

Ryan splutters an incredulous laugh as Annie grabs the razor from my hand. "You'll *shave* your *head*?" Annie says, looking down at the razor as though it's a bomb.

"Yes," I insist. "I'm finally going to fulfill my Sinéad O'Connor dream from the D.A.R.E. pageant. I thought you guys would be stoked."

"Isn't your mom going to freak out?" Annie says. "My mom would freak out."

The idea came to me the night before as Jody was packing for her bachelorette party. She was piling every last bit of pleather she had left in her wardrobe into an oversize suitcase as Sinéad O'Connor's cover of "All Apologies" blasted from her phone. It reminded me of the D.A.R.E. pageant, the years afterward, and all the things Ryan and Annie swore they'd do if I shaved my head. Though I know most if not all of the time it was just a joke, maybe this would be the one time it wasn't. My last chance.

"Are you kidding me?" I say. "Jody will eat this up. Sinéad O'Connor is her third favorite style icon from the nineties, behind Cher from *Clueless* and Gwen Stefani."

"Do you have any idea what year it is right now?" Annie says. "The Sinéad O'Connor reference was outdated when we were ten. It's even more outdated now." She waves this thought away. "Never mind. Even if you were actually prepared to keep your word, which, there's no way you are—"

"I am," I say. My fingers tighten around the razor. "I promise. If you guys make it the whole way to the Hotel Del on completely neutral terms, I swear I'll shave my head. Plus, Sinéad O'Connor is never outdated." They both stare back at me with matching bewildered expressions. "This was always your bargaining chip," I say. "Now I'm finally agreeing and you're getting weird about it?"

"That was a joke," Ryan says.

"But why?" Annie says to me. "What's in this for you?"

"Being right," I lie. "I know you guys can do this, and if this is what it takes to show you, then fine. I'll be bald for a few months."

"It's going to take a lot longer than a few months—"

Annie's cut off by the sound of Ryan opening her car door. She retrieves her purse from the passenger seat and tosses her keys inside.

"Fine," she says, slamming the door behind her. "Let's do this."

It's Annie's turn to give a confused laugh. "Are you kidding?" she says.

Ryan skips up the curb toward the bike shop, the skirt of her floral dress fluttering behind her. When she turns back around, her eyes are on me, her mouth turning up into a smile that makes my skin prickle.

"I don't lose, Wilson," she says. "You know this about me. So you'd better hope you've got a good-shaped head."

I fully expected to have to shave my head by the end of this bike ride. Vindicated and like a majestic mermaid, I would stand at the edge of Coronado Beach with my hair falling down in clumps as the razor buzzed across my scalp, all in the name of friendship. What I did not expect was for Ryan and Annie to stay completely silent from the moment we left the bike shop, each one of us teetering on our slightly-too-tall bikes, a heavy quiet weighing between us.

As we pedal onto the pathway, the bay opens up on our left, down a slight cliff of rocks. The downtown San Diego skyline stretches over the water, looking as perfect as a screen saver, the endless blue sky expanding overhead. On the other side of the path is an open park, just one long stretch of green grass. Ryan pedals ahead, her long brown hair whipping in the wind behind her.

Before we set off, I should've made some sort of rules. Something like, we all actually have to talk, that they can't win just by avoiding each other. That by the end of this, I won't be friendless *and* hairless.

"Have you heard from your mom?" Annie asks as she evens her pace out so our bikes run parallel on the path.

I shake my head, my hair getting trapped under the helmet's strap. Maybe for the last time. The drive will take Jody and her friends at least five hours, so the earliest I should expect to hear from my mother is later this afternoon, when they check in.

"Where's your mom?" Ryan shouts back.

"Bachelorette trip in Vegas," I say.

"For Ashley's seventeenth birthday party," Annie says, "her parents bought everyone tickets to see Lady Gaga's Vegas show. The dress code was you had to go in one of her weird looks. Ashley wore the Kermit the Frog dress."

I nod as though I'd know what my mom having enough money to do something like that for me and my friends would feel like. My mom, who's currently on her way to stay at Circus Circus, a hotel infamous for being the cheapest and most disgusting one in a land infamous for being cheap and disgusting.

Ryan appears at my other side, her eyes glowering. "What'd you go as?" she asks. "Besides a thirsty show-off."

The question is asked innocently enough, as though Ryan is genuinely curious. If you only listened to the tone of her voice and not the question itself, you wouldn't know Ryan was being antagonistic except by the way Annie glares back. Worry swirls in my stomach as I prepare for the oncoming argument.

But eventually Annie swallows and says with heroic evenness, "I'm pretty sure that's every Lady Gaga costume since the dawn of time."

I laugh before I can stop myself, and instead of biting back with something that'll cut a little deeper, Ryan gnaws her lip and nods, as though accepting Annie's one-up.

The pathway narrows as we cross under the darkness of the giant concrete bridge that arcs over San Diego Bay, connecting Coronado Island to the mainland. Cars rush over us as we bike through and turn right, swerving onto the path that edges along a golf course. We fall into silence again as we follow the gentle slope of the bike path that eventually spills us out onto a wide street busy with cars. We straddle our bikes, feet planted on the blacktop as we wait for a gap in the traffic. When one appears, we pedal across the street, where a long line of sweet little houses extends around a bend and leads toward the beach.

As we get closer and closer to the hotel, dread squeezes tighter in my chest. Only fifteen more minutes and we'll be there, where Annie and Ryan still won't be friends and I'll have less hair than a naked mole rat.

We curve with the sidewalk, now facing a suburban street with more beach-style houses. At the end of the block underneath a giant eucalyptus tree is a small one-story house in a pristine cream, with baby-blue edges and a yellow front door. Normally I wouldn't know what a eucalyptus tree looks like, but this is the house Jody would always make us drive past at Christmas, the first place she'd go to spend her millions. She'd keep everything about the house the same—the rosebushes under the porch, the white lantern lights hanging on either side of the front door—but she'd put a swinging chair underneath the eucalyptus tree, where I could read comics, Jody could paint her nails, and Bernie could quiz us on some useless topic, like chemistry.

I'm at the very back of our silent bike train, so Annie and Ryan don't notice right away when I hit my brakes in front of the house. Because underneath the tree is the exact swinging chair Jody said she'd buy, a big wooden bench with an off-white awning hanging over the top. And she was right: it is perfect.

After dropping my bike onto the lawn, I pat my pockets, looking for my phone. The sharp smell of eucalyptus reminds me of Jody when she gets off work, all doctory and clinical. Finally, having noticed me missing, Ryan and Annie circle back and walk their bikes in the street until they reach the house.

"What're you doing?" Annie asks, one hand held up to shield her face from the sun.

"Trying to find my phone," I say.

I drop my backpack onto the sidewalk and lean down to unzip it, but before I can, something shoves me from behind, knocking me forward so I have to reach my hands out onto the grass to steady myself. A man in a red T-shirt and denim shorts barrels past and glares at me from over his shoulder.

"Sorry," I say, even though I'm not the one who bumped into him.

"You're standing in the middle of the sidewalk," he calls out to me. "Get your head out of your ass."

I open my mouth to respond, but the shock of someone I don't even know swearing at me punches me straight in the throat. But before I can say anything back, something else rushes past me; this time it's air as Ryan charges onto the sidewalk.

"How about you watch where the fuck you're going?" she says. "She's literally been there for two seconds and you just bashed into her."

The guy turns around again, a look of pure disgust on his face. "If you stand in the middle of the sidewalk, prepare to get bashed."

Annie drops her bike into the street and joins us on the curb. "Look," she says as she puts her hands on her hips, "you're doing a really great job of showing the three of us what it looks like to be a sad, angry little dude whose funeral is attended by his mom and nobody else, but why don't you do us all a favor and go back to the misogynistic corner of the dark web you crawled out of and stop screaming at random girls in the street?"

The man takes a step forward, his hands clenching and un-clenching at his sides. Under the sun, his face is basically the same color as his shirt, beads of sweat speckling his forehead.

"What did you say to me, you little bitch?"

"Guys," I say nervously, but they both ignore me.

"Oh my god, *yes*," Ryan says with a bark of a laugh. "Please come charging at three teenage girls in broad daylight. That is such a macho look for you."

"Honestly, dude"—Annie brushes dust from her hands—"I

would love nothing more than to kick you in your teeny, tiny wiener." She gives him her sweetest smile. "Believe me when I say I have literally nothing to lose by ensuring you never procreate."

The man's eyes shift between the two of them, weighing what to say next. By this point, a few people have assembled on the lawns of nearby houses, watching. He notices them too, his grayish mouth flattening into a line.

Finally he just shakes his head and mutters, "Crazy bitches."

He turns away, his pace considerably faster than it was before. The sounds of him mumbling angrily to himself filter back to us, but I can't make out what he's saying, which is probably for the best.

Ryan snorts with laughter, her hands clutched around her stomach. "Oh my god, look at how fast he's going," she says as he disappears down the street. "What a little shit."

And then something miraculous happens. Ryan lifts her hand toward Annie, and instead of making some bad joke about how the lines on Ryan's palm suggest she's going to die a spinster who survives solely on human tears, Annie gives her a high five. At the sight of it, I blink so hard it feels like my eyes are spasming, trying to convince myself that this is actually happening. Even Ryan and Annie look stunned, the slap of their hands meeting bringing them back to reality. They both stare at each other with matching expressions, Ryan clutching her hand against her chest as though it's broken.

"We should probably go," she says eventually.

Ryan weaves around Annie, careful not to touch her as she moves toward her bike and retrieves it from the street. Annie nods, following suit.

"Yeah, definitely," she says.

"Did you find your phone?" Ryan asks.

"Oh, no," I say. "It doesn't matter anymore."

As they both hop back onto their bikes, everything in me is fighting the urge to squeal. Because I know that if I do, I'll only bring more attention to their obvious embarrassment, effectively murdering any chance of them bonding again for real. I don't even care that it's me getting screamed at by a random middle-aged man in the street that brought them together. If it meant Ryan and Annie would be friends again, I'd let him and all eight million of his angry internet friends berate me for hours and turn it into a podcast.

Annie and Ryan are practically two blocks away when I finally snap my attention back to the street. I have to rush for my bike and pump my legs on the pedals so hard that my thighs burn. Annie glances over her shoulder at me when I finally catch up. When she sees the goofy smile on my face, she rolls her eyes, but I don't care because she's smiling too.

FOURTEEN

The sand is warm and powdery underneath my feet as I trudge over the ridge leading down to the sea. Behind me towers the Hotel Del Coronado, a massive white castle with deep red spires that poke up into the sky. I weave around the families and kids throwing footballs and sprinting in and out of the brownish waves, making my way toward a cluster of boulders, against which the waves crash in big, explosive bursts. Annie is standing beside them, her back to me and her hands cradled in the pockets of her shorts.

Once the three of us finally reached the hotel, Ryan and I offered to get the ice cream while Annie found us a good spot on the beach, but after waiting in the line—which extended up the stairs from the ice cream shop and wrapped around to the front of the hotel near the valet—for twenty minutes, I went in search of Annie to give her an update.

The waves are the tallest I've ever seen them out here, roaring deeply as they collapse in on themselves. It's too loud for Annie to hear me calling her name until I'm only a few feet away, but from the moment I reach her, I can tell something's wrong. Her long blond hair streaks across her face, whipping against her nose and getting caught in her mouth. Her cheeks are wet and red, but not from the sea spray misting over the rocks; she's crying.

I trace her gaze out to the waves, looking for the source. A cute family of dolphins or a really harrowing rescue we'll all applaud when the lifeguard drags the grateful near-victim back to shore, but there's nothing. Just water.

"What happened?" I say. I haven't left her and Ryan alone together all afternoon, for fear that one or both might try to escape or murder the other. But that doesn't mean Ryan couldn't have muttered something under her breath when I was out of earshot. "Did Ryan say something?"

Annie shakes her head and wipes her nose with the back of her hand. "That night," she says, smiling sadly before she turns her attention back to the sea.

I open my mouth to ask what night she's talking about, but then, as another tear, muted by the sound of the waves, slips down her face, I stop. Though Annie died at home, the water must be making her think of that night. The night she died, her drowning. It's so unexpected, this sudden reference to Annie's death after our bike ride, after near weeks of virtual normalcy and pretending like it never happened, but of course it's on Annie's mind. How could it not be?

"I'll never be in love or see the *Mona Lisa* in person," she says. "I'll never know what the rainforest smells like."

My muscles tense as I search the shoreline for Ryan, wondering what to do. Part of me wants to back away, give Annie space with her grief. But the last time I backed away, my best friend died and I wasn't there. It's something I'll never be able to take back, and probably couldn't have even controlled in the first place, but it doesn't mean history needs to repeat itself. That I can't control how I respond here.

Without another word, I slip my arm around Annie's waist and lay my head on her shoulder. There's nothing I can think to say that will make this better or less real, so I just push myself into her side, hoping my presence is enough.

Annie simply rests her head on top of mine and cries.

Ryan, Annie, and I stretch out on the beach, our cups of ice cream resting in our laps. I have coffee ice cream with Oreos and fudge, Annie has strawberry cheesecake, and Ryan has mint chocolate chip. After a few more minutes of standing on the beach, Annie gave me a quiet nod before we found a spot to sit on the dry sand. We didn't say anything more about it, much less that night, but judging by the way Annie instantly started talking about the time she buried her mom's legs in the sand at Torrey Pines Beach and she got bitten to death by sand fleas, I'm pretty sure she preferred it that way.

"Thanks for your help," Ryan said to me when she found us, our three cups of ice cream balanced precariously in her arms. But when she saw Annie's red eyes and still-wet cheeks, she closed her mouth and distributed our ice cream in silence.

When we finish, Annie stacks our cups into a tower and wedges them in the sand so they don't blow away.

"Okay, hand over the razor, baby Sinéad," Ryan says, wiping the corners of her mouth with her thumb. "Let's do this."

"What?" Annie says. "She's not actually shaving her head."

"Yes, she is. We kept up our end of the bargain. Now Wilson has to shave her head."

I let out a long sigh and retrieve the razor from my backpack. "She's right," I say.

"She is not right," Annie says. Ryan and I both give her a look. "Okay, *technically* she's right," she relents. "But that doesn't mean you should do it. In fact"—Annie lifts up her right hand—"I officially give up my half of the bargain. Wilson, you do not need to shave your head on my account."

"Fine," Ryan says as she snatches the razor from my hand. "Do it on mine."

"Ryan," Annie snaps. "We're supposed to be helping her *into* the twenty-first century, not leaving her to rot in the nineties." She gives me a pained smile. "No offense."

"We're not doing this again," I say. "I said I was gonna shave my head, so I'm gonna shave my head."

I realize as I'm saying this that I'm actually arguing in favor of going bald prematurely, but making this bargain has gotten us this far. This new peace between Ryan and Annie feels precious and fragile, and I don't want to break it already by going back on my word.

The razor comes to life in Ryan's hand with a high-pitched buzz.

"You're doing this *now*?" Annie says, leaning across me.

"Why do you think I brought the razor?"

"As a prop!"

Ryan shrugs. "If we do it on the beach, we don't have to clean all the hair up."

I pull in a deep breath. "Just do it."

"What if the razor dies right in the middle of it and you're not done? Are you just gonna walk around with half a shaved head?" Annie says.

"First of all, that's a very popular hairstyle right now," Ryan says. "Second of all, the razor runs on batteries, so if they die, we'll go buy more."

Annie bites her lip. It's obvious she's trying to think of another excuse to slow us down, but she's coming up short. Ryan shuffles around on her knees so that she's kneeling in front of me, the razor poised at the top of my forehead. Her eyes flick around my face, searching. She's waiting for me to break, to take it all back, to start laughing and tell her it was just a joke, like all the other times. But she's not going to find it. When it comes to making things work between the three of us, I'm serious.

When the razor first hits my scalp, a shiver runs down my back, the metal vibrating against my skull. Ryan gently guides it from my hairline all the way down to my neck, long strips of hair falling delicately onto my shoulders. Her left hand is cold as her fingertips press lightly into my neck, holding my head steady and sending little lightning bolts zipping down my spine from where her skin meets mine.

"I can't believe this is happening," Annie whispers from beside me, her hands against her cheeks.

"Believe it, baby," Ryan says from above me.

I know I should be nervous, but I'm not. I feel weirdly powerful. I brought Ryan and Annie together again. It worked. I did this. For once, I feel fearless. For once, I feel strong.

. . .

At the sight of myself in the ice cream store's bathroom mirror, I burst into tears. In what I can now only describe as my utter state of delusion, I failed to seriously consider what I would look like with a shaved head, which is not an alt-rock star, but a Q-tip with eyes.

"You look weirdly amazing," Annie says for the forty millionth time. Back on the beach, my hair sits in a pile on the sand, enough to look like a small dog taking a nap. "Not many people can look cool with a shaved head. It's basically you and Millie Bobby Brown."

I can tell my crying is making her uncomfortable by the way she won't look me in the eyes. This only makes me cry harder. Ryan stands with her back against the bathroom door and her hands crossed over her chest as she watches me in the mirror. I hate that I can't read her cool expression. Ever since we were kids, Ryan and her scowls have always been basically unreadable beyond conveying her general disapproval, which only made me crave her approval more. I wish more than anything I could hear what she's thinking, but I know that if I did, I'd probably feel even worse.

Reaching my hand up to feel my naked scalp, I instantly recoil. "Do you think I look weird?" I say to Ryan. I can't help it.

"No."

She says it with such little emotion, I can't tell if she's serious or just trying not to laugh. Annie pulls my phone out of her shorts pocket and grimaces at the screen. I forgot she had it.

"Maybe we should go get food or something," she says.

"In Coronado?" I say between hiccupping sobs. "Are you serious? All this fancy island has is black-tie-only restaurants and they definitely won't let in a skinhead like me." The last part comes out as a wail.

"What about PB?" Ryan says. "I can drive us."

"Yes, Pacific Beach!" Annie says. She retrieves my phone again and types something in. "That is a splendid idea."

We agree I'm not in a state of mind to drive, so Ryan takes us in her car. On the drive to find food, I lie across the back seats, tears dripping down my face sideways as I wonder how I'm ever going to go outside again. I'm going to have to become one of those people who have all their groceries delivered and are so pale, you can see the blue of their veins through their skin.

Annie, as if reading my mind, turns around from the front seat to look at me with a sad smile. "It's gonna grow back," she says. "Trust me, in three weeks, it's gonna be at least a centimeter long."

"In three weeks, I'm gonna—" I start to say, but then the realization of what's happening over the next three weeks hits me. "Holy shit, Jody's wedding is next week," I exclaim. "Oh my god, I'm gonna have my hair like this for my mom's wedding. It's going to be commemorated in pictures that I'm going to have to look at for the rest of my life. *Oh my god.*"

The tears that follow make my vision go so blurry, it's as if I'm underwater, the lights around me melting into hazy blobs as Ryan arcs off the highway and stops at an intersection.

"What is wrong with me?" I wail. "Why did nobody stop me?"

"I tried—" Annie begins, but Ryan shoots her a look that shuts her up.

Even though Ryan's back windows are tinted a murky black, a rainbow of colors pours in and drenches the seats in bright lights. It means we must be in Pacific Beach, a pseudo-hippie neighborhood that, as the name suggests, sits along the beach. The main road leading in from the highway extends all the way to the shore and is at first lined with grocery stores and apartment complexes. Eventually this narrows to a series of tacky bars and restaurants, all of which are remarkably quiet tonight. As Ryan parks in one of the spots along the main road, I bury my face in my hands.

The car door just beside my head swings open, letting in a rush of air that sends goose bumps speckling along my scalp. I didn't even know it was possible to get goose bumps on your head.

"Wear this."

Something soft lands on my face. I yank it down and hold it up: it's a gray UCSD sweatshirt. Ryan looms over me from the street as I sit up, my neck cracking from the awkward angle of lying across the three leather seats.

"Thanks," I say quietly as I pull the sweatshirt on and leave the hood up so it covers my naked head.

Annie and Ryan cross the street without a word to each other as I stand beside the SUV and watch them. I have the option to get back in the car and go to sleep, waiting patiently for me to wake up from what I'm realizing belatedly is my worst nightmare, but my stomach rumbles at the thought. The sun is slowly falling behind where Grand Avenue meets the beach, sending the sky into a blur of Starburst-colored pastels. A cloud shaped like a fire hydrant scuds along the bottom of the sun as I hug the sweatshirt hood tighter around my head and dash across the street and into a taco restaurant, where Annie stands at the counter ordering us California burritos.

The restaurant can barely be categorized as a hole-in-the-wall. It's only about ten feet wide by ten feet long, and that's including the counter and a small strip of space the guy behind it has between the register and the serving hatch. The three of us sit in a window booth whose chairs consist of hard laminated wood and nothing else. On the table is a bowl of tortilla chips with a glob of guacamole and sour cream in the middle, along with two Styrofoam cups whose insides are cherry red. Sitting across from me and Annie, Ryan nudges the cups in our direction.

"I still don't get how you dressing like Marilyn Monroe fits the theme of America the Beautiful," Ryan says.

Annie bites down on the straw poking out of her cup. "Because Marilyn Monroe was American and beautiful." She takes a long sip of her drink. "I feel like you're overcomplicating things."

"So, okay, let me get this straight." Ryan sets all ten fingertips on the surface of the table. "You're going to stand on top of the Fourth of July float dressed as Marilyn Monroe because she was pretty." She blinks. "I'm sorry. Am I blacking out, or is that not the most misogynistic bullshit you've ever heard?"

Annie smiles, the straw still between her teeth. "There's plenty of room for you on the float," she says.

Ryan scoffs. "Yeah, never."

I glance between the two of them, surprise poorly hidden on my face. "You invited her on the float?" I say to Annie.

Annie turns to me. "Was I not allowed to?"

"No—I mean, yeah, you were," I say as I shovel a tortilla chip into my mouth. "I just didn't think you—yeah."

As I'm speaking I realize I should probably stop, so as not to remind the two of them that only a few hours ago, they could barely be within three feet of each other.

Ryan sits up straight in her seat, her eyes focused on something over my shoulder. "What is my brother doing here?" she says.

Annie and I turn toward the taco shop's front door at the same time. Standing on the other side of the street, waiting for the stream of cars on Grand Avenue to slow down, is Mark Morton. His hands are shoved into the pockets of his black jeans, the thick red straps of a backpack looped around his shoulders and the wind blowing his hair across his face.

With one finger, Annie slides my phone toward me. "Surprise," she says weakly.

Instinctively, I pull down the strings on Ryan's sweatshirt, cinching the hood around my face until I look like I'm posing behind one of those giant wooden boards with the faces cut out.

"You called Mark Morton?" I say. "Why would you call Mark Morton? He's gonna see my head and think I joined a cult or something."

Mark Morton being physically repulsed by me will join the list of things I didn't consider before semi-impulse-shaving my head, behind the fact that I can under no fucking circumstances pull off a headscarf and wigs make my neck itch.

Ryan leans across the table. "I'm sorry, why are you talking to my brother?"

"I thought it'd be fun if we all hung out in San Diego," Annie says. She turns to me. "I invited him before you shaved your head, I swear."

"Then why didn't you tell me *before* I shaved my head?" I say.

"I told you not to do it," she insists.

"Yeah, but you could've said it was because Mark was coming out here."

Annie swivels around and eyes the restaurant's front door nervously. "Oh yeah, because that would've been super feminist. *Oh, Wilson, don't shave your head because a hot guy is coming to hang out and you don't want to look weird for him.*"

Ryan blinks as though someone has just blown sand into her eyes. "Did you just say *hot* in reference to my brother?"

"You seemed so confident about it," Annie says to me. "I didn't know you were gonna flip out, and by the time you did, he was already on his way. I couldn't just tell him not to come."

"Yes, you could have," I say. "You could've called him and said, *Hello, Mark, please do not come anymore. Goodbye.*"

I prop my elbows up on the table and dig my hands into my eyes. The one time somebody cool looks like they might actually like me, I shave my head.

"Excuse me, I realize I'm sounding like a broken record here," Ryan says, "but are we genuinely talking about my brother? The same guy who got a boner at my seventh-grade pool party?"

"I'm gonna throw up," I say, my stomach churning. "Oh my god, I'm actually gonna throw up."

There's a murmur of voices around me as the restaurant's front door dings open. I don't need to look up to know who's there.

"Whaddup, Moss?" Mark says, the bench groaning as he slides in beside Ryan. "Cool sweatshirt. You look like Luke Sky-walker."

I glance up as he reaches over and grabs a chip from the bowl, making sure it has enough guacamole on it before he drops it into his mouth. On his white T-shirt is a picture of a bulldog riding a skateboard, some album cover for a band I've never heard of.

"What're you doing here?" Ryan says.

Mark shrugs. "Crashing your day trip."

One of the guys from the shop brings over our burritos on a red plastic tray that he deposits in the middle of the table. Annie distributes the three fat rolls, each as chunky as my fist and wrapped in greasy wax paper. Wrapped inside the tortilla is steak, guacamole, cheese, and french fries, something I'd ordinarily be all over, but that now just makes me feel kind of sick. As I unpeel my burrito, I think of all the ways I can avoid Mark seeing my naked head: I could say I've developed an allergy to the sun, or that my body has somehow acclimatized itself to the weather of somewhere even warmer than Southern California, somewhere like Brazil, and is anyone else chilly in here? Or I could fake being sick and Uber back to the bike shop parking lot.

Sense points out that Mark will likely, at some point, see my hair before it grows to a normal length, but fear says that a year is not that long of a time to stay inside and away from the rest of the human race.

Annie swallows a bite of her burrito. "So," she says, a hint of nervousness in her voice I'm pretty sure only I can hear, "what do you guys wanna do after this?"

She doesn't bother looking at me as she asks this question, because she already knows my answer.

Mark drums his fingers against the table. "What if I told you we could go somewhere where all your dreams will come true?" he says.

"You know Harry Styles?" Annie says.

"Our cousin works at a karaoke sushi bar down the street," Mark says. "He'll let us in for free. Just think about it." Mark spreads his hands out in front of his face, painting the picture. "A private room, nobody can hear us. Ryan singing 'Gangnam Style.'"

There's a loud thump as Ryan kicks Mark under the table. He laughs as they start to argue and Ryan throws a french fry at him.

"What do you think?" Annie says to me over the noise. She nudges me with her elbow. "It could be kinda cool. You can sing Nirvana and Pearl Band and all the Spice Girls songs you want and nobody will make fun of you."

Mark lifts his hand in a half wave. "I'll make fun of you," he says.

As she says this, I can tell Annie feels bad about surprising me with Mark. Her voice is so earnest I don't even have the heart to tell her it's Pearl *Jam* and not Pearl Band. I bite into my burrito, considering this, but when I look up again, everyone at the table is staring at me.

My chewing slows as I lower my burrito to the table. This is when it dawns on me that they're not just staring at me, they're waiting for me to say something. For my answer, my approval. I'm the one who gets to decide what we do.

I bite my tongue. At least at a karaoke bar, everyone will be so distracted by the music, the thought that it's sort of weird that I'm wearing a hood inside won't even cross Mark's mind. And honestly, what else would I do tonight? After this, I'd drive Annie home and then sit in my empty house while my mother dances on a party bus and my sister plays Scrabble with her new family.

I swallow and let out a long breath. "Okay, fine," I say eventually.

Mark beams at me as Annie calls dibs on some niche One Direction song and Ryan rolls her eyes. For a second, I forget that I'm completely bald. Instead all I'm thinking is that maybe, just maybe, my whole Ryan and Annie plan might actually work.

FIFTEEN

DAYS UNTIL ANNIE LEBLANC DIES: 14

The private room at Wok N' Roll looks vaguely like IKEA's version of a dungeon: the walls are made of the same padded, scratchy material that's on the carpet, as are the staircase-looking seats that climb three levels. In the middle of the room is a large rectangular coffee table in bright pink plastic that's surrounded by green and purple beanbags. All of this is dwarfed by the giant screen, which covers an entire wall and is illuminated by a projector at the back of the room.

Before the waitress who led us into the room leaves, Mark orders four orange juices.

"Vitamin C for our vocal cords," he says to me, shrugging.

The door shuts behind her and then the lights go out, replaced by a shower of rainbow lights that sparkle off a disco ball hanging from the ceiling. Annie makes a dive for the coffee table and thick binder of karaoke songs sitting on top while standing above her, Ryan and Mark argue over who gets to sing "Old Town Road."

I sit on the lowest step and watch them, my fingernails picking at the frayed ends of the pull strings on Ryan's sweatshirt. For the whole walk over here from the taco shop, Ryan and Annie didn't argue. Not once. We even walked in a line, the three of us, Annie's arm looped through mine. As I watch them flip through the songs in the binder, all I can think is, *Is this what friendship looks like?* Will it really not become clear that I've righted a wrong until Annie is waiting for the bus back to the afterlife, or will there be some sort of indication that Lennon says she can stay? For a second I actually catch myself wishing Jody were here. She's the reason I'm even in this karaoke bar in the first place, that this whole thing with Annie and Ryan has had any sort of success. It was her idea to play the nostalgia card, and for some freaky reason I'm not sure I'll ever understand, it worked.

The waitress returns with a tray of orange juices that she leaves on the coffee table as Annie plays with the remote for the projector. Mark settles in beside Ryan on one of the carpeted stairs and pulls an entire bottle of tequila from his backpack.

"Have you had that the whole time?" I say.

He dribbles tequila into each of the glasses as Ryan stirs hers with her pinkie finger.

"Did you really think any of us would sing karaoke with nothing to drink?" she says. She leans down to sip from her glass and grimaces. "Woof, that's strong."

Mark nods at the glass that's supposed to be mine. "Moss, the real question is," he says as he wipes his hands on his pants, "will you be the Billy Ray Cyrus to my Lil Nas X?"

"You're not singing that song," Ryan says.

"It's my song," Mark fires back.

I lift the glass of orange juice to my nose and inhale, the sharp smell shooting up my nostrils and making me cough.

"It's easier to drink the first time if you hold your nose," Annie says, correctly identifying my uncontrollable hacking as a result of me never having had tequila before.

Ryan scowls. "Why not just tattoo 'underaged' on your forehead?"

"We should've gotten rum," Annie says. "It tastes way better with orange juice."

"How do you know?" I say.

Annie shrugs. "Del Monte kids are weird."

I glance down at my drink. "How're we gonna get home?" I say.

"We can stay at Jessie's house," Mark says. "He always lets us crash in the living room when we come to PB."

Jessie is Mark and Ryan's cousin. When I saw him working behind the Wok N' Roll bar, I could tell they were vaguely related. They all have the same chiseled jaw, but Jessie is way taller.

"What about your parents?" I say to Annie. "Aren't they gonna be mad you aren't home?"

"I'll call them," she says. "Besides, I'm spending the next three days with them at my cousins' house. They can give me another night off."

I glance down at my drink and think of Jody again. I've gotten this far because of her; what would she do now? Without even having to think, I know the answer; she would drink the tequila. She would obviously drink the tequila. Even though she's so tone-deaf that she got kicked out of her fourth-grade patriotic pageant, she would sing "Old Town Road" next to one of the most beautiful boys she'd ever met. She would forget the past two years, forget the flying shrimp and the lonely nights and the birthdays that didn't feel like birthdays without her two best friends and have the best freaking night of her life.

With the drink lifted to my lips, I take the tiniest sip possible and wince at the burning that blossoms in the back of my throat. The tequila leaves a sour trail of fire all the way down and settles in my stomach with a dull warmth.

"Holy shit, that's disgusting," I say, sticking out my tongue.

Mark reaches over and pats my hand. "Welcome to tequila."

I try again, this time careful to let the tequila slide over my tongue, and it's not as bad. The more I sip, the less it burns my mouth. The more it just feels warm instead of painful, comforting instead of gross. Annie raises her glass into the middle of the room.

"To karaoke," she says.

Mark stands and clinks glasses with her. "To cool people," he says, looking at me.

Ryan and I exchange glances before I join the circle and lift my own glass. "To tequila," I say.

Ryan snorts. "Lightweight."

"Yes!" Annie cheers. "To that. Definitely to that."

Karaoke is the single greatest invention of all time. Light bulbs, toilets, Facebook—none of them have anything on the karaoke binder. I want to make a shrine to karaoke and bow down to it. If there was karaoke church, I would be at that altar scream-singing the Spice Girls to the congregation and they would hold up their phones and worship me. Because that's what happens at karaoke: everybody loves you.

So far I've sung Lit's "My Own Worst Enemy," a million things by Nirvana, and Hanson's "MMMBop." For most of them, I don't even need the lyrics projected up on the screen in a flash of tie-dye colors because I already know them all by heart. Instead of watching the screen, I bob on my heels or dance around with Annie, jumping from carpeted stair to carpeted stair. At first, I was nervous about singing, my eyes trained on Ryan as the opening bars of "On a Plain" crunched to life, but as I made it through the first chorus, it was impossible not to close my eyes and fall into it, my body swaying to Kurt Cobain's *mmm*s. When I opened my eyes again, Ryan was just smiling and shaking her head, but not in a way that suggested she was embarrassed on my behalf.

There are a few times when I catch myself wishing Jody were here so I could prove to her that I really am her kid, that the nurses didn't swap me at the hospital and some other boring, antisocial family got her cool baby. But then I remember that if Jody were here, she would probably be the one dominating the karaoke stage and I simply could not let that happen.

After my third tequila and orange juice, I stop counting. The waitress just keeps bringing the orange juices and Annie keeps passing them to me.

I'm in the middle of doing my best Courtney Love impression as I sing "Celebrity Skin"—which mostly involves me dancing around like a beauty queen while simultaneously flipping people off—when Annie shrieks.

"Oh my god, I know what we're doing for the Fourth of July parade."

She scrambles across the seats toward Ryan and shouts something into her ear. Ryan's eyes widen as she erupts into laughter and claps her hands.

"That's it!" she shouts back. "We're doing it. We're definitely doing it."

"You're gonna come on the float with us?" I say into the microphone.

Mark watches this exchange with half interest, the karaoke binder open on his lap. Ryan purses her lips as though she's still mulling it over, but I can see the smile trying to push its way through.

Finally she rolls her eyes and says, "Fine."

Annie lets out a high-pitched squeal and wraps her arms around Ryan's shoulders, practically knocking her flat. The grungy guitars hum around me as I bounce on my feet, arms shooting up toward the ceiling. That's when it happens: my hood slips back, sending a cool rush of air around my ears.

The hood barely touches my shoulders before I flip it back onto my head, and for a second I let myself think that nobody even saw it. Then my eyes shoot to Mark, who's looking at me with his jaw dropped. The song fades into nothing, plunging immediately into Annie's next pick. She smacks a button on the control panel that's fixed into the wall, cutting off the opening notes.

"Holy shit," Mark says.

My ears are ringing from the new silence, the tequila leaving me feeling like there are a billion ants crawling under my skin. Mark's face is all confusion as he stands and moves closer to me, almost as if he's convinced he's in the middle of a very hairless hallucination.

"I made Ryan and Annie a deal that if they could ride bikes around Coronado without arguing, I'd shave my head," I say to him quickly. "I didn't think it through, I just did it, I didn't want them to think I was a wuss and then they'd start arguing again and why are you looking at me like that, does it really look that ugly?"

His eyes squinted, Mark edges my hood back a few inches and leans over so his nose is so close to my scalp; it's as though he's examining a specimen under a microscope. I half expect him to say "hmmm" and take a swab of my head.

"It looks . . ." he says, pulling away from me slightly so he can take in the whole picture again, "fucking *awesome.*"

A gust of air shoots through my lungs. "Are you serious?" I say. "Are you just being a dick?"

"What? No," Mark says. "You look like Eleven from *Stranger Things.*"

"That's what I said," Annie exclaims.

He lifts his hand to touch my head but pauses. "Is it okay if . . . ?" he says. I nod. His fingers are cold on my scalp, but every other part of me is warm. "Oh my god, I love this, it's like petting velvet." He drops his free hand under my chin and tips it up so I can meet his eyes. "Seriously, Moss, it's really cool."

A heaviness that I can't describe settles in my stomach as Mark takes a step closer to me. His face is framed by the disco lights so that a ring of red shines around his hair, and with just that tiny step, narrowing the space between us to no more than an inch, I know with every atom in my body that he's about to kiss me.

"My turn!"

Annie rips the microphone out of my hand, shaking me awake to the room around us. The mysterious sounds of harps, a spooky piano, and jungle noises are building from the speakers that hang from the ceiling. Annie widens her eyes and nods unsubtly over her shoulder at Ryan before claiming her spot at the head of the room. Mark takes the hint, his hand dropping from my face as he returns to the stairs.

With the microphone pressed to her lips, Annie says, "This one goes out to the Amazon rainforest. I'm sorry I never got to see you IRL."

It's "Earth Song," the weirdly intense song about conservationism that used to be Annie's anthem. When Annie first discovered it, it was all she listened to for a good three months; she even danced to it for our elementary school's talent show in third grade when, just before going onstage, she streaked her face with red paint and put on a T-shirt that read SILENCE = MURDER.

I grab my drink and sit beside Ryan, my body still buzzing with the residual energy left over from almost kissing Mark. She lifts her drink to her mouth and gives me a look from the corner of her eye.

"Are you happy now?" she says.

At first I think she's talking about Mark, but when I follow her eyes, they land on Annie, who's doing what looks like an impression of water. Her arms wiggle above her head, body swaying from side to side. I don't know if it's the tequila, but I lean my head on Ryan's shoulder. She tenses but doesn't pull away.

"All my friends are here and I look like a human golf ball," I say.

My voice is slurry and my body feels like Jell-O. Ryan laughs into her drink, orange juice exploding across her mouth. She wipes away the bubbles with the back of her hand.

"I know I'll regret saying this, but Annie and my annoying brother are right. You do look weirdly cool."

I drop my jaw in mock-horror. "Did you just admit somebody *other than you* could be *right*?" I say.

She shakes her head and looks down into her drink. "Don't make me hate you."

I sling my free arm around her. "You love me," I say as I nuzzle her neck with the top of my head.

She's so warm, like the night of the graduation party, when the heat of the fire radiated off her skin. The memory of it sends a flush spreading across my neck, like caramel in my veins. The ease with which my hands moved up her sides, the feeling of her fingers in my hair.

Ryan reaches over and taps my glass. "I'm cutting you off," she says.

I pull back and run a hand down my face, shivering away the thought. "Probably a good idea," I say, blinking.

The song crescendos around us as the gospel choir goes into full swing. Annie raises one hand to the sky and sways. When I look over at Ryan again, her eyes are fixed on my face, the sparkle of the disco ball reflecting back at me.

"What?" I say.

Her gaze falls to her drink and the ice cubes slowly dissolving on its surface. She mumbles something, but Annie is on the verge of screaming the song's bridge, so Ryan's words are lost in her chest. I lean over so her mouth is pressed right against my ear.

"I said I'm sorry," she shouts.

I frown. "What?" I repeat.

"I'm sorry," she says again. "And I'm sorry I didn't say it sooner."

This time when I lean away, Ryan looks at me, but for once she isn't daring me to argue. She actually looks soft, almost vulnerable. I can't remember the last time I saw her like this, but I know it hasn't been since we were kids.

I tilt in so it's my mouth that's on her ear. Even though she hasn't specified what exactly she's sorry for, she doesn't need to. It's everything.

"I know," I say, loud enough so that she can hear me but quiet enough so that it's only for her.

Because I know how much that admission must've cost her, Ryan the sarcastic, Ryan the indestructible, so I don't want her to be any more embarrassed than I imagine she already is. Ryan, sensing this, smiles with just one corner of her mouth. Seeing her like this, with Annie behind us collapsed on the floor in laughter as the song fades into nothing, I feel something like real happiness melt across me. For a second I swear I could close my eyes and it would feel like the last two years never happened.

SIXTEEN

DAYS UNTIL ANNIE LEBLANC DIES: 13

It's only just before eight o'clock when we leave Pacific Beach the next day, but Mark and Ryan have to open the Country Kitchen and Annie and I don't feel like sticking around and eating the pancakes that Jessie is making in a broken frying pan. Ryan drives us back to Coronado to get Jody's car, and before I even get there, I already have a few texts from Mark waiting for me.

Mark
Last night was really fun
Mark
I feel like I pet your head a creepy
amount of times though 😕
Mark
Hang out this week?

My phone is dying, but if anything, it gives me more time to think about what I'll say back. In the meantime, if I concentrate hard enough on it, I can still feel Mark's fingers on my face. So close to my mouth. It's weird and confusing and all I can think about as Annie and I drive across the giant blue bridge towering over the bay and back into Downtown San Diego.

Instead of staying on the highway that will eventually lead us back to Lennon, I turn off at the exit for Balboa Park. From the passenger seat, Annie frowns at me.

"What're you doing?" she says.

But I keep my eyes pointed forward. "You'll see."

This morning, as I lay between Annie and Ryan on the lumpy pullout couch, Annie's hand wedged under my back and Ryan's breath on the side of my face, I had an idea. What I could remember of the night before played over and over again in my head: Ryan's apology, Mark's goofy smile, Annie screaming "Earth Song" for a second time, so loud that Jessie had to come in and tell us other booths were complaining about the noise. It brought back a random memory I didn't know I had, one of me in the Lennon Historical Society as I waited for Ruth Fish. A quick stop at a gas station in Coronado and a Google consultation before my phone died confirmed my plans.

I park Jody's car on the street outside the zoo, Annie trailing behind me as we cross the hill underneath the big gnarled trees that cloak the grass in shade.

"Is this the part where we get a giant disgusting breakfast?" Annie says. "Because I'm not sure I can make it back up all those windy roads to Lennon without one."

The thought makes my stomach groan. Currently my head feels like it's being continually run over by the back wheels of a tractor, while my stomach burns with hunger. But I can't let it distract me.

"Afterward," I say over my shoulder.

Ahead of us is a massive water fountain that, from this distance, looks like a geyser has erupted in the middle of the plaza. Its circular base blends in with the concrete around it, only materializing as we get closer to the ice-blue water. Behind it sits a pale red-brown building with a terra-cotta roof, its windows cut with geometric designs—the Bailey Higgins Science Center.

"Okay, close your eyes," I say to Annie once we reach the building's front doors. "I want this to be a surprise, but I'm pretty sure there're gonna be like eight million posters that'll give it away."

"Give what away?" she says.

"Just trust me."

With a sigh, Annie shuts her eyes and holds out her hand. Inside is a long wraparound desk with digital screens strung above it detailing today's programs. I quickly scan them for the one I want, then buy our tickets while Annie hovers behind me, not saying anything.

I lead her through the brightly lit halls, past the dinosaur bones and the entrance to the kids' zone, until we reach the Burbidge Dome Theater. The theater itself is a literal dome, with a massive white screen extending up all the sides and over the ceiling, giving the audience the feeling of being trapped inside a giant golf ball. Everything is lit with a soft purple glow, from the screen to the seats and the worn carpet lining the stairs. I carefully lead Annie up, slowing down when she stumbles and almost falls into a man and his grandson. Outside of them, it's just me and Annie, so I guide her to what look like the most central seats.

I wait until she's settled in before saying, "Okay, you can open your eyes."

Her eyelids spring open, followed quickly by a confused frown. "Where are we?"

"Don't you remember this from third grade?" I say, gesturing to the empty seats. "We came and saw that movie about Antarctica."

Annie's frown disappears as the memory must return. "Is that the movie where the killer whales chased that baby seal and ripped it to pieces?"

My mouth drops open. "I think—"

"If this is something like that, I hope you brought a barf bag, because I am already two bloody hunks of seal blubber away from yacking all over these seats."

The man a few rows down turns around, giving us a startled look. I sink a few inches into my seat so I can't see his eyes.

"Just wait," I whisper to Annie. "This isn't about whales or penguins or any—"

As I'm speaking, the lights speckling the walkway and beaming up at the screen begin to dim, sending the theater into darkness. An image from a forest floor takes shape before us, framed by tall moss-covered trees that reach up to the sky. Only fragments of blue show up through the millions and millions of leaves, the sun a bright orb behind. Because the theater's screen is so big, it gives the effect of us actually being there, surrounded by endless trees. Loud birdsong and croaks swirl around us, filtering in from hidden speakers.

"What is this?" Annie says, her eyes unable to leave the screen.

But I don't answer as the scene changes to a wide, sweeping view of the treetops from above, a thick mist rolling over the uneven vista. And then, just as fast, there's an image of a person dressed in what looks like waterproof overalls wading through a brown-green river that comes all the way up to their chest. The person moves slowly through the murky water, their arms held up and hovering over the surface. A title screen appears, the letters blocky and red: THE AMAZING AMAZON.

Annie breathes out a long sigh.

"I know it's not the real thing," I say. "And you can't actually smell it, but I figured if you couldn't visit it while you were here, this was better than nothing."

There's a chance Annie could still get to visit the real Amazon one day, if I make her and Ryan friends again. I can feel that I'm getting close: last night Ryan and Annie sang "Love the Way You Lie" in a non-ironic way to each other. But even so, I know deep down that guaranteeing this whole plan works is out of my control. Ultimately, it's up to Lennon.

When Annie turns to me, her eyes are sparkling with tears. She finds my hand in the dark and squeezes it, a single tear making its way down her face. I smile as bravely as I can before squeezing her hand back.

Because if I don't succeed and Annie *does* have to go back to the afterlife, at least I'll have given her this.

I drop Annie off at her house before returning to mine, where I stand outside on the lawn for a solid three minutes staring up at the same faded paint job and the porch lights that have never worked. It's almost disappointing how normal it all looks. After last night, I can't help but feel like everything in my life has been turned upside down again, but in a good way; now here I am and everything looks exactly the same.

I groan as I trudge up the porch steps, my body aching from the sofa bed and tequila orange juices. All I want to do today is put on my sweatpants and eat Cheetos in front of the TV. After that, I might pick up *The Walking Dad* again, but recently I haven't been able to find my sketchbook. With how much of a bomb site Bernie's and my room has become since Annie came back and I haven't been cleaning it, this isn't actually that surprising. But these plans pretty much die when I open the front door and find Jody sitting at the dinner table.

"What're you doing here?" I say.

The three suitcases she packed just two nights ago are strewn out on the living room floor, her purse and sandals discarded nearby. She shoots to her feet.

"What did you do to your hair?" she says as she pulls my head down to examine my scalp. "Did you shave your head?"

"No, it spontaneously combusted," I say.

Her fingers dance across my skin from my forehead to my neck, as if searching for the telltale line of a bald cap. "You went full Sinéad O'Connor. Why did you go full Sinéad O'Connor?"

"It was the only way to get Annie and Ryan to hang out," I say, pulling away. "I promised if they could do it without arguing, I'd shave my head."

"Oh, Wilson," Jody says, shaking her head. "Wilson, Wilson, Wilson."

"You're the one who was proud when I said I wanted to shave my head in fifth grade," I say.

Now standing a few feet back, Jody blinks rapidly as though to wake herself up from a dream. "How do you even— Never mind," she says. "Where in the hell have you been? I've called you four *billion* times."

"My phone died," I say. "I went to San Diego to ride bikes around Coronado with Ryan and Annie, like you told me to."

"I told you to re-create your childhood memories, not get trashed at a karaoke bar."

"Wh—" I start to say, but my brain is suddenly moving too fast for someone with this much tequila still in their system. "How did you know where I was last night? Are you following me?"

"No, I'm not following you," Jody says. "I got your incredibly drunk voicemail."

I blink her words into focus. What is she talking about?

"I didn't leave you a voicemail," I say. "It must've been Pam, or—"

"Pam? You mean my best friend, who was literally standing next to me all night?"

She says this as she reaches for her phone, which is lying on the kitchen table. Without another word she scrolls through, looking for something before putting her phone on speaker and holding the screen up to me. There's a loud crackling on the other line before a blur of shouting and then one voice.

"Jody. Jody."

"Oh my god," I whisper under my breath. It's me. *"Guys, shut up!"* voicemail-me shouts to everyone. *"I'm talking to Jody."*

"Why are you calling your mom?" Ryan says.

"Hi, Jody, hi, Mrs. Baker." It's Annie now, screaming into the phone. *"Oh shit, is she even Mrs. Baker anymore? What's your mom's maiden name? Hi, Mrs. Dr. David. Mrs. Future Dr. David."*

There's a snort of laughter before I return to the phone. *"Jody, I did it. I actually did it. Ryan and Annie are hanging out and nobody's dead. Well, okay, not fully dead. Annie is still kind of dead, but"*—my voice drops to an exaggerated whisper—*"not for long."*

I fall onto the couch and bury my head in my hands. "This is so embarrassing," I moan.

Jody follows me, the phone still held up in my face. "Oh, not so fast," she says. "It's just about to get good."

"Did you know that I'm really good at karaoke?" drunk-me says. *"I bet you didn't even know that. Honestly, Jody, you would be so proud of me right now. I, like, had tequila and I didn't even barf. I feel* amazing. *I know you probably think I'm just this boring, sad loser but not anymore. I sang the Beastie Boys tonight—would a boring person do* that? Here, listen to this, hold on." There's a rustling as I put the phone down and wrestle whoever's on the microphone. Then there's the earsplittingly loud intro for the Beastie Boys' "Fight for Your Right," followed by me shrieking the opening lyrics.

Jody finally ends the voicemail.

"It mostly goes on like that for the next seven minutes," she says.

"I don't even remember that," I say.

It must've been somewhere after Annie's second rendition of "Earth Song," when the tequila and orange juice turned into straight shots of some unidentified blue liquor that appeared out of nowhere. The couch sags as Jody sits next to me. I wait for her to replay the voicemail, to show me that she's made a ringtone out of me screaming the Beastie Boys like she did that time Pam sang some cheesy eighties love song in our shower after her ex-boyfriend broke up with her for the ninth time. There's so much I have to tell her about Ryan and Annie, about the Fourth of July float and how the three of us are actually going to ride on it. Together. But when I peek up at Jody from around my hands, she's watching me with one brow bent.

"What?" I say.

Her eyebrows shoot into her forehead. "*What?* Did we not just listen to the same voicemail?"

I rub my hands into my eyes until my vision goes from black to white. A dull pain pounds behind my left eyebrow in time with my heartbeat, and the thought enters my head about how lame it'd be if I puked here after making it all the way up the twisty mountain roads back to Lennon completely fine.

"Look, I know you're disappointed I didn't sing 'Sabotage,' because that's your favorite Beastie Boys song, but my throat would've gotten road burn if I tried," I say.

Jody's jaw drops open. "Is that— Are you serious right now?" she says, her voice laced with an anger that instinctively makes me wince. "Do you really think that's why I'm here? Why I spent five hundred dollars on a flight back from Vegas and missed my own bachelorette party, because you sang the third best Beastie Boys song at karaoke?"

"'No Sleep Till Brooklyn' is not—"

"Again," Jody says, holding her hand up to silence me, "not the point."

At the sound of her obvious frustration, I push myself into the far corner of the couch without thinking. Jody's never directed anger at me before, not really. I've never given her a reason to. We've always had a kind of understanding that I wouldn't do anything worth worrying about and she wouldn't worry about me.

"It wasn't like I had everybody here and we trashed the house," I say. "We were in San Diego."

"Wilson, you're allowed to have your friends over," Jody says. "That's not the issue."

I frown. "Oh, I'm *allowed* to?" I say.

"Yeah, because news flash"—she waves her hands around— "I'm the mom here and you're the kid. I make the rules. And you can't be getting completely wasted while I'm out of town. You can't even be getting a little bit wasted. You're seventeen."

As she speaks, the frustration in her voice only grows. I watch as her hands curl into fists, a slow realization dawning on me.

"Wait, are you—are you mad I was *drinking*?" I say.

The thought is so unbelievable, it almost makes me laugh. This is Jody, who famously got pregnant with me at a bonfire party at Lake Cuyamaca, and I'm sorry, nobody can have sex on a lakeside beach without being completely hammered. That's not a thing. This is the woman who, at this very second, is wearing the hot pink T-shirt Pam made for her and all the other women on the bachelorette trip, with the phrase JO'S A HOE NO MO ironed on the front in sparkly silver letters.

"Of course that's why I'm mad," Jody exclaims. "Do you have any idea how freaked out I've been? I didn't know where you were, who you were with, and you call me so obviously face-plant drunk. I'm surprised you're even standing right now. I thought for sure you had alcohol poisoning."

"But I—I thought you wanted me to."

"Get alcohol poisoning?"

"No." I shake my head. "Have fun, take a risk. You're the one who has all these stories about your wild nights out and the parties from when you were my age. Just last week, you said you were happy I was going to Grant's party."

"I meant, I was happy to see you go out with your friends,

not give me all the sordid details about what you're drinking, which, by the way, do I even want to know how you got the alcohol? You know what, never mind. One thing at a time." She opens and closes her mouth to speak a couple of times, carefully choosing her next words. "Does this have anything to do with David and the wedding?"

It takes a few seconds for her words to land, but when they do, they send a heat spreading throughout my chest.

"What?" I say.

She glances up at the ceiling as though this conversation could possibly be more awkward for her than it is for me. "I just mean, is that why you're acting like this, trying to get my attention, because you're worried things are going to change when we move in with David? I know you and Cass are still close, but—"

"I don't— I can't even— *No.* How would that even make sense?"

"I don't know. Sometimes kids do that, act out when they feel out of control. And I can't help but feel like it's just a *tiny* bit convenient that you do this while I'm on my bachelorette trip."

"I'm almost eighteen," I say. "You don't control me anymore. You've never controlled me. I've always been the responsible one trying to control *you.*"

At this, Jody laughs darkly. "Oh, you're right, because all those years I went to work so you could eat and have somewhere to live, you were being the responsible one."

My next words sting my tongue, but they're out of my mouth before I can think twice. "That was *Cass,*" I say.

Jody recoils as though I've just spit poison in her face. "Last time I checked," she says slowly, once she's recovered, "you were five years old when I met Cass, and doing just fine."

I cradle my head in my hands, for once not caring about how jarring it is to feel cold skin instead of hair. "Are we really going to talk about this right now?" I say.

"Wilson, talk about what? What is going on here? This drinking, this party stuff—this isn't you."

My head snaps up. "Oh, and this is you?" I say. "The person who used to wear six-inch heels to the doctor's office and now owns four pairs of Crocs."

"Yeah, because I don't hate myself anymore."

"Exactly," I say with a laugh that borders on maniacal. Pressure is building behind my eyes. "You're exactly who you want to be now. You're Mrs. Perfect. You said so yourself: Dr. David makes you whole."

Jody frowns. "I never said that," she says.

"Yes, you did, at Blushing Brides. You told that saleslady that Dr. David makes you feel whole, apparently something *being my mother* never did."

"Wilson, that's not what I meant—"

"You sure?" I say.

And then, to my utter horror, the pressure behind my eyes gives way to tears.

"Of course I'm sure," she says. "I just meant that I'm finally in the right place to get my life on track. I thought you'd be happy for me."

"I *am* happy for you," I insist.

"It doesn't sound like it," she says. "Look, I know you're still upset about everything with Cass and I'm sorry. But I've finally found someone who makes me want to be better, not just for you and your sister, but me, too."

"There you go," I say, clapping my hands. "*I* wanted to be the person who made you better. Being good didn't do it, making sure our bills got paid didn't do it, and then the one time I actually go out and do something that you used to do *all the time,* you suddenly have a problem with it." I shake my head. "Once again, I'm not enough for you. Even with Cass, I'd finally found a family. *We* were a family. I was happy, but that wasn't good enough for you either. You had to go and fuck it all up."

"Wilson!" Jody exclaims. "It's not that simple."

"No?" I say. "It's the truth. The only person who could make you change is some lame-ass dentist who probably spent his first allowance on a burial plot with a good view."

I know I'm being mean when Dr. David has been nothing but nice to me, but I'm on a roll. And it might not be something I've ever fully realized before, but it's true: I *am* mad at Jody for choosing chaos over my happiness, my only family. *She* is the reason I never feel good enough. Not for her, not for Ryan and Annie, not for anyone.

When Jody and I meet eyes again, she looks exhausted. Her face is pale and her eyes are half-closed, as though she might just sprawl out on the couch and fall asleep. Finally her eyes slip down to her lap and she sighs sadly.

"David is a good person who loves you and your sister very much. And if you can't be happy for us, then maybe you shouldn't come to the wedding on Thursday."

Her words cut into my lungs like razors, but I stretch my lips into a sarcastic smile and nod. After everything I've just said, finally laying out my fears for her like a fucking buffet, that's all she can do. Uninvite me to her wedding, the party that wouldn't even be happening if it weren't for me. I shouldn't be surprised, but for some reason, my stomach still sinks.

"Sure," I say, wiping my eyes with the heels of my hands. "I wouldn't want to get in the way of your perfect new life. Please pass along my congratulations to the happy couple."

Without another word, I stand from the couch and push past my mother, fast-walking into the hallway as tears slide down my face. She calls to me as I go, but I slam my bedroom door before I can register her words. The only thing I hear from her for the rest of the night is the sound of suitcases wheeling across the carpet and her car backing down the driveway.

SEVENTEEN

DAYS UNTIL ANNIE LEBLANC DIES: 10

Mark Morton will be at my house in approximately eight minutes. This thought circles my head as I scramble around my kitchen straightening all the food I bought at the deli this morning after making a meticulously planned snack list, as I triple-check that I've stashed all the embarrassing baby pictures of me away in dark closet corners, where they belong. During all this, I keep my eye on the microwave clock, even though it's always two minutes off. Mark, like Ryan, is never late for work, so I know he'll be here on time, and I don't know if this thought makes me more or less nervous.

I've changed my outfit at least four times, from one of Jody's plaid skirts and a weirdly itchy crop top, to the black shirtdress she let me borrow for Grant's party, to a pair of shorts and another, even itchier crop top, then back to the black shirtdress. Logically, I know I should wear something different from what I wore to Grant's party, but a) I know Mark thinks it looks okay because he may or may not have planned on kissing me while I was wearing it before and b) he's a boy, so he probably doesn't notice these things.

Jody hasn't been back since our fight. All I can picture is her sitting on Dr. David's couch with a glass of expensive red wine, loudly recounting the way I cried and making some joke about teenage hormones. Every time I think about what I said, I'm filled with a renewed sense of shame. I can't help but think it's a good thing that I'm not invited to the wedding anymore. After what I said, I don't think I could face my mother again anyway. This is where Mark comes in. I know I should be obsessing about keeping Annie back, but she's still in Los Angeles with her parents, which means inviting Mark to my house was the only thing that could take my mind off Jody; it was the perfect way to funnel my nervous energy into a completely different, equally ridiculous scenario.

I check the fridge again, take in the Diet Coke strung together in neat rows, the chips and the candy lined up on the counter. I'm behaving like someone who googled "how to make people like me," but hopefully Mark either isn't paying attention or finds my awkwardness kind of endearing.

Only three minutes to go, and my phone rings. Without looking at the screen, I know it'll be Annie. Ever since Mark and I decided our first official solo hangout would happen at my house, I've been calling Annie almost nonstop, desperate for ideas of things to do with Mark. My DVD player skips on everything that was made before 2015 and the only board game in my house is Trivial Pursuit, which mostly asks questions about the 1970s, and not even I could get into that decade. I briefly considered asking Mark to help me work on Ryan's, Annie's, and my outfits for the parade on Monday, since I somehow got stuck on seamstress duty even though I can't sew, but Annie swore me to secrecy on our adaptation of Ruth Fish's theme.

"Oh my god, my cousin Kelsey is actually bananas," Annie says when I answer the phone. "Her entire bedroom is covered in crystals, and she keeps trying to get me to drink this weird orange tea that smells like cough syrup. Honestly, you die for a little bit and everyone becomes a freaking weirdo." She finally pauses for a breath. "Sorry I missed your calls. You'd think being in LA County would mean you'd automatically have service. What's going on?"

"It's okay," I say. "Mark Morton is sort of coming over . . . to my house."

There's a beat of silence as this information stretches the 150 miles between us.

"I'm sorry, what?" Annie says slowly. "When?"

I glance at the microwave clock. "Two minutes?"

"Two minutes?"

Though she's trying to control it, panic still creeps in around the edges of Annie's voice. Hearing it sends a whole new wave of worry rushing through me.

"We were trying to find something to do and nothing else was working," I say quickly. It's true. We spent four hours texting about it last night. "We can't go for a hike because Mark has a bad ankle from track and we can't rob a bank because I said we've filled our quota of breaking the law for one month, so him coming over just seemed like the next best option."

Annie makes an incredulous sound. "Did you just say your three options were hanging out at your house, hiking, and *robbing a bank*?"

"It was a joke," I say. My throat feels tight with anxiety now, my heart picking up speed. "After San Diego, me and Jody got in this big fight and I didn't tell you about it because it's super embarrassing, and then having Mark over seemed like the perfect distraction. I—I don't know, it sounded way better in my head. I just figured since Bernie is at Cass's house and Jody went—"

"Wait, wait, wait," Annie says, cutting me off. "He's coming to your house, where you'll be *alone*?"

I swallow. "Yeah."

"Oh my god." Annie pulls the phone away from her face, where she does some quiet, incredulous mumbling. After a few seconds, she brings the phone back to her mouth. "Oh my god. You know what this means, right? He's gonna think you want to have sex with him."

"What?" I say. "Why would he think that?"

"Because you invited him to your empty house. That's basic Teenage Boy 101 for 'I'm going to bang you.'"

"I—I didn't mean—I definitely didn't mean that. You really think he's gonna think that?"

"Of course he's going to think that," Annie shouts. "That's what I would think. That's what literally everyone would think."

I sink onto the couch and rest my forehead against my knees. "Oh my god," I moan into the fabric of my dress. "I'm so pathetic. Do you know how pathetic I am? I made a snack list. I made a fucking snack list."

Even though the thought of having sex with Mark Morton lights a confusing kind of warmth in my stomach, it's not something I want to do here, now, in my bed, which is currently covered in a bunny-themed sheet set I've had since I was eight.

It's already weird enough that the last person I kissed shares his DNA, much less that she vomited violently afterward. Maybe it's something in their genes that makes me so repulsive to them.

"What am I supposed to do?" I say into the phone. "He's gonna be here in—" But before I can finish the sentence, there's a knock at the door. "Shit, he's here. What do I do?"

"ABORT, ABORT," Annie shouts into the phone. "I REPEAT, DO NOT LET HIM IN."

"I have to let him in," I whisper. "He knows I'm here. I'm the one who told him to come over."

"Tell him you're sick," Annie says. "Tell him your mom's sick. Tell him anything. Just don't. Let. Him. In."

Mark knocks again. I can see his shape in the front door's frosty glass panels; it's all wiry frame with strong shoulders, and then that hair. So much hair. What would it feel like to touch his hair?

Annie is still screaming into the phone, but without listening I whisper "I'm going now" and press end on our conversation.

There's a small, heart-shaped mirror hanging just beside the front door. In it, I check my nose and teeth for anything gross, hands shaking with a mixture of panic and excitement. I don't have enough hair for it to be messed up, so I just pat my head instead.

Mark is waiting on our doormat, its surface so old and stepped on that the WELCOME HOME has been worn down to just WEL HO. Against his chest, he hugs a big, plastic Tupperware container.

"Hey," he says, smiling at the sight of me. He lifts the container. "I made cupcakes."

Mark follows me inside and sets the cupcakes down on the

kitchen counter. He's wearing black jeans and a mustard-colored T-shirt. It's a good color on him, making the darkness of his gold-brown eyes look even warmer. I catch myself watching him as he peels the cover off the Tupperware container, then blush when he looks at me.

"They're chocolate chip cookie dough," he says, sweeping a hand over the open container.

Inside are twelve identical cupcakes, each topped with a swirly brown frosting that's dotted with mini chocolate chips.

"Holy shit, these look amazing," I say, peering inside. "You made these?"

"With my own two little hands," he says, wiggling his fingers.

I pluck up one of the cupcakes and hold it in the palm of my hand. Everything about the frosting is symmetrical, every crystal of sugar perfectly in place.

"The frosting is incredible," I say.

"That would be the piping kit I got for my birthday last year. I'm still mastering my decorations. Ryan says I have a tendency toward showmanship."

The frosting is cotton-ball light, wisping off the edge of my fingertip when I swipe the top.

"Does Ryan know you're here?" I say.

I pop my finger into my mouth, savoring the salty-sweet flavor on my tongue. I think back to the way Annie looked at me when Mark held my face in the karaoke bar, the way she jerked her head toward Ryan as if she were a sleeping baby we had to tiptoe around. Even after that, I've only really been concerned with Mark knowing about me and Ryan, not the other way around. Would she care if she knew he was at my house? What would that do for our newfound truce?

"Nah, she's obsessed with getting ready for college," he says. "She basically stays in her room packing all day and night and only leaves to go to work. I thought her bossiness was unbearable, but turns out, her weird silence is just as bad."

"She's already packing?" I say. "I thought she wasn't leaving till next month."

Mark nods. "Yeah, but I think she's pretty much counting down the days. Homegirl's hatred for Lennon is *strong*." He shuffles around the dining room table toward the pile of plastic bags that are stacked up against the wall. Before I can tell him not to, Mark leans down and grabs a broken piece of wood lying next to one of the bags on the floor, its ends jagged from where I broke it off an old table leg on the side of the road near the library. "Do I wanna know?" he says, then shakes his head. "That was ridiculous. I obviously wanna know."

"It's for my costume for the Fourth of July parade," I say, snatching the table leg out of his hands. I shove it back into one of the bags and bury it under Jody's old leather jacket.

"And you're going as a biker pirate?" he says.

I smirk. "No, and Annie would kill me if I told you," I say. "You've already seen too much."

Mark raises his hands in fake surrender. "Forget I asked."

I tap my fingers against my sides and glance around the empty living room. Calling Annie to figure out what I should do with Mark served no purpose other than making me even more nervous than I already was. I should've had something set up, something for us to do so we didn't have to just stand in my living room staring at each other. Then I remember the food.

"Do you want something to drink?" I say.

But Mark shakes his head. "Nah, I just came from work. I

can never seem to drink the right amount of coffee. It's either I pass out from exhaustion or pass out from caffeine overload."

"Which one are you on right now?" I ask.

"My entire body is vibrating."

I nod. At least that makes two of us.

"We could listen to music," I say. Anything but the sound of my brain caving in on itself with worry.

Mark shrugs. "Yeah, cool. But only if it's Nirvana."

"I love Nirvana," I say.

"Yeah, I know. You sang their entire catalog at karaoke."

I laugh and say, "I'll get my speaker."

Careful not to look too panicked, I zigzag down the hallway to my bedroom and grab the speaker from my desk. When I turn back to my door, Mark is standing in the threshold, his eyes scanning my room.

"Holy cow, are those the *Angel & Faith* comic books?" he says, edging around me toward the shelf of comics above my bed.

"Did you just say 'holy cow'?"

Mark pretends to scowl at me over his shoulder and looks way too much like Ryan. "Maybe," he says, then turns back. "I've always wanted to read them."

Hoisting himself up on his tiptoes, Mark pulls down the first book in the series of the *Buffy the Vampire Slayer* spin-off and sits on my bed. I hop over a discarded pair of shoes and sit next to him.

"Have you read *Buffy*?" I ask.

Mark shakes his head as he flips through the first couple of pages. "I've read a little bit on the internet but not the whole thing. Are they good?"

"They're amazing. The *Buffy* universe works way better as a comic than it does on TV. All the craziness is multiplied by ten thousand. And it doesn't matter, because you can get away with a ridiculous monster and superpowers in a comic infinitely more than you can with cheesy special effects."

That's why I love comics so much in general. Every idea I have, every cartoon I draw, is completely limitless.

"I almost like *Angel & Faith* more than the *Buffy* comics," I say. "They're even funnier, and Angel and Faith have way better banter."

Buffy the Vampire Slayer as a whole is about as perfect as it gets in terms of a franchise, but there's something about *Angel & Faith*—the chronicles of Buffy's vampire ex-boyfriend, Angel, and her former arch nemesis, Faith—that's so much smoother. It's funny and edgy and, in spite of myself, I kind of want Angel and Faith to bang.

"Yeah, but Angel sucks," Mark says. "And so does Faith, kind of."

"I won't disagree with you about Angel," I say, wrinkling my nose at the thought of Angel's boring moodiness. "He's the actual worst. But Faith is a million times cooler in the comics than she is on the TV show."

Mark nods. "Do you wanna hear something embarrassing?" he asks. Then, without waiting for my answer: "I think I might've had my sexual awakening to Eliza Dushku."

I want to make fun of him, but I can't. Eliza Dushku as Faith in the *Buffy* TV show is basically perfect.

"Oh my god, same," I say. "Remember that scene where her and Buffy go off the rails and do all that hot dancing at the Bronze?"

Mark pretends to fan himself with his hand.

"Still, though," I say, "Annie is gonna be so offended."

Mark's jaw drops as he nudges my foot playfully. "I take back what I said about forgetting you're going as Captain Hells Angel for the Fourth of July parade," he says. "I actually already texted Annie and she said you should be ashamed of yourself. Shame. Shame!" He wiggles his fingers down the front of my face and I push him off, giggling. He turns his attention back to the comic. "Didn't you used to like drawing, or did I make that up? I feel like Ryan used to say you made your own comics."

My face flushes, but I tip it down toward my lap. "Not really," I say. "I mean, I drew a little bit, but it was just kid stuff."

"I always thought it would be really cool to be able to draw," Mark says. "But every time I even try to draw a circle, it always comes out looking like I did it with my feet."

"But you're great at baking," I say, desperate to change the subject. "The stuff you make is awesome."

He side-eyes me, half smiling.

"Do you think you'll ever own your own restaurant, like your mom?" I say. "You do come from a long line of apple pie people."

Mark scoots himself backward so that he can lean against the wall bordering my bed, legs stretched out across my comforter and feet dangling.

"There's this cool culinary school in LA I've been thinking about. I mean, I wouldn't go right away; I want to take a year off first, help my mom with the Country Kitchen. I think she'd let me have it when she wants to retire."

I bite down on my lip. "You're not desperate to get away like Ryan?"

"Nah, I like it here. I mean, I get why Ryan wants to go. The fact that we don't have a movie theater is an abomination. But I don't know. I sorta like how lame it is. It's kinda hilarious. What about you?"

Part of me knows what Mark is talking about. Lennon's quaintness, the dream catchers hanging in shop windows, and the deli, whose walls are lined with gold rush–era mug shots. For most people who live here, Lennon is permanent. They've ended up here for a reason, and Lennon let them. To a lot of people, that means something.

"I don't know yet," I say. "Part of me wants to get the hell out of here and move to San Diego, but the other part still thinks my mother can't reheat pizza in the microwave without me being there to make sure she doesn't burn the house down." At least until she marries Dr. David and he takes over microwave duty. "But she's getting married, so I guess it'll be her husband's problem now."

"My mom did that," he says. "Ran away from Lennon, I mean, not burn our house down with the microwave. She hated all this boring mountain crap and went to New York for a while and met my dad. But when my grandma got sick, Mom came back to take care of her and eventually she took over the Country Kitchen. She hates apple pie, but she said there's something in her that just couldn't really forget Lennon. When you're out in a big city or whatever, I guess you start to crave something small again."

"Maybe me and Ryan just need to get it out of our systems," I say.

Mark shrugs. "Maybe, maybe not. If you decide to stay out there though, that's cool. San Diego's close enough to visit."

When I look at him, smiling at me, I can't tell if he means

San Diego is close enough for me to visit Lennon or for him to visit me. Either way, my face goes hot again.

"Wait, did you say your mom hates apple pie?" I say suddenly.

Mark whips his body around toward me. "Yes, but that's a secret you have to take to your grave," he says. "If my mom ever finds out anyone knows, she'll skin me alive and use my shell for a Halloween costume."

In the lamplight, Mark's hair picks up streaks of gold between the brown. It's way lighter than Ryan's, probably from the sun. Ryan talks a big game about liking San Diego and the California weather, but I happen to know for a fact that she'd much rather read books in her bedroom or watch the old Mary-Kate and Ashley tapes we used to check out from the library in a haphazardly made tent fort than go to the beach.

"You can borrow those if you want," I say, gesturing to the comic still in Mark's lap. "I didn't know you liked *Buffy*. You just became way cooler."

"Why do you underestimate me, Moss? Other people can like *Buffy* and Nirvana, not just hipsters like you." His face takes on a mischievous look, his eyes glinting. "Is this the part where you're so into me, we make out?"

If I thought my face was hot before, it's on fire now. How can he be so blatantly flirty, when I'm such a blatant dork? But then, maybe I don't have to feel so nervous; Mark is here because he likes me, even if a large chunk of that revolves around wanting to take off my dress. And knowing this, maybe I can just be cool for once. Maybe I can just accept that I'm enough for him to be here in this exact moment. Enjoy him being here, wanting to be here with me.

I swallow down my nerves. "Not anymore," I say, pretending to be offended.

"Look, let's just call this what it is," Mark says. He tucks his legs underneath him. "You're super into the fact that I like *Buffy* and Nirvana because you secretly just want to make out with yourself."

Before I can talk myself out of it, I reach up and smooth Mark's hair back, tugging it away from his face so it's pulled down tight. Not expecting it, Mark leans his head back slightly with the yank of my hand, his smile going from mischievous to a little surprised.

"There," I say, squinting at him. "Now I can pretend you're bald."

Mark's gaze goes from my mouth to my eyes again in a move that's so fast, I almost miss it. With a quick breath, I lean in and kiss him, my hand releasing his hair and sliding down to the back of his head. His hands move to my waist as I ease him backward onto my pillow and crawl up so my legs are on either side of his stomach.

But as my hands reach up to dig into his hair, I can't help but feel like something's not right. It's not even that the kissing isn't good; we're pretty much in sync, our mouths moving together in a slow, easy tempo. He's sliding his hands down the back of my bare legs and he's actually really good at managing the exact right ratio of tongue in my mouth, but there's something about it that's just . . . *meh*. A giant shrug of a make-out, like two Barbie dolls bashing their heads together.

I pull away, vaguely out of breath.

"What?" Mark says.

"Oh, I just—" I say, briefly considering if I should lie about this feeling off, if I should just keep trying. Maybe it's something I need to work myself up for, like warming up before a run. But then, this is Mark. Mark, who's never been anything but sweet and understanding toward me. Do I really want to lie to him? "This is just—"

But Mark cuts me off. "Weird?" he says.

"Yeah?" I say, relief crashing over me. "You feel it too?"

He grimaces. "Please don't hate me, but it kind of feels like I'm making out with my cousin," he says.

I raise my eyebrows. "Do you have a lot of experience with that?"

"Only at Christmas."

I roll off of Mark, who makes room for me on the bed. We stare up at the ceiling, our arms folded across our stomachs so we don't touch.

"Is it me?" I say.

But Mark shakes his head quickly. "No, you're fine," he says. "Is it me?"

"I don't think so," I say.

I sigh through my nose. This is the part where my heart should be pounding. There's a very cute boy in my room. A very cute boy who's willing to kiss me. A very cute boy with whom I've been waiting weeks for this to happen. This thing right here, after all the buildup. The shameless flirting. The dancing at the karaoke bar, the texting.

The same thought is clearly going through Mark's head, because he curls onto his side and waves me back over.

"Okay, forget the cousin stuff," he says. "Let's try again."

I reach my right hand up around to the back of his neck again and kiss him so deeply, I can practically taste his tonsils. If this were a movie, red hearts and naked babies would be dancing around our heads.

"Still weird," Mark says, pulling away.

"Still weird," I agree.

But what about the electric shock that went up my arm at the feeling of his hand in mine? The way my thoughts go fuzzy whenever we talk, when he makes me laugh? At least when Ryan kissed me, I—

"Oh my god," I groan, cutting off the thought.

Why can't I be around Mark without thinking about Ryan? No wonder this is weird. Because *I* am weird.

At the sight of Mark's frown, I add quickly, "It's just—this shouldn't be weird. I don't want this to be weird."

"I know, dude, me too," he says.

I lift my hands to cover my face. "Please don't call me dude," I say into my palms. "That just makes it worse."

"Sorry," he says, patting my shoulder awkwardly, "pal."

We both exchange glances before bursting into laughter. I know I should be embarrassed, but something about the way Mark is smiling at me just makes this whole thing feel like an elaborate prank we both planned. We didn't reject each other; some higher power did.

"God, does this mean there's something wrong with us?" I say.

"Nah," he says with a shrug. "I think I just like to keep things in the bloodline and you have very high standards for hair, like a reverse height requirement on a roller coaster. You know, 'You must have no more than this much hair to make out with Wilson.'"

I shove him with my elbow and laugh again. If anything, a

little well of sadness pools in my stomach. Mark is genuinely awesome. He's funny and cute and smart and he likes comic books, but kissing him feels like putting my lips on a giant block of ice.

We don't even talk about what to do next; it's unspoken that Mark is leaving. I follow him to the front door and past the bags with the Fourth of July costumes, the fridge full of Diet Cokes I know now probably won't get opened.

"I don't want you to think I'm leaving because we're not gonna make out anymore," Mark says once we reach the porch.

"Yeah, no, I know," I say quickly.

To be honest, that thought hadn't even occurred to me.

Mark smiles at me again, except this time, it's kind of sad. With one hand holding the back of his head, he waves the other and turns to walk down the porch.

Once I get back inside my house, I unwrap another cupcake and lay the little paper cup down carefully on the dining table. Before I can think too much about it, I shove the entire cupcake into my mouth in one bite, almost completely blocking my windpipe so that I nearly choke. I'm almost done chewing when there's a knock at the front door. A shape has returned to the glass panels. Mark.

I swallow the last remaining hunks of cupcake. "I'm keeping the cupcakes," I shout through the door.

Sure enough, standing on the other side is Mark, who, as soon as I swing the door open, springs forward and kisses me again, his hands cupping my cheeks. It's like something out of a romantic comedy, except we're supposed to be at an airport or in the rain. A Taylor Swift song should be playing in the background.

Mark pulls away, smiling into my lips. "I thought that might surprise us into feeling something," he says. His forehead touches mine and this should be so hot and why is it not hot? "Still weird."

I nod, my eyes closed. "Still weird."

"Okay, bye for real, Moss."

And then he's gone. Again.

EiGHTEEN

DAYS UNTIL ANNIE LEBLANC DIES: 10

When I was younger and everything felt like it was falling apart, I walked. It was never to anywhere in particular, just wandering around Lennon in circles until my legs ached and my brain felt somewhat clearer or too exhausted to care anymore. With the Fourth of July parade outfits still unfinished, a walk is basically the last thing I have time for right now, but with Mark still on my brain, the thought of sitting in my house alone makes me feel itchy.

Lennon is quiet around this time. A few things are still open—bars and restaurants, mostly—but all the tourists go home once the sun starts to set, Lennon gently pushing them out with reminders of Starbucks and Chicken McNuggets. The sun is melting the sky from pumpkin orange to blue to black, leaving a thin line of light glowing over the wooden buildings on Main Street. Lennon's night sky and the eruption of stars scattered across it used to be my favorite thing about this town, but I don't go out that much at night anymore because there's not much to do and nobody to do it with.

"Wilson?" a voice calls through the dark. "What're you doing over here?"

Somehow I've ended up in front of Cass's house, which probably isn't that surprising, seeing as it's the place I've lived the longest in my life. It used to be the foundation for my walks, the start and end of everything when it all slanted. Cass is sitting on the porch in one of two rocking chairs, his outline lit by the haze coming from the windows behind him. A small circle of orange sits right around where his mouth should be, turning into a stream of smoke that filters up to the porch's wooden overhang.

"Good job quitting smoking," I say from the bottom of the porch.

He smiles sheepishly before snuffing the cigarette out on the ashtray at his feet. "You're not supposed to be here until tomorrow," Cass says as he claps stray ash from his hands. "You enjoying your freedom?"

I throw my arms out to either side, a burst of cold rushing into their place. "Obviously," I say.

"You want to sit down?" Cass says. He nods to the open rocking chair beside him.

"Am I allowed to?" I ask.

"Wh— Of course you're *allowed* to," he says. "Don't be ridiculous. You want a cup of coffee?"

He points to the tin mug and thermos on the wicker coffee table between the chairs. I shrug and he goes inside. Hands shoved into the pockets of the oversize jacket I slung on before heading out, I trudge up the porch steps and slump into one of the empty rocking chairs. A breeze brushes over the porch, jangling the wind chimes that used to belong to Cass's mom. It's surprisingly cold for a July night.

"Oh my god," Cass says when he returns. He hands me a mug that matches his and pats me on the shoulder. "Wilson Sinéad O'Connor Phillips, you finally achieved your dream. I'm so proud of you, buddy."

I shrink into my jacket, giving him my best scowl. Now I really never will live down that fifth-grade pageant.

Cass sits in the chair beside me. For once, he's not in his sheriff's uniform, but a dark green sweater and jeans that are baggy around the ankles, hanging over his scuffed Nikes. He looks like such a dad.

Steam clouds out of the thermos as Cass unscrews the lid and pours a dark liquid into my mug. The thick scent of coffee fills the air.

"I finally finished volume one of *Ms. Marvel*," Cass says.

"Finally," I say. "I only gave you that comic four months ago. And?"

He shrugs. "It was okay."

"*Okay?*" I say, unable to keep the astonishment out of my voice. I take a tentative sip of my coffee. The mug stains it with a slight metallic taste that reminds me of camping. "It's basically perfect."

"I mean, you know I'm not into superheroes, so it was always gonna be a stretch. But I just don't really get the whole Ms. Marvel thing. Is she Captain Marvel or is she something else?"

"She's *Ms.* Marvel," I insist. "She takes the name when Carol Danvers becomes Captain Marvel. She's a completely different thing."

"Then why not give her a new name?"

"Because she finds out she's Inhuman and chooses to be like her hero, Captain Marvel." Basically, this normal, everyday girl discovers she has secret super abilities locked inside her. Adrenaline bubbles throughout my body at the memory of the comic. "She's just this average teenage girl who feels super awkward about herself. She doesn't fit in with her Muslim family and she doesn't fit in with the white kids at school. That's, like, basically the story of every teenager, in some way or another. Marvel is trying to bring the saga down to a new generation. I thought if anyone would get that, it'd be you."

"I do get that. I guess it's just been too long since I was a teenager." Cass chuckles. "So," he says, "are you working on anything new? You always used to show me your comics."

"I sort of had a new idea," I say slowly, wondering if I should risk it, "something based on what you said that time I came to pick up Bernie after Annie came back. *The Walking Dad.*"

Shoving my worries down for a second, I try to explain the basic gist of *The Walking Dad,* about Jerry and his daughters. His endless struggle for acceptance as an undead dad in the land of the living. I haven't worked on it since Annie first got back, but talking about it now, the panels flying around my brain, I can feel the familiar sense of excitement at having a new idea, the pull of wanting to *create* alive in my fingers.

"Now *that* sounds like something I'd read," Cass says when I'm finished.

I'm grateful for the darkness on the porch as my cheeks heat. The occasional car rumbles down Cass's street, lighting up the houses and their drying lawns.

"So, where's Amanda?" I say quietly.

Even though we don't say it, we both know the only reason

I'm allowed to go near his porch for a prolonged period of time is because Amanda isn't here. Cass, sensing that I'm thinking this, sighs.

"She took your sister out for dinner and a movie in Rosita. They've been buying clothes for the new baby all day, which your sister was obviously very excited about." He sips from his mug and gives me a tired look that says the exact opposite is true. "But Amanda just wants her to feel like she's part of things, get her ready to be a big sister and all that."

I hold my mug up to my face, let the steam warm my mouth. "Must be nice," I mutter into my drink.

The air thickens as this statement sits between us, and for a second I wish I could take it back. It's too much to get into right now, with Mark and Annie and Ryan and Jody. But it's true, and Cass knows it.

Cass runs a hand down his face, scratching his stubbly chin. "I know things with you and Amanda aren't great," he says as he sets his mug back on the table. "But she doesn't hate you."

"Then she's a super-awesome actress," I say. "Is she in, like, movies and stuff?"

"She's just insecure," he says. "I gave her a lot to be insecure about when we first got together and I'm not proud of it." He folds his arms across his chest, waiting for me to say something, but when I don't, he sighs again. "When I first met her, I was still very much in love with your mother and Amanda knew it. She stuck around, hoping it would break, and eventually it did. But I think sometimes, because I've got Bernie, which means you and your mom will always be in my life, Amanda feels threatened. So sometimes she takes it out on you, which isn't right."

I can feel his eyes on me, but I'm too nervous to meet his

gaze. I've never heard Cass talk like this, about how much he loved Jody. Everything meaningful we ever said to each other was always between the lines, hidden in shrugs.

"It doesn't help that I moved her into the house I shared with you and your mom. But it's a good house, close to the station. It's my home. I can't just leave."

He doesn't need to explain himself to me, but I'm not sure he is. Cass shakes his head.

"I think when Amanda has her own baby and sees that some things are bigger than the past, she'll feel better. She needs something that's just mine and hers. Does that make sense?"

I nod. As I drain the coffee from my mug, it leaves me with a warmth that spreads down my arms. Cass holds the thermos out to me but I shake my head.

"How's your mom doing in Vegas? Bernie said she was going skydiving or some crap," he says before pouring himself the remaining drops of coffee.

"Bungee jumping," I say as I set down my mug and tuck my legs underneath me. "She was supposed to do it yesterday, but I haven't heard anything. We're kind of not talking."

I know Jody didn't go back to Las Vegas, because I've been keeping an eye on Pam's Instagram. I also know that Cass wouldn't mind having the extra days with Bernie, but something stops me from telling him my mother came home early.

Cass leans back in his chair so that the light from inside slashes across his face. "Why? What'd she do this time?"

I look down at my lap and smirk. If this were any other mother and daughter, his question would be flipped around. I'm the one who's supposed to be irresponsible.

"It was me for once," I say. When Cass's eyebrows shoot into his hairline, I sigh. "I may or may not have gone into San Diego with Ryan and Annie and done something . . . not great. Many somethings." Despite this little heart-to-heart we're having, I can't bring myself to go into more detail. Even though I know Cass wouldn't yell at me, his quiet disappointment would be harder to take. "Let's just say it was something straight out of the Jody playbook," I say. "And she caught me. Well, I sort of caught myself and told her, because I didn't think she'd be mad. I know this sounds absurd, but I actually thought she'd be happy I was being more like her."

Cass rocks back and forth in his chair, the wood creaking. "And why would you think that?"

"I don't know," I say. "You know how she is. Or how she used to be. Ever since she met Dr. David, she's become weirdly normal. No more tube tops or Chinese food at three in the morning. She bought travel insurance for her bachelorette party. *Travel insurance.*"

"What does that have to do with you?"

My shoulders shrug into my ears. "It feels like she's becoming this new person because there was something wrong with the old one," I say. "Like, I know it's not normal to have to talk your drunk mother out of booking a singles cruise to the Bahamas, but we made it work." My rocking chair has been painted white, but the left armrest is chipping. I scratch at it with my fingernail until a little piece flakes off. "Sometimes I can't help but feel like she's only doing this now because what we had before wasn't good enough. That this is all because of me."

As this statement lingers, I have to fight every urge in my body not to scramble off the porch and run into the night from embarrassment. But ever since I admitted this out loud to Jody,

I realized that this thought has been clinking around in my head for the last year in broken little pieces, the shards sticking into me every time she scheduled a dentist appointment for me, or when she threatened to punish me after San Diego. Why pull the responsible mom card now, after all this time, if something wasn't missing before?

I wait for Cass to correct me, to reassure me that this whole thing isn't my fault, but it doesn't come. Instead he nods and says, "I'm sure she is doing this for you." When I pull in a sharp breath, he looks at me and elaborates. "Not for the reasons you're saying. People change, Wilson. Sometimes even though you're making it work, there's a lot going on under the surface that you don't know about. Your mom's seen a lot in her thirty-five years. Maybe she's just tired and ready to cool down. You and I both know she needed to grow up, not just for herself but for you and Bernie."

We're quiet as this new idea sinks in: Jody not changing because of me, but for me. It sort of makes sense, but maybe it's the skeptic in me that doesn't want to trust it yet. Because I'm nearly eighteen now. Where was all this when I was younger, when I didn't want to have to take care of myself? She might be changing for Bernie, but Bernie has Cass and Amanda. Who did I have except Jody?

Cass leans backward, his arms folded across his chest. "Something I've always known about you is that you seem to be happiest when other people are happy," he says. "And when they aren't, you blame yourself."

A pair of headlights swings into Cass's driveway, belonging to a little red car that parks next to his cruiser. Bernie hops out of the passenger seat and frowns at the sight of me on the porch.

"Wilson?" she says. "What're you doing here?"

Behind her, Amanda has slowly pushed herself out of the driver's seat with a groan. I pull my jacket tight around my middle and stand. Cass watches this with his mouth open, scrambling to the edge of his seat.

"You don't have to—" he starts to say, but I'm already halfway down the porch steps.

I wrap my arms around Bernie's neck, pulling her close. She slides her arms around my stomach and lays her head on my chest as I bury my nose in her scalp. Her hair, pulled back into a loose ponytail, smells like apples.

"Just missed you, I guess," I say into her hairline.

Bernie squints up at me. "As much as you miss your hair?" she says.

I snort. "Debatable."

Cass follows me down the porch and rounds the car so he can help Amanda with the eight thousand bags piled high in the trunk. When I finally pull away from Bernie, Amanda is watching me over the hood of the car. One hand is gripping the trunk's lid while the other rests on her baby bump.

"Wilson, what—" she says, but stops when I give a tight-lipped smile and cross past them into the street.

What Cass said about Amanda might be true, but that doesn't mean it's happened yet. I know that look on her face, what it means.

"Don't worry, I'm leaving," I say, and disappear into the dark.

Nineteen

"We look amazing."

Annie, Ryan, and I are huddled together around the bathroom mirror of the Country Kitchen, putting the finishing touches on our outfits for the Fourth of July parade. Annie is wearing what's supposed to be a long black judge's robe, but is really just a hairdresser's cape, giant circular glasses pushed high on her nose, and her hair slicked back in a low bun. Draped around her neck is a chunky yellow necklace with turquoise beads that her dad let her borrow from one of his Western collections. Ryan is in a floor-length baby-blue dress I found at the back of Jody's closet, her brown hair long and silky, topped with a spiky rhinestone-encrusted crown. Her mascara is smudged halfway down her cheeks, making it look like she's just taken a shower with a full face of makeup.

Ryan leans toward the mirror and adjusts one of her fake eyelashes. "On a scale of one to ten, how pissed off is Ruth Fish gonna be?"

"What's she gonna be pissed about?" Annie says. She sweeps her hands down the front of her robe. "I'm Ruth Bader Ginsburg, a beacon of American justice. What could be more beautiful than that?"

"Yeah," I say as I straighten my wig. "And since when do you care what Ruth Fish thinks?"

It's easily eight thousand degrees outside and I'm wearing a leather jacket, but to take it off now would ruin my entire outfit. The blond wig that itches like a rash and keeps slipping down the side of my head was from Jody's dressing-up section of her closet, and the long silky white dress I'm wearing is really just a nightie I bought at the Thrifty Coyote. Tucked into one of the jacket pockets is the broken table leg, my makeshift stake. Because I'm dressed as season one Buffy the Vampire Slayer, when she leaves the prom to kill the Master, the leader of the vampire race.

Annie claps her hands and rubs them together. "Okay, people," she says. "It's go-time."

Ryan grabs her bouquet of roses and follows Annie to the front door of the restaurant, but I break away and move toward the back office instead.

"Just give me a second. I have to put my stuff in my locker," I say.

The Country Kitchen is quiet for once because it, along with all the other businesses on Main Street, is closed for the morning. I drop my backpack into my locker, but before closing it again, I quietly slip out my Annie notebook. Ever since I realized what I had to do to keep Annie back, I've been taking notes of all the ways in which Annie and Ryan's attitudes toward each other have shifted over the last couple of weeks, how they've patched up their friendship. Grabbing a pen from Terri's desk, I find my list and scribble, *Group costume successful. Teamwork!!* Even though we're not technically dressed the same and our costumes aren't even that related, it still counts. The point is, we came up with the idea together.

Somewhere from Main Street, drums begin to pound.

"Wil, the parade's starting!" Annie calls.

"Coming," I shout back. I shove the notebook into my locker and scramble out to find Ryan and Annie waiting by the front door, watching me. "Are we really doing this?" I say.

Annie pushes open the door. "Obviously."

The air is heavy with the smell of barbecue from the booths lined up just in front of the post office, lawn chairs stacked along Main Street. Draped from the gutter of every single storefront is an American flag that blows lightly in the breeze.

The only thing I hate more than Lennon's Fourth of July parade is how much I love Lennon's Fourth of July parade. Every summer, our town puts together all the weirdest things it can possibly imagine and then directs them down Main Street: old-timey fire trucks, the local Zumba class, bejeweled ATVs, and bearded men playing bagpipes. One year they even had the ladies from the local Women's Association dress up in belly-dancer outfits and guide farm animals down the street. What does any of it have to do with the birth of America, one might ask? Who the eff knows. What I do know is that, instinctively, I should be morally opposed to something so ridiculous, but no matter how much it makes me physically ill to admit, I was born here; this freak show is in my DNA.

The Welcome Back float sits near the end of the parade. Hitched up to a black pickup truck and stacked on a wheeled platform, the float towers over the rest of the parade participants.

The platform itself is divided into four even squares: one that's dusted with red-orange sand and spiked with brightly colored cacti piñatas; another consisting of what I think is supposed to be a field of wildflowers, but that's actually just Astroturf speckled with yellow silk flowers; a forest scene with two giant mushrooms surrounded by stuffed animals; and a tangle of sparkly blue sheets with an inflatable palm tree on top. At the front of the platform sits a papier-mâché mountain carved with steps that lead to a metal banister. A stuffed parrot is perched on it, except the parrot has been redecorated to look like a bald eagle.

As we approach the float, Ruth Fish materializes in front of us completely out of nowhere, as though she's climbed up from a trapdoor in the asphalt. At her sudden appearance, the three of us scream in surprise.

"Oh my god!" Annie shrieks.

Ryan clutches my arm. "You're like a fucking jack-in-the-box," she says to Ruth.

"Where have you girls been?" Ruth says. We were supposed to get in place on the float twenty minutes ago, which is probably why she looks so panicked. She clutches a clipboard against her lavender pantsuit. "Where are your outfits?"

"These are our outfits," Annie says. "I'm RBG."

"And I'm Buffy the Vampire Slayer," I say.

"What about you?" Ruth says to Ryan. "Are you supposed to be Carrie?"

"I'm the girl from Courtney Love's album cover." Ryan's face morphs into an open-mouthed smile as she lifts the bouquet to her cheek, perfectly mimicking the pseudo prom queen. When Ruth says nothing, Ryan shrugs. "I don't know, ask Wilson."

"It's actually Hole's album cover," I say. "*Live Through This*. It was based on Stephen King's *Carrie,* so you're not that far off."

"We wanted Ryan to go as Carrie, but we figured if we drenched her in blood, it'd be super messy," Annie adds.

But Ruth isn't really listening. "The theme is America the Beautiful," she says, her voice climbing in pitch. She gestures to the platform's frame, which is ringed with red, white, and blue streamers.

Annie squints. "Yeah." She says it slowly, in a way that makes it sound like she's speaking to a five-year-old. "And our costumes are of people who are American and beautiful."

"And also badass," Ryan says.

"Oh, for god's sake, we don't have time for this," Ruth says. She points to the papier-mâché mountain. "Annie, you're standing on top of Freedom Mountain."

Annie hikes her robe up around her knees. "Of course it has a name," she says as she climbs onto the platform.

"Wilson, Ryan, you're in the Redwood forest." Ruth gestures toward the mushrooms before waving her clipboard at the llamas on leashes a few groups behind us. "Carol, I told you they can't eat the window boxes!" she exclaims before clacking down the street in her off-white heels.

Ryan and I climb onto the platform and take our seats on the mushrooms. They're surprisingly squishy, the caps made of foam with white felt circles glued on top. As soon as we're settled, the truck lurches forward and Ryan and I grip each other's arms, giggling, to stop us from tipping backward.

Within seconds of moving, the two of us are enveloped in a cloud of exhaust. Annie, who's at least a few feet above the platform, isn't hit by it; she just waves half-heartedly at the crowd while Ryan and I gag. We pivot on the mushrooms so that our backs face the tail end of the platform, which means we can now at least breathe. The parade runs from one end of Main Street to the other, so we'll only be on the float for fifteen minutes, tops. At the front is the Lennon Union Marching Band, who are currently playing an almost frantic version of "Kids in America." Already they're nearly halfway down Main Street, Mr. Martin, the band teacher, waving his sparkly red baton at the crowd in front of the Country Kitchen.

As we chug slowly down Main Street, the float is surrounded by a sea of red, white, and blue. There are kids in bedazzled Uncle Sam top hats waving tiny American flags on sticks, their other hands filled with corn dogs, caramel apples, or ice cream cones from the food stands. Because Lennon is so small, most people know at least someone in the parade, and so at one point or another, everyone is taking pictures as the parade passes by. But whenever Annie comes into view, every single person lifts their phone, almost like they're doing the wave. This time Annie doesn't look uncomfortable; she just grins and waves, banging an inflatable gavel she pulls from her robe pocket on the mountain's metal banister.

"People get that nobody outside of Lennon will think their pictures of Annie are interesting, right?" Ryan says. "Don't they think it'll be kind of weird to outsiders, them having a bunch of pictures of some random girl?"

"I think you're overestimating the people of Lennon," I say.

Ryan nods, considering this.

Most of the noise is incoherent cheering from the crowd, until suddenly it morphs into a steady chanting, just a few voices that cut above the rest. They're shouting Ryan's name.

"Oh my god, I'm gonna kill them," Ryan growls under her breath.

Standing in front of the Wells Fargo are Grant, Mark, and two guys from the track team. They each have their shirts off and a single letter from Ryan's name drawn on their chests in red paint. At first, they're out of order, their chests spelling RANY, until Mark, the *Y*, realizes his mistake and rushes into the right place.

"That's my sister!" Mark screams, his hands cupped around his mouth.

His face is smeared with matching red paint, little slash marks cutting across his cheeks. He and I haven't talked since he came over to my house, where we both declared each other asexual mannequins and very maturely went our separate ways. Seeing him now, in his Ray-Ban sunglasses and his hair pushed back, I know I should feel the heat of embarrassment, but I'm too busy watching Ryan, who has one hand slapped across her forehead. Her shoulders are shaking, and at first I think it's from rage, but when I look closer, I see that she's actually laughing. Up on her mountain, Annie is laughing so hard, she's gasping for breath.

Ryan outstretches both arms, middle fingers pointed upward. Mark boos her.

"Un-American," he shouts, giving her two thumbs down.

As we pass them, Ryan turns her eyes forward and stares into nothing, as though lost in thought. Her tongue creeps over her teeth as she absently half smiles. At the sight of it, the skin on my arms rises with goose bumps. It's only now that I notice her hair as it catches the sun. The way it curls out at the ends, spilling across her back and brushing lightly against her tanned shoulders. She looks really grown-up all of a sudden, not like the Ryan I remember from when we were kids. The one curled up under a blanket fort, Miley Cyrus playing out of her iPod and bright green nail polish smudged across her toes. She looks beautiful.

"What?" she says, catching me staring.

I shake my head as if to clear fog out of my brain. "Nothing," I say, fingers playing with the Atomic Fireball in my pocket. I still haven't been able to eat my last one, opting to carry it around like an edible good luck charm. "You just look really pretty."

"Oh," she says simply. "Thank you." Her eyes sweep across the crowd as a swallow travels down her throat. "Thank god this is my last parade."

"You're moving to San Diego," I say. "It's an hour away."

"Doesn't mean I have to come back here," she says. "I can't deal with another summer of apple pie and Mark's earnest laughter."

"You never know," I say, my eyes flicking up toward Annie, "there might be something you want to come back for." When I look at her again, Ryan is staring at me with squinted eyes. I can tell by the way her gaze shoots up to Annie and then back to me that she's turning something over in her brain. Trying to work something out. But she doesn't know about my plan. She can't. "Like your family," I add quickly.

Ryan finally looks away. "Yeah, I guess," she says.

The float passes in front of Ma's Diner, where Jody, Dr. David, and Bernie are camped out. Last night my mother finally came back to our house, but instead of having the mature conversation we clearly needed to have, we both stayed in our rooms and avoided each other. She's sitting in one of the chairs we used to bring when we went camping at Lake Tahoe, wearing a Calvin

Klein T-shirt and matching fanny pack over jean shorts. When our eyes meet, she waves.

"What about you?" Ryan says, cutting into my thoughts.

I blink myself back onto the float. "What do you mean?"

"Are you staying in Lennon?"

"Where else would I go?" I say. "I mean, I've thought about going to San Diego. Not to follow you, though."

Ryan laughs quietly. "I wouldn't think that, even if you were," she says.

A few groups in front of us is a pack of men in Civil War clothes strutting down the pavement, their plastic guns *pop, pop, pop*ping toward the sky. I watch as one of them stops to answer his phone, one finger pressed into his free ear.

"What would you do if we ran into each other in San Diego?" I say to Ryan.

"I thought you said you weren't following me."

"I said I wasn't following you *to* San Diego," I say. "I didn't say anything about not following you *in* San Diego."

She smirks and looks down at her dress. Around the waist is a strip of tiny silver beads. Ryan picks at them with her fingernail until one of the strands pops free. Watching her do this, I feel my mouth go dry and I can't help but fidget on my mushroom. For some reason her answer feels huge here, as though the wrong one could send me backward like a punch.

"Would you hang out with me?" I say quietly.

At this, Ryan glances up. And just like that, the parade is done. Our float pulls into the parking lot behind the town hall, and before the truck even stops, Annie is scrambling down the fake mountain. Ryan and I are still staring at each other when Annie yanks the robe over her head and discards it on top of a stuffed fox's head.

"I need a thousand showers after that," she says. She tugs her ponytail holder out, unleashing her hair across her shoulders. "Plus, I'm starving." She wrinkles her nose. "Oh my god, what is that smell? Is that from the float? Have you guys been smelling that the whole time?"

Ryan is the first to break our eye contact. "My dad made five thousand pizzas last night for his golf club, so the garage fridge is crammed with leftovers. You guys could come over for lunch, if you— you know, if you wanted."

She says this with her eyes trained on the sky over Annie's head, as though she couldn't care less how we answer. But it's obvious by the way she trips over her words that this question hasn't come naturally.

Annie's jaw hangs open for a second, but she's quick to pull it back up. "Yeah, cool," she says. Then her head snaps toward me. "Wait, don't you have wedding stuff to do? Isn't the rehearsal dinner tomorrow?"

I slide the wig off my head, the itchy cap replaced with cool air. "Nope and yes," I say simply.

I still haven't told either of them about the fact that I'm not invited to Jody's wedding anymore, and somehow right now, as I'm dressed in a secondhand nightgown with suspicious blue stains on the back, doesn't feel like the right time.

"If I come over," Annie says to Ryan, "do you promise not to throw anything at me?" For once, there's no edge to her voice. Annie is actually smiling as she says this.

Ryan rolls her eyes and bites back her own smile. "I can never make that promise, and you know it."

They both laugh and turn away from me, walking so closely together toward the Country Kitchen that their shoulders almost touch. I'm too preoccupied with watching them to move.

Because just like that, in this one exchange, I know I've done it. I've actually done it. Annie and Ryan are friends again.

After the parade, Main Street is a hive of noise as everyone disperses. Crowds push past us, lawn chairs folded under their arms. Already the Country Kitchen has a line of people extending out the front door, so Annie and I wait on the sidewalk while Ryan goes inside to grab our stuff. My body is still electric with the fact that I'm pretty sure this isn't the last summer I'll have with my best friends, my head buzzing with all the things I'll have to do tonight when I get back from Ryan's house.

Just showing Ruth Fish my notebook might not be enough to make my case, so I'll need to make a presentation. A poster or something, or a PowerPoint. I know Ruth says she's not the one who makes the decisions, but she could at least give me feedback on my arguments. Because I'm fully prepared to make a case for Annie staying back if I need to. I'll give it to the grim reaper bus driver who's supposed to take Annie back to the afterlife myself, for all I care.

Because I've done the impossible. I made two people who were once inseparable and then couldn't be in the same room together actually want to hang out again. Ryan Morton and Annie LeBlanc, two of the most stubborn people I've ever met in my life.

"Why's she taking so long?" Annie stands on tiptoe to look over the crowd and into the Country Kitchen windows. "It's been like ten minutes."

I glance down at my phone, which is tucked into one of my

leather jacket's inner pockets. She's right. "Maybe she can't carry everything," I say. "I'll be right back."

The Country Kitchen is so crammed with people, I have to crab-walk sideways to the back office. Mark's face is still covered in red paint as he rushes around behind the counter, shouting pie orders to Taylor. I feel kind of bad, watching him scramble to make change; ordinarily I'd climb behind the counter and help until the rush died down, but Ryan invited us to her house *willingly,* and I don't want to screw that up lest it was part of some fever dream from which she's on the verge of waking up.

Ryan is sitting at her mom's desk, her back to me when I make it into the office. She doesn't stir as I shut the door behind me, instantly plunging the room into quiet. Over the lip of the office chair, all I can see is the top of her head and her spiky crown.

"Should we help Mark?" I say, a little out of breath. "I'm kind of worried the crowd might mob him."

But Ryan doesn't turn. At her feet is my backpack, Annie's black duffle bag, and the long plastic bag Ryan brought for Jody's dress.

"What're you doing?" I say, taking a step toward her.

This time, Ryan does swivel the chair around so that she faces me. Except she doesn't look up, because sitting open in her lap is my Annie notebook.

My stomach plummets. "Where— What are you doing with that?" I say.

She's flipped to the page where I've listed out all the ways in which Ryan and Annie have interacted not like two lions fighting for territory on the savanna, but actual human beings who are actual friends. I lean down to grab the notebook, but Ryan pulls it back, taking it out of my reach.

"That's just— It's my diary," I say weakly. "I've been taking notes on everything we've done this summer. I was gonna give it to Annie at the end so she'd have something to remember us when she goes back to, you know, wherever. I mean, not that I actually know if she's allowed to take—"

Ryan flips back to the first page of the notebook. "That's really interesting," she says. "Because it says here"—she begins reading directly from the notebook—"'Ruth Fish says how to keep Annie back for good equals righting a wrong.' Then you list a bunch of terrible ways you could do this. Here's my favorite: 'Convince David Boreanaz to rerecord the 'Becoming (Part 1)' episode of *Buffy* without his horrible fake Irish accent.' And then all the way down at the bottom, we have a winner. 'Make Ryan and Annie friends again.'"

"That— It was just an idea," I stammer.

She jams her finger into the notebook so hard, it leaves nail prints in the paper. "You literally circled and underlined it four thousand times like a serial killer," she says. Ryan slams the notebook shut and tosses it at my feet. "This fell out of your locker when I was grabbing your backpack. So that's what this whole thing was about? You just wanted me and Annie to be friends again so she could stay back?"

"That," I say slowly, "and because I knew you guys were fighting over nothing. If you could just—"

"Bullshit," Ryan says. She stands, her hands balled at her sides. "You don't care about me. This was never about me."

Behind me, the office door creaks open. Annie's face appears in the gap. "What're you guys doing?" she says. "I thought we were getting pizza."

"Just give us a second," I say to Annie.

But Ryan waves, beckoning Annie into the room. "Oh no, please come in. We wouldn't want you to miss the big reveal."

Annie frowns but steps inside and closes the door behind her. She stands between me and Ryan, her mouth hanging open in question. "What's going on?" she says slowly.

I take a step toward Ryan, my voice low and shaky as I shove my hands into my pockets. The Atomic Fireball is still there, crinkling against the fabric of my jacket.

"Ryan, please," I say. My throat is already thick with tears. What if this ruins everything? That can't happen, not when I've gotten so close. "Obviously I care about you."

"Do you care about me?" Ryan says. "Do you actually? Because I'm not even sure you care about Annie, either." She folds her arms across her chest and cranes her neck so she can see around me. "By the way," she says to Annie, "Wilson has only been trying to make us friends again because she thinks it's the key to you staying back for good."

Annie's gaze goes between me and Ryan rapidly, as though she's trying to shuffle her words into the right order. Eventually she just says, "What?"

I turn to face her, panic coursing through me. "Ruth Fish said if we could right some kind of wrong, there was a chance you could stay back," I say. "Other people have done it before. I couldn't tell you because it had to be genuine, and it was. You guys are friends again. We did it."

"But you did this for yourself," Ryan says. "You went straight into your little plan to keep Annie around because you wanted things to go back to how they used to be. But news flash, Wilson: I told you in Coronado, we're not those people anymore.

And if you stopped, even for just a single second, to actually *ask* what *we* wanted, maybe you would've realized that."

They both look at me, waiting for my response. When there is none, Annie says quietly, "Wilson?"

Before I can answer, tears spill down my face. "I missed you guys," I say. "I missed how things were, before you both left. Annie, you just left. You *disappeared*."

"And how do I fit into that?" Ryan says.

She stares at me with her mouth flattened into a line. Too many thoughts are flying around my head for me to answer. How does Ryan fit into that? How does she *not* fit into it? Without Ryan, we're not a triangle. Annie and I are just a tent without its base. A capital *A* without the middle and therefore gibberish. I try to blink these thoughts into focus, but the words won't stop moving long enough for me to fit them into a sentence. While Ryan waits for my answer, a tear slips down her cheek.

"Yeah," she says as she wipes it with the back of her hand and pushes past me, "that's what I thought."

There's a momentary burst of noise as Ryan opens the office door and slams it shut behind her. Annie has slumped into the office chair, her eyes wide and staring into her lap.

"That is not how I thought this was gonna go," she says.

I step backward again until I reach the door, my shoulders lining up with the cold wood. Without Ryan's anger heating the room, things should feel more manageable. Smaller, somehow. But all I feel is broken, like half of me is missing. How did this all get so backward so fast? All I wanted to do was bring my two best friends back together again, for us to have one amazing month that could turn into something more. The long friendship we always should've had. The one they both obliterated when they decided I wasn't good enough for them anymore. And now here I am, still not good enough.

This thought makes my stomach knot. But as I stand here, swaying slightly, the only thing I can think to do is ask the question I've been wanting to ask ever since Annie came back. Because if this is all going to fall apart anyway, this might be my last chance.

I grip the Atomic Fireball in my pocket so hard, my hand shakes. "What happened before you died?" I say, swallowing.

Annie looks up, her dazed expression swapped for one of confusion. "What are you talking about?" she says. "I drowned. Case closed."

"No, I mean, the year before you died. You know, the one where you ignored me? Where you pretended I didn't exist? Where I literally saw you outside your school and you acted like you'd never met me before?"

At the mention of this moment, Annie flinches. "Wilson, I don't want—" she starts to say as she stands.

"Why can't you just admit it?" I say, centering my body against the door so there's nowhere for her to go. If she started screaming, half of Lennon would hear her and think she was being murdered. But Annie stands still, her eyes fixed on my face. She actually looks afraid. As though I'd hurt her, as though she's not the one who did all the hurting. "Admit that I wasn't cool enough for you when you transferred schools. I was just your pathetic childhood friend. You only wanted to hang out with all the other rich kids, even though my whole life was falling apart. Cass and Jody splitting up, Ryan leaving—"

"I didn't know Ryan would disappear too," Annie says.

"Is that supposed to make it better?" I say. My fingers grip tighter around the Atomic Fireball. Tighter and tighter. "Your parents didn't want you to have anything to do with me because I reminded them too much of all this." I nod to the office around us. "And while I was packing up the only place that ever felt like home, you were out at parties with your precious Ashley and all your other friends. I'd accuse you of forgetting about me, but that would have to mean you actually cared in the first place."

"If I don't care about you, why am I here?" she says.

"Because where else would you be? None of your old friends recognize you. You're basically trapped in Lennon. It's the only way I could get you to hang out with me instead of the other rich assholes."

Just a few weeks ago, these were positives in my head. But now I see these points for what they really are—the sad, demented reasonings of a friendless loser. Me human-hoarding my friends, *The Lennon Chronicles* all over again.

Annie smiles tightly and nods. "You're right," she says. "My life was so fucking perfect. Me and all my rich friends." She throws her arms out and lets them slap against her sides. "You got me, Wilson. We've now established that you didn't care about me, and I didn't care about you, so what are we doing here? Let's cut our losses and stop pretending we're friends."

"Fine," I fire back.

With a rustle, something gives way with a tiny *pop* in my pocket. The Atomic Fireball slips from my hand and bounces onto the floor, rolling somewhere I can't see.

"I should never have brought you back," I say to Annie. "This whole thing was a big fucking mistake, and I'm sorry for wasting your time." Even as I'm saying this I know I'll regret it, but there's a part of me that wants to make her hurt, to feel the cold sting of rejection I've had to sit with for the last two years. It's not right, but I can't help it. "You can go back to acting like I don't exist."

I slam the door before Annie has a chance to say anything else.

TWENTY

DAYS UNTIL ANNIE LEBLANC DIES: 7

When I reach the Country Kitchen just after nine o'clock, the windows are completely dark. The bakers come in around midnight to start putting together the day's apple pies, but I won't be long.

After the parade yesterday, all I could manage when I got home was shrugging my dress off into a heap by the TV and changing into an oversize pajama shirt before watching an entire season of *Buffy the Vampire Slayer* on DVD—the outrageously depressing season six, for the express purpose of torturing myself—and crying until four o'clock in the morning. Jody and Bernie were thankfully at Pam's house celebrating Jody's last few days as an unmarried woman, so I could slowly dissolve into the couch in relative peace. In the absence of the sound of them arguing over how Bernie will do her hair for the wedding—a showdown I *know* has been brewing over the last three months—all I could think about was my argument with

Ryan and Annie, their voices getting colder as I replayed the moments in my head.

Let's cut our losses and stop pretending we're friends.

Maybe Annie was right. Maybe we weren't ever friends, not me, not her, and not Ryan. Maybe childhood was the only thing that bound us, and like Ryan has been saying all along, we aren't those people anymore. I'm now the type of person who downs shots and screams the Beastie Boys in front of an audience. I ran my hands through Mark Morton's hair. But Annie is the one who had helped me get there; without her, I'd probably still be drawing comics in my dark bedroom, ignoring Mark and tip-toeing around Ryan. Could that all really have been possible if Annie and I weren't friends?

And then there's Ryan.

You did this for yourself.

Yeah? And so what? Maybe it *was* about me to some degree. Was that such a bad thing? After the two of them ditched me, they owed me a few days of actually being nice, of acknowledging what they did. I'm so sick and tired of having to prove myself to Ryan, especially when I'm not the one who left in the first place. When I'm with her, my chest fizzes with the need to impress her, to make her happy or laugh, her anger alive and sparkling under my skin. And for the first time in years, she actually looked like she cared. Like she noticed. On the float, when I asked if she would hang out with me in San Diego, she gave me this look that made my stomach flip. Obviously, I care about her. Obviously, I care a weird amount about her. I always have.

And the worst part of all is that after everything, I doubt either of them even cares that it's all fallen apart. Because what have they really lost? Things are now exactly as they had been, with all of us on our own. Like they wanted.

The Country Kitchen's alarm is a shrill beeping designed to deafen burglars and small animals. I have fifteen seconds to turn it off before the beeping staggers into one long beep, then ten seconds before the alarm company alerts the cops. With quick, practiced strides I cross the front floor to the alarm system next to the door by the kitchen and punch in the code, sending the restaurant into silence. I flip on the lights to the back office; sitting exactly where I left it in a pile on the floor next to Ryan's dress bag is my backpack. Annie's duffle is gone. I know it's weird that I waited until the cover of darkness to grab my stuff, but I couldn't stomach the thought of running into Ryan or Mark, in case she'd told him what'd happened and even he started to hate me.

When I crouch down to grab my stuff, my eyes snag on a pinprick of red that stands out against the beige floor tiles, under the desk. I crawl on my hands and knees to reach it, nestled all the way at the back by the computer cords. It's my last Atomic Fireball, its once shiny surface now coated in dust, dirt, and hair that's not mine. The thought to wash the debris off and actually keep the candy crosses my mind, but I throw it away in the trash can by the cubbyholes instead. It's a fitting tribute, it being the only thing Ryan gave me in the last two years, now ending up in the trash.

My notebook is lying closed on the office desk; I grab it, not letting myself wonder if anyone else has read it, because I can't deal with another humiliation right now. As I shove my notebook into my backpack and sling it over my shoulder, it skims against Ryan's bag, which is still open from when she changed into Jody's dress. The insides ruffle, revealing the edge of a book buried underneath Ryan's sneakers and makeup bag. Even though I know there's nobody else here, I poke my head out of the office door to check before rooting through the bag. The book is season eight, volume one of the *Buffy the Vampire Slayer* comics, *The Long Way Home*. On its cover is a sword-wielding Buffy flanked by Willow and one-eyed Xander, the military operation that is all the other slayers gathered behind them. It's an old copy, the pages crinkled and the corners bent. Inside the front cover is a handwritten note.

TO WILSON.

GOODBYE, KINDERGARTEN. HELLO, FIRST GRADE!

LOVE, CASS

It's my copy. The one I put in the time capsule. The one Ryan said she threw away.

"How—" I whisper to myself.

How is this here? Right now? Why would Ryan lie about getting rid of it?

But my confusion quickly gives way to anger. Because there's only one real reason Ryan would pretend she threw away one of my most prized possessions—she wanted to torture me. The thrill she must have gotten to see the disappointment on my face, especially knowing she'd kept my comic all along. Knowing she could bring it out at any moment and my confused joy would follow. She probably wanted the privilege of shredding it in front of my face, the perfect payback for daring to repair things between her and Annie. Technically, though, in order for her to get any payback by bringing the comic to the parade, that would mean she'd already had to have known about my Annie plans. That, or she was hiding her hatred for me all along. But then maybe she just wanted to save the big confrontation for a time she knew Annie would be there, when the potential for humiliation would be at its highest. Maybe that's why she invited us to her house for pizza, to give me the false hope that I'd succeeded. It was all just an act.

Anger and hurt hot in my veins, I cram the comic into my backpack and stomp back out onto Main Street. Locking up the Country Kitchen and storming over to Ryan's house is all a furious blur, one that only lifts when Mark materializes in the front doorway of his house. I don't even remember ringing the doorbell.

"Moss?" he says. He's wearing bright yellow track shorts and thick-rimmed glasses I've never seen before. "What're you doing here?"

"Where's Ryan?" I growl.

Between the sound of my voice and the way my entire body is tensed, Mark skips asking any more questions and leads me inside. Ryan's room is at the front of the house, her door shut. I swing it open without knocking.

She's sitting on her bed, cross-legged, reading from a small red book. I recognize the lavender pajama shirt she's wearing, one we all got from selling Girl Scout cookies when we were little. At the unannounced entrance, she whips her head up.

"What the hell—" she starts to say, but at the sight of me, she stops. "What're you doing here?"

I rifle through my backpack and pull out the comic. "Why did you have this?" I say, throwing it onto the bed. It lands on her comforter without a sound.

Ryan picks up the comic, but I can tell from the look on her face that she doesn't need to examine it in order to know what it is.

"What, so you're going through my stuff now?" she says in what I guess is supposed to be outrage. But her eyes don't meet mine.

I take a slow step toward her, my hands clenched at my sides. "Why did you lie?" I say, my voice shaking with anger.

Pushing herself off her bed, Ryan moves toward the doorway. At first I think she's trying to escape, but she holds on to the door and faces Mark, who's still hovering in the hall.

"Do you mind?" she says to him.

He leans against the wall. "Actually, I'd really like to stay for this," he says.

Ryan makes a sound of annoyed fury before slamming her bedroom door. "I kept it, so what, Wilson?" she says when she turns back around. "I thought you'd be happy."

"So you did want to shove it in my face," I say. Tears grow heavy at the back of my throat. "Did you love the fact that you could just pull it out whenever you wanted and I'd be grateful? Poor, pathetic Wilson, who'd be so happy to have her little comic back from the person who took it in the first place?"

Ryan squints at me. "What the fuck are you talking about?"

Her confusion is so convincing that for a second I can feel my resolve crumbling. But I won't let her make me feel crazy. I didn't imagine this.

"Why did you lie?" I say again, swallowing my tears.

"I was trying to give it back to you," Ryan says. "But not because I wanted to get some sick thrill out of it. I'm not a sociopath."

"You're not answering my question."

"Because I'm not doing this with you, okay?" She charges past me and stops in the middle of the room, arms folded across her chest. "I'm leaving next week because I don't want to do this, not after yesterday."

For the first time, I notice the cardboard boxes scattered around Ryan's room. There are at least seven of them, two of which are tall enough to reach her waist. Written on their sides are descriptions of their contents: BOOKS, BED STUFF, and (MORE) CLOTHES.

"What do you mean?" I say.

Ryan gestures to the open boxes. "I'm moving to San Diego next week and staying with my cousin until school starts. I just can't—I don't want to be here anymore."

Defeat rushes through me, one I don't understand. Ryan was always going to leave. That was always the plan. After yesterday and now this, with my comic, I shouldn't care. But somehow, still, after everything, I do.

"Why?" I say, the tears returning. "You really hate me and Annie that much that you'd leave early?"

"No," Ryan says. Her eyes dart up to the ceiling, as though my inability to understand her is so frustrating, she can't even look at me. "It's the *situation* that I hate."

"But Annie's leaving soon," I say.

"But you'll still be here!" Ryan throws her arms out, giving the impression that she's two sizes bigger. "When are you going to realize that I hate Annie because of *you*?"

This question hits me with such force, I feel almost breathless. I blink it into focus, not sure if I even heard her right. "What?" I say, nearly a whisper. Then, after I swallow: "Why?"

"Because it's always been you and Annie, for as long as I can remember. I know you like to pretend that we were all best friends, but anyone with a brain could see I was just your third wheel."

"That's not true," I say.

"Are you kidding me?" Ryan says. "You picked her over me for everything. *Everything*. Remember when you broke your arm riding your bike and you let Annie design your entire cast so nobody else had room to sign it? Or when we went to the Del Mar Fair that summer, and you wanted to ride the Ferris wheel for hours. You sat next to Annie *every time*."

I rub my eyes, trying to remember. Those were just two times. It wasn't always like that. Was it?

"And then when you gave us that comic, that was it," Ryan continues. "I couldn't do it anymore. I had to get away from you."

"But *why?*"

"Because it was the last straw!" Ryan throws her hands onto her head and paces around the boxes in circles. "That comic proved everything I'd ever been scared of, everything I'd tried to ignore." She gives me a look, her eyes pleading, but I still don't understand. "You made it so that the first chance I got, I sided with the vampires and you and Annie saved the day. It was you guys against the world. Even me."

I take a deep breath through my nose, the instinct to argue at the front of my mouth, but I don't say anything. I can't. Because she's right: I did make her the villain, if only for a few pages.

"That's not—I didn't mean for it to seem like that."

"I know you didn't," Ryan says. "And that made it even worse. You were too busy thinking about Annie to see that you'd crushed me." Tears gather along the bottoms of her eyes. When Ryan blinks, they fall. "And then everything about this summer. You never wanted to be friends with me; you just wanted to keep Annie back. I've always been a footnote in your fairy-tale friendship."

"That's not true. I never wanted to stop being friends with you," I say, taking a step toward her. "I hate that you and me can't make fun of the way Mark's voice drops like four octaves when a hot girl comes into the Country Kitchen and I hate that I can't call you when I want to kill my mother and I hate that you're moving to San Diego. I hate that you hate me."

Ryan drops her eyes to the floor and the plush cream-colored carpet underneath her bare feet. "I don't hate you," she says quietly. "I've tried. If I hated you, this would be so much easier."

"Then what?" I say, taking another step closer. "If you don't hate me, then why couldn't we be friends after Annie died? Why did you leave?"

"Because I don't want to be your friend." When Ryan looks up, her face is streaked with tears. "I want to be *with* you."

She's looking at me so plainly, her eyes more nervous than I've ever seen before. Ryan wanting to be with me would mean she . . . actually likes me? Like . . . *likes* me, likes me? But that can't be true. Not when everything she's ever said to me has been chocolate-dipped in rage. Even after she kissed me, I never thought for a single second that she did it because she liked me, mostly because the interaction ended when she *literally threw up*.

"You—" I start to say. "What?"

The only thing I can seem to do is ask questions. Because none of this makes any sense.

"After the comic I—I knew I was kidding myself, that I just

needed to get over you," she says. "And the only way I was gonna do that was by leaving. I mean, as much as I could in Lennon. And in the meantime, apparently the only way I could deal with being around you was by acting like a six-year-old who has to push someone down on the playground to say she likes them." Ryan wipes her nose with the back of her hand. "I thought if you shaved your head, things might get easier."

Outside, a pair of headlights cuts through the darkness of the street, flooding Ryan's bedroom with a bright white glow that's gone as fast as it came. Hearing Ryan say this, I feel something click in my head. Is that why she was so adamant about me shaving my head? Because she thought it would make me look ugly and she wouldn't like me anymore?

I frown. "That's kind of fucked-up," I say.

She laughs softly. "Yeah, well, if it makes you feel any better, it completely backfired." She glances up, shy, before looking away. "You weren't supposed to be this cute with a shaved head."

I don't know what to say to this. Even though only days ago Mark was acting like he also thought I wasn't the grossest person on the planet, hearing Ryan say this fills me with an embarrassed warmth. It's my turn to look down at my feet.

"Ever since Annie got back, I went right back to being the old me, the one who put up with her just so I could be around you," Ryan says. "And don't pretend that Annie likes me either. She only hung out with me because she wanted to hang out with you, too, just not for the same reasons." Ryan straightens up. She's wearing her gold necklace with the *R* charm, its delicate chain curving over her sharp collarbones. She runs her finger along its ridges, nail catching in the gaps. "I just need to get out of here," she says absently, her eyes scanning the boxes scattered across her room. "I can't feel like this anymore, like I'm drowning."

A new round of tears falls, snaking along her nose and pooling in the bow of her top lip. With one more step, I close the gap between us. Being this close to her, feeling her warmth just inches away, that same spark zigzags up my spine, the one I felt when Ryan kissed me, or when I accidentally saw her half naked. For the first time, it occurs to me that maybe I didn't just like kissing Ryan. Maybe I actually *like* Ryan. But because it was hidden behind my nerves, the need to impress her, to make this work, I'd been able to reason it away as something else.

Without thinking, I reach my hands up to either side of her face and touch her forehead to mine. She doesn't pull away, just lifts her eyes, her gaze glittering with tears.

"Please don't go," I whisper.

And then, before I can stop myself, I lean in and kiss her. Within seconds, the spark has multiplied by thousands, swirling up my back, across my arms and into my legs. Up my neck and even into my scalp, as though every millimeter of me is on fire. Ryan's hands make their way to my waist, her fingers grabbing the cotton fabric of my T-shirt in hungry handfuls.

A few seconds later when I finally pull away, I'm almost totally out of breath. "I think I've been kissing the wrong Morton," I say.

Ryan's eyes spring open. "You've been kissing my *brother*?"

I'd forgotten there was a chance Ryan didn't know about me and Mark, but of course she's not aware I had him at my house, that I let myself obsess over what it would be like to touch his hair. And obviously Mark doesn't talk about girls with his twin sister, especially not ones who are supposed to be her friends.

"Wh— No," I stammer quickly. "I mean yes, but also no. Not anymore. It's a really long story and I promise I'll tell you about it, but can it please be later?"

It looks as though Ryan is weighing her options as her eyes float up to her ceiling again. Finally she sighs and moves back in, her mouth finding mine. With her hands never leaving my hips, she skillfully maneuvers me over to her bed, where we fall backward onto her polka-dot comforter. Her mouth travels down to kiss my neck, but before she can get any further, she pulls away. Her eyes bounce around my face without ever meeting mine, her breathing heavy and fast. As her hair falls across her forehead, all I can think about is how beautiful she is, so beautiful I feel slightly sick.

Her gaze somewhere on the bed behind me, she gnaws her lower lip. "Is this okay?" she says quietly.

I've never seen her this nervous before. There's something sweet about it. Irresistible. I push myself onto my elbows and kiss her again, the weight of her hips pressing into mine.

I know it's not what she meant when she asked, but there's only one thing I can think to say: "Better."

After making out for a truly unbelievable amount of time, Ryan and I lie in her bed still fully clothed because she insists she doesn't want to take advantage of me by pushing me into moving too fast, even though I'm the one trying to take off her pajama shorts. We stay like that all night, legs and arms intertwined under her comforter, only breaking apart so she can tell her parents I'm here and I can change into a pair of sweatpants. It takes me a couple of hours to catch her up on everything: the plan with Annie, my fight with Jody. Even Mark. She makes me speed through this part, pretending to gag when I tell her about him ambushing me on my porch.

"He's such a drama queen," Ryan says. "He likes to make it seem like he's super cool, but he actually loves all that cheesy romantic shit. Did you know his favorite movie is *The Fault in Our Stars*?"

Hearing this gives me a little pang of despair. Not because I wish things had worked out with Mark instead of Ryan, but because I feel kind of bad. Now that I'm here with Ryan, it's so obvious to me how this whole thing is supposed to feel, and that it never did with Mark. I was nervous and weird around him just like I was with Ryan, but maybe that was because nobody had ever really acted as if they liked me like that before. And with the combination of me trying to forget the way it felt to kiss Ryan mixed with my excitement over the thought of someone so great as him feeling that way, I never actually stopped to ask myself if I felt that way too, or if I just liked being liked.

I tell her about Jody and the way I basically accused her of being a terrible mom until Cass forced her into normalcy. Ryan has the decency not to laugh in my face when I mention that Jody was upset when I called her drunk, maintaining the same pensive expression when I say that we've barely talked since and Jody's wedding is tomorrow. And that after all that work, I'm not actually going to see my mom walk down the aisle on what I know is her dream day. After I did everything I could to make sure it's her dream day.

When I get to the part about Annie, Ryan is so quiet it's almost weird. She doesn't give me a high five when I confess that I told Annie I wished I'd never brought her back in the first place, that I finally told her how she made me feel all those years ago.

"I'm so sorry I hurt you," I say to Ryan, wrapping my legs in hers. "All those times in the past, and then since Annie's been back. I never meant to be closer to Annie. It's just—things with her always felt easy. My feelings for you felt more . . . complicated." Only now am I realizing that our different dynamics aren't the way they are because I necessarily like Annie more than Ryan, at least not in a way that's so simple; my feelings for them are just very, very different.

"I'd be madder, but," Ryan says, "*this* happened." She slides her hands along my bare stomach for emphasis. "Maybe it was always meant to be like this. Annie as your best friend and me as . . ." She lets her sentence trail off, her eyes searching mine.

I press my mouth to hers, sparks lighting up every inch of my skin. When I pull away, her eyes are still closed as I say, "Everything else."

The next morning, I wake up with one of Ryan's arms flung over my waist. I curl into her side and breathe in the smell of her T-shirt until her eyes flutter open. A rectangle of light cuts in through the window, making her peach-orange walls glow. As I trace the constellation of freckles speckling Ryan's hip with my finger, I can't tell which one feels weirder: me being with her, like this, or the fact that it took us this long to get here. Everything about lying next to her, in the sleepy warmth of her bed, feels right, like the crevice in her sheets was made exactly for the shape of my body. Now that we're finally here, leaving again feels impossible.

"You know you have to talk to Annie, right?" Ryan says into the top of my head.

I push my face into my pillow and groan. "I was literally just thinking about the fact that I'm never leaving this bed."

"There'll be plenty of time for this," Ryan says.

"Not really," I say, suddenly quiet.

For a few seconds Ryan doesn't answer. I pull my head up to see her expression, but it's blank. Her chest rises and falls slowly as my words, something that's been in the back of my head since we first kissed yesterday, hang above us in the dim morning light of her bedroom. Just next week, she's leaving. All her stuff, shifts at the Country Kitchen with her, Ryan—it'll all be gone. Now that I've acknowledged it out loud, the air in the room feels too heavy, the thrill of having finally found each other squashed by the crushing fist of reality.

From the way Ryan's eyes fly around my face, I can tell she's trying to think of something to say. This is when I realize that what I've just said is beyond needy, even in spite of the fact that I just spent the entire night in Ryan's bed while she spooned me and muttered dream words into my neck. Because this is *Ryan Morton,* who can walk into a room and leave with whoever she wants. Who hasn't been in a relationship before not because she wants to but can't, but because she doesn't want to be tied down.

"I just mean, because I know you're going to college or even, like, moving to San Diego next week," I say, my words rushed and nervous. Even though just last night I more or less told Ryan she was everything to me, images of her and Maddie on that bench at Grant's house flood my head against my will. "Plus, I don't know if you're still hanging out with Maddie, or whatever, or anyone else—"

"Wilson." Ryan shimmies down her bed so that we lie directly parallel to each other. "Stop." She lifts a hand and rests it on the side of my face, fingertips absentmindedly playing with my earlobe. "I've basically loved you my whole life. I loved you when you picked Annie, I loved you when you made out with my brother. Me moving to San Diego is the least of my worries."

"But I know you don't like relationships and I—"

She snorts a laugh. "I didn't want a relationship with any of *them,*" she says. "I know I've hooked up with a lot of people, and I'm not ashamed about that. It was my way of looking for someone I could care about as much as I cared about you. It's like how you felt with Mark. On paper, yeah, you're into it, but then when you actually try to do something, it just feels weird and numb. There's nothing wrong with that person; they're just— not for you."

"That makes sense, I guess," I say, nodding.

Maybe Mark, though gorgeous and cool and so funny it hurts, just isn't my person and never would be, no matter the circumstances. Because Ryan Morton is.

"Although, it was definitely easier making out with people I didn't care about," she says. "At least I never threw up in front of them."

My head snaps back against the pillow at this memory. The fact that I haven't thought about it in the last twelve hours feels impossible, especially because it's almost always at least in the back of my mind whenever I'm within ten feet of Ryan.

"Which, by the way, was the most embarrassing moment of my life," Ryan continues. "I specifically told Mark not to get vanilla vodka because it always makes me sick."

"Wait, what?" I say. "You were drinking that night?"

Ryan frowns. "Yeah," she says slowly. "Why else would I have puked?"

"I don't know," I say, suddenly feeling shy. My arms prickle with goose bumps I try to smooth down with my fingers. "Because I was gross?"

It's Ryan's turn to pull away, her expression becoming so comically shocked, I almost laugh. "Are you serious right now?" she says. She glances around her bedroom as if to look for hidden cameras. "No. Oh my god, no. I'd had three very poorly mixed vodka orange sodas and then every time I'm near you I already feel like I'm gonna barf because I'm so nervous, so put that all together and that's me throwing up into my hands."

I stare up at the ceiling, blinking. Ryan and everyone drinking that night never occurred to me before, but it would explain Mark repeatedly holding up the orange soda bottle to me and lifting his eyebrows.

I turn my head toward Ryan. She's actually blushing.

"Wait," I say, "did you say *I* make you nervous?"

She squints at me. "Uh, absolutely," she says, as though it's the most obvious thing in the world. "More than anyone I've ever met."

Curling onto my side again, I inch toward her, fingers skimming the chain of her *R* necklace, whose charm is hidden somewhere in the neck of her T-shirt. "But Ryan Morton does not get nervous," I say, a warmth spreading in my stomach when the feeling of my fingers on her collarbone makes her shiver.

"I do when I'm with you," she says.

The firework is back, shooting up from my stomach and into my throat. I edge toward Ryan as close as I can until there's no space left between us and our faces are only millimeters apart.

"Are you nervous right now?" I ask.

She furrows her brow, a question bright on her face, as though she doesn't recognize me and, honestly, I don't know where this is coming from either. But something about being with Ryan makes me feel strong and safe. Gutsy.

Ryan's voice is quiet, but charged. "A little bit."

I know I should be thinking about Annie and my mom. I should be kicking down their respective doors and making things right, but Ryan's skin is so soft and she looks impossibly beautiful in spite of the fact that she hasn't brushed her hair. As if she can read my thoughts, Ryan leans in and kisses me, her hands gripping the sides of my head so they would be knotted in my hair if I had any. With one skillful movement, she rolls me on top of her and then before I can think about it, I lift my shirt over my head. I shiver with both the new cold and nerves over Ryan seeing me naked, but as she looks up at me, her eyes are still bright and, for once, I'm not the only one who looks like they can't say no.

Her hands move to my back, carefully tracing the notches of my spine as I lean down to kiss her again, but before I can, there's a knock on her bedroom door.

"Shit!" Ryan hisses as I clamber off of her and grope around the bed for my shirt.

It's probably more surprising that we haven't been interrupted yet, especially because Ryan's entire family was home all night. We heard them through the door talking loudly about football and Mark leaving the bathroom light on, but after Ryan told her parents I was sleeping over, they pretty much left us alone.

The pajama shirt is just over my head again when Ryan says to whoever's in the hallway, "You can come in."

I scrub my hair down before forgetting there's nothing to scrub, so instead I busy myself arranging my limbs on top of Ryan's comforter in a way that makes it look like I would never even consider going underneath.

The bedroom door creaks open.

"You lovebirds decent?" Mark says as he pokes his head around the corner. He's smiling mischievously and raising his eyebrows at his sister, who scowls in response.

"How did—" I say, shooting a glance at Ryan, but I stop myself.

Though Mark obviously knows Ryan likes girls, I'm not sure how much of this situation she's ready to reveal.

But without blinking, Ryan folds her arms across her chest and says, "Yeah. What do you want?"

I suck in a sharp breath, fighting off a smile. When Ryan's eyes meet mine, I can see a shy smile of her own trying to cut through her scowl, but she looks away quickly before it can.

"How did you know?" I say to Mark as I bite my lip.

He glances over his shoulder before stepping farther into Ryan's room. In his hand is a half-wrapped Slim Jim that he takes a bite from with his back teeth. "Wow, okay, where to start?" he says as he shuts the door. "First of all"—he turns back to us, chewing—"nobody says 'shit' when someone knocks on their door unless they're banging. Second, you guys haven't whispered a single thing since you got here, Wilson, and my room is literally *right there*." He reaches over my head and knocks on the wall behind Ryan's bed. I can't bear to look at him; my face is so red, I don't know how I haven't burst into flames. "And for the record, my favorite movie is *Paper Towns,* not *The Fault in Our Stars*." He points a finger in Ryan's face. "Get your fucking facts straight."

Ryan slaps his hand away. "Are you done?"

"No," Mark says. He gestures to me with the Slim Jim. "I haven't gotten to the third reason I knew about you two, which is, Wilson, your shirt's on backward."

I glance down at my shirt. Sure enough, the tag is sticking up right in my face, the fabric a plain navy blue and missing the star logo it's supposed to have on the front pocket.

"Oh my god," I mumble as I bend my arms so I can tuck them inside and twist my shirt around the right way.

Ryan rolls her eyes at her brother, but then bites her lip. "So," she says, dropping her voice. "You're not mad?"

Mark sits on the edge of the bed closest to Ryan. "Nah," he says, patting her arm. He clears his throat and pauses, bobbing his head as whatever he's about to say next races through his mind. Maybe he's come to the same conclusion as me, that we just weren't right for each other on some sort of cosmic level. When he finally leans in and swallows, his eyes look somber, his smile understanding. "Because," he says to his sister softly, "the bottom line will always be, Wilson was always into me first."

Without meaning to, I bark a laugh as Ryan shoves Mark off her bed and throws a pillow at the back of his head. He turns around, still laughing, arms going up to cover his face as a second pillow arcs through the air.

"Did you actually need something, or are you just here to be a dick?" Ryan says.

Mark's face is red from laughing. He nudges one of the pillows with his toe before taking another bite of his Slim Jim and nodding his chin at me.

"Oh, yeah," he says. "Wilson, your mom's here."

TWENTY-ONE

DAYS UNTIL ANNIE LEBLANC DIES: 6

Jody stands in the foyer of the Morton house in a pair of sweat-pants and an oversize button-down that probably belongs to Dr. David. Her forehead crinkles as she takes in the sight of me. In one hand she holds a coffee cup from the Country Kitchen, while at her feet are a few shopping bags and a duffle. I spent the entire walk trailing Mark down the hallway smoothing down my shirt and rubbing my eyes, as though that'll somehow hide the fact that I've got Ryan all over me. Mark doesn't attempt to hang around this time; when we reach Jody, he quietly slips into the kitchen without another word.

"Aren't you supposed to be getting ready for the wedding?" I say to my mother.

"I've been calling you all morning," Jody says. "When you didn't answer, I had to start calling your friends' houses. Why aren't you picking up your phone? Why do you never pick up your phone anymore?"

I chew my tongue. "It's in my backpack," I say. Between charging over here and having the most intense sleepover of my life, I haven't checked it. "Why, what's wrong? Did Pam forget to give the florist the key to the clubhouse at the orchards? Because they can't start putting the centerpieces together unless—"

"No, it doesn't have anything to do with the wedding," Jody says. She puts both hands on her hips. "It's Annie. She's missing."

With just those few words, the room seems to shrink.

"Wh— Wait, what? How?" I say. "I saw her two days ago."

"Well, her mom says she's not home. They don't know where she is."

The last time I saw her was when I stormed out of the Country Kitchen. I just assumed she'd go home after that, but what if she didn't? There aren't any public buses or taxis in Lennon—much less Ubers—that go to San Diego, so what if she hitchhiked to Rosita? Ashley and the rest of her friends won't remember Annie, but what if she went down there to try to rekindle things anyway, to remember what real friendship was like? But then on the way, the person that was driving her got in a horrible accident and swerved their car off into the canyons. One of the last things I would've said to Annie was that I wished I'd never brought her back.

Jody sips from her coffee, her eyes closing with the quiet happiness that comes with ingesting caffeine early in the morning.

"Um, hi, my best friend is *missing*," I say, waving my hands in front of her face. "Can you please act like this is a big deal?"

Over the lid of her coffee cup, Jody blinks. "Okay, maybe 'missing' was a little strong," she says. "All signs point to her running away."

"Running away?" I say, the coldness of my worst fears sinking in. "How do you know that?"

"Mary LeBlanc called this morning." Jody shifts her weight to her other hip. "Apparently Annie went up to her room after dinner yesterday and they didn't hear from her again all night. This morning when her mom went to check on her, she was gone. She left a note."

"A note?" I repeat. "What kind of note?"

Jody nods. "She said she'd had enough of this whole thing and just wanted to let everyone get back to their lives."

I cover my face with my hands. "Oh my god," I groan. "This is all my fault."

"What're you talking about?"

Though the TV is on in the family room just off the kitchen, I'm still acutely aware of the fact that Mark can probably hear fragments of our conversation.

"Can we talk about this outside?" I say under my breath.

Jody follows me out to Ryan's porch. On the front step is a white mailbox decorated with hand-painted tulips and a welcome mat with a rainbow flag. Jody and I settle onto the porch's top step, my mother setting her coffee cup between us so she can splay her hands across her knees.

"So, why are you the reason Annie ran away?" she asks.

I rub my forehead, a pit forming in my stomach. "The day of the parade me and Annie got in a fight and I told her I wished I'd never brought her back." I say this part quickly, hoping that if my mother misses some of it, it won't be as bad as I think. But when I look up and see Jody's stricken face, I know it's a lost cause. "It was awful, I know," I insist. "Now she's probably dead in some ditch and I'll never get to say sorry."

"Let's not jump that far ahead," Jody says. "Mary says they heard her moving around upstairs just before she went up to check on her, which means she can't have gotten very far. They've already called the sheriff's department, which means Cass is on it, and you know how worked up he gets when anything happens to you and your friends. Remember Chuck E. Cheese?" At this, Jody raises an eyebrow.

For Bernie's fifth birthday we went to Chuck E. Cheese and I got to bring Ryan and Annie along. When Annie came out of the ball pit crying because some older boy had called her a "little bitch," Cass squeezed himself through the mesh curtains and pulled the kid out by the neck of his T-shirt. And that's why Cass isn't allowed in any Chuck E. Cheese franchises anymore.

"Cass thinks you should go over there and look at the note. You might be able to read something into it he can't."

I squint at my mother. I can't help it. "You talked to Cass?"

She glances away, her gaze landing on something above my head. "Believe it or not, I can be mature," she says.

Something in the way she says this, ever sarcastic but tinged with a little bit of hurt, makes my eyes drop to my lap. I swallow, Cass's words from that night at his house echoing in my ears. *You seem to be happiest when other people are happy, and when they aren't, you blame yourself.* Is that really what I've been doing this entire time? Holding myself accountable for my mom's unhappiness?

"About what I said a few days ago—"

"Don't worry about it," Jody says, cutting me off. "Let's talk about it after you've found Annie."

"But I shouldn't—"

"Wilson," she says, softly but firmly. "You had every right

to say what you did. Would I have used the same bitchy tone?" She shrugs theatrically. "Probably not. But still, I deserved it." Jody reaches over, searching for my hand. When our fingers find each other, she interlaces hers with mine. "You *are* enough for me," she says, barely above a whisper. "You always have been, you and Bernie. I wasn't enough for myself. It had nothing to do with you."

I open my mouth to speak, maybe even argue, but Jody keeps going.

"I think I always thought that you came out of me the way you are, so responsible and mature and independent. It never occurred to me that maybe I made you this way, that you became how you are because I wasn't there to take care of you." Jody's voice hitches, tears suddenly spilling down her cheeks. "I took advantage of it. Of you. I wasn't who you needed me to be and I'm so sorry." She looks up at me, her face near crumpling. "I need you to know that. I know it doesn't mean much, now that you're old enough not to need me anymore, but I still wanted you to know."

I nod slowly. "It's not like you abandoned me . . ." I start to say, but I know that's not what she means.

Because she's right. She wasn't there when I needed her, when my family self-destructed, when my best friends disappeared. Even still, I want to believe her when she says that I'm enough for her. And I think I can. Maybe there's a part of me that already does. But it's going to take time for this to fully sink in.

Jody shakes her head. "I love you so much, but I was selfish and young."

"I know you love me," I say. "But you were going through your own stuff too and, I don't know, when I said all that stuff about you and Cass, I think I—"

"No, no, can you not be the mature adult in this scenario, and let me apologize?" Jody squeezes my hand. "My stuff isn't your stuff, and I never should've made it that way. You were a kid who didn't need to be worrying about whether or not dinner got made or if I was grieving over a breakup. End of story." She straightens up, teeth creeping over her bottom lip. "And everything with Cass—he's an amazing person and such a good dad, but I wasn't ready for him. I was so young when we met and the idea of slowing down scared me. But when I met David, I knew it was finally time to *accept* the love I deserved and be the person I should've been a long time ago. For you and Bernie, and for me."

Somehow during all of this I've started crying too, but this time I don't really care. Jody's tears pool at the edge of her chin and drop onto the triangle of chest visible above her shirt.

I wipe my nose with the back of my hand. "I thought you didn't want to talk about this right now," I say with a sniff.

"All right, fine, maybe I wanted to talk about *some* things," she says. Jody glances up at the porch covering, still strung with white Christmas lights. "So, what's going on here? Are you and Ryan Morton friends again?"

The easy thing to do here would be to nod quietly and move on, if only to avoid having this conversation with my mom now. Here. But at the same time, it feels wrong to pretend like what I have with Ryan isn't real, especially if she's already willing to do the same.

"Um, maybe more?" I say, braving a glance at my mom. Her eyes widen. "We're still figuring it out."

"Are you telling me you had a naked sleepover here last night?" she says.

"Wh— Naked sleepover?" I stammer. My voice drops to a whisper. "I did not have a naked sleepover. Why would you even say that?"

Technically I only got half naked and that was after the sleeping part.

She laughs softly and turns her gaze toward the street, where a family of squirrels skitters across the road and disappears into a rosebush. "So," she says eventually. "Ryan Morton, huh?"

I swallow. "Ryan Morton," I say. "I only just worked it out, but now that I have, it feels . . . I don't know. Perfect."

Jody nods. "Good," she says. "That's how it's supposed to feel. I always liked Ryan. She's sweet. Very, very intense. But sweet." She puts a hand on my shoulder and says with seriousness, "Does this mean Ryan and her family might want to come over for fajita night?"

I drum my fingers against my knees and push myself to my feet. "This is the part where I go find Annie," I say.

With my arms hugged around my chest, I open Ryan's front door. Behind me, Jody is laughing.

"Fine," she calls after me, "but don't forget, the wedding guests start arriving today at—"

"Two o'clock," I say without thinking. But once the words are out of my mouth, I freeze. "Wait," I say, turning back. "I didn't think I was invited anymore."

Jody swivels around and gives me a look. "Do you really think I'd get married without you?" she says. "You and your sister are everything to me. Plus, Pam cannot be my only bridesmaid. That's too depressing, even for me."

I roll my eyes, pretending to look annoyed, but there's a warmth in me that I can't describe.

As I step back into Ryan's house, Jody shouts, "And don't think we've finished this Ryan conversation."

The front door clicking softly back into place, I pause, smiling to myself like an idiot in the darkness of the foyer. I know we haven't finished our conversation, and for once, I kind of like it.

TWENTY-TWO

DAYS UNTIL ANNIE LEBLANC DIES: 6

From the bottom of the driveway, Annie's house looks exactly like I remember: crisp white paint, navy-blue trim with matching shutters, and a front door in candy-apple red. At Halloween, Mrs. LeBlanc used to arrange the pumpkins on their porch by size and color so that it all looked as precise as a window display for a big New York City department store. The last time I went inside was the weekend before the incident at the Fish Grotto, when Ryan and I slept over. Annie's dad had just bought a vintage pinball machine for his home office, the whirling lights making the ceiling glow rainbow.

Standing just at the bottom of Annie's long pebbled driveway, I feel even more awkward than normal.

"Are you sure we have to do this?" I say.

Though I already know the answer, I can't stomach the idea of what might lie inside: a new home movie theater or an outbuilding in the backyard reserved exclusively for head massages.

Ryan nods just once and says, "Yep."

Together, we crunch our way up the driveway, through the narrow gap left between the LeBlancs' Range Rovers. There's a long white streak cut down the driver's side of one, as though someone zigzagged their key from the door handle all the way to the car's nose. My finger drags along it as we pass, hovering in the air even when the trail falls behind.

A small wooden bench is pressed up against the side of the house on the porch, faded red, white, and blue pillows scattered across its surface. The metal lanterns on the porch steps are unlit, their candles inside just plastic instead of wax.

"I think I'm gonna throw up," I say to Ryan, goose bumps rising on the back of my neck.

"Why?" Ryan says.

"Because," I say, glancing around the porch. The paint around the doorframe is chipped and worn, the navy-blue flakes shivering in the wind. "If Mary LeBlanc hated me before, she definitely hates me more now. Now that I'm the reason her undead daughter who has less than a week to live has disappeared."

Ryan's hand slips into mine. We didn't bother going back to my house so I could change, so I'm just wearing a pair of her shorts and the T-shirt I wore to bed last night. Standing there in it, knowing what we did, makes me blush.

She squeezes my hand. "She never hated you," she insists. "She was a weirdo, but at least she was nice to us."

"Yeah, maybe before Annie transferred to Del Monte, but that was only because we were around all the time and she probably felt like she had to," I say, remembering the way Mary LeBlanc actually fled the deli at the sight of me. "When Annie started ignoring me, she could finally do it too."

Ryan squints at me. "People with this much money don't have to be nice to—"

The front door sweeps open, cutting her off. Mary LeBlanc stands in the doorway, her hands clutched at her chest. It's obvious from her red eyes that she's been crying for the last three hours. I suck in a deep breath and try to think of something to say. I'd do anything to skip this part, where Mrs. LeBlanc has to force herself to acknowledge us, but only because we're actually worth something to her now. A window into her daughter's whereabouts.

But then, without warning, Mrs. LeBlanc lunges forward and wraps me in her arms, her face resting in the crook of my neck.

"Oh, girls, I'm so glad you're here," she says, reaching out and groping for Ryan, who she pulls into me.

At first, it's impossible not to freeze under her bony grip, but as she sobs into my shoulder, my body somehow manages to relax. The whole time, I can feel Ryan watching me, my hand resting awkwardly on Mary LeBlanc's back. Basic tolerance, disgust, even indifference at my presence: any of these reactions, I would've expected. But this? I don't know what to do with this.

After what feels like ten minutes, Mrs. LeBlanc finally pulls away. "Here, come in," she says, one hand dabbing at her eyes and the other waving us through the threshold.

Hanging from the foyer's ceiling is a chandelier so bright, my eyes water. I step into the LeBlanc house blinking back tears, waiting for my eyes to adjust. When they finally do, I glance into the living room just off the front door, expecting to see nothing but velvet and gold, a really elaborate armchair made out of crocodile skin, and a silver statue of a greyhound towering over a marble fireplace. Instead it's the exact living room from years ago: the same glass coffee table, latte-colored carpet, and blue corduroy couches, except the arms are shredded from what look like cat claws. Hanging over the plain plaster fireplace is Annie's school picture from junior year, the one her parents used in her obituary in the *Lennon News,* its frame a simple black. The walls are striped with red-and-white wallpaper, the same stuff Mrs. LeBlanc put up after Mr. LeBlanc's company opened a third warehouse in the desert.

The same family photos in tacky collages are on the walls, the fake leather recliner Mr. LeBlanc got from Cass after his mom died and we cleared out her house still in the far corner of the room. Even their TV is the same, perched on the trunk me and Annie used to pretend was a treasure chest when we played pirates in her backyard.

Though she doesn't say anything, Ryan is clearly thinking the same thing, her eyes narrowing as she takes in the room. We follow Mrs. LeBlanc upstairs as she recounts the morning. It's mostly stuff we already know: Annie was home yesterday, didn't say much and went up to her room after dinner. This morning, they heard her rummaging around upstairs, and when Mrs. Le-Blanc went to see what she wanted for breakfast, Annie was gone. All she found was a handwritten note on Annie's desk. Chaos ensued, Mary called the cops.

"They only just left," Mrs. LeBlanc says as she opens the door to Annie's room. "Ordinarily they wouldn't come if it's a clear-cut runaway case, and Annie's eighteen. But because Cass knows you, Wilson, he came anyway."

My mouth lifts in a half smile. I'll have to thank him later.

She leads us into Annie's room, which, like downstairs, hasn't changed since we were kids, lit with a yellow tinge from the sun streaming in through the open shutters, catching specks of dust as they swirl and dance through the light. A pink-and-white-striped comforter hangs halfway off what has to at least be a queen-size bed, while the floor is littered with eighteen thousand tiny pillows. Anchoring the room is a giant white desk in the corner, the walls surrounding it covered in pictures, certificates, ribbons, and playbills from the San Diego Civic Theatre. I move toward it, my eyes scanning the memories. The pictures are mostly group shots, ones I vaguely recognize from Facebook: Annie with the cast of her high school musical, Annie with her field hockey team, Annie with the school government dorks. And then, in the middle of it all, stuck to the wall with a single red thumbtack is *The Lennon Chronicles*.

I touch an edge of the front cover to make sure it's real. "She kept it?" I whisper.

But neither of them hears me. Mrs. LeBlanc is still talking, Ryan nodding and making quiet sounds of acknowledgment.

"Here's the letter," Mrs. LeBlanc says, tapping her finger gently against a single sheet of lined paper.

It sits atop the lid of Annie's laptop in the middle of her desk. I reach down for it but stop at the last second.

"Am I allowed to . . ." I say, trailing off.

Mrs. LeBlanc nods. "Go ahead," she says.

The paper is smooth and crisp, as though Annie deliberately kept it pristine. I'm careful not to wrinkle it as I pick it up.

Mom and Dad,

This is probably the lamest thing I've ever done, but I'm sorry. I'm glad I got to come back and see you, but I

*can't help but feel like it wasn't a good idea. I want you
and everybody else to just move on, okay? I can't be here
anymore, so it's time for me to go. Please tell Wilson I'm
sorry. For everything.*

I love you guys.

*Love,
Annie*

Mrs. LeBlanc gives me a few seconds to read before she pokes
her head up over my shoulder and says nervously, "What do you
think it means?"

I turn to face her. She almost looks like a different person,
wringing her hands over her stomach, her once perfectly tanned
skin now pale and stretched. All I can think is, is this seriously
the person who kept me from Annie? The one who decided I
was bringing her daughter down? She looks nothing like what
I remember, nothing like the monster I've had in my head.

"I think it means she left," I say softly as I set the note back
on Annie's desk.

"But left where?" Mrs. LeBlanc says. "Where would she go?"
She takes a step back, her eyes filling with tears again. "You don't
think she'd hurt herself—"

"No," I say firmly. I can't know this for sure, but I also can't
let myself even consider it. It's too terrifying. "If anything, I
think she probably went to Rosita. Do you have Ashley Turner's
phone number?"

I've been thinking about it since I found out Annie was gone.
No matter how much I don't want to admit it, I have a feeling
Ashley Turner is the key to finding Annie. Mrs. LeBlanc's forehead

creases as she lets this question sink in. When it finally does, her face unravels, her eyes growing brighter.

"I should have all the numbers of the parents from the girls' field hockey team," she says, shuffling quickly toward the door. "Let me go find it."

Once we're alone again, Ryan leans against Annie's bed and watches me pace back and forth between the door and Annie's desk.

"What're you gonna do if she gets you this girl's phone number?" Ryan says. "Even if Annie does find her or her friends, none of them will recognize her."

"I know," I say. "But she might know where Annie would go. If we find Ashley, maybe we can find Annie."

The plaza outside Blushing Brides is the most obvious choice, so it's at the top of my list for places to check. But if we can just talk to Ashley, maybe she can tell us if there were any other places Annie liked to hang out when she was still alive.

Mrs. LeBlanc reappears, nearly breathless, clutching a piece of paper to her chest. On it is a list of all the home phone numbers of the Del Monte girls' field hockey team. As I scan it for Ashley's number and type it into my phone, Ryan sits at Annie's desk and opens her laptop. Mrs. LeBlanc holds both her hands up and takes a step toward the door.

"I'm going to call the sheriff's office and see if they have any updates," she says before jogging downstairs again.

With Ashley's number now in my phone, I zero in on the green call button. I'd be lying if I said I never considered messaging her to find out more about how Annie was in the weeks before she died. I thought about it almost constantly right after it happened, but every time I pulled up Ashley's Instagram, I'd get too nervous and chicken out. But if I can't muster up the courage to talk to her now, I never will. Staring down at my phone, I click on the little green circle.

Someone answers after a few rings: "Hello?"

The voice on the other line is male. Young, bored. As his low baritone fills my ear, I realize I don't actually know what to say.

I swallow. "Hi, is Ashley home?"

There's a long pause. As it stretches on, my stomach clenches, a thousand ridiculous excuses as to why I'm calling stacking up in my head, until finally the guy just says, "Yeah."

On the other end is a thunk, followed by muffled shouting.

Covering the bottom half of the phone with my hand, I bob from foot to foot and whisper to Ryan, "What do I say? I can't tell her why I'm actually calling."

"I don't know, tell her you're calling from the yearbook committee and you want to do an RIP feature on Annie," Ryan says.

The voices on the other line are getting louder.

"Who works on a yearbook in the middle of summer?" I say back.

Ryan shoots me a look. "I said I didn't know!"

"Hello?"

The baritone voice is swapped for one that's slightly higher, but equally bored. This must be Ashley Turner.

"Um, yeah, hi, Ashley?" I say. "My name is Wilson Moss. I used to be friends with Annie LeBlanc, you know, before she, um, died."

"Oh," Ashley says.

From the way her voice drops, this is obviously not what she was anticipating. And why would it be? This might be just as weird for her; she was Annie's friend too. Maybe thinking or talking about Annie makes her insides curl, the way mine used to whenever I thought about her. About what I lost.

"I'm sorry to call you about this out of the blue," I say quickly, "but I'm on the yearbook committee, you know, for my school—" Out of the corner of my eye, I can see Ryan whirling her finger around in a circle, urging me to wrap it up. I clear my throat, willing myself to sound like someone who would be on the yearbook committee. Someone who shouldn't have to care what other people think of them. Someone who's confident and cool enough to not be afraid. Someone Ryan already thinks I am. "I'm doing a memorial project on Annie for the yearbook, and I was hoping you could help me."

"Oh," Ashley says again. Her voice is muffled by the sound of clanking silverware. I can almost picture her in her big white-walled house, her brunch cooling on the dining table. "I'm not sure I can help. I didn't really know Annie that well."

I frown. "Didn't you do field hockey together?"

"Well, yeah. But it's a big team, and Annie only joined junior year. Most of us have been playing together since middle school."

It's obvious from the way Ashley's voice drifts that our conversation isn't her main focus. I've interrupted her, and she's probably looking for a way to get me off the phone and back to her eggs Benedict.

"That's okay," I rush. "I just wanted to know if there were any places you guys hung out a lot. You know, after practice or whatever."

"I mean, yeah, we did, but Annie never went."

"What about places you went a couple of times?"

"Um, nowhere, kind of. We didn't really hang out."

"But I saw you—" I bite my tongue. Ashley Turner does not

need to know I stalked Annie online. "I mean, I think Annie mentioned once or twice that you hung out."

"Her mom went to yoga near my house, so sometimes I drove her there after practice."

"Oh," I say, the word falling flat. "Then did she mention anywhere else she liked to go? Maybe somewhere she got coffee, or did her homework? Like a library or something?"

Annie isn't likely to go back to the place where she studied for tests or did her algebra homework, but I'm getting desperate.

"I don't know," Ashley says. "She never really talked much when I drove her back from practice. I told you, we weren't really friends."

"But you guys went to parties together," I insist, remembering Annie's story as we walked to Grant's house. "The one where you played make-out bingo and kissed five random dudes."

"Oh god." Ashley laughs. "It was actually four. I'm not that big of a mess. But how do you know about that? Annie wasn't at that party."

"What?" I say.

At the sound of my confusion, Ryan glances over her shoulder at me and mouths, *What's happening?*

I wave her away.

"She must've heard that story when I talked about it at practice and then pretended she was there," Ashley says. "God, that's so weird."

I run a hand across my scalp and breathe loudly through my nose. None of this is adding up. "Okay, do you know who else might know where Annie is—I mean, where she liked to hang out?" I say.

Ashley sighs. "I mean, not really. I don't think people actually knew her. I never saw her with anyone at school or anything. She never went to our parties, mostly because I don't think she was invited."

"But she was in a million clubs," I say, glancing again at the collage of pictures over Annie's desk. "Theater, field hockey—"

"That doesn't mean she had friends."

But that can't be right. I've seen the pictures, her arms around her classmates. Their arms around her. I've seen the memorial Facebook page. People cared about Annie.

"Then who made the RIP ANNIE LEBLANC page on Facebook?" I say.

"Oh god, I did," Ashley says. "I mean, technically my mom went on my account and made it. She's PTA president and I think she felt bad that nobody really did anything after Annie died. She still posts on it, I think. She has all my passwords after she found out I was talking to this guy in Australia last summer."

The phone almost slides from my hand as I listen to Ashley talk about the forty-six-year-old mother of three who catfished her last year. If this is true, that nobody ever really knew Annie, then that would mean—

"Ashley, I gotta go," I say, hanging up just as she launches into a tirade against American Airlines and their refund policy. "Oh my god," I say, turning slowly toward Ryan. From the look on her face, I can tell she's heard the entire conversation. "Annie didn't have any friends."

"But that would mean she's been lying this whole time. All those stories about the parties and Ashley and guys, all the posts— none of it was true."

For the last five minutes, I haven't stopped pacing. It's basically impossible with the number of pillows littering Annie's floor, but somehow I'm making it work. Because with all the thoughts spinning around in my head, I can't sit still. All I can think about are the pictures in Annie's bedroom, the way she threw in stories about Ashley and her other "friends." It was all just an elaborate act to look . . . what? Important? Loved? Wanted?

Ryan watches me from the desk chair.

"Why would she do this?" I ask.

"She was probably trying to impress you," Ryan says.

"But I'm the last person she needed to impress," I say. "I didn't care about any of that stuff."

"Didn't you?" Ryan says.

When I pause to look at her, she's giving me a sad smile. "No," I insist. "All I wanted was for her to be back. With me."

"But, Wil, you can't say you weren't jealous of how many friends you thought she had."

"That was because I thought she picked them over me." I lean against Annie's bed and rub my forehead. "Now I finally know the truth and we only have less than a week left. And I don't even know where she is."

Ryan hops over a mountain of pillows and wraps her arms around my neck. I relax into her, resting my head on her shoulder.

"We're gonna find her," Ryan says. "We just need to think strategically. Where would Annie go? Is there a Rosita chapter of friendless dorks who pretend they have social lives?"

I pull away from Ryan and scowl.

"I'm just trying to lighten things up," she mutters. "Jesus."

"She can't have gone that far, right?" I say. "She doesn't have any money and not many people—if anybody—in Rosita who knew her before can recognize her."

"They also probably wouldn't care since, you know, they didn't like her," Ryan says.

I shrug her off. "Do you still have to be like this?" I say. Her eyes glint and I hate how beautiful she is when she's being sarcastic. "You don't have to be jealous and weird about Annie anymore. You won. You've seen me mostly naked now."

"I'm just listing the facts!"

I roll my eyes. "What if she got hurt? She doesn't have a place to sleep. Somebody could have taken her."

The more I list off these possibilities, the more terrifying they become. Annie really could be in danger. Rosita is just outside of Poway, which is easily the seediest suburb of northern San Diego. The number of drug dealers who hang outside the AMC movie theater on any given night confirms this.

"Just slow down," Ryan says. She sidesteps the pillow pile and retrieves Annie's note. "Let's look at this again. There's got to be something in here that'll tell us where Annie is."

I squint down at the paper, Annie's neat handwriting. Of course she would handwrite a note instead of sending an email or leaving a Word doc up on her laptop, for the same reason I have eighteen thousand notebooks stashed under my bed. It's why she's my best friend.

"It's time for her to go," Ryan says, reading from the note. She frowns at the words. "It's time for her to *go*. Go where?"

"That's the problem," I say. "The only place she used to really go when she was alive was Rosita. And why would she go back there if she didn't have any friends? She wouldn't want to remind herself of that."

When we went with Jody to try on her dress at Blushing Brides, Annie was so quiet in the car. I thought it was because she was missing her old hangouts, but it was because she was remembering how awful her time in Rosita was. How lonely.

"Okay," Ryan says, "then where else could she go?"

I swallow. There's only really one other option. "Maybe she means she's going back to the afterlife," I say. "When she said she can't be *here* anymore, maybe she doesn't mean Lennon. Maybe she means here, like Earth."

Ryan chews the inside of her mouth before saying quietly, "But I thought you said she wouldn't hurt herself."

"She wouldn't," I say quickly. "But maybe there's another way. What if she—"

Before I can finish the sentence out loud, I finish it in my head. If Annie wanted to go back to the afterlife early, there's one easy, direct route open only to her.

"Oh my god," I say under my breath, the pieces clicking into place.

"What?" Ryan says.

I scramble over the pillows on the floor, nearly tripping face-first on one shaped like a seashell.

"Where are you going?"

I'm basically through the door when I shout back to her, "I know where Annie is."

TWENTY-THREE

DAYS UNTIL ANNIE LEBLANC DIES: ???

Even though the drive through Lennon to the edge of town takes only about seven minutes, it feels like Ryan and I are in the car for hours. It helps when she rests her hand on the inside of my left knee, her fingers moving slowly over my skin, but I still can't help worrying. What if I'm wrong and Annie's not there? What if she *was* there, but we're too late? Or worse, what if I get there and she won't talk to me?

"We'll find her," Ryan says, reading my mind. "Don't worry."

Almost imperceptibly, the car creeps up in speed.

Main Street is fringed with pine trees, their rigid tops an ever-present backdrop over the roof slopes, but when we pass the last storefront, the trees become a solid block of dark green. The road is paved, but it quickly gives way into a chalky dirt, the plants brown and charred after the last time Southern California was on fire. I try to focus on them as they streak past us, the browns and greens melding together in an indecipherable blur, but all I can think about is my fight with Annie, how impossible it would be to carry on normally knowing the last thing I said to her was that I wished we hadn't had this extra time together. Especially now that I know nothing about her last year alive was true.

The only indication that a bus stop is coming up is a tiny circular sign with what I assume is supposed to be a bus but that looks more like a rectangle propped up by two smaller squares. About fifty feet from it is a wooden bench that doesn't even have a Plexiglas roof or anything to protect the person sitting on it from the blinding sun.

Annie.

"There," I say, lurching up and out of my seat.

Ryan manages not to roll her eyes and point out that obviously Annie is right there. In the middle of the empty road and endless line of pine trees, she's the only thing around.

At the sound of the car's wheels crunching off the pavement and onto the gravel that lines the road, Annie glances up. I think she might smirk slightly, but I can't be sure.

"I'll wait here," Ryan says as I scramble to unbuckle my seat belt and open my door.

Before climbing out, I grab Ryan's hand and squeeze it.

"I had a feeling you'd find me," Annie says as I slam the car door and start to walk toward her.

For the entire drive, I was too focused on finding Annie, worrying if she'd even be here, to plan out what I'd say if I actually did find her. Sitting on the bench with her legs outstretched over the dirt, Annie's dressed in a plain white T-shirt and a pair of cotton shorts. She's significantly underdressed compared to how she arrived nearly a month ago in her pink sparkly dress.

Once I'm only a few feet away from her, I blurt out, "I'm sorry."

Annie shrugs. "It's not your fault you're a good detective," she says.

"No, I mean about everything," I say. "What I said, about wishing I didn't bring you back. You know I didn't mean it, but I shouldn't have said it anyway."

The bench is only about two feet long, but I cram myself into the empty space, the left half of my body pressed up against Annie.

"Wil, I deserved it," she says. "I hard-core ditched you junior year."

"So what?" I say. "You had one month to be alive again and I made you live it out by following my sad little plan. And it was all for nothing. You and Ryan aren't friends and probably never would've been, no matter what I did."

I glance over at Ryan who, when we lock eyes, looks away nervously.

"She is insufferable," Annie says under her breath, only half joking.

I turn back to Annie. "But she was right: this whole thing was never about you. I should've asked what you wanted to do, but I was too busy being a selfish dick. Why didn't you say anything?"

"*Because,* Wilson. I knew you were only trying to help."

"Yeah, help myself," I say.

"No, help keep me back."

At this, the thoughts in my head go fuzzy. Annie *knew*? But how? Had she somehow found my notebook too and didn't tell me because . . . why? She felt bad for me? It was too hilarious watching me try to achieve the impossible?

"You knew," I say slowly. "You knew what I was trying to do. You knew it was never going to work. And you didn't tell me not to waste my time?"

Annie shakes her head. "I only figured it out in San Diego," she says. "You trying to push me and Ryan back together again—it didn't make sense. It wasn't until you shaved your head that I realized how desperate you were, and then it all started to fall into place."

"But how did you know it was possible? You staying back for good."

"Because my parents have been trying to figure it out too." Annie rolls her eyes, but beneath the exasperation is an undercurrent of sadness. "Except they pretty much told me about it from the beginning. That's why we went to LA. My mom's been trying to find some family secrets she could fix, but turns out that in spite of the fact that I'm pretty sure my cousin Kelsey eats bath bombs, our family is really freaking boring."

Even though what Annie's saying is fairly clear, it still doesn't make any sense. How could she let me think I could keep her around for good when there was never any chance? How could she let me have hope?

"Why didn't you tell me you knew?" I say.

Annie's eyes slide toward me, the sadness from just moments before swapped for a mischievous smile. Seeing it, I curl my hands into fists, anger welling up in my chest. Does she think this is funny?

"I saw the way Ryan looks at you. The way you look at her," she says. "You're right: I knew me and her were never going to be friends, not like we used to, but I thought that maybe if I just swallowed whatever weirdness there was between us and kept you guys together for long enough, you'd figure it out. You get that she's obsessed with you, right?"

I lean so far away from Annie, I almost fall off the bench. "Wh— How did you know that?" I splutter.

"Um, because I have *eyes*?" she says. "You should've seen the look on her face when she was shaving your head. The sexual tension between you both is just bizarre." At the incredulous look on my face, Annie bursts into laughter. "Why do you think I backtracked so hard on Mark?" she says. "As soon as I spent a day with the two of you, I realized what was going on. But I'd already invited her *brother* out to flirt with you." She blinks. "Wil, I wanted to die. Again."

As this new thought dawns on me, I slump. That's why Annie didn't want me to kiss Mark in front of Ryan at Wok N' Roll, why she was so adamant I shouldn't let Mark into my empty house. Finally I laugh too. Somehow Annie saying all this is the least unbelievable thing to happen to me in the last twenty-four hours.

"I'm pretty sure she actually really likes you," Annie says.

"Yeah," I say, looking at Ryan. "I think so too."

Annie slings an arm over my shoulder. "You guys can be my lasting legacy," she says. "After everything I did to you—" Annie pauses, her voice fading. Eventually she clears her throat. "It's the least I could do."

I swallow a deep breath, biting back nerves. I know I have to say this next part, no matter how uncomfortable. "Annie," I say quietly. I say this looking at her, even though my brain is begging me to look away. "I know about Ashley and everyone else."

The sky is a dizzying shade of blue, unfurling like a never-ending puddle of water above the trees. Annie's arm slides from around my shoulders as she leans her head back to stare at the sky, her eyes squinting into the sun.

"How?" she says simply.

"Your mom asked us to come over and help find you. I thought you might've gone down to Rosita, so I called Ashley."

At this Annie nods slowly but doesn't say a word.

"Why did you lie?"

A full minute of silence passes. I wait patiently, watching Annie as a series of emotions flicker across her face: sadness, embarrassment, frustration, and then just resignation.

"My whole life, I knew I was gonna go to Del Monte," she says. "One of my first memories is of me in a green-and-gold T-shirt at a varsity field hockey game, sitting on my mom's shoulders. I knew it was going to suck leaving you, but going there had been part of my life plan since I was born. I couldn't not do it. It meant everything to my mom."

I nod wordlessly.

"When I got there, I joined a billion different clubs, but it was such a weird time to start a new school. Even though it'd been closed for the last two years, all the people who were enrolled there had been doing their classes in Poway, so they all knew each other. Plus, they'd been going to school together basically since birth. Everyone was nice to me, but they didn't *need* me. They already had their circles, they already had best friends."

"Then why didn't you just come back?" I say.

"Because I *couldn't*," she says. "I wanted to. My mom begged me, but Dad's business, it—" Her voice catches.

"Your dad's— What?" I say. "What happened?"

Annie shakes her head. "It started sophomore year. Everything grew too fast; one second, my dad had one tiny antiques shop on Main Street and then the next, he had seven ware-houses scattered across Southern California. The moment busi-ness slowed down, he had too much to pay for and not enough cash to pay it."

"But I thought—"

"Yeah, I know what you thought," Annie says. "But my parents were so embarrassed. If anybody found out how many overdue bills we had crammed into our mailbox every day, they would've died. Thank god Dad inherited our house from Grandpa, other-wise we would've been homeless."

Their house, which they'd sunk so much money into when the business had started to take off. Their house, which hadn't changed since we were kids. But could I really have been that wrong about Annie's parents? That their wealth was all just an act?

"Then how'd you go to Del Monte?" I say. "Isn't it like—"

"Twenty thousand dollars a year?" Annie laughs darkly. "Yeah. I got a scholarship for field hockey. They gave me a full ride. And if I wanted to go to college, I'd need a scholarship for that, too." She turns to me, her eyes shining. "That's why I couldn't go back to Lennon Union. There's no field hockey team. I'm not creative like you, or smart like Ryan. If I wanted to get out of here and do something with myself, this was the only way."

"Then why would your mom beg you to leave? You made it sound like she was so stoked about all the Del Monte parties."

"She was, until she realized I wasn't actually going to them. She could tell something was wrong, that I never hung out with anyone, never even had people over to study."

"But she was so cold to me," I say, thinking about all the times she recoiled at the sight of me in town. "I thought she was happy to have me out of your life."

"That's because I made her promise not to tell you what was going on," Annie says. Tears have started streaking down the sides of her nose. She wipes each one with the back of her hand. "It killed her to be so mean. That's why she stopped talking to you, because she didn't want to lie. She told me about the time at the deli when she ran out. After that, she said she was done. If I didn't tell you what was going on at school, she would, but I couldn't let that happen, not after I'd been so shitty. I knew you would've forgiven me, and I didn't deserve it."

This realization hits me like a slap to the face. Mrs. LeBlanc's hug this morning, the awkward smile she gave me when Annie first came back; she was trying to apologize for the way she'd treated me.

"I told her I needed one more chance," Annie says. "My birthday was coming up, and I was going to turn everything around."

Annie's birthday.

"But you died," I say, wrapping my fingers so tightly around my knees that my knuckles turn white.

More silent tears slip down Annie's face. When she eventually nods, the tears drip onto her chest, leaving little dark stains on her white T-shirt. She turns to me, her eyes barely able to meet mine as she draws in a shaky breath, one hand clenched into a fist on her lap. Prying her fingers apart, I weave mine in with hers and rest my head on her shoulder.

"Turning eighteen is a BFD," Annie says into my scalp. "I thought if I could throw this big party, maybe that'd be my ticket in." She laughs, but it's cold. "I'm so pathetic. I was literally trying to buy friends."

I squeeze her hand.

"I begged my mom to let me throw a huge party at the

house. She felt really weird about it, but I promised it was gonna be my last try. If this didn't work, I'd go back to Lennon Union. My mom bought all this food and rented a chocolate fountain; my dad put up all these Christmas lights and paper lanterns in the backyard. I invited everyone from every single club I'd ever joined: field hockey, student government, theater. Even the debate team. I got super dressed up, my parents went out for the night. Everything was so perfect."

Annie's voice is thick with tears as she takes in a deep breath.

"Oh, Annie—" I say.

But she doesn't hear me. I can tell by the way her voice floats over the road that she's lost in the memory of her house that night, the backyard lit by the soft glow of a thousand bulbs.

"Nobody came," she whispers. "Not a single person. At first I thought I must've put the wrong time. I mean, how could *nobody* come? Like, not even the debate kids? I'm pretty sure none of them had ever seen a real party in person before. They should've been psyched. But now I realize it wasn't that they necessarily didn't want to go to a party—they didn't know me. They must've seen the invite and been like, *Who even is this girl?*"

"But what about all those people on the RIP ANNIE page?" I say. "Maybe they got your address wrong, or—"

Annie silences me with a shake of her head. "Nope," she says. "Believe me, I double-checked a hundred times that night. All those people saying how sad they were that I died, that I was so nice and wasn't it so awful—none of them knew me. They were all hopping on the demented bandwagon, pretending they were my friends so people would feel sorry for them."

I open my mouth to refuse this, to voice my outrage and denial, but it *does* sound like something people would do.

"So, the night goes on and I'm sitting there eating Oreos by myself," Annie continues. "It gets to ten o'clock, then eleven. By midnight I gave up and texted my parents to come home, told them everyone had left. I was still so obsessed with making this work, even after everyone blew me off, so I knew that if my mom was going to let me stay at Del Monte, I had to make it look like there'd actually been a party." Annie tucks her hair behind her ears and sighs. "I started drawing hearts all over the windows with lipstick, streaking streamers across the lawn. I even threw empty Diet Coke cans in the pool. I bought these heinous heels that were way too tall, and I rolled my ankle when I was trying to throw stuff in the pool and I must've hit my head, because the next thing I knew, I was at Welcome Back. My mom said when she and Dad got home, they found me floating."

Annie and I let her story sit between us for a moment as a red minivan speeds past, ruffling her hair with a breeze. Desperation courses through me as I try to think of something helpful to say here. Something comforting, something that can take away the fact that Annie died completely alone and completely by accident.

Without another word, Annie crumples over so her face presses into the tops of her knees. "I ruined everything," she sobs, her whole body shaking. I rub circles into her back, wishing I wasn't so useless. "I ditched you, my mom thinks it's her fault that I died. She's slept with me every night since I got back."

My throat feels tight with tears, but I swallow them down. "Annie, I'm so sorry," I say. "I wish I'd known. I should've said something to them, your mom and your dad—"

"My dad's been so good about the whole thing," she says.

"He said my mom's been getting better. He drives her to therapy every week, he barely goes to LA anymore. But ever since I've been back, I can tell it's making my mom slide backward. She was finally starting to take on work again, but I showed up and ruined that too."

"You didn't ruin anything," I say. "We love you. We all wanted you back."

Annie lurches herself up into a sitting position and rubs her nose until it's red. When she turns back to me, her faint smile is all sadness. She shuts her eyes tight, squeezing out more tears.

"I'm so sorry for blowing you off," she says as she leans into me. I wrap my arms around her and pull her close. "You're my best friend, you always have been. You should've been the one at my party, I never should've lied about all my quote, unquote *friends*."

"It doesn't matter now," I say. "I just wish I could've been there."

She nods into the crook of my neck. "Me too."

It's too hot for us to be this close, but I don't want to pull away. "I'm still sorry I tried to force you and Ryan to be friends," I say. "I genuinely didn't know you guys hated each other." When Annie glances up at me with her eyebrows raised, I backtrack. "Okay, the signs might've been there, but I always thought what you guys had was like what me and Ryan had, a kind of, like, *ha ha ha I hate you but I really love you* kind of thing. Like sisters."

Annie snorts. It's a cross between a laugh and a sniffle, but even still, hearing it makes my chest feel lighter, as though someone has inflated a balloon in my rib cage.

"I don't hate her," Annie says. "I'll always love her in my own weird way, but things will never be like they were. We're too different now." She sucks air in through her teeth. "And by the way, if you and Ryan are sisters, I'm pretty sure what's going on between you is illegal."

As a pickup truck streaks past, the whole reason I'm even here on the side of this road hits me like a cake to the face. I snap my head toward Annie.

"Please don't go back early," I say.

Annie's eyes are on the road leading out of town, where the bus will likely appear. Nerves rush through me as I rake my fingers down my thighs. What if the bus appears and Annie can't take it back? What if she still wants to go?

But when she turns back to face me, Annie is smirking.

"Only if you buy me at least two hot chocolate bombs every day."

I smile so wide, it creases my eyes. "Deal."

Somewhere far off, a bird sings a high-pitched song that echoes across the empty road. Annie and I both blink up at the sky as an airplane streaks across the sheet of blue, leaving a trail that stretches over us like a puffy white rainbow. I consider telling her about what Ryan and I did last night, but decide to leave it for another time. We still have six days left together; six days without lying, without secrets, without having to plan my mom's—

"Holy shit, my mom's wedding!" I exclaim. "What time is it?"

Annie overturns her empty hands and looks at me helplessly. Ryan opens the driver's door and steps onto the gravel, waving her phone.

"It's one forty-five," she calls out.

"Oh my god, I'm gonna be so late," I say.

I jog back to Ryan's car, adrenaline sizzling through me, as Annie follows close behind. Ryan turns the car on before we even close our doors, and then we're back on the road again, speeding toward the apple orchards on the other side of town. I glance up and peer into the rearview mirror as the bus stop fades in the distance. Somehow with it behind us, it feels like the past is too. All the hurt and confusion and secrets left on the side of the road leading out of Lennon.

"I'm obviously really happy not to be dying and all," Annie says, cutting through my thoughts, "but I had a bet going in my head on what color pantsuit Ruth Fish would be wearing, and I'm not gonna lie, it's kind of a bummer that I'll never know."

Without hesitating, Ryan says, "Avocado green, obviously."

"Nope." Annie waves a finger through the air. "The correct answer is periwinkle."

"With her hair color?" Ryan says. "It would totally wash her out. She'd look like a vanilla cupcake."

"Exactly," Annie says. "Which is why—"

They argue like that for the entire drive, and I love every minute of it.

THREE DAYS LATER

This is the fifth hot chocolate bomb I've had in three days, but I don't care. Every time I ask Annie what she wants to do when we're together, it always starts with a hot chocolate bomb and apple pie at the Country Kitchen, so that's what we do. Her, Ryan, and I are seated at our old booth, three plates of apple pie and our white porcelain mugs of milk steaming on the table in front of us. We each have a solid ball of chocolate as big as an oversize jawbreaker—the bomb part of a hot chocolate bomb—that we drop into our milk and swirl around with teaspoons. The chocolate takes a lot longer than you'd think to melt and so I wait patiently, stirring and stirring and stirring as the milk gradually goes from white to brown.

"Did they change the recipe?" Annie says through a mouthful of pie. She points with the spires of her fork at the chunks of apple smeared across her paper plate. "I swear to god, it tastes better than I remember."

Underneath the table, Ryan's legs are intertwined with mine, the toe of her sandal gently skimming my calf. She scoops up another hunk of pie and nods. "Mark convinced Mom to start using cardamom and ginger instead of just cinnamon to spice the apples," she says.

The three of us glance over at Mark, who's behind the counter refilling the napkin dispensers.

"So, he's more than just hot," Annie says. From the way her voice trails off, it sounds like she's just discovered a new element or something. "Interesting."

Ryan pretends to gag.

Annie's parents were too relieved that she was home again to be upset with her when Ryan dropped her off a few days ago. That night, she explained everything to them, my attempts at keeping her back for good, the RIP ANNIE LEBLANC page, Ashley Turner, and how I managed to unravel the story. After that, Annie went to therapy with her mom under the pretense that she was Annie's cousin and was there to role-play *as though* she were Annie in an effort to help Mrs. LeBlanc work through her grief. Apparently, it was as weird of an experience as it sounds, but oddly comforting, and ever since, Annie says Mrs. LeBlanc's laugh sounds more like it used to. Now, whenever I go over to their house, Mrs. LeBlanc starts by wrapping me in a hug so tight, she practically crushes the air out of my lungs.

At my feet is my backpack, phone tucked in the front pocket. I can feel it buzz against my leg and Ryan must too, because she leans down and fishes it out for me.

"Is it Jody?" she says as I type in my password.

I shake my head. My mom and Dr. Dav—*just David,* I correct myself—are on their honeymoon in San Francisco, where they've spent the last couple of days riding bikes along the bay and taking elaborately themed wine tours. But it's not more pictures of my mother posing in front of the *Full House* house. It's from Cass.

Cass
Thurs 4 dinner?

I type my response and wait as three dots appear.

> **Wilson**
> Thursday could be good. I don't think Jody is working, but I'll check when I get home

Cass
👍👍 u can bring Ryan 2 if u want

This makes my eyes bug out of my head. Ryan, seeing this, leans in.

"What's wrong?" she says.

"Nothing," I say, obscuring my phone.

> **Wilson**
> How do you know about Ryan?

Cass
Ur mom has Amanda's # now. U did this to urself

When I first saw Cass and Amanda in the crowd at Jody's wedding, I thought I was hallucinating: Cass, in a dark green shirt and khaki sport coat; Amanda, in a pretty blue sundress with her hair braided loosely to one side. Turns out, Jody's definition of being "mature" extended beyond just talking to Cass, to inviting him and Amanda to the wedding.

"I told you I could be a grown-up," Jody said to me later that night.

I actually sat with Amanda and Cass for almost an hour after dessert, talking to Amanda about how she was planning to decorate the baby's room, and what corners got too hot in the summer. After Cass told her I liked to draw, she even commissioned me to paint a mural of wildflowers on the wall. Though it was weird and surreal at times, talking to the both of them, together, made a good night even better.

Because Jody's wedding was freaking perfect. Outside of the fact that I showed up literally two minutes before I was due to walk down the aisle with my sister, the only other hiccup on the day was that Jody's old boss from the Thrifty Coyote got too drunk and knocked over the gift table. The food was amazing, though, the cake was perfect, and the centerpieces lit up the orchard at night with a soft glow, as though the whole place was covered in fireflies. Jody even surprised me with a flower crown she'd persuaded the florist to make at the last second to decorate my naked head. When I sent a selfie to Ryan of me wearing it, she said it was probably good she wasn't there because she'd want to bite my face off, but in a good way.

Since Jody and David have been gone, Ryan has basically been living at my house aside from the night I spent at Annie's eating ice cream and watching old Adam Sandler movies. Ryan has now seen me totally naked and I haven't gotten embarrassed once.

I lean in toward Ryan and kiss her shoulder. "Do you wanna come to dinner at Cass and Amanda's house with me?" I say.

She turns her face so that her lips are in my hair, which is already about a half centimeter long, thank you very much. "Do I have to?" she says, only kind of joking.

I shrug. "No."

She makes a scoffing sound. "Oh my god, Wilson, don't be such a nag. I'll go to your awful dinner."

Annie laughs as she shovels another forkful of pie into her mouth and I glance up at Ryan and smile. She's smiling too as she closes the gap and kisses me.

Once I pull away, I tuck my phone back into my backpack. Annie is staring at me, her shoulders pressed into the booth.

"Okay, there's something I have to tell you," she says.

This instantly makes a bolt of fear fire up my spine. "What?" I say uneasily.

"Well"—she shoots a nervous glance at Ryan, who nods—"I may or may not have done something you probably would've hated but that I think is actually a really good idea."

My eyes ping-pong between Ryan and Annie, but neither of them elaborates.

"Guys," I say slowly, "what did you do?"

Annie leans over so she can retrieve something from her purse. She pulls out a series of papers stapled together and folded in half. As she smooths them out on the table, I can see that they're emails, but not from who, or what they're about.

"Okay, so." Annie swallows, her fingers playing awkwardly with the bent edges of the paper. "I may have sort of, you know, I don't know, just—"

"Just tell her," Ryan demands.

Annie jolts at the bark in Ryan's voice and launches into a nervous ramble: "Okay, I might have emailed the editor of the

Lennon News and told him how big of a travesty it is that there aren't any comics in the newspaper anymore especially when he's got such a talented artist on his doorstep, so I stole your sketchbook and photocopied it and sent it to him and I'm so sorry but I just couldn't stand the idea of you being this good and doubting yourself and never doing anything with it."

She finally pauses to breathe, but I've pretty much stopped taking things in since Annie first started speaking.

"You stole my sketchbook and sent it to the editor of the *Lennon News*?" I say slowly.

Annie shoots a panicked glance at Ryan.

"And what did he say . . ." Ryan prompts.

"Oh!" Annie exclaims. "He loved it. He's obsessed with you. He wants to meet and talk with you about doing a weekly cartoon strip for them. Here, look."

She shoves the papers toward me and points to the most recent email. My eyes scan the top page, but my heart is thumping so fast, I can only process the information in snippets. *Wilson. Talented. Homegrown. Hysterical. Meeting. Tuesday?*

I flip through the rest of the emails. "Oh my god," I whisper. It's just more of the same, including the panels from *The Walking Dad* that Annie sent over. "This . . . this is . . ."

But I can't bring myself to say it. The words are too big for my mouth, my brain spinning at a dizzying speed.

"I know you're probably really mad at me, but I was just trying to help," Annie says.

Ryan looks between me and Annie. "Yeah," she says after a few seconds, "I was the one who told her it was a good idea. If you're gonna be mad at anyone, blame—"

"Incredible," I finally say. "It's incredible."

Annie blinks. She looks like I've slapped her. "Are you serious?" she says. "You're not mad?"

"You got me my dream job," I say, on the verge of breathless. "I mean, the *Lennon News* isn't exactly the *New Yorker,* but it's something. Someone believes in me. Somebody thinks I'm good enough for this."

Ryan's arm snakes around my shoulders. "You *are* good enough for it," she says, before kissing me on the side of my head.

Mark slides into the booth beside Annie and picks up the comic. "And what do we have here?" he says as he begins to flip through it.

The three of them start talking about *The Walking Dad,* Annie pointing at the panels she's scanned in. While they do this, I sit quietly, stunned. Because how did I get here? This summer, kicked off just because Ruth Fish picked my name out of a bowl, has somehow resulted in me being surrounded by the best people I could ever imagine the universe creating. And even though it's ending soon, the fact that it happened at all is everything.

Annie laughs at something Jerry says about being a zombie stereotype while Ryan and Mark argue over whether the love interest should be his yoga instructor or the mailman, and then they're all musing about what Jerry's future will be, as though this story, these characters, are already actually real. As I watch them, for the first time in two years the thought of other people seeing my creations doesn't make me want to cower.

It makes me excited.

EPILOGUE

DAYS SINCE ANNIE LEBLANC DIED: 30

Even though Ryan is driving, she lets me curate our playlist the whole way back to Lennon. I try to intersperse her weird indie music with my songs, but there's something about The Smashing Pumpkins that's just too perfect for a road trip, so we mostly end up driving to the sounds of reverb and Billy Corgan's raspy voice. Wedged between my knees is my backpack, so crammed with tubs of Atomic Fireballs that the zipper almost broke twice as I tried to yank it closed. Ryan and I spent the day in Orange County, pilfering the candy shop she found with her mom, eating our weight in fish tacos, and holding hands on the beach. She hasn't spoken much to me in the last two hours, since I bet her she couldn't eat an entire Atomic Fireball without spitting it out. Winner got to choose what we watched tonight. And that's how we've ended up with the OG *Buffy the Vampire Slayer* movie on our horizon.

As we cross the line from Santa Ysabel into Lennon, the trees arcing over the highway are somehow already starting to shed, leaves in rich oranges and reds fluttering to the ground. They swirl up and over the car as we drive through, dancing delicately in a way I can't help but think isn't natural, that is most likely concocted by Lennon to look beautiful, but this time I don't care. Over the last few days, the air has developed a distinctly crisp edge: shorts turning into pants, T-shirts into sweaters. Summer is slowly fading behind us, making way for fall.

For the eight thousandth time since Annie died again, I pull out my phone and flick through my pictures: ones Jody took of me, Ryan, and Annie on the Fourth of July float, pictures of the three of us and Mark in Annie's pool, even some I don't remember taking on karaoke night of Annie and Mark with their eyes closed and mouths open wide as they screamed something likely incoherent into the microphone. I know I should be grateful that I got this opportunity to take these pictures, to have Annie back in the first place, but all I feel right now is an ache in my chest I'm not convinced will ever go away.

"Don't be ridiculous," Annie said on the morning she went back to the afterlife, when I wailed that I wasn't sure how I'd ever live without her again. She'd invited me to go to the bus stop with her parents, but I'd declined. They deserved that time together, just the three of them. Annie had both hands on my shoulders, her forehead only a millimeter from mine. "You are the glue that keeps all of us together. Look around."

We broke apart and turned toward the porch, where Mark, Ryan, Cass, Amanda, Bernie, Jody, David, and Annie's parents stood. They were all careful to keep their distance, giving me and Annie space to say goodbye, but at the break in our conversation, they each turned and gave me their own smile. Mark's, sweet; Ryan's, fierce; Jody's, warm but with sadness glittering behind her eyes.

"You did this," Annie says, giving my shoulders a shake. "Without you, we, us, together—we don't exist."

The last picture in my phone is of all of us on my porch, the camera angle slightly off since we had to take it on a timer and lean the phone on Cass's cruiser so we could all be in it. In the middle is me with Annie on one side and Ryan on the other, our arms draped over one another's shoulders while everyone else is huddled around us, Bernie sticking out her tongue, Mark giving Ryan bunny ears, Amanda with a hand on her bump. It was a weird mash-up of people, one I never could have predicted, but we all fit together perfectly. We were exactly where we belonged.

A tear I didn't know was forming slips down my cheek. I turn my face toward my window and quickly wipe it away. I don't want Ryan to think I'm upset, not after the perfect day we've had together. But she's Ryan; within seconds her hand slips into mine and gently squeezes. When I look over, she's shooting glances at me in between watching the road, her face soft and concerned.

"Have I ever told you your head is shaped like a pistachio?" she says.

I bark out a laugh that's half sob, snot peeking out of my nose. I swipe it with my free hand and lean back on the headrest, face tilted out toward my window as Ryan turns off the main highway and residential streets begin sprawling out on either side of the car. As we pass Annie's street, I force myself not to look away, because I know this is the only way it'll ever get easier. The same U-Haul that's been parked there the last few times I went to Cass's house is still in Annie's driveway. Eyes trained on it until we pass, I wonder how long it'll take for me to stop calling it Annie's house, if I ever will.

Because the day after Annie returned to the afterlife, Mr. and Mrs. LeBlanc were gone too. They disappeared overnight, their house newly on the market and a pack of movers in to sell all the furniture they'd left behind. Mr. LeBlanc sold his antiques shop on Main Street to a lady who was going to turn it into a cat salon. And while I wished I'd had the chance to say goodbye to them, I got it. Nostalgia was an intrinsic part of Lennon, and when the memories were so powerful they made it hard to breathe, sometimes you needed to move somewhere else to keep going. To start over. Annie's parents had tried after she died, but having to do it twice—it was too much. I was only just starting to understand how it could be possible to let the hard memories power you instead of hold you back, to live *with* them, not in spite of them; it wasn't something I was sure I could do yet, but I was trying.

We're silent as Ryan pulls into my driveway and we get out of the car. She skips up the porch steps while I grab the mail, my heavy backpack slung over one shoulder. In the living room, my mom is on the couch with Bernie tucked at her feet, *Wheel of Fortune* on the TV, and David on the recliner reading a book.

"How was the OC?" my mom asks.

Bernie wrinkles her nose. "Nobody calls it that," she says.

"Excuse me, but you're ten," my mom says, nudging my sister with her foot. "I distinctly remember having three more years before you devolve into a snarky teenager."

David looks up from over his book and shrugs at my mom. "She's right, though," he says. "That was very early 2000s of you."

"Orange County was good," Ryan says. She rounds the kitchen island and rests her elbows on the counter. "Wilson cleaned the candy shop out of Atomic Fireballs. I'd be impressed if I wasn't so disgusted."

I sling my backpack onto the floor and sit at the dining room table, mail splayed across its surface. "You're just mad I won the bet," I say.

She scowls at the reminder. "I'm mad you have such terrible taste."

"Says my girlfriend."

At this, Ryan rolls her eyes.

The mail is mostly junk: a water bill, a letter from the electricity company confirming the closure of our account for next week when we move, a belated wedding card for my mom and David. The very last piece of mail, hidden behind coupons for a Pizza Hut that Lennon doesn't even have, is a postcard. On its front is a picture of a rope bridge extending out toward a tall, perfectly shaped tree that's surrounded by impossibly green forest. *The Tambopata National Reserve* is written across the bottom in white cursive.

Frowning, I flip the postcard over. It's addressed to me. Ryan is rustling around in our cabinets looking for popcorn while Bernie shouts at the TV, but at the sight of the inscription on the postcard, scrawled in a neat handwriting I'd know anywhere, my breath catches in my throat. The room around me fades into nothing, drowned out by the sound of blood rushing in my ears. Tears return to my eyes, blurring my vision as I read the words on the postcard again and again, until I've got them tattooed on my brain. It's not until I read it for what must be the twelfth time that I realize I'm smiling.

The rainforest smells like wet dirt—it's perfect.

ACKNOWLEDGMENTS

I both love and hate this part of writing a book—love, because I'm so grateful to the people in my life and want them to know it, and hate, because I'm petrified of leaving someone out. So here goes (sorry in advance to anyone I forget).

The first thank-you goes to my parents for their bottomless support for not just my writing and dreams but our family. *You* are the glue that keeps us together.

Thank you also to my lovely agent, Chloe Seager; my editor, Eileen Rothschild; and the rest of the fabulous team at Wednesday Books. This book has seen so many versions of itself before it reached this last, best one, which would never have happened without you all. Shout-out too to the Chicken House gang and Kesia Lupo, whose good vibes I can still feel all the way from her new home in the States.

As ever, I am seriously indebted to the many talented writers I'm fortunate enough to call my friends. Abby Erwin, Anna

Pook, Dani Redd, Bikram Sharma, and Rowan Whiteside, thank you for reading the bizarreness I continue to put in front of you and somehow, impossibly, sticking with me through it all.

Thank you to Girl Scout Troop 8239 for all the camping trips and jaunts to Dudley's Bakery that inspired so much of this book. I'd say sorry for killing you off in my increasingly wild bedtime stories, but we'd all know it wasn't sincere.

I received so many gorgeous messages after the publication of my first book and truly cherished them all. Thank you to the friends, family, and new faces that sent them. I could try to describe how happy each one made me, but it'd never be enough.

I'm from Southern California, and so many of the anecdotes in this story are ones I also experienced in real life. To the girl by my side through most of them—thank you. Emily Morris, you are the definition of "feisty little sister," and I wouldn't have it any other way.

To Adam, my sense of humor soulmate and best friend— long may we find the silliness in everything together. Thank you for caring about me and this book.

And finally, always, to Margot. You keep me inspired, motivated, and at the ready with chocolate every day. I'm so, so grateful.